The daughter of a town marshal, **Linda Lael Miller** is a *New York Times* bestselling author of more than one hundred historical and contemporary novels. Linda's books have hit #1 on the *New York Times* bestseller list seven times. Raised in Northport, Washington, she now lives in Spokane, Washington. Visit her at www.lindalaelmiller.com.

Patricia Davids has led a storied life, so it is no wonder she enjoys writing books. She has been in turn a Kansas farmer's daughter, a nurse, a pen pal to a lonely sailor, a navy wife, a mother, a neonatal transport nurse, a champion archer, a horse trainer, a grandmother times two, a widow, a world traveler and finally an award-winning, bestselling author. Pat now lives on the Kansas farm where she grew up. She loves to hear from readers. You can contact her through her website at patriciadavids.com or follow her on Facebook at Author Patricia Davids.

#1 *New York Times* Bestselling Author

LINDA LAEL MILLER

A CREED COUNTRY CHRISTMAS

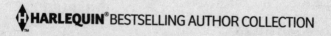

HARLEQUIN® BESTSELLING AUTHOR COLLECTION

ISBN-13: 978-1-335-92846-7

A Creed Country Christmas

Copyright © 2019 by Harlequin Books S.A.

The publisher acknowledges the copyright holders of the individual works as follows:

A Creed Country Christmas
Copyright © 2009 by Linda Lael Miller

The Doctor's Blessing
Copyright © 2010 by Patricia MacDonald

Recycling programs for this product may not exist in your area.

This edition published by arrangement with Harlequin Books S.A.

For questions and comments about the quality of this book, please contact us at CustomerService@Harlequin.com.

® and TM are trademarks of Harlequin Enterprises Limited or its corporate affiliates. Trademarks indicated with ® are registered in the United States Patent and Trademark Office, the Canadian Intellectual Property Office and in other countries.

Printed in U.S.A.

CONTENTS

A CREED COUNTRY CHRISTMAS

Linda Lael Miller

For Jean Woofter
With love and gratitude

CHAPTER ONE

Stillwater Springs, Montana
December 20, 1910

THE INTERIOR OF Willand's Mercantile, redolent of saddle leather and wood smoke, seemed to recede as Juliana Mitchell stood at the counter, holding her breath.

The letter had *finally* arrived.

The letter Juliana had waited for, prayed for, repeatedly inquired after—at considerable cost to her pride—and, paradoxically, dreaded.

Her heart hitched painfully as she accepted the envelope from the storekeeper's outstretched hand; the handwriting, a slanted scrawl penned in black ink, was definitely her brother Clay's. The postmark read Denver.

In the distance, the snow-muffled shrill of a train whistle announced the imminent arrival of the four o'clock from Missoula, which passed through town only once a week, bound for points south.

Juliana was keenly aware of the four children still in her charge, waiting just inside the door of a place where they knew they were patently unwelcome. She turned away from the counter—and the storekeeper's disapproving gaze—to fumble with the circle of red wax bearing Clay's imposing seal.

Please, God, she prayed silently. *Please.*

After drawing a deep breath and releasing it slowly, Juliana bit her lower lip, took out the single sheet folded inside.

Her heart, heretofore wedged into her throat, plummeted to the soles of her practical shoes. Her vision blurred.

Her brother hadn't enclosed the desperately needed funds she'd asked for—money that was rightfully her own, a part of the legacy her grandmother had left her. She could not purchase train tickets for herself and her charges, and the Indian School, their home and hers for the past two years, was no longer government property. The small but sturdy building had been sold to a neighboring farmer, and he planned to stable cows inside it.

Now the plank floor seemed to buckle slightly under Juliana's feet. The heat from the potbellied stove in the center of the store, so welcome only a few minutes before when she and the children had come in out of the blustery cold, all of them dappled with fat flakes of snow, threatened to smother Juliana now.

The little bell over the door jingled, indicating the arrival of another customer, but Juliana did not look up from the page in her hand. The words swam before her, making no more sense to her fitful mind than ancient Hebrew would have done.

A brief, frenzied hope stirred within Juliana. Perhaps all was not lost, perhaps Clay, not trusting the postal service, had *wired* the money she needed. It might be waiting for her, at that very moment, just down the street at the telegraph office.

Her eyes stung with the swift and sobering realization that she was grasping at straws. She blinked and forced herself to read what her older brother and legal guardian had written.

My Dear Sister,
I trust this letter will find you well.
   Nora, the children and I are all in robust health. Your niece and nephew constantly inquire as to your whereabouts, as do certain other parties.
   I regret that I cannot in good conscience remit the funds you have requested, for reasons that should be obvious to you....

Juliana crumpled the sheet of expensive vellum, nearly ill with disappointment and the helpless frustration that generally resulted from any dealings with her brother, direct or indirect.

"Are you all right, miss?" a male voice asked, strong and quiet.

Startled, Juliana looked up, saw a tall man standing directly in front of her. His eyes and hair were dark, the round brim of his hat and the shoulders of his long coat dusted with snow.

Waiting politely for her answer, he took off his hat. Hung it from the post of a wooden chair, smiled.

"I'm Lincoln Creed," he said, gruffly kind, pulling off a leather glove before extending his hand.

Juliana hesitated, offered her own hand in return. She knew the name, of course—the Creeds owned the largest cattle ranch in that part of the state, and the *Stillwater Springs Courier,* too. Although Juliana had had encounters with Weston, the brother who ran the newspaper, and briefly met the Widow Creed, the matriarch of the family, she'd never crossed paths with Lincoln.

"Juliana Mitchell," she said, with the proper balance of reticence and politeness. She'd been gently raised, after all. A hundred years ago—*a thousand*—she'd called one of the finest mansions in Denver home. She'd worn imported silks and velvets and fashionable hats, ridden in carriages with liveried drivers and even footmen.

Remembering made her faintly ashamed.

All that, of course, had been before her fall from social grace.

Before Clay, as administrator of their grandmother's estate, had all but disinherited her.

Mr. Creed dropped his gaze to the letter. "Bad news?" he asked, with an unsettling note of discernment. He might have had Indian blood himself, with his high cheekbones and raven-black hair.

The train whistle gave another triumphant squeal. It had pulled into the rickety little depot at the edge of town, right on schedule. Passengers would alight, others would board. Mail and freight would be loaded and unloaded. And then the engine would chug out of the station, the line of cars rattling behind it.

A full week would pass before another train came through.

In the meantime, Juliana and the children would have no choice but to throw themselves upon the uncertain mercies of the townspeople. In a larger community, she might have turned to a church for assistance, but there weren't any in Stillwater Springs. The faithful met sporadically, in the one-room schoolhouse where only white students were allowed when the circuit preacher came through.

Juliana swallowed, wanting to cry, and determined

that she wouldn't. "I'm afraid it *is* bad news," she admitted in belated answer to Mr. Creed's question.

He took a gentle hold on her elbow, escorted her to one of the empty wooden chairs over by the potbellied stove. Sat her down. "Did somebody die?" he asked.

Numb with distraction, Juliana shook her head.

What in the world was she going to do now? Without money, she could not purchase train tickets for herself and the children, or even arrange for temporary lodgings of some sort.

Mr. Creed inclined his head toward the children lined up in front of the display window, with its spindly but glittering Christmas tree. They'd turned their backs now, to look at the decorations and the elaborate toys tucked into the branches and arranged attractively underneath.

"I guess you must be the teacher from out at the Indian School," he said.

Mr. Willand, the mercantile's proprietor, interrupted with a *harrumph* sound.

Juliana ached as she watched the children. The storekeeper was keeping a close eye on them, too. Like so many people, he reasoned that simply because they were Indians, they were sure to steal, afforded the slightest opportunity. "Yes," she replied, practiced at ignoring such attitudes, if not resigned to them. "Or, at least, I *was*. The school is closed now."

Lincoln Creed nodded after skewering Mr. Willand with a glare. "I was sorry to hear it," he told her.

"No letters came since you were in here last week, Lincoln," Willand broke in, with some satisfaction. The very atmosphere of that store, overheated and close, seemed to bristle with mutual dislike. "Reckon you can wait around and see if there were any on today's train, but my guess is you wasted your money, putting all those advertisements in all them newspapers."

"Everyone is sorry, Mr. Creed," Juliana said quietly. "But no one seems inclined to help."

Momentarily distracted by Mr. Willand's remark, Lincoln didn't respond immediately. When he did, his voice was nearly drowned out by the scream of the train whistle.

Juliana stood up, remembered anew that her situation was hopeless, and sat down again, hard, all the strength gone from her knees. Perhaps she'd used it up, walking the two miles into town from the school, with every one of her worldly possessions tucked into a single worn-out satchel. Each of the children had carried a small bundle, too, leaving them on the sidewalk outside the door of the mercantile with Juliana's bag.

"There's a storm coming, Miss—er—Mitchell," Lincoln Creed said. "It's cold and getting colder, and it'll be dark soon. I didn't see a rig outside, so I figure you must have walked to town. I've got my team and buckboard outside, and I'd be glad to give you and those kids a ride to wherever you're headed."

Tears welled in Juliana's eyes, shaming her, and her throat tightened painfully. Wherever she was headed? *Nowhere* was where she was headed.

Stillwater Springs had a hotel and several boarding houses, but even if she'd had the wherewithal to pay for a room and meals, most likely none of them would have accepted the children, anyway.

They'd hurried so, trying to get to Stillwater Springs before the train left, Juliana desperately counting on the funds from Clay even against her better judgment, but there had been delays. Little Daisy falling and skinning one knee, a huge band of sheep crossing the road and blocking their way, the limp that plagued twelve-year-old Theresa, with her twisted foot.

Lincoln broke into her thoughts. "Miss Mitchell?" he prompted.

Mr. Willand slammed something down hard on the counter, causing Juliana to start. "Don't you touch none of that merchandise!" he shouted, and Joseph, the eldest of Juliana's pupils at fourteen, pulled his hand back from the display window. "Damn thievin' Injuns—"

Poor Joseph looked crestfallen. Theresa, his sister, trembled, while the two littlest children, Billy-Moses, who was four, and Daisy, three, rushed to Juliana and clung to her skirts in fear.

"The boy wasn't doing any harm, Fred," Lincoln told the storekeeper evenly, rising slowly out of his chair. "No need to raise your voice, or accuse him, either."

Mr. Willand reddened. "You have a grocery order?" he asked, glowering at Lincoln Creed.

"Just came by to see if I had mail," Lincoln said, with a shake of his head. "Couldn't get here before now, what with the hard weather coming on." He paused, turned to Juliana. "Best we get you to wherever it is you're going," he said.

"We don't have anyplace to go, mister," Joseph said, still standing near the display window, but careful to keep his hands visible at his sides. Since he rarely spoke, especially to strangers, Juliana was startled.

And as desperate as she was, the words chafed her pride.

Lincoln frowned, obviously confused. "What?"

"They might take us in over at the Diamond Buckle

Saloon," Theresa said, lifting her chin. "If we work for our keep."

Lincoln stared at the girl, confounded. "The Diamond Buckle...?"

Juliana didn't trust herself to speak without breaking down completely. If she did not remain strong, the children would have no hope at all.

"Mr. Weston Creed said he'd teach me to set type," Joseph reminded Juliana. "Bet I could sleep in the back room at the newspaper, and I don't need much to eat. You wouldn't have to fret about me, Miss Mitchell." He glanced worriedly at his sister, swallowed hard. He was old enough to understand the dangers a place like the Diamond Buckle might harbor for a young girl, even if Theresa wasn't.

Lincoln raised both hands, palms out, in a bid for silence.

Everyone stared at him, including Juliana, who had pulled little Daisy onto her lap.

"All of you," Lincoln said, addressing the children, "gather up whatever things you've got and get into the back of my buckboard. You'll find some blankets there—wrap up warm, because it's three miles to the ranch house and there's an icy wind blowing in from the northwest."

Juliana stood, gently displacing Daisy, careful to keep the child close against her side. "Mr. Creed, we couldn't accept..." Her voice fell away, and mortification burned in her cheeks.

"Seems to me," Lincoln said, "you don't have much of a choice. I'm offering you and these children a place to stay, Miss Mitchell. Just till you can figure out what to do next."

"You'd let these savages set foot under the same roof with your little Gracie?" Mr. Willand blustered, incensed. He'd crossed the otherwise-empty store, shouldered Joseph aside to peer into the display window and make sure nothing was missing.

The air pulsed again.

Lincoln took a step toward the storekeeper.

By instinct, Juliana grasped Mr. Creed's arm to stop him. Even through the heavy fabric of his coat, she could feel that his muscles were steely with tension—he was barely containing his temper. "The children are used to remarks like that," she said quietly, anxious to keep the peace. "They know they aren't savages."

"Get into the wagon," Lincoln said. He didn't pull free of Juliana's touch, nor did he look away from Mr. Willand's crimson face. "All of you."

The children looked to Juliana, their dark, luminous eyes liquid with wary question.

She nodded, silently giving her permission.

Almost as one, they scrambled for the door, causing the bell to clamor merrily overhead. Even Daisy, clinging until a moment before, peeled away from Juliana's side.

After pulling her cloak more closely around her and raising the hood against the cold wind, Juliana followed.

LINCOLN WATCHED THEM GO. He'd hung his hat on one of the spindle-backed wooden chairs next to the stove earlier, and he reached for it. "There's enough grief and sorrow in this world," he told the storekeeper, "without folks like you adding to it."

Willand was undaunted, though Lincoln noticed he stayed well behind the counter, within bolting distance of the back door. "We'll see what *Mrs.* Creed says, when you turn up on her doorstep with a tribe of Injuns—"

Lincoln shoved his hat down on top of his head with a little more force than the effort required. His wife, Beth, had died two years before, of a fever, so Willand was referring to his mother. Cora Creed would indeed have been surprised to find five extra people seated around her supper table that night—if Lincoln hadn't left her with enough bags to fill a freight car at the train depot before stopping by the mercantile. She was headed for Phoenix, where she liked to winter with her kinfolks, the Dawsons.

"I'll be back tomorrow if I get the chance," he said, starting for the door. With that storm coming and cattle to feed, he couldn't be sure. "To see if any letters came in on today's train."

Willand glanced at the big regulator clock on the wall behind him. "My boy's gone to the depot, like always, and he'll be here with the mail bag any minute now," he said grudgingly. "Might as well wait."

Lincoln went to the window, looked past his own reflection in the darkening glass—God, he hated the shortness of winter days—to see Miss Mitchell settling her unlikely brood in the bed of his wagon. Something warmed inside him, shifted. The slightest smile tilted one corner of his mouth.

He'd been advertising for a governess for his seven-year-old daughter, Gracie, and a housekeeper for the both of them for nearly a year; failing either of those, he'd settle for a wife, and because he knew he'd never love another woman the way he'd loved Beth, he wasn't too choosey in his requirements.

Juliana Mitchell, with her womanly figure, indigo-blue eyes and those tendrils of coppery hair peeking out from under her worn bonnet, was clearly dedicated to her profession, since she'd stayed to look after those children even now that the Indian School had closed down. A lot of schoolmarms wouldn't have done that.

This spoke well for her character, and when it came to looks, she was a better bargain than anyone all those advertisements might have scared up.

Glancing down at the display, with all the toys Willand was hoping to sell before Christmas, Lincoln's gaze fell on the corner of a metal box, tucked at an odd angle under the bunting beneath the tree. He reached for the item, drew it out, saw that it was a set of watercolor paints, similar to one Gracie had at home.

Was this what the boy had been looking at when Willand pitched a fit?

For reasons he couldn't have explained, Lincoln was sure it was.

He held the long, flat tin up for Willand to see, before tucking it into the inside pocket of his coat. "Put this on my bill," he said.

Willand grumbled, but a sale was a sale. He finally nodded.

Lincoln raised his collar against the cold and left the mercantile for the wooden sidewalk beyond.

The kids were settled in the back of the wagon, all but the oldest boy snuggled in the rough woolen blankets Lincoln always carried in winter. Juliana Mitchell waited primly on the seat, straight-spined, chin high, trying not to shiver in that thin cloak of hers.

Buttoning his coat as he left the store, Lincoln unbuttoned it again before climbing up into the box beside her. Snowflakes drifted slowly from a gray sky as he took up the reins, released the brake lever. The streets of the town were nearly deserted—folks were getting ready for the storm, feeling its approach in their bones, just as Lincoln did.

Knowing her pride would make her balk if he took off his coat and put it around her, he pulled his right arm out of the sleeve and drew her to his side instead, closing the garment around her.

She stiffened, then went still, in what he guessed was resignation.

It bruised something inside Lincoln, realizing how many things Juliana Mitchell had probably had to resign herself to over the course of her life.

He set the team in motion, kept his gaze on the snowy road ahead, winding toward home. By the time they reached the ranch, it would be dark out, but the horses knew their way.

Meanwhile, Juliana Mitchell felt warm and soft against him. He'd forgotten what it was like to protect a woman, shield her against his side, and the remembrance was painful, like frostbitten flesh beginning to thaw.

Beth had been gone awhile, and though he wasn't proud of it, in the last six months or so he'd turned to loose women for comfort a time or two, over in Choteau or in Missoula.

The quickening he felt now was different, of course. Though anybody could see she was down on her luck, it was equally obvious that Juliana Mitchell was a lady. Breeding was a thing even shabby clothes couldn't hide—especially from a rancher used to raising fine cattle and horses.

Minutes later, as they jostled over the road in the buckboard, Juliana relaxed against Lincoln, and it came to him, with a flash of amusement, that she was asleep. Plainly, she was exhausted. From the way her face had fallen as she'd read that letter, which she'd finally wadded up and stuffed into the pocket of her cloak with an expression of heartbroken disgust in her eyes, she'd suffered some bitter disappointment.

All he knew for sure was that nobody had died, since he'd asked her that right off.

Lincoln tried to imagine what kind of news might have thrown her like that, even though he knew it was none of his business.

Maybe she'd planned to marry the man who'd written that letter, and he'd spurned her for another.

Lincoln frowned, aware of the woman's softness and warmth in every part of his lonesome body. What kind of damned fool would do that?

His shoulder began to ache, since his arm was curved around Juliana at a somewhat awkward angle, but he didn't care. He'd have driven right past the ranch, just so she could go on resting against him like that for a little while longer, if he hadn't been a practical man.

The wind picked up, and the snow came down harder and faster, and when he looked back at the kids, they were sitting stoically in their places, bundled in their blankets.

The best part of an hour had passed when the lights of the ranch house finally came into view, glowing dim and golden in the snow-swept darkness.

Lincoln's heartbeat picked up a little, the way it always did when he rounded that last bend in the road and saw home waiting up ahead.

Home.

He'd been born in the rambling, one-story log house,

with its stone chimneys, the third son of Josiah and Cora Creed. Micah, the firstborn, had long since left the ranch, started a place of his own down in Colorado. Weston, the next in line, lived in town, in rooms above the Diamond Buckle Saloon, and published the *Courier*—when he was sober enough to run the presses.

Two years younger than Wes, Lincoln had left home only to attend college in Boston and apprentice himself to a lawyer—Beth's father. As soon as he was qualified to practice, Lincoln had married Beth, brought her home to Stillwater Springs Ranch and loved her with all the passion a man could feel for a woman.

She'd taken to life on a remote Montana ranch with amazing acuity for a city girl, and if she'd missed Boston, she'd never once let on. She'd given him Gracie, and they'd been happy.

Now she rested in the small, sad cemetery beyond the apple orchard, like Josiah, and the fourth Creed brother, Dawson.

Dawson. Sometimes it was harder to think about him and the way he'd died, than to recall Beth succumbing to that fever.

Juliana straightened against Lincoln's side, yawned. If the darkness hadn't hidden her face, the brim of her bonnet would have, but he sensed that she was embarrassed by the lapse.

"We're almost home," he said, just loudly enough for her to hear.

She didn't answer, but sat up a little straighter, wanting to pull away, but confined by his arm and the cloth of his coat.

When they reached the gate with its overarching sign, Lincoln moved to get down, but the Indian boy, Joseph, was faster. He worked the latch, swung the gate wide, and Lincoln drove the buckboard through.

His father and Tom Dancingstar had cut and planed the timber for that sign, chiseled the letters into it, and then laboriously deepened them with pokers heated in the homemade forge they'd used for horseshoeing.

Lincoln never saw the words without a feeling of quiet gratification and pride.

Stillwater Springs Ranch.

He held the team while the boy shut the gate, then scrambled back into the wagon. The horses were eager to get to the barn, where hay and water and warm stalls awaited them.

Tom was there to help unhitch the team when Lincoln drove through the wide doorway and under the sturdy barn roof. Part Lakota Sioux, part Cherokee and part devil by his own accounting, Tom had worked on the ranch from the beginning. He'd named himself, claiming no white tongue could manage the handle he'd been given at birth.

He smiled when he saw Juliana, and she smiled back.

Clearly, they were acquainted.

Was he, Lincoln wondered, the only yahoo in the countryside who'd never met the teacher from the Indian School?

"Take the kids inside the house," Lincoln told Juliana, and it struck him that rather than the strangers they were, they might have been married for years, the two of them, all these children their own. "Tom and I will be in as soon as we've finished here."

He paused to lift the two smaller children out of the wagon; sleepy-eyed, still wrapped in their blankets, they stumbled a little, befuddled to find themselves in a barn lit by lanterns, surrounded by horses and Jenny Lind, the milk cow.

"I'll tend to the horses," Tom told him. "There's a kettle of stew warming on the stove, and Gracie's been watching the road for you since sunset."

Thinking of his gold-haired, blue-eyed daughter, Lincoln smiled. Smarter than three judges and as many juries put together, Gracie tended toward fretfulness. Losing her mother when she was only five caused her to worry about him whenever he was out of her sight.

With a ranch the size of his to run, he was away from the house a lot, accustomed to leaving the child in the care of his now-absent mother, or Rose-of-Sharon Gainer, the cumbersomely pregnant young wife of one of the ranch hands.

The older boy's gaze had fastened on Tom.

"Can I stay here and help?" he asked.

"May I," Juliana corrected with a smile. "Yes, Joseph, you may."

With that, she leaned down, weary as she was, and lifted the littlest girl into her arms. Lincoln bent to hoist up the smaller boy.

"This is Daisy," Juliana told him. "That's Billy-Moses you're holding." The girl who'd spoken of working for her keep at the Diamond Buckle ducked her head shyly, stood a little closer to her teacher. "And this is Theresa," she finished.

Leaving Tom and Joseph to put the team up for the night, Lincoln shed his coat at the entrance to the barn, draped it over Juliana's shoulders. It dragged on the snowy ground, and she smiled wanly at that, hiking the garment up with her free arm, closing it around both herself and Daisy.

They entered the house by the side door, stepping into the warmth, the aroma of Tom's venison stew and the light of several lanterns. Gracie, rocking in the chair near the cookstove and pretending she hadn't been waiting impatiently for Lincoln's return, went absolutely still when she saw that he wasn't alone.

Her cornflower-blue eyes widened, and her mouth made a perfect O.

Daisy and Billy-Moses stared back at her, probably as amazed as she was.

"Gracie," Lincoln said unnecessarily. "We have company."

Gracie had recovered by then; she fairly leaped out of the rocking chair. Looking up at Juliana, she asked, "Did you answer one of my papa's advertisements? Are you going to be a governess, a housekeeper or a wife?"

Lincoln winced.

Understandably, Juliana seemed taken aback. Like Gracie, though, she turned out to be pretty resilient. The only sign that the child's question had caught her off guard was the faint tinge of pink beneath her cheekbones, and that might have been from the cold.

"I'm Miss Mitchell," she said kindly. "These are my pupils—Daisy, Billy-Moses and Theresa. There's Joseph, as well—he's out in the barn helping Mr. Dancingstar look after the horses."

"Then you're a *governess!*" Gracie cried jubilantly. Young as she was, she could already read, and because Lincoln wouldn't allow her to travel back and forth to school in Stillwater Springs, she was convinced that lifelong ignorance would be her lot.

"Gracie," Lincoln said, setting Billy-Moses on his

feet. "Miss Mitchell is a guest. She didn't answer any advertisements."

Gracie looked profoundly disappointed, but only for a moment. Like most Creeds, when she set her mind on something, she did not give up easily.

For the next little while, they were all busy with supper.

Tom and Joseph came in from the barn, pumped water at the sink to wash up and joined them at the table, while Gracie, who had already eaten, rushed about fetching bread and butter and ladling milk from the big covered crock stored on the back step.

His daughter wanted to make Miss Mitchell feel welcome, Lincoln thought with a smile, so she'd stay and teach her all she wanted to know—and that was considerable. She hadn't asked for a doll for Christmas, or a spinning top, like a lot of little girls would have done.

Oh, no. Gracie wanted a dictionary.

Wes often joked that by the time his niece was old enough to make the trip to town on her own, she'd be half again too smart for school and ready to take over the *Courier* so he could spend the rest of his life smoking cigars and playing poker.

As far as Lincoln could tell, his brother did little else but smoke cigars and play poker—not counting, of course, the whiskey-swilling and his long-standing and wholly scandalous love affair with Kate Winthrop, who happened to own the Diamond Buckle.

Gracie adored her uncle Weston—and Kate.

Casting a surreptitious glance in Juliana's direction whenever he could during supper, Lincoln saw that she could barely keep her eyes open. As soon as the meal was over, he showed her to his mother's spacious room. She and Daisy and Billy-Moses could share the big feather bed.

Joseph bunked in with Tom, who slept in a small chamber behind the kitchen stove, having given up his cabin out by the bunkhouse to Ben Gainer and his wife. Theresa was to sleep with Gracie.

Lincoln's young daughter, however, was not in bed. Wide-awake, she sat at the table with Lincoln, watching as he drank lukewarm coffee, left over from earlier in the day.

"Go to bed, Gracie," he told her.

Tom lingered by the stove, also drinking coffee. He smiled when Gracie didn't move.

"I couldn't possibly sleep," she said seriously. "I am entirely too excited."

Lincoln sighed. She was knee-high to a fence post, but sometimes she talked like someone her grandmother's age. "It's still five days until Christmas," he reminded her. "Too soon to be all het up over presents and such."

"I'm not excited about *Christmas*," Gracie said, with the exaggerated patience she might have shown the village idiot. Stillwater Springs boasted its share of those. "You're going to marry Miss Mitchell, and I'll have Billy-Moses and Daisy to play with—"

Tom chuckled into his coffee cup.

Lincoln sighed again and settled back in his chair. Although he'd thought about hitching up with the school-teacher, he'd probably been hasty. "Gracie, Miss Mitchell isn't here to marry me. She was stranded in town because the Indian School closed down, so I brought her and the kids home—"

"Will I still have to call her 'Miss Mitchell' after you get married to her? She'd be 'Mrs. Creed' then, wouldn't she? It would be really silly for me to go around saying 'Mrs. Creed' all the time—"

"Gracie."

"What?"

"Go to bed."

"I told you, I'm too excited."

"And *I* told *you* to go to bed."

"Oh, for heaven's sake," Gracie protested, disgruntled.

But she got out of her chair at the table, said goodnight to Tom and stood on tiptoe to kiss Lincoln on the cheek.

His heart melted like a honeycomb under a hot sun when she did that. Her blue eyes, so like Beth's, sparkled as she looked up at him, then turned solemn.

"Be nice to Miss Mitchell, Papa," she instructed solemnly. "Stand up when she comes into a room, and pull her chair back for her. We want her to like it here and stay."

Lincoln's throat constricted, and his eyes burned. He couldn't have answered to save his hide from a hot brand.

"You'll come and hear my prayers?" Gracie asked, the way she did every night.

The prayers varied slightly, but certain parts were always the same.

Please keep my papa safe, and Tom, too. I'd like a dog of my very own, one that will fetch, and I want to go to school, so I don't grow up to be stupid....

Lincoln nodded his assent. Though it was a request he never refused, Gracie always asked.

Once she left the room, Tom set his cup in the sink, folded his arms. "According to young Joseph," he said, "he and his sister have folks in North Dakota—an aunt and a grandfather. Soon as he can save enough money, he means to head for home and take Theresa with him."

Lincoln felt a lot older than his thirty-five years as he raised himself from his chair, began turning down lamp wicks, one by one. Tom, in the meantime, banked the fire in the cookstove.

They were usual, these long gaps in their conversations. Right or wrong, Lincoln had always been closer to Tom than to his own father—Josiah Creed had been a hard man in many ways. Neither Lincoln nor Wes had mourned him overmuch—they left that to Micah, the eldest, and their mother.

"Did the boy happen to say how he and the girl wound up in a school outside of Stillwater Springs, Montana?"

Tom straightened, his profile grim in the last of the lantern light. "The government decided he and his sister would be better off if they learned white ways," he said. "Took them off the reservation in North Dakota a couple of years ago, and they were in several different 'institutions' before their luck changed. They haven't seen their people since the day they left Dakota, though Juliana helped him write a letter to them six months back, and they got an answer." Tom paused, swallowed visibly. His voice sounded hoarse. "The folks at home want them back, Lincoln."

Lincoln stood in the relative darkness for a few moments, reflecting. "I'll send them, then," he said after a long time. "Put them on the train when it comes through next week."

Tom didn't answer immediately, and when he did, the whole Trail of Tears echoed in his voice. "They're just kids. They oughtn't to make a trip like that alone."

Another lengthy silence rested comfortably between

the two men. Then Lincoln said, "You want to go with them."

"Somebody ought to," Tom replied. "Make sure they get there all right. Might be that things have changed since that letter came."

Lincoln absorbed that, finally nodded. "What about the little ones?" he asked without looking at his friend. "Daisy and Billy-Moses?"

"They're orphans," Tom said, and sadness settled over the darkened room like a weight. "Reckon Miss Mitchell planned on keeping them until she could find them a home."

Lincoln sighed inwardly. *Until she could find them a home.* As if those near-babies were stray puppies or kittens.

With another nod, this one sorrowful, he turned away.

It was time to turn in; morning would come early.

But damned if he'd sleep a wink between the plight of four innocent children and the knowledge that Juliana Mitchell was lying on the other side of the wall.

CHAPTER TWO

THE MATTRESS FELT like a cloud, tufted and stuffed with feathers from angels' wings, beneath Juliana's weary frame, but sleep eluded her. Daisy slumbered innocently at her right side, sucking one tiny thumb, while Billy-Moses snuggled close on the left, clinging to her flannel nightgown—the cloth was still chilled from being rolled up in her satchel, out in the weather most of the day.

Juliana listened as the sturdy house settled around her, her body still stiff with tension, that being its long-established habit, heard a plank creaking here, a roof timber there. She caught the sound of a door opening and closing just down the corridor, pictured Lincoln Creed passing into his room, or bending over little Gracie's bed to tuck her in and bid her good-night. Would he spare a kind word for Theresa, who was sharing Gracie's room, and so hungry for affection, or reserve all his attention for his little daughter?

Gracie was a charming child, as lovely as a doll come to life, with those thickly lashed eyes, golden ringlets brushing her shoulders and the pink-tinged porcelain perfection of her skin. Privileged by comparison to most children, not to mention the four in Juliana's own charge, Gracie was precocious, but if she was spoiled, there had been no sign of it yet. She'd greeted the new arrivals at Stillwater Springs Ranch with frank curiosity, yes, but then she'd ladled milk into mugs for them, even served it at the table.

Juliana's heart pinched. Gracie had a strong, loving father, a home, robust good health. But behind those more obvious blessings lurked a certain lonely resignation uncommon in one so young. Gracie had lost her mother at a very early age, and no one understood the sorrows of that more than Juliana herself—she'd been six years old when her own had succumbed to consumption. Juliana's father, outraged by grief, torn asunder by it, had dumped both his offspring on their maternal grandmother's doorstep barely two weeks after his wife's funeral and, over the next few years, delivered himself up to dissolution and debauchery.

Clay, nine at the time of their mother's passing, had changed from a lighthearted, mischievous boy to a solemn-faced man, seemingly overnight. In a very real way, Juliana had lost him, in addition to both her parents.

Victoria Marston, their grandmother, already a widow when her only daughter had died, dressed in mourning until her own death a decade later, but she had loved Juliana and Clay tirelessly nonetheless. Grandmama had given them every advantage—tutors, music lessons, finishing school for Juliana, who had immediately changed the course of her study to train as a schoolteacher upon the discovery that "finishing" involved learning to make small talk with men, the proper way to pour tea and a lot of walking about with a book balanced on top of her head. There had been college in San Francisco for Clay, even a Grand Tour.

Juliana had stayed behind in Denver, living at home with Grandmama, attending classes every day and letting her doting grandmother believe she was being thoroughly "finished," impatiently waiting for her life to begin.

For all the things she would have changed, she appreciated her blessings, too; she'd been well-cared-for, beautifully clothed and educated beyond the level most young women attained. Yet, there was still a childlike yearning inside Juliana, a longing for her beautiful, laughing mama. The singular and often poignant ache was mostly manageable—except when she was discouraged, and that had been often, of late.

After graduating from Normal School—her grandmother had died of a heart condition only weeks before Juliana accepted her certificate—she'd begun her career with high hopes, pushed up her sleeves and flung herself into the fray, undaunted at first by her brother's cold disapproval. He'd wanted her to marry his business partner, John Holden, and because he controlled their grandmother's large estate, Clay had had the power to disinherit her. On the day she'd given back John's engagement ring and accepted her first teaching assignment at a school for Indian boys in a small Colorado town a day's train ride from Denver, he'd done that, for all practical intents and purposes.

Juliana had been left with nothing but the few modest clothes and personal belongings she'd packed for the journey. Clay had gone so far as to ban her from the family home, saying she could return when she "came to her senses."

To Clay, "coming to her senses" meant consigning herself to a loveless marriage to a widower more than twenty years her senior, a man with two daughters close to Juliana's own age.

Mean daughters, who went out of their way to be snide, and saw their future stepmother as an interloper bent on claiming their late mother's jewelry, as well as her home and husband.

Remembering, Juliana bit down on her lower lip, and her eyes smarted a little. She might have been content with John, if not happy, had it not been for Eleanor and Eugenie. He was gentle, well-read, and she'd felt safe with him.

In a flash of insight and dismay, Juliana had realized she was looking for a father, not a husband. She'd explained to John, and though he'd been disappointed, he'd understood. He'd even been gracious enough to wish her well.

Clay, by contrast, had been furious; his otherwise handsome features had turned to stone the day she'd told him about the broken engagement.

In the six years since, he'd softened a little—probably because his wife, Nora, had lobbied steadily on Juliana's behalf—writing regularly, even inviting Juliana home for visits and offering to ship the clothing and books she'd left behind, but when it came to her inheritance, he'd never relented.

Even when John Holden had died suddenly, a year before, permanently disqualifying himself as a possible husband for the sister Clay had once adored and protected, teased and laughed with, he had not given ground. After months of working up her courage, she'd written to ask for a modest bank draft, since her salary was small, less than the allowance her grandmother had given her as a girl, and Clay had responded with words that still blistered Juliana's pride, even now. "I won't see you squandering good money," he'd written, "on shoes and schoolbooks for a pack of red-skinned orphans and strays."

A burning ache rose in Juliana's throat at the memory.

Clay would cease punishing her when she stopped teaching and married a man who met with his lofty approval, then and only then, and that was the unfortunate reality.

She'd been a fool to write to him that last time, all but begging for the funds she'd needed to get Joseph and Theresa safely home to North Dakota and look after the two little ones until proper homes could be found for them.

The situation was further complicated by the fact that Mr. Philbert, an agent of the Bureau of Indian Affairs and therefore Juliana's supervisor, believed the four pupils still in her charge had been sent back to their original school in Missoula, along with the older students. Sooner or later, making his rounds or by correspondence, Philbert, a diligent sort with no softness in him that Juliana could discern, would realize she'd not only disobeyed his orders, but lied to him, at least in part.

As an official representative of the United States government, the man could have her arrested and prosecuted for kidnapping, and consign Daisy and Billy-Moses to some new institution, far out of her reach, where they would probably be neglected, at best. Juliana knew, after working in a series of such places, all but bloodying her very soul in the effort to change things, that only the most dedicated reformers would bother to look beyond the color of their skin. And there were precious few of those.

To keep from thinking about Mr. Philbert and his inevitable wrath, Juliana turned her mind to the students she'd had to bid farewell to—Mary Rose, seventeen and soon to be entering Normal School herself; Ezekiel, sixteen, who wanted to finish his education and return to his tribe. Finally, there was Angelique, seventeen, like her cousin Mary Rose, sweet and unassuming and smitten with a boy she'd met while running an errand in Stillwater Springs one spring day.

Part Blackfoot and part white, Blue Johnston had visited several times, a handsome, engaging young man with a flashing white smile and the promise of a job herding cattle on a ranch outside of Missoula. Although Juliana had kept close watch on the couple and warned Angelique repeatedly about the perils of impulse, she'd had the other children to attend to, and the pair had strayed out of her sight more than a few times.

Privately, Juliana feared that Angelique and her beau would run away and get married as soon as they got the chance—and that chance had come a week before, when Angelique and the others had boarded the train to return to Missoula. Should that happen—perhaps it already had—Mr. Philbert would bluster and threaten dire consequences when he learned of it, all the while figuratively dusting his hands together, secretly relieved to have one less obligation.

Footsteps passed along the hallway, past her door, bringing Juliana out of her rueful reflections. Another door opened and then closed again, nearer, and then all was silent.

The house rested, and so, evidently, did Lincoln Creed.

Juliana could not.

Easing herself from between the sleeping children, after gently freeing the fabric of her nightgown from Billy-Moses's grasp, Juliana crawled out of bed.

The cold slammed against her body like the shock following an explosion; there was a small stove in the room, but it had not been lit.

Shivering, Juliana crossed to it, all but hopping, found matches and newspaper and kindling and larger chunks of pitchy wood resting tidily in a nearby basket. With numb fingers, she opened the stove door and laid a fire, set the newspaper and kindling ablaze, adjusted the damper.

The floor stung the soles of her bare feet, and the single window, though large, was opaque with curlicues and crystals of ice. A silvery glow indicated that the moon had come out from behind the snow-burdened clouds—perhaps the storm had stopped.

Juliana paced, making no sound, until the room began to warm up, and then fumbled in the pocket of her cloak for Clay's crumpled letter. Back at the mercantile, she'd been too overwrought to finish the missive. Now, wakeful in the house of a charitable stranger—but a stranger nevertheless—she smoothed the page with the flat of one hand, hungry for a word of kind affection.

Not wanting to light a lamp, lest she awaken the children resting so soundly in the feather bed, Juliana knelt near the fire, opened the stove door again and read by the flickering flames inside, welcoming the warmth.

Her gaze skimmed over the first few lines—she could have recited those from memory—and took in the rest.

You will be twenty-six years old on your next birthday, Juliana, and you are still unmarried. Nora and I are, of course, greatly concerned for your welfare, not to mention your reputation....

Juliana had to stop herself by the summoning of inner forces from wadding the letter up again, casting it straight into the fire.

Clay had accepted the fact, he continued, in his usual brisk fashion, that his sister had consigned herself to a life of lonely and wasteful spinsterhood. She was creating a scandal, he maintained, by living away from home and family. What kind of example, he wondered, was she setting for Clara, her little niece?

He closed with what amounted to a command that she return to Denver and "live with modesty and circumspection" in her brother's home, where she belonged.

But there was no expression of fondness.

The letter was signed *Regards, C. Mitchell.*

"'C. Mitchell,'" Juliana whispered on a shaky breath. "Not 'Clay.' Not 'Your brother.' 'C. Mitchell.'"

With that, she folded the single page carefully, held it for a moment, and then tossed it into the stove. Watched, the heat drying her eyeballs until they burned, as orange flames curled the vellum, nibbled darkly at the edges and corners, and then consumed the last forlorn tatters of Juliana's hopes. There would be no reconciliation between her and Clay, no restoration of their old childhood camaraderie.

As much as she had loved the brother she remembered from long ago, as much as she loved him still, for surely he was still in there somewhere behind that rigid facade, she *could not* go home. Oh, she would have enjoyed getting to know little Clara and her brother, Simon. She had always been fond of Nora, a good-hearted if flighty woman who accepted her husband's absolute authority without apparent qualms. But Clay would treat her, Juliana, like a poor relation, doling out pennies for a packet of pins, lecturing and dictating her every move, staring her down if she dared to venture an opinion at the supper table.

No. She definitely could not go home, not under such circumstances. It would be the ultimate—and final—defeat, and the slow death of her spirit.

"Missy?" The lisp was Daisy's; the child could not say Juliana's whole name, and always addressed her thus. "Missy, are you there?"

"I'm here, sweetheart," Juliana confirmed quietly, closing the stove door and getting back to her feet. "I'm here."

The assurance was enough for Daisy; she turned onto her side, settled in with a tiny murmur of relief and sank into sleep again.

Even with the fire going, the room was still cold enough to numb Juliana's bones.

Having no other choice, she climbed back into bed and pulled the top sheet and faded quilts up to her chin, giving a little shiver.

Billy-Moses stirred beside her, took a new hold on her nightgown.

Daisy snuggled close, too.

Juliana stared up at the ceiling, watching the shadows dance, her heart and mind crowded with children again. At some point, she could send Joseph and Theresa home by train to their family in North Dakota.

But what of Daisy and Billy-Moses? They had no-where to go, besides an orphanage or some other "school."

In her more optimistic moments, Juliana could convince herself that some kindly couple would be delighted to adopt these bright, beautiful children, would cherish and nurture them.

This was not an optimistic moment.

Poverty was rampant among Indians; many could not

feed their own children, let alone take in the lost lambs, the "strays," as Clay and others like him referred to them.

A lone tear slipped down Juliana's right cheek, tickled its way over her temple and into her hair. She closed her eyes and waited, trying not to consider the future, and finally, fitfully, she slept.

THE COLD WAS BRITTLE; it had substance and heft.

Lincoln had carried in an armload of wood and laid kindling on the hearth of the big stone fireplace directly across from his too-big, too-empty four-poster bed that morning before dawn, the way he always did after the weather turned in the fall. He'd gotten a good blaze crackling in the little stove in Gracie's room, so she and Theresa would be snug—he'd seen children sicken and die after taking a chill—but that night he didn't bother to get his own fire going.

He stripped off his clothes and the long winter underwear beneath them, and plunged into bed naked, cursing under his breath at the smooth, icy bite of the linen sheets. It was at night that he generally missed Beth most, recalling her whispery laughter and the warmth of her curled against him, the sweet, eager solace of their lovemaking.

Tonight, it was different.

He couldn't stop thinking about Juliana: her new-penny hair; her eyes, blue as wet ink pooling on the whitest paper; the way she'd rested against his side, under his coat, soft with the innocent abandon of sleep, on the wagon ride home from town.

He reckoned that was why he wouldn't light a fire. He was punishing himself for betraying Beth's memory in a way that cut far deeper than relieving his body with dance-hall girls in other towns. God Almighty, he'd had to study the little gilt-framed picture of his late wife on Gracie's night table earlier just to reassemble her features in his mind. They'd scattered like dry leaves in a high wind, the memory of Beth's eyes and nose and the shape of her mouth, with his first look at Juliana that afternoon, in the mercantile.

Beth would have understood about the loose women. Even a mail-order bride.

But he'd vowed, sitting beside this very bed, holding Beth's hand in both his own, to love her, and no one else, until they laid him out in the cemetery alongside her.

Lincoln's eyes stung as he remembered how brave she'd been. How she'd smiled at his earnest promise, sick as she was, and told him not to close his heart, for Gracie's sake and his own.

She hadn't meant it, of course. She'd read a lot of novels about love and chivalry and noble sacrifice, that was all. A woman of comparatively few flaws, at least as far as he was concerned, Beth had nonetheless been possessive at times, her jealousy flaring when he tipped his hat to any female under the age of sixty, or returned a smile.

He'd been faithful, besotted as he was, but Beth's wealthy father had kept a mistress while she was growing up, and her mother had withdrawn into bitter silence in protest, becoming an invalid by choice. Though the instances were rare, Beth had fretted and shed tears a time or two, certain that it was only a matter of time before Lincoln tired of her and wanted some conjugal variety.

He'd reassured her, of course, kissed away her tears, made love to her, sent away to cities like New York and San Francisco and Boston for small but expensive presents he hadn't been able to afford, what with beef prices bottoming out and his mother spending money as if she still had a rich husband, and his brother Wes running the ranch into near bankruptcy while he, Lincoln, was away at college.

No, he thought, with a shake of his head and a grim set to his mouth, his hands cupped behind his head as he lay still as fallen timber, waiting for the sheets to warm up. Beth hadn't meant what she'd said that day, only hours before she'd closed her eyes for the last time; she'd merely been playing out a scene from one of those stories that made her sniffle until her face got puffy and her nose turned red. She'd believed, being so very young, that that was how a lady was supposed to die.

If it hadn't been for the seizing ache in the middle of his chest and the sting behind his eyes, Lincoln might have smiled to remember the earlier days of their marriage, when he'd come in from the barn or the range so many evenings and found his bride with a thick book clutched to her bosom and tears pouring down her cheeks.

"She died with a rose clasped between her teeth!" Beth had expounded once, evidently referring to the heroine of the novel she'd been reading by the front room fire.

His mother, darning socks in her rocking chair, wanting them both to know she disapproved of such nonsense, and saucy brides from Somewhere Else, had muttered something, shaken her head and then made a tsk-tsk sound.

"*Someone* had better start supper cooking," Cora Creed had huffed, rising and stalking off toward the kitchen.

Waited on by servants all her short life, Beth had never learned to cook, sew or even make up a bed. None of that had bothered Lincoln, though it troubled his mother plenty.

He had merely smiled, kissed Beth's overheated forehead and said something along the lines of "I hope she was careful not to bite down on the thorns. The lady in the book, I mean."

Beth had laughed then, and hit him playfully with the tome.

Now, alone in the bed where they'd conceived Gracie and two other children who hadn't survived long enough to draw even one breath, Lincoln thrust out a sigh and rubbed his eyes with a thumb and forefinger.

Morning would come around early, and the day ahead would be long, hard and cold. He and Tom and the few ranch hands wintering on the place would be hauling wagonloads of hay out to the range cattle, since the grass was buried under snow. They'd have to break the ice at the edge of the creek, too, so the cattle could drink.

He needed whatever sleep he could get.

Plainly, it wouldn't be much.

JULIANA HAD BEEN an early riser since the cradle, and she was up and dressed well before dawn.

Even so, when she wandered through the still-dark house toward the kitchen, there was a blaze burning in the hearth in what probably passed for a parlor in such a masculine home. The furniture was heavy and dark and spare, all hard leather and rough-hewn wood, the surfaces uncluttered with the usual knickknacks and vases and doilies and sewing baskets.

Perhaps Lincoln's mother—gone traveling, Gracie had said at supper, with marked relief—had packed away her things in preparation for a lengthy absence. As far as

Juliana could tell, the woman had left no trace at all—even her room, where she and the children had passed the night, was unadorned.

Entering the kitchen, Juliana stepped into lantern-light and the warmth of the cookstove. Lincoln stood at a basin in front of a small mirror fixed to the wall, his face lathered with suds, shaving. He wore trousers and boots and a long-sleeved woolen undershirt, and suspenders that dangled in loose, manly loops at his sides.

He was decently clothed, but there was an intimacy in the early-morning quiet and the glow of the kerosene lamps that gave Juliana pause. She stopped on the threshold and drew in a sharp breath.

He smiled, rinsed his straight razor in the basin, ran it skillfully under his chin and along his neck. "Mornin'," he said.

Juliana recovered her inner composure, but barely. "Good morning," she replied, quite formally.

"Coffee's ready," Lincoln told her. "Help yourself. Cups are on the shelf in the pantry." He cocked a thumb toward a nearby door.

Juliana hurried in to get a cup, desperate to be busy. Came back with two, since that was the polite thing to do. She poured coffee for Lincoln, started to take it to him and was suddenly tongue-tied again, and flustered by it.

He chuckled, rinsed his face in the basin, reached for a towel and dried off. His ebony hair was rumpled, and glossy in the lamplight. "Thanks," he said, and walked over to take the steaming cup from her hand.

Tom entered while they were standing there, staring at each other, his bronzed skin polished with the cold. Behind him walked Joseph, carrying a bucket steaming with fresh milk.

Juliana smiled, feeling as though she'd been rescued from something intriguingly dangerous. "You're up early," she said to the boy. At the school, Joseph had been something of a layabout mornings, continually late for breakfast and yawning through the first class of the day.

"Tom needed help," Joseph said solemnly.

Juliana felt a pang, knowing why Joseph was so eager to be useful. He hoped to land a job on Stillwater Springs Ranch, earn enough money to get himself and Theresa home to North Dakota. With luck, the Bureau of Indian Affairs would leave them alone.

"We can always use another hand around here," Lincoln said.

Juliana shot him a glance. "Joseph has school today."

Some of the milk slopped over the edge of the bucket as Joseph set it down hard in the sink. A flush pounded along his fine cheekbones.

"School?" Lincoln asked.

Just then, Gracie burst in, dressed in a light woolen dress and high-button shoes and pulling Daisy behind her by one hand and Billy-Moses by the other. Both children stared at her as though they'd never seen such a wondrous creature, and most likely they hadn't.

"School?" Gracie chirped, her eyes enormous. "Where? When?"

Juliana smiled, rested her hands lightly on her hips. She hadn't bothered to put up her hair; it hung in a long braid over her shoulder. "Here," she said. "At the kitchen table, directly after breakfast."

Joseph groaned.

"Can I learn, too?" Gracie asked breathlessly. "Can I, please?"

"May I," Juliana corrected, ever the teacher. "And I don't see why you shouldn't join us."

"Will you teach me numbers?" Gracie prattled, her words fairly tumbling over one another in her eagerness. "I'm not very good with numbers. I can read, though. And I promise to sit very still and listen to everything you say and raise my hand when I want to speak—"

"Gracie," Lincoln interrupted.

Releasing Daisy and Billy-Moses, Gracie whirled on her father. "Oh, Papa," she blurted, "you're *not* going to say I can't, are you?"

Lincoln's smile was a little wan, and his gaze shifted briefly to Juliana before swinging back to Gracie's up-turned face. "No," he said. "I'm not going to say you can't. It's just that Miss Mitchell will be moving on soon and I don't want you to be let down when she does."

The words shouldn't have shaken Juliana—they were quite true, after all, since she *would* be moving on soon, though the means she would employ to do that were still a mystery—but they did. She felt slightly breathless, the way she had the day Clay told her she was no longer welcome in the mansion on Pine Street.

Gracie's eyes brimmed with tears, and Juliana knew they were genuine. She longed to embrace the child, the way she would Daisy or Billy-Moses, if they ever cried. Which, being stoic little creatures, they didn't.

"I just want to *learn things* while I can, Papa," she said.

Tom broke into the conversation, pumping water at the sink. Washing up with a misshapen bar of yellow soap. "I'll get breakfast on the stove," he interjected. His gaze moved to Juliana's face. "We could use Joseph's help today, if you can spare him."

Joseph looked so hopeful that Juliana's throat tightened.

"I'll hear your reading lesson after supper," she relented.

Joseph's grin warmed her like sunshine. "I promise I'll do good," he said.

"Well," Juliana said. "You will do *well,* Joseph, not 'good'."

He nodded, clearly placating her.

When Juliana turned back to Gracie, she saw that the child was leaning against Lincoln's side, sniffling, her arms around his lean waist. The flow of tears had stopped.

"Saint Nicholas is going to bring me a dictionary for Christmas," Gracie announced. She looked up at her father. "Do you think he got my letter, Papa? He won't bring me a doll or anything like that, just because you already *have* a dictionary on your desk and he thinks I could use that instead of having one of my own? Yours is *old*—a lot of words aren't even in it."

Lincoln grinned, tugged lightly at one of Gracie's ringlets. "I'm sure Saint Nick got your letter, sweetheart," he said.

"Who's that?" Theresa asked, trailing into the room, hair unbrushed. Juliana wondered if Lincoln had heard her prayers, as he probably had Gracie's. Told her to sleep well.

"You don't know who Saint Nicholas is?" Gracie asked, astounded.

"We'll discuss him later," Juliana promised, "when we sit down for lessons after breakfast."

"I could recite," Gracie offered. "I know all about Saint Nicholas."

"Gracie," Lincoln said.

"Well, I *do*, Papa. I've read Mr. Moore's poem *dozens* of times."

"We'll have cornmeal mush," Tom decided aloud. "Maybe some sausage."

"What?" Lincoln asked.

"Breakfast," Tom explained with a slight grin. Then he turned to Joseph. "You know how to use a separator, boy?"

Joseph nodded. "We had a milk cow out at the school," he said. "For a while."

Separating the milk from the cream had always been Theresa's chore, since Joseph considered it "woman's work." Mary Rose and Angelique had taken turns churning the butter.

And then the cow had sickened and died, and Mr. Philbert hadn't requisitioned the government for another.

Sadness and frustration swept over Juliana, and it must have shown in her face, because, to her utter surprise, Lincoln laid a hand on her shoulder.

Something startling and fiery raced through her at his touch. She nearly flinched, and she saw by his expression that he'd noticed.

"Sit down," he said, watching with amusement in his dark eyes as she blushed with an oddly delicious mortification. "I'll get you some coffee."

CHAPTER THREE

THE SKY WAS A CLEAR, heart-piercing blue, and sunshine glittered on fields of snow rolling to the base of the foothills and crowning the trees. Creek water shimmered beneath sheets of ice, and the cattle, more than a hundred of them, milled and bawled, impatient for the first load of hay to hit the ground. Lincoln sat in the saddle, his horse restless beneath him, and pulled his hat down over his eyes against the dazzling glare.

He watched as Joseph climbed into the back of the sleigh—the snow was too deep out on the range for a wagon to pass—while Tom soothed the two enormous draft horses hitched to it.

Ben Gainer, a young ranch hand who'd stayed on for the winter because his wife, Rose-of-Sharon, was soon to be delivered of their first child, rode up alongside Lincoln on a spotted pony, a shovel in one hand.

"Best break up some of that ice on the creek," Gainer said.

Lincoln nodded, swung down from the saddle. It was there to be done, as his father used to say. When cattle weren't hungry, they were thirsty, and they weren't smart enough to eat snow or trample the ice with their hooves so they could get to the water beneath. He went to the sleigh, helped himself to one of the pickaxes Tom had brought along.

Wishing, as he sometimes did, that he'd chosen an easier life—Beth's father had offered him a partnership in his Boston law firm—Lincoln went to the creekside and began shattering ice an inch thick, two in some places.

If he'd stayed in Boston, he reflected, Beth might have lived, the two babies, too. Gracie would have been able to go to a real school, too.

Inwardly, Lincoln sighed. Left in Wes's incapable hands, the ranch would be gone by now, his mother displaced, Tom Dancingstar ripped up by the roots and left to wander in a world that not only underestimated him, but often scorned him, too. All because he was an Indian.

He'd been caught between the devil and the deep blue sea, Lincoln had, and if he'd made the wrong choice, there was no changing it now. The ranch wasn't making him rich, but he'd gotten it back in the black with a lot of hard work and Creed determination.

But what a price he'd paid.

Tom appeared beside him, toting another pickax. Sent Gainer and Joseph back to the hay barn, nearer the house, where the two remaining ranch hands, Art Bentley and Mike Falstaff, waited to load the sleigh up again.

"You look mighty grim this mornin'," Tom observed.

"Hard work," Lincoln said without looking at his friend.

"You've been working since you were nine. I don't think it's that."

Lincoln stopped to catch his breath, sighed. Cattle nosed up behind him, scenting the water. "You going to insist on chatting?" he asked.

Tom chuckled. Cattle pushed past them to get to the

creek, so they moved a little farther down the line, out of their way. "Something's thrown you, that's for sure. I reckon it's Miss Juliana Mitchell."

Lincoln felt a surge of touchy exasperation, which was unlike him. He started swinging the pickax again. "I might have had a thought or two where she's concerned," he admitted.

Tom laid a hand on his arm. "She needs a place to light. You need a wife and Gracie needs a mother. Why don't you just offer for Juliana and be done with it?"

A growl of frustration escaped Lincoln. He drove the pickax deep into the hard ice, felt satisfaction as the glaze splintered. "It's not that simple," he said in his own good time.

"Isn't it?" Tom asked.

"I'm paying you to work," Lincoln pointed out, humorless, "not spout advice for the lovelorn."

"Is that what you are?" Tom asked, and looking sidelong, Lincoln saw amusement dancing in the older man's eyes. "Lovelorn?"

"No, damn it," Lincoln snapped.

Tom was relentless. "You're a young man, Lincoln. You ought to have a woman. Gracie ought to have a mother, brothers and sisters. If you were willing to bring in a stranger from someplace else and put a wedding band on her finger, why not Juliana?"

"I was hoping for a governess or a housekeeper," Lincoln said. "Taking a wife was a last resort."

"All right, then," Tom persisted, "Juliana's a teacher. She would make a fine governess. Maybe even a decent housekeeper."

"She won't want to stay out here on this ranch," Lincoln argued. "She's a city girl—you can see that by the way she moves, hear it in the way she talks."

"Beth was a city girl, and she liked the ranch fine."

It was all Lincoln could do not to fling the pickax so far and so hard that it would lodge in the snow on the other side of the creek. Tom sometimes went days without talking at all; now, all of a sudden, he was running off at the mouth like a lonely spinster at high tea. "Why? Why is this different, Lincoln? Because you think you could care about Juliana?"

Lincoln didn't answer because he couldn't. His throat felt raw, and a cow bumped him from behind, nearly sent him sprawling into the cold creek water. "I loved Beth," he said after a long time, because Tom would have kept at him until he gave some kind of answer.

Tom laid a hand on his shoulder. "I know that," he said. "But Beth is gone, and you're still here. You and Gracie. That child is lonesome, Lincoln—sometimes it hurts my heart just to look at her. And you're not doing much better."

"I'm doing fine. And there are worse things than being lonesome."

"Are there? You going to tell me you don't lie in there in that bed at night and wish there was a woman beside you?"

Again, Lincoln couldn't answer.

Mercifully, the talk-fest seemed to be over. Tom went back to work, another load of hay arrived, Joseph and young Gainer threw it to the cattle and went back for more.

Toward noon, satisfied that the stock would neither starve nor perish of thirst, Lincoln sent the whole crew back to have their midday meal in the bunkhouse kitchen and then tend to other chores around the place, like splitting firewood and mending harnesses and mucking out stalls in the barn. Winter work could be miserably hard, but the season had its favorable side. There was a lot of time for catching up on lost sleep and sitting around a potbellied stove, swapping yarns.

Gainer, Lincoln knew, was always anxious about his wife, fearing she'd run into some kind of baby trouble, alone in the tiny cabin they shared, and he wouldn't be there to help.

God knew, the possibility was real enough. Beth might have bled to death with the first miscarriage if Cora hadn't been around. She'd gone out onto the back porch, Lincoln's mother had, and clanged at the iron triangle with vigor until they'd heard the signal, out on the range, and ridden for home.

What if Beth had been alone with Gracie, who was only two at the time?

Lincoln stuck a foot into the stirrup and swung up onto his horse's back. No sense in agonizing over something that was over and done with. He'd raced to town for the doctor, but it had been Tom Dancingstar who'd stopped Beth's bleeding. By the time Lincoln returned with help, Cora had bathed and bundled the lifeless baby, a boy.

Lincoln had sat in the rocking chair in the kitchen, holding his son, and wept without shame until sunset when he'd carried him out to the graveyard beyond the orchard, dug a tiny grave and laid the child to rest. Eighteen months later, Beth had given birth to a second daughter, stillborn.

He'd wept then, too, though not in front of his distraught wife. That time, Tom and Wes had done the burying, and more than a month had gone by before the circuit preacher stopped by to say prayers over the grave.

Turning his horse homeward, Lincoln set the memories aside, but they seemed to trail along in his wake like ghosts. Clouds gathered, black-gray in the eastern sky, bulging with snow.

Feeding the cattle would be harder tomorrow, cold work that would sting his hands, even inside heavy leather gloves, but mostly likely the creek wouldn't freeze again.

His heart seemed to travel on ahead of him, drawn to the light and warmth of the house. Drawn to Juliana.

Reaching the barn, he unsaddled his horse, rubbed the animal down with a wad of burlap and gave him a scoop of grain in the bottom of a wooden bucket. He was putting off going into the house, not because he didn't want to, though. No, he was savoring the prospect.

The first snowflakes began to fall, slow and fat, as he left the barn, and the sun was veiled, bringing on a premature twilight.

Lanterns shone in the kitchen windows, and Lincoln raised the collar of his coat, ducked his head against the wind and quickened his stride.

Gracie met him at the back door, her face as bright as any lantern, her eyes huge. "I'm learning the multiplication tables!" she fairly shouted. "And I gave a recitation about Saint Nicholas, too!"

Lincoln smiled, bent to kiss the top of Gracie's head, then eased her backward into the kitchen, out of the cold. The table was clear of the slates and books that had come out of Juliana's satchel that morning after breakfast was over, and she was at the stove, stirring last night's venison stew.

She turned her head, favored him with a shy smile, and it struck him that she was not just womanly, but beautiful. She made that faded calico dress of hers look like the finest velvet, and he wanted to touch her fiery hair.

Instead, he hung his hat on its peg, shrugged out of his coat and hung that, too. "School over for the day?"

She nodded. "We accomplished a lot," she said quietly.

Lincoln smiled down at Gracie again. "So I hear," he replied. "Where are the others?"

"Theresa's putting Daisy and Billy-Moses down for their naps," Juliana answered, seeming pleased that he'd asked. "Joseph is with Tom—they spotted a flock of wild turkeys and they're hoping to bring back a big one for Christmas dinner."

Christmas. He'd forgotten all about that, and it was coming up fast. Fortunately, he'd already bought Gracie's dictionary, and his mother had taken care of the rest. There was a stash of peppermint sticks, books, doll clothes and other gifts hidden away on the high shelf of Cora's wardrobe; she'd shown him the loot before she left on her trip, and admonished him not to forget to put up a tree.

As though reading his mind, Gracie tugged at his sleeve. "Are we getting a Christmas tree?"

Lincoln thought it was a foolish thing to cut down a living tree, minding its own business in some copse or forest, and he flat-out refused to allow any lighted candles in the branches. But he always gave in and hiked out into the woods with an ax, and nailed two chunks of wood crisscross for a stand, because it meant so much to his little girl. "Don't we always?" he countered.

"I thought you might change your mind this year," Gracie said. "You said it was a very *German* thing to do. What's German?"

It was Juliana, the schoolmarm, who answered. "Germany is a country, like the United States and Canada. People from Germany are...?"

"Germans!" Gracie cried in triumph.

"Very good," Juliana said, with pleasure growing in her eyes.

"Go take a nap," Lincoln told his daughter.

"Papa, I never take naps," Gracie reminded him. "I'm not a *baby*."

"Neither are Daisy and Billy-Moses," Lincoln said. "Go."

Gracie turned to Juliana. "Is *Theresa* going to take a nap?"

At that moment, Theresa entered the kitchen, and it was apparent, by the sparkle of collusion in her eyes, that she'd heard at least part of the exchange. She held out a hand to Gracie. "Come," she said. "We'll just lie down for a while and rest. We don't have to sleep, and I'll read you a story."

"I'll read *you* a story," Gracie insisted.

Theresa smiled, nodded slightly.

Gracie could never resist any opportunity to show off her uncanny mastery of the written word. When she was barely three years old, Beth had taught her the alphabet, and after that, she'd been able to divine the mechanics of the reading process. It was as if the child had been *born* knowing how to make sense of books.

Lincoln felt a pang, thinking of Beth when he wanted so badly to be alone in that kitchen with Juliana, for whatever time Providence might allot them. It wasn't as if he meant to touch her, or "offer for her," the way Tom had suggested out there by the creek. She warmed him deep down, that was all. In places where the heat from the cookstove didn't reach.

When Gracie and Theresa were gone, though, he just stood there, mute as a stump.

"Wash up," Juliana told him, keeping her gaze averted. "You must be hungry."

He went to the sink, rolled up his sleeves, pumped some water and lathered his hands with soap. It was harsh stuff, fit to take the hide off, as his mother complained.

Juliana fetched a bowl and spoon, dished up stew for him. The task was ordinary enough, but it made Lincoln think about the conversation with Tom again.

He drew back his chair at the table, sat down. "Did you eat?" he asked, because he wanted Juliana to join him.

She nodded. "Coffee?"

"You don't have to wait on me, Juliana," he replied.

"Nonsense," she replied, bustling off, returning to the table with a steaming mug. "You've given us food and shelter, and I want to show my gratitude." A twinkle sparked in her eyes. "But I draw the line at polishing your boots, Mr. Creed."

"I guess you wouldn't be looking for a housekeeper's job," Lincoln said, and then wished he could bite off his tongue. Juliana Mitchell might have fallen on hard times, but she wasn't cut out to be a servant, even if she *had* poured him coffee and heated up last night's stew for lunch.

She sat down, though, and that was encouraging.

"Are you offering?" she asked, almost shyly.

Lincoln went still, his spoon midway between the bowl and his mouth. "Would you accept if I did?"

Juliana shifted in her chair. Folded her hands in her lap. "My brother would probably come here and drag me back to Denver by the hair if I did," she said, and she sounded almost rueful.

"Your brother?" *Yes, fool,* taunted an impatient voice in his head. *You know what a brother is. You have two of them yourself, three if you count poor Dawson, lying out there in the cemetery next to your pa.*

A fetching blush played on her cheekbones. Lincoln tried to imagine her scrubbing floors, beating rugs, ironing shirts and emptying chamber pots, and found it impossible. For all that her dress had seen better days, there was something innately aristocratic about this woman, something finely honed in the way she held herself, even sitting in a chair.

"Clay had enough trouble reconciling himself to my being a teacher," Juliana said after a few awkward moments during which she swallowed a lot. "So far he's left me alone, but he'd have a fit if I took to keeping house. Unless I was married—"

Her voice fell away, and the blush intensified. Now, Lincoln suspected, *she* was the one wanting to bite off her tongue.

"What if you were a governess?" he ventured, lowering the spoon back to his bowl even though he felt half-starved.

She shrugged both shoulders and looked miserable. "I suppose he'd see that as an improvement over teaching in an Indian School," she allowed.

Lincoln wanted to close his hand over hers and

squeeze some comfort into her, but he didn't. "You do everything your brother tells you?" he asked, surprised.

"No," she said, meeting his eyes at last, trying to smile. He'd intended no criticism by his question, and to his great relief, she seemed to know that. "If that were so, I'd be a wealthy widow now, living in Denver."

Lincoln raised one eyebrow, waited.

She did some more blushing. "Clay wanted me to marry his business partner. I'd resigned myself to that, even though I was going to Normal School. But then my grandmother died and I'd graduated, and I realized I wanted to *use* what I'd learned."

There was more she wasn't saying, Lincoln knew that, but he didn't push. The situation seemed too fragile for that. Slowly, to give her a chance to recover a little, he looked down at his bowl, stuck his spoon into the stew and began to eat.

"This Clay yahoo wouldn't like your being a governess?" he asked carefully, when some time had passed.

She laughed softly, probably at the term *yahoo* applied to her no-doubt powerful brother. "Probably not."

"Why? Because he'd think it was beneath you?" Again, there was no scorn in the inquiry.

"No," Juliana said, with quiet bitterness. "He'd think it was beneath *him,* and he's already despairing of my reputation. To Clay, my teaching other people's children—especially *Indian* children—is tantamount to serving drinks in a saloon."

Again, Lincoln waited. Some process was unfolding, and it had to be let alone.

"It's starting to snow," Juliana said wistfully, her gaze turned to the window again.

"What will you do, then?" Lincoln asked. "After you leave here, I mean?"

She sighed. Met his gaze. "I don't know," she confessed.

"I guess we could get married," Lincoln said.

Juliana opened her mouth, closed it again.

Lincoln felt crimson heat climbing his neck, pulsing along the underside of his jawline. "You heard Fred Willand say it in the mercantile yesterday," he said, his voice raspy. "I've been advertising for a housekeeper or a governess, or both, for better than a year. Failing that, I'd settle for a wife."

Juliana began to laugh. Her eyes glistened with unshed tears, and she put a hand to her mouth to silence herself.

"I didn't mean 'settle,' exactly—"

"Yes, you did," Juliana said. Her look softened. "You loved Gracie's mother a lot, didn't you?"

"Yes," Lincoln answered readily.

"So much that you can't make room in your heart for another woman," Juliana speculated. "That's why you'd marry a stranger, someone answering a newspaper advertisement. Because you wouldn't have to care for that person."

She wasn't accusing him of anything; he knew that by her tone and her bearing. Most likely, the words stung the way they did because they were only too true.

"And that person wouldn't have to care for me," he replied.

"But you'd expect her to—to share your bed?"

"Sooner or later, yes," Lincoln said. "That's part of being a wife, isn't it?"

Juliana propped an elbow on the table, cupped her

chin in her palm. They might have been discussing hog prices, she was so unruffled and matter-of-fact. "I suppose," she agreed.

Before things could go any further, Tom and Joseph banged in through the back door, their faces white-slashed with broad smiles.

"Christmas dinner's outside," Tom said. Then his glance traveled between Juliana and Lincoln, and he sobered a little.

Joseph, being so young, and buoyed by the pride of accomplishment, didn't notice that they'd interrupted something, he and Tom. "We got two turkeys," he announced proudly. "Tom's already gutted them, but we have to pluck them yet, and I might have to pick some buckshot out of the one I got."

Juliana winced.

Lincoln smiled. Pushed back his chair and stood, carrying his bowl and spoon to the sink.

"Better have some stew," he told Tom and the boy.

"And then I'll hear you read today's lesson," Juliana told Joseph.

The boy's face fell briefly, then he smiled again. A deal, he must have decided, was a deal. Juliana had allowed him to skip his schoolwork earlier so he could work with the men out on the range. Now she wanted her due.

"After I pluck the turkeys?"

"After you pluck the turkeys," Juliana conceded with a fond sigh. "And you're not bringing those poor dead creatures into the house to do it."

The command was downright wifely, and that pleased Lincoln, though he didn't let it show. The idea had taken root in his mind, and in Juliana's, too, and for now, that was enough.

Joseph's grin faltered a little. "Remember last Christmas, Miss Mitchell, when you tried to roast that turkey that farmer's wife gave us and it smoked so much that we had to open the doors and all the windows?"

"Thank you, Joseph," Juliana said mildly, "for that reminder."

Tom smiled at that.

Lincoln glanced at the windows, saw that the snow was coming down harder and faster. Through the flurries, he glimpsed his brother Wes riding up, leading a pack mule behind him, a huge pine tree bound to its back.

"I'll be damned," he muttered with a low, throaty chuckle, and headed for the back door, pausing just long enough to put on his coat.

Wes wore no hat, and snowflakes gathered in his dark chestnut hair and fringed his eyelashes. His grin was as white as the snowy ground, and even from ten feet away, Lincoln could smell the whiskey and cigar smoke on him.

"Ma said she'd have my hide if I didn't make sure Gracie had a Christmas tree," Wes said cheerfully. "So here I am."

Lincoln laughed and shook his head. "Did you happen to credit that there's another blizzard coming on and it'll be pitch-dark by the time you get back to town?"

"I've got enough whiskey in me to prevent any possibility of freezing," Wes answered. He took a cheroot from the pocket of his scruffy coat, fitted at the waist like something a dandified gambler would wear, and clamped it between his perfect teeth. "Fact is, I might need a swallow or two before I head home, just the same."

Dismounting, Wes went back to the mule and began untying the ropes that secured the Christmas tree to the animal. The lush, piney fragrance his motions stirred reminded Lincoln of their boyhood. They hadn't been raised to believe in Saint Nicholas, but there had always been fresh green boughs all over the house, and modest presents waiting at their places at the breakfast table on Christmas morning.

"Are you just going to stand there," Wes grumped, grinning all the while, "or will you lend me a hand getting this tree into the house?"

"It's too wet to be in the house," Lincoln said, sounding a mite wifely himself. "We'll set it in the woodshed, let it dry off a little."

"Whatever you say, little brother," Wes replied affably, even though he was six inches shorter than Lincoln and only two years older. "Fred Willand told me when I stopped off at the mercantile to see if you'd gotten any mail—you didn't—that you've got a woman out here. That pretty teacher from the Indian School."

Lincoln took hold of the sizable tree. It was a wonder the weight of the thing hadn't buckled that poor old mule's knees—he'd have to saw a good foot off the thing to stand it up in the front room. "Fred Willand," he said, through the boughs, "gossips like an old woman."

Wes laughed at that. "Hell," he said, "if it weren't for Fred, I wouldn't know what you were up to half the time. It's not as if you ever stop by the saloon or the newspaper office to flap your jaws."

"I don't have much time for flapping my jaws," Lincoln answered. In spite of nearly losing the ranch because of Wes's well-intentioned mismanagement, he'd always loved his brother. After Dawson's death, the old man had taken his grief out on his second son, since Micah, being the eldest, would have given as good as he got. Lincoln, taking Dawson's place as the youngest in the family, had stayed clear of his pa and taken to following Tom Dancingstar everywhere he went.

Wes looked up, his eyes serious now. "Ma's gone," he said. "I can feel the peace even from out here."

Their mother didn't approve of Wes's drinking, his poker playing and cigar smoking, or the woman he loved, and she made that clear every time she got the opportunity. So Wes stayed away from the ranch house when she was around.

Lincoln started for the woodshed, dragging the massive tree behind him. "Go on inside and have some of Tom's venison stew," he called over one shoulder. "It's probably been a month since you've had a decent meal."

"I wouldn't miss a chance to drag my eyeballs over a good-looking woman," Wes responded.

Lincoln didn't dignify that with an answer, but it made him grin to himself just the same.

When he came out of the woodshed, he saw that Wes had left the horse and mule standing. Lincoln led them both into the barn, out of the icy wind, unsaddled the horse, fed and watered both creatures, and rubbed them down the way he'd done with his own mount earlier.

He'd been doing things his brother should have done for as long as he could remember, but he didn't mind, because Wes was always the one who showed up at the most unlikely times with the most unlikely gifts.

ALTHOUGH JULIANA PUT ON a good show, she was shaken inside, and it wasn't just because Lincoln Creed had all but proposed marriage to her at his kitchen table a little while before. She might actually say yes, if he did, and that jarred her to the quick.

John Holden would have made a perfectly acceptable husband, despite his obnoxious daughters, but she'd refused him. Other men had tried to court her during the intervening years, too, though she'd discouraged them, as well. She'd always imagined that if she ever married, it would happen in a fit of wild, romantic passion. She'd be swept off her feet, overcome with desire.

Lincoln stirred something in her, something almost primal—that was undeniable. But wild, romantic passion? No.

On the other hand, she knew he was kind, generous. That he worked hard, was an attentive father and didn't judge people by the culture they'd been born into. That he let his suspenders loop at his sides in the mornings while he shaved.

She smiled at the image, even as Tom introduced her to Weston Creed, and Gracie ran shrieking for joy into the kitchen, hurling herself into her laughing uncle's arms.

He swung her around. "Brought you a Christmas tree," he told her. "Your papa is putting it in the woodshed to dry off a little. What's Saint Nicholas going to bring you this year?"

Gracie paused at the question and her lower lip trembled. A troubled expression flickered across her perfect face.

"I hope he doesn't come," she confided, in a whisper that carried.

Weston looked genuinely puzzled, though Juliana suspected everything he said and did was exaggerated. "Why would you hope for a thing like that?"

"Because he doesn't know the others are here," she said, near tears. "And I don't want any presents if Billy-Moses and Daisy and Joseph and Theresa don't get some, too."

Juliana's heart melted and slid down the inside of her rib cage. If Lincoln *did* propose, she might just accept. She wasn't in love with him—but she adored his daughter.

CHAPTER FOUR

WHEN LINCOLN GOT back inside the house, he found Wes standing in the middle of the kitchen, holding a dismayed Gracie in his arms.

"Well," Wes told his niece solemnly, "we'd better get word to Saint Nicholas right quick, then."

Shedding his coat, Lincoln raised an eyebrow.

"Christmas is only four days away," Gracie fretted. "And the train won't come through Stillwater Springs again until *next* week. So how can I write to him in time?"

Lincoln and Juliana exchanged looks: Lincoln's curious, Juliana's wistful.

"Papa," Gracie all but wailed, "could we send a telegraph to Saint Nicholas?"

"What?" Lincoln asked, mystified.

"He won't bring anything for the others, because he doesn't know they're here!" Gracie despaired.

Something shifted deep in Lincoln's heart, and it wasn't just because he was standing so close to Juliana that their shoulders nearly touched. When had he moved?

He thought of the gifts on the shelf in his mother's wardrobe, the box of watercolor paints he'd bought on impulse back at the mercantile the day before. "Oh, I already did that," he lied easily.

Gracie was not only generous, she was formidably

bright. Her forehead creased as Wes set her gently on her feet. "When?" she asked skeptically.

"In town yesterday," Lincoln said. "Soon as I knew we were going to have company, I went straight to the telegraph office and sent the old fella a wire."

Gracie's eyes widened, while her busy mind weighed the logistics. Fortunately, she came down on the side of relief rather than reason, and Lincoln felt mildly guilty for deceiving her, pure motives or none.

She beamed. "Well," she said. "That's fine, then."

"'Course, he'll probably have to spread things a little thinner than usual," Lincoln added. "Saint Nicholas, I mean. Times are hard, remember."

Gracie was undaunted. "All I want is a dictionary," she said. "So I can learn all the words there are in the whole world."

Lincoln wanted to sweep her up into his arms, the way Wes had apparently done upon arrival, but he figured that would be laying things on a little thick, so he just replied quietly, "I'm proud of you, Gracie Creed."

Beside him, Juliana sniffled once, but when he looked, he saw that she was smiling. Her eyes glistened a little, though.

Seeing he was watching her, Juliana turned quickly and busied herself scraping the last of the stew from the kettle into a bowl and basically herding a clearly charmed Wes over to the table.

She didn't even make him wash up, which might have galled Lincoln a little, if he hadn't been so busy thinking what a fine daughter he and Beth had brought into the world.

Although Wes loved his woman, Kate, and to Lincoln's knowledge his brother hadn't been unfaithful from the day the two of them had taken up with each other, his amber-colored eyes trailed Juliana's every movement, danced with mischief whenever he met Lincoln's gaze.

He *knew,* damn it. Wes knew Juliana had his younger brother's insides in a tangle, and he was bound to rib him without mercy.

"You'd better spend the night," Lincoln said to his brother, even though, at the moment, that was about the last thing he wanted. "Snow's coming down hard."

Wes shook his head, shifted slightly so Gracie could plant herself on his knee. "I've gotta get back. Poker game."

It wasn't long before he'd finished his meal and said goodbye to Gracie. This, too, was like Wes—he'd been uncomfortable in the house since Dawson died. Once, he'd even confided privately that he half expected their murdered brother to tap him on the shoulder from behind.

Gracie went off in search of the other children, and Tom and Joseph were still outside plucking turkeys. Avoiding Juliana's eyes, just as he sensed she was avoiding his, Lincoln put his coat on again, followed Wes into the cold and walked alongside him toward the barn.

About midway, Wes chuckled and shook his head, then gave a low whistle. He hadn't even hesitated when his horse and mule weren't where he'd left them; he knew Lincoln would have attended to anything he'd left undone.

"What?" Lincoln asked, sounding peevish because he knew what the answer would be.

"You," Wes said happily, snow gathering on his hair and shoulders and eyelashes again. "Every time you looked at that schoolmarm, I thought I was going to have to roll your tongue up like a rug and shove it back in your mouth."

Lincoln felt his neck warm. He was half again too stubborn to honor Wes's good-natured taunt with a reply of any kind.

Wes laughed outright then, and slapped Lincoln hard on the back as they slogged heavily through the snow. "She's smitten with you, little brother," he went on. "I figured I'd better tell you that, since you can be a mite thickheaded when it comes to women."

"I suppose *you're* an expert?" Lincoln bit out, raising his collar again. Damn, it was colder than a well-digger's ass. If he could have willed green grass to sprout up right through the snow, he would have done it.

Wes laughed again. "If you don't believe me, just ask Kate," he said lightly.

Lincoln happened to like Kate, even if she was a "light-skirt," as his old-fashioned mother put it, but he wasn't about to put any questions to her, especially when it came to something that personal.

He was silent until they entered the barn, now nearly dark. Both of them knew every inch of the place, and neither of them hesitated to let their eyes adjust to the lack of light.

"Thanks," Lincoln said awkwardly. "For the tree, I mean."

Wes found his horse and opened the stall door, began saddling up. "That was for Gracie," he said. "You want me to stop by Willand's Mercantile and get some presents for those other kids?"

The offer touched Lincoln. "No," he said, his voice sounding gruff. "Ma laid in a good supply of stuff before she left. There'll be plenty to go around."

Wes nodded. "That's good," he said.

"I guess you must have seen Ma recently?" Lincoln ventured. Their mother was a sore spot between them; Lincoln accepted that she was a little on the irritating side, while Wes still seemed to think she ought to change anytime now. "I dropped her off at the depot myself, and there was no sign of you."

There was no humor in Wes's chuckle this time. "She sent Fred Willand's boy, Charlie, around to the newspaper office with a note. 'Course, I'd have lit a cigar with it if it hadn't been for Gracie."

Lincoln frowned. Just as their mother wasn't fixing to change, Wes wasn't, either. Both of them were waiting for the other to see the error of their ways and repent like a convert at a tent meeting, and that would happen on the proverbial cold day in hell. "You think it's wrong, letting Gracie believe in this Saint Nicholas fella?"

Wes lowered the stirrup, gave the saddle a yank to make sure it was secure, then swung up. "She's a child," he said. Lincoln couldn't make out his features in the shadows. "Children need to believe in things while they can. I'll leave the mule here for a day or two, if it's all the same to you."

Lincoln nodded, stepped forward, hoping in vain for a better look at his brother's face, and took hold of the reins to stop Wes from riding out. "Do you believe in anything, Wes?" he asked, struck by how much the answer mattered to him.

Wes sighed. "I believe in Kate. I believe in five-card stud and whiskey and the sacred qualities of a good cigar. I believe in Gracie and—damn it, I must be sobering up—I believe in your good judgment, little brother. Use it. Don't let that schoolmarm get away."

"I've only known her since yesterday," Lincoln reasoned. He was always the one inclined to reason. Wes just did whatever seemed like a good idea at the time.

"Maybe that's long enough," Wes answered.

Lincoln let go of the reins.

Wes executed a jaunty salute, there in the shadows, and rode toward the door of the barn, ducking his head as he passed under it.

"Rub that horse down when you get back to town," Lincoln called after his brother. "Don't just leave him standing at the hitching post in front of the saloon."

Wes didn't answer; maybe he hadn't heard.

More likely, he'd heard fine. He just hadn't felt called upon to bother with a reply.

THE TURKEY CARCASSES had been trussed with twine and tied to a high branch in a tree so they'd stay cold and the wolves and coyotes wouldn't get them. Looking out the window as she stood at the sink, Juliana watched the pale forms sway in the thickening snow and the purple gathering of twilight.

She was certain she would never be hungry again.

Behind her, seated at the table, Tom Dancingstar puffed on a corncob pipe, making the air redolent with cherry-scented tobacco, while Joseph droned laboriously through the assigned three pages of a Charles Dickens novel. The other children had gathered in the front room near the fireplace; the last time Juliana had looked in on them, Theresa and Gracie were playing checkers, while Daisy examined one of Gracie's dolls and Billy-Moses stacked wooden alphabet blocks, knocked them over and stacked them again.

The afternoon had dragged on, and Juliana wondered

when Lincoln would come back into the house, when they'd get a chance to talk alone again, whether or not she ought to attempt to start supper.

It wasn't that she didn't *want* to cook. She hadn't been allowed near the kitchen as a young girl—Cook hadn't wanted a child underfoot—and every school she'd taught at until Stillwater Springs had provided meals in a common dining room.

Now, resurrected by Joseph's account, the image of last Christmas's burned turkey rose in her mind. They'd managed to save some of it and eaten around the charred parts. After that, probably tired of oatmeal and boiled beans, the construction of which Juliana had been able to discern by pouring over an old cookery book, Theresa and Mary Rose had taken to preparing most of the meals.

A snapping sound made Juliana jump, turn quickly.

Joseph had closed the Dickens novel smartly. "Finished," he said. "Can— *May* I go out and help Tom with the chores?"

Juliana blinked. A fine teacher *she* was—for all she knew, Joseph might have been reading from the back of a medicine bottle instead of a book. She had no idea whether he'd stumbled over any of the words, or lost track of the flow of the narrative and had to begin again, the way he often did.

So she bluffed.

"Tell me what happened in the story," she said.

Joseph was ready. "This woman named Nancy got herself beat to death by that Bill Sykes fella."

He'd been reading from *Oliver Twist,* then.

"He was a bad'un," Tom remarked seriously. "That Sykes, I mean."

"He was indeed," Juliana agreed. "You may help with the chores, Joseph."

Tom sighed, rose to his feet. "You reckon you could start that story over from the first, next time you read?" he asked the boy. "I'd like to know what led up to a poor girl winding up in such a fix."

Joseph would have balked at the request had it come from Juliana. Since it came from Tom instead, he beamed and said, "Sure."

"When?" Tom asked, starting for the back door, bent on getting the chores done, his pipe caught between his teeth.

"Maybe after supper," Joseph answered.

Supper. Renewed anxiety rushed through Juliana.

And Tom gave his trademark chuckle. The man probably couldn't read, at least not well enough to tackle Dickens, but he soon proved he *could* read minds.

"I'll fry up some eggs when we're through in the barn," he told Juliana. "And Mrs. Creed put up some bear-meat preserves last fall—mighty good, mixed in with fried potatoes."

Bear-meat preserves? That sounded about as appetizing to Juliana as the naked turkeys dangling from the tree branch outside, but she managed not to make a face.

"You have enough to do," she said, with a bright confidence she most certainly didn't feel. "I can fry eggs."

"No, you can't," Joseph argued benignly. "Remember when...?"

"Joseph."

The boy shrugged both shoulders, and he and Tom let in a rush of cold air opening the door to go out.

The instant they were gone, Juliana hurried to the

front room and beckoned to Theresa with a crooked finger.

Theresa obediently left her checker game and Gracie to approach.

"Quick," Juliana whispered, fraught with a strange urgency. "Come and show me how to fry eggs!"

WHEN LINCOLN CAME IN with an armload of firewood, he found Juliana and Theresa side by side in front of the stove, working away, and the kitchen smelled of savory things—eggs, potatoes frying in onions, some kind of meat. Gracie was busy setting the table.

His stomach grumbled. The venison stew had worn off a while ago.

"Where have you been, Papa?" Gracie asked, all but singing the words, and dancing to them, too. "Did you ride all the way to town with Uncle Wes so he wouldn't get lost in the snow?"

Lincoln smiled and shook his head no. "Wes's horse knows the way home, even if your uncle doesn't," he said. Actually, he'd been in the Gainers' cabin, admiring the spindly little Christmas tree Ben had put up for his child-heavy wife and drinking weak coffee. And at once avoiding and anticipating his return to the house, to Juliana.

Gracie nodded sagely. "That's a good horse," she said.

Lincoln proceeded through the kitchen, then the front room, and along the hallway to Juliana's door. Tonight, he thought, entering with the wood and kindling, he wouldn't have to lie awake worrying that she and the little boy and girl were cold.

Oh, he'd probably lie awake, all right, but there would be something else on his mind.

He'd made a damn fool of himself, with all that talk about governesses and housekeepers and—he gulped at the recollection—taking a wife.

Unburdening himself of the wood, Lincoln bent to open the stove door. Methodically, he took up the short-handled broom and bucket reserved for the purpose and swept out the ashes. When that was done, he crouched, crumpling newspaper and arranging kindling. In an hour or so, the cold room would be comfortably warm.

"Lincoln?"

Startled, Lincoln turned his head, saw Juliana standing in the doorway, looking like a redheaded angel hiding wings under a threadbare dress. His heart shinnied up into the back of his throat and thumped there.

"Supper's ready," she said.

Another wifely statement. He liked the sound of it. Smiled as he shut the stove door and rose to his full height to adjust the damper on the metal chimney. "Thanks," he said.

She lingered on the threshold, neither in nor out.

Lincoln enjoyed thinking how scandalized his mother would have been if she'd known. Straitlaced, she'd have had a hissy fit at the idea of the two of them standing within spitting distance of a bed—especially when that bed was her own. "Was there something else?"

Juliana swallowed, looked away, visibly forced herself to meet his gaze again. "About the presents—the children would understand. They aren't used to a fuss being made over Christmas, anyway, and—"

Lincoln smiled and went to his mother's massive wardrobe, opened the door. Gestured for Juliana to come to his side.

Reluctantly, she did so.

He pointed to the top shelf. Games. Dolls. Books. A set of jacks. A fancy comb-and-brush set. Enough candy to rot the teeth of every child in the state of Montana, twice over.

Seeing it all, Juliana widened her eyes.

"There's plenty," he said. "My brother Micah lives a long way from here, in Colorado, so Ma never sees his boys. Wes never married, and as far as we know, he's never fathered a child. That leaves Gracie, and Ma's been bent on spoiling her from the first."

Juliana stepped back, watched as Lincoln closed the wardrobe doors again. "You don't approve?"

"Of what?"

She went pink again. Fetchingly so. "Your mother, buying so many gifts for Gracie."

Lincoln considered, shook his head. "No," he said. "I guess I don't. But it doesn't seem to be hurting her any—Gracie, I mean—and anyhow, my mother is a force to be reckoned with. Most of the time, it's easier to just let her have her way."

Juliana moved closer to the stove, though whether the objective was to get warm or put some distance between the two of them, Lincoln didn't know. What she said next sideswiped him.

"The Bureau of Indian Affairs is probably going to put me in jail."

Lincoln's breath went shallow. "Why?"

"I was supposed to send these children to Missoula for placement in another school," Juliana said. "Joseph and Theresa have a family, a home, people who want them. Daisy and Billy-Moses will either be swept under some rug or placed in an orphanage. I couldn't bear it."

Lincoln went to her then, took a gentle hold on her

shoulders. Tried to ignore the physical repercussions of touching her. "I'll pay the train fare to send Joseph and Theresa home," he said. "But how do you know the bureau won't just drag them out again?"

Gratitude registered in her face, and a degree of relief. "They won't bother," she said with sad confidence. "It would take too long and cost too much."

"The two little ones—they don't have anyone?"

"Just me," Juliana said. "I shouldn't have gotten attached to them—I was warned about that when I first started teaching—but I couldn't help it."

A solution occurred to Lincoln—after all, he was a lawyer—but even in the face of Juliana's despair, talking about it would be premature. His right hand rose of its own accord from her shoulder to her cheek. She did not resist his caress.

"After Christmas," he said, very quietly, "we'll find a way to straighten this out. In the meantime, we've got two turkeys, a tree—" he indicated the wardrobe with a motion of his head "—and enough presents to do Saint Nicholas proud. For now, set the rest aside."

She gazed up at him. "You are a remarkable man, Lincoln Creed. A remarkable man with a remarkable daughter."

Embarrassed pleasure suffused Lincoln. "I think we'd better go and have supper."

Juliana smiled. "I think we'd better," she agreed.

SUPPER WAS A BOISTEROUS AFFAIR with so many people gathered around the table, their faces bathed in lantern light and shadow. And to Juliana's surprise—she forced herself to try some, in order to set a good example for the children—the bear meat turned out to be delicious.

Tom and Joseph did the dishes, while Gracie sat in a rocking chair nearby, feet dangling high above the floor, reading competently from *Oliver Twist*.

Juliana, banking the fire in the cookstove for the night, stole a glance at Tom and noted that he was listening with close and solemn interest.

Gracie finally read herself to sleep—Billy-Moses and Daisy had long since succumbed, and Lincoln had carried them to bed, one in each arm—and Tom seemed so letdown that Joseph took the book gently from the little girl's hand and picked up where she'd left off.

Juliana hoisted Gracie out of the chair and felt a warm ache in her heart when the child's head came to rest on her shoulder.

She met Lincoln in the corridor leading to the bedrooms. She thought he might take Gracie from her, but he stepped aside instead, his face softening, and watched in silence as she carried his daughter to her bed. A lamp glowed on the nightstand, and Theresa, a pillow propped behind her, was reading one of Gracie's many books.

Juliana set Gracie on her feet, helped her out of her dress and into her nightgown.

Gracie, half awake and half asleep, murmured something and closed her eyes as Juliana tucked her in, kissed her forehead, and then Theresa's.

She took the book from Theresa's hands with a smile, and extinguished the lamp, aware all the while of Lincoln standing in the doorway, watching.

He stepped back again, to let her go by, and smiled when she shivered in the draft and hugged herself.

"I want to show you something," he said.

Curious, she allowed him to lead her to the end of the hallway, where he opened a door, stepped inside and lit a lamp, causing soft light to spill out at Juliana's feet. She hesitated, then followed, and drew in a breath when she saw a porcelain bathtub with a boiler above it, exuding the heat and scent of a wood fire.

Juliana hadn't enjoyed such a luxury since she'd left her grandmother's mansion in Denver. There, she'd taken gaslights and abundant hot water for granted. Since then, she'd survived on sponge baths and the occasional furtive dunk in a washtub.

"I mean to put in a commode and a sink come spring," Lincoln said, sounding shy. "They say we'll have electricity in Stillwater Springs in a few years."

Juliana was nearly overcome. She put a hand to her heart and rested one shoulder against the door frame.

He moved past her, their bodies brushing in the narrow doorway.

Heat pulsed at Juliana's core.

Without another word, Lincoln Creed left her to turn the spigots, find a towel and fetch her nightgown and wrapper from the toasty bedroom, where Daisy and Billy-Moses were already deeply asleep.

The bath was a wonder. A gift. Juliana sank into it, closed her eyes and marveled. When the water finally cooled, she climbed out, dried herself off and donned her nightclothes. A bar of light shone under the door to the room she supposed was Lincoln's, and if it wouldn't have been so brazen, she would have knocked lightly at that door, opened it far enough to say a quiet "Thank you."

Instead, she made her way back to the kitchen, walking softly.

Joseph was still reading from *Oliver Twist,* seated at the table now, and Tom was still listening, smoking his pipe and gazing into space as though seeing the story unfold before his eyes.

Without making a sound, Juliana retreated, smiling to herself.

That night, she slept soundly.

THE SNOW HAD STOPPED by dawn, but it reached Lincoln's knees as he made his way toward the barn. Even the draft horses would have a hard time getting through the stuff, but the cattle had to be fed, and that meant hitching up the sled and loading it with hay.

Lincoln thought of Wes, hoped his brother had made it safely home to the Diamond Buckle Saloon. There would be no finding out for a while, since the roads would be impassable.

He thought about Juliana, and how pleased she'd been when he'd shown her the bathtub. His mother had insisted on installing the thing, saying she was tired of heating water on the stove and bathing in the kitchen, ever fearful that some man would wander in and catch her in "the altogether."

At the time, he'd thought it was plain foolish, a waste of good money, but then Beth—destined to die in just a few short months—had pointed out that she'd had a bathtub of her very own back in Boston, and she missed it.

Lincoln had ridden to town the same day and placed an order at Willand's Mercantile. Weeks later, when the modern marvel arrived by train, shipped all the way from Denver in a crate big enough to house a grand piano, half the town had come out to the ranch to see it unloaded and set up in the smallest bedroom.

Husbands pulled Lincoln aside to complain; they were

being hectored, they said. Now the wife wanted one of those infernal contraptions all her own.

He'd sympathized, and proffered that a bathtub with a boiler was a small price to pay for a peaceful household. Hell, it was worth the look of delighted disbelief he'd seen on Juliana's face when she saw it.

Guilt struck him again like the punch of a fist as he entered the barn, lit a lantern to see by so the work would go more quickly. He'd bought that bathtub for *Beth,* not Juliana.

The cow began to snuffle and snort, wanting to be milked.

Lincoln soothed her with a scratch between the ears and gave her hay instead. Once he'd fed all the horses and Wes's mule, he undertook the arduous task of hauling water from the well to fill the troughs.

By the time he'd finished that, milked and started back toward the house, bucket in hand, it was snowing again.

For a moment, Lincoln felt weary to the core of his spirit. Ranching was always hard work, always a risk, but in weather like this, with cattle on the range, it could be downright brutal.

Finding Juliana in the kitchen, and the coffee brewed, he felt better.

Tom was nowhere around, though, and that was unusual enough to worry Lincoln. He was about to ask if Juliana had seen him when Tom came out of his room just off the kitchen, tucking his flour-sack shirt into his pants.

"Too much reading," he said. "That Oliver feller has me worried."

Lincoln chuckled, poured himself some coffee. "What's for breakfast?" he asked. "Gruel?"

Tom looked puzzled, but Juliana smiled. "How about oatmeal?" she suggested brightly.

"No gruel?" Lincoln teased.

She laughed. "You haven't tasted my oatmeal."

The gruel, he soon discovered, would have been an improvement.

Joseph, turning up rumpled at the table, made a face when he saw it. "Is there any of that bear hash left?" he asked, his tone plaintive.

Only Tom accepted a second bowl of oatmeal.

When the three men left the house, they met Ben Gainer in the yard, and he looked worried. His freckles stood out against his pale face and his brownish-red hair stuck out in spikes under his hat. "Rose-of-Sharon is feelin' poorly this morning," he said.

"You'd better stay with her, then," Tom said quietly.

"I told her she ought to let you come and see if the baby's on its way, but she said—" Ben fell silent, blushed miserably. Turned his eyes to the snowy terrain and looked even grimmer than before.

All of them knew what Rose-of-Sharon Gainer had said. She didn't want an Indian tending her, no matter how "poorly" she might feel.

"It's all right, Ben," Tom told the boy. "Things get bad, you send Joseph out to the range to fetch me."

Glumly, stamping his feet to get the circulation going, Ben nodded, his breath making puffs of steam in the air, like their own. "With all this snow, I don't see how I could get to town to bring back the doctor."

Joseph had turned to Tom. "Don't I get to go with you? Out to the range?"

"Mike can do that. You'll stay here and help Art load the sled with hay."

There was a protest brewing in the boy's face, but it soon dissolved. He sighed and went on toward the barn.

They hauled the first load of hay out to the range half an hour later, and found the cattle in clusters, instinctively sharing their warmth and blocking the wind as best they could. The air they exhaled rose over them like smoke from a chimney.

The creek was slushy, but it flowed.

They went back to the barn for another load of feed, and then another. Tom scanned the surrounding plain for wolf or coyote tracks, and found none.

They headed back and met a panicked Joseph, all but stuck in snow reaching to his midthighs and waving both arms.

Lincoln, driving the team while Tom rode behind him on the sled, felt a sinking sensation in the pit of his stomach.

The boy shouted something, but Lincoln couldn't make out the words. It didn't matter. Something was wrong, that was all he needed to know.

He drove the draft horses harder, and Tom scrambled off the sled and crow-hopped his way through the snow toward the boy.

CHAPTER FIVE

LINCOLN HEARD THE SCREAMS as he left the horses with
Joseph to be unhitched, led to their stalls, rubbed down
and fed. He followed Tom toward the cabin out by the
bunkhouse, moving as fast as he could.

Glancing once toward the main house, he saw Gracie and Theresa standing at the window, both their faces
pale with worry.

The cabin was only about eight by eight feet, so it was
impossible to overlook the straining form in the center
of the bed. Juliana was seated nearby, holding Rose-of-
Sharon Gainer's hand and speaking softly, and the sight
of her calmed Lincoln a little.

Nothing was going to calm Ben, though.

He paced at the foot of the bed, frenzied, shoving both
hands through his hair every few steps. He looked like
a wild man, some hermit from the high timber, baffled
by his new surroundings.

"You go on over to the big house," Tom told the young
husband firmly. "You'll be of no help to us here."

Ben set his jaw, glanced at his weeping, sweating
wife, and looked as though he might throw a punch. Finally, though, he bent over Rose-of-Sharon, kissed her
forehead and did as he'd been told, putting on his coat,
passing Lincoln without a word or a look and closing
the cabin door smartly behind him.

Lincoln, unsure of whether to stay or follow right on Ben's heels, stood just inside the door, turning his gaze to the pitiful little Christmas tree with its strands of colored yarn and awkwardly cut paper ornaments. Two packages, wrapped in brown paper and tied with coarse twine, lay bravely beneath it.

"Breathe very slowly, Rose-of-Sharon," he heard Juliana say, her voice soft and even, but underlaid with a tone of worry.

Lincoln slowed his own breathing, since the idea seemed like a good one.

"You'll be all right," Tom told the girl.

Rose-of-Sharon, a pretty thing with glossy brown hair, was well beyond fussing over letting an Indian attend her. "Is—is the doctor coming?" she asked, between long, low moans and ragged breaths it hurt to hear.

Lincoln thought of the snow, so deep now that the draft horses had had all they could do to get through it, plodding to and fro as they hauled hay to the cattle.

"Yes," Tom lied, rolling up his sleeves and inclining his head slightly in Juliana's direction. "He's on his way for sure."

An unspoken signal must have gone from Tom to Juliana. She nodded and raised the bedclothes.

The sheets and Rose-of-Sharon's nightgown were crimson.

Lincoln turned his back, busied himself building up the fire in the little stove that served for both cooking and heating the cabin. Because the chinking between the logs of the structure was good and the ceiling was low, the room would stay warm.

Rose-of-Sharon shrieked, and the sound scraped

down Lincoln's insides like a claw. For a few moments, it was Beth lying in that bed, not Ben Gainer's child-bride.

He wondered again if he ought to leave, get out from underfoot the way Ben had, but something held him there. He'd go if Tom told him to; otherwise, he'd remain. Do what he could, which was probably precious little.

"Put some water on to heat," Tom said from the fraught void behind Lincoln. "Then go to the house for my medicine bag."

Lincoln nodded—no words would come out—found a kettle, went outside to pack it full of snow, since the water bucket was empty, and set it on the stove. He carried the bucket to the well next, worked to fill it, carried it back inside. Next, he made his way to the house, frustrated by the slow going, found all the kids and Ben gathered at the kitchen table, staring down at their hands.

For some reason, the sight left him stricken, unable to move for a few moments. When he managed to break the spell, he headed for Tom's room, really more of a lean-to, and grabbed the familiar buckskin pouch from its place under the narrow bed. Joseph's pallet, fashioned of folded quilts and blankets, lay crumpled against the inside wall.

Leaving the room, he nearly collided with Ben.

"Rose-of-Sharon?" Ben asked, his voice hoarse, his eyes hollow with quiet frenzy.

"Too soon to know," Lincoln said, and sidestepped past him.

"I'm going for the doctor," Ben said, following him to the back door.

Lincoln turned. "No," he said. "You'd never make it that far, and even if you did, old Doc Chaney wouldn't budge in this weather."

"My wife could die!"

Lincoln looked past him, his gaze connecting with Gracie's. She was white with terror, no doubt remembering Beth's passing, and he longed to go to her, assure her everything would be all right.

The problem was, it might not.

Lincoln laid a hand on Ben's shoulder. "Yes," he said gravely, because nothing but the stark truth would have done. "She could die. But there's no point in your freezing to death somewhere between here and Stillwater Springs, whether she does or not. Besides, if Rose-of-Sharon and the baby survive this, they'll need you."

Ben considered that, swallowed hard and gave a grudging nod.

Lincoln turned and bolted out the door, wading hard for the cabin, the long strap of Tom's medicine pouch pressing heavy into his shoulder.

JULIANA HAD NEVER, in the whole of her life, been so frightened. At the same time, she was oddly calm, as though another self had risen within her, pushed the schoolmarm aside and taken over.

The scene was nightmarish, with all that blood, and poor Rose-of-Sharon shrieking as though she were being torn apart from the inside.

When Lincoln returned with the bag Tom had sent him for, Tom took the bag, plundered it, solemn-faced, then brought out a smaller pouch with strange markings burned into it. His own hands covered in blood, he extended the pouch to Juliana and instructed her to put a pinch of the seeds under Rose-of-Sharon's tongue.

Trembling, she obeyed.

"Don't swallow," Tom told the girl. "It'll ease the pain

some, in a few minutes, and then we'll see about getting that baby born."

"Am I going to die?" Rose-of-Sharon pleaded, her eyes ricocheting between Juliana and Tom. She looked so small and so young—no more than fifteen or thereabouts. It was only too common for girls of her station to marry at an early age. "Is my baby going to die?"

Tom spoke in the Indian way, some of his syllables flat. "No," he said, with such certainty that Juliana glanced up at him. She saw the determination in his face, at once placid and stalwart. "But this could take a while. You'll have to be as brave as you can."

Rose-of-Sharon bit down hard on her lower lip, nodded, her skin glistening with perspiration, her eyes catching Juliana's, begging. *Hold on tight,* they seemed to say. *Don't let me go.*

"I'm here," Juliana said, in the same tone she'd used when one of the children was sick or frightened in the night. She squeezed Rose-of-Sharon's small hand. "I'm right here, Rose-of-Sharon, and I'm not going anywhere."

The words, spoken so quietly, were at complete odds with her every instinct. Given her druthers, Juliana would have jumped up and run out into the snow, turning in blind, frantic circles, gasping at air and screaming until her throat was raw.

What was calming her?

Surely, it was necessity, at least in part. Tom's quiet confidence helped, too. In the main, though, it was knowing Lincoln was there, feeling his presence through the skin of her back, as surely as she felt the heat from the stove.

He seemed as strong and immovable as any of the mountains rising skyward in the distance.

Tom asked for a basin, once the water had been heated, and instructed Lincoln to prepare more. Juliana bathed Rose-of-Sharon, helped her into her spare nightgown, while Tom removed the soiled sheets, replacing them with a blanket.

And Rose-of-Sharon's travails continued.

Between keening screeches of pain, her body straining mightily, she rested, eyes closed, pale lips moving constantly in wordless prayer or protest.

The light shifted, dimmed, became shadow-laced.

Lincoln lit lanterns. Left the cabin again to make sure the children were all right and the barn chores got done.

Juliana, as preoccupied with tending to Rose-of-Sharon as she was, barely breathed until he came back.

It was well into the night when the crisis finally came; too exhausted to scream, Rose-of-Sharon convulsed instead, her eyes rolling back into her head, her back curved high off the mattress in an impossible arch.

The baby slipped from her then, a tiny, bluish creature, soundless and still.

Tom caught the little form in his cupped hands.

Was the child dead? Juliana waited to know, felt Lincoln waiting, too.

And then Tom smiled, grabbed up one of the discarded blankets and wrapped the baby in a clean corner of the cloth. "Welcome, little man," he said. "Welcome."

The infant boy squalled, such a small sound. So full of life and power.

Tears slipped down Juliana's cheeks.

Rose-of-Sharon, spent as she was, seemed lit from

within, like a Madonna. She reached out for the baby, and Tom laid him gently in her arms.

"Get Ben," Rose-of-Sharon murmured. "Please get my Ben."

Juliana heard the door open as Lincoln rushed to do the girl's bidding, felt a rush of cold air, and shielded mother and child from the draft as best she could. Only minutes later, Lincoln returned with the new father.

Ben approached the bed slowly, a man enthralled, hardly daring to believe his own eyes.

"Come see," Rose-of-Sharon said, the last shreds of her strength going into her wobbly smile. "Come and see your son, Ben Gainer."

The room seemed to tilt all of the sudden, and the world went dark. Juliana was barely aware of being lifted out of her chair next to the bed, bundled tightly into her cloak, lifted into strong arms.

Lincoln's arms.

She felt his coat enfold her, too, the way it had in the wagon, on the way out from town. "I've got to stay," she managed to say, blinking against the blinding fatigue that had risen up around her between one moment and the next. "They'll need—"

"Hush," Lincoln said.

Even in the bitter cold, she felt only the warmth of him as he carried her through the snow and into the main house. A single lantern burned in the middle of the kitchen table, but the room was empty. What time was it?

"The children…?"

"Theresa put them to bed hours ago," Lincoln said, making no move to set her on her feet. Instead, he took her through the house, along the corridor, into a room several doors down from hers.

He laid her on the bed, covered her quickly with a quilt, tucked it in tightly around her.

The fatigue reached deep into her mind, into her very marrow. She tried to get a handhold on consciousness, but the strange darkness kept swallowing her down again.

She was aware of Lincoln moving about, now removing her shoes, now opening a bureau drawer.

"Lincoln?" she asked, scrambling back up the monster's throat only to be swallowed once more.

She knew when he left the room, knew when he came back, after what seemed like a long time, but could not have said which of her senses had alerted her to the leaving and the returning. She could not seem to fix on anything; she wasn't asleep, and yet she wasn't fully awake, either.

Lincoln was lifting her again, carrying her again, still cocooned in the quilt. When had she last felt so safe, so cared-for? Surely not since early childhood, when she'd had two loving parents and a brother.

"Where...?"

"Shh," he said.

The sound of running water and the misty caress of steam roused her a little. Lincoln stood her on her feet, supporting her with one arm, peeling away her clothes with the other hand.

He was *undressing* her.

But suddenly it seemed the most normal thing in the world for him to be doing. There was no fear in her, no resistance.

He helped her into the bathtub, and the warmth of the water, the soothing, blessed heat, encompassed her.

Of course, she thought, drifting. She'd been soaked in poor Rose-of-Sharon's blood.

Her dress had surely been ruined, and she could not spare it.

Helpless tears welled in her eyes.

"My dress," she lamented in a despairing whisper. In that moment, she was grieving over so much more than the best of her three calico gowns. Her mother, her father. Grandmama and Clay. She had lost them all, and she could bear no more of such losing.

"There are other dresses," Lincoln told her, lifting her again, drying off her bare skin with soft swipes of a rough towel, pulling a nightgown on over her head. It felt soft and worn, and the scent—rosewater and talcum powder—was not her own.

Supporting her with one arm around her waist—*why* was she so weak?—he guided her out into the corridor again. Past the door to the room she'd been sharing with Billy-Moses and Daisy.

"The children," she protested.

"Theresa's with them," he told her.

He took her back to his room—a slight, wicked thrill flickered through her at the realization—and put her into his bed.

She began to weep, with weariness and with relief, because, out in the little cabin, sorrow had drawn so near and then passed on. For now.

Lincoln sat down on the edge of the mattress. Kicked off his boots. In the next moment, he was under the covers with her, fully clothed, holding her close. Just then, Juliana knew only two things: she'd be ruined for sure, and she'd die if he let her go.

He did not let her go—several times during the night,

she awakened, gradually growing more coherent, and felt his arms around her, felt his chest warm beneath her cheek.

When she opened her eyes the next time, all weariness gone, she found herself looking straight into Lincoln's face. By the thinning darkness, she knew dawn would be breaking soon.

"Since we just spent the night in the same bed," Lincoln said reasonably, as though they'd been discussing the subject for hours and now he was putting his foot down, "I think we'd better get married."

Juliana stared at him, her eyes widening until they hurt. "Married?"

He merely smiled.

She swallowed. "But—surely—"

The door creaked open. "Papa?" Gracie's voice chimed. "Theresa can't find Miss Mitchell and—"

Juliana wanted to pull the covers up over her head, hide, but it was too late. Gracie, fleet as a fairy, was beside the bed now.

"Oh," she said, in a tone of merry innocence, "*there* you are!"

"Gracie—" Lincoln began.

But she cut him off by shouting, "Theresa! I found Miss Mitchell! She's right here in Papa's bed!"

Juliana groaned.

Lincoln laughed. "Miss Mitchell has something to tell you, Gracie," he said.

"What?" Gracie asked curiously.

Juliana drew a very deep breath, let it out slowly. "Your father and I are getting married," she said.

"I'm going to have a mama?" Gracie enthused. "That's even better than a *dictionary!*"

"You go on back to bed now," Lincoln told his daughter.

She obeyed with surprising alacrity, fairly dancing through the shadows toward the door.

"That," Juliana told Lincoln, in a righteous whisper, "was a *very* underhanded thing to do."

He sat up, clothes rumpled, swung his legs over the side of the bed, then leaned to pull his boots back on. He was humming under his breath, a sound like muted laughter, or creek water burbling along under a spring sky.

"Soon as the snow melts off a little," he said, as though she hadn't spoken at all, "I'll send for somebody to marry us. Probably be the justice of the peace, since the circuit preacher only comes through when the spirit moves him."

She could have protested, but for some reason, she didn't.

Lincoln added wood to the hearth fire and got it crackling again. "You might as well go back to sleep," he said. "Rest up a little."

Juliana lay there, the covers pulled up to her chin, and reviewed what had just happened. She'd accepted a proposal of marriage—of sorts. It was as unlike what she'd imagined, both as a girl and as a grown woman, as it could possibly have been.

It was all wrong.

It was wildly *un*romantic.

Why, then, did she feel this peculiar, taut-string excitement, this desire to sing?

Sleeping proved impossible. The children were up; she could hear their voices and footsteps. Besides, she was rested.

She must get dressed, do something with her hair, put on her cloak and go out to the cabin to look in on Rose-of-Sharon and the baby. Suppose the fire had gone out and they took a chill?

Rising, she realized that yesterday's calico, no doubt beyond salvaging anyhow, had disappeared. A pretty blue woolen frock with black piping lay across the foot of the bed—Lincoln's doing, she reflected with a blush. A garment his wife must have owned, since it did not look matronly enough to belong to his mother, as the oversize nightgown probably did.

For a moment, she considered her remaining dresses, both frayed at the seams and oft-mended, both worn threadbare. Both inadequate for winter weather.

She put on the lovely blue woolen, buttoned it up the front. Except at the bosom, where it was a little too tight, it fit remarkably well.

The children, she soon discovered, had assembled in the kitchen. Seated around the table, they all stared at her as though she'd grown horns during the night. Lincoln was making breakfast—eggs and hotcakes—and Tom was just stepping through the back door, stomping snow off his boots.

Juliana forgot her embarrassment. "Rose-of-Sharon?" she asked, her breath catching. "How is she? How is the baby?"

Tom's smile flashed, bright as sunshine on snow. "She's just fine, and so is the little man," he said. "I don't reckon she'd mind some female company, though."

Juliana nodded, looking back at the children. "No lessons today," she said. With the exception of Gracie, they looked delighted. "And I expect you all to behave yourselves."

They all nodded solemnly, from Joseph right on down to Billy-Moses and Daisy. Their eyes were huge, though whether that was due to the blue dress or the fact that she'd spent the night in Lincoln Creed's bedroom and everyone in the household seemed to know it, she could not begin to say.

She looked about for her cloak, realized that it had probably been hopelessly stained, like her dress.

"Take my coat," Lincoln said.

Juliana hesitated, then lifted the long and surprisingly heavy black coat from its peg and put it on, nearly enveloped by it. With one hand, she held up the hem, so she wouldn't trip or drag the cloth on the ground.

She stepped outside into the first timorous light of day, and immediately noticed that the eaves were dripping. The snow was slushy beneath her feet.

Would Lincoln ride to town and fetch back the justice of the peace, now that the weather was changing? A quivery, delicious dread overtook her as she hurried toward the Gainers' cabin. Light glowed in the single window, and smoke curled from the stovepipe chimney.

She *could* refuse to marry Lincoln, of course—even though she'd slept in his room, in his *bed,* nothing untoward had taken place. Why, he hadn't even kissed her.

She blushed furiously and walked faster, remembering the bath, trying to outdistance the recollection. He'd undressed her, seen her naked flesh, *washed* her. At the time, she had been too dazed by exhaustion and the delivery of Rose-of-Sharon's baby to protest. The experience hadn't seemed—well—*real.*

Now, however, she felt the slickness of the soap, the heat of the water, the tender touch of Lincoln's hand, just as if it were all happening right then. She quickened her steps again, but the sensations kept up with her.

It was a relief when Ben Gainer opened the cabin door to greet her, smiling from ear to ear.

"Rose-of-Sharon's been asking for you," he said.

Juliana hurried inside so the door could be closed against the soggy chill of the morning. A fire crackled in the stove, and the cabin was cozy, scented with fresh coffee and just-baked biscuits. Even the pitiful little Christmas tree had taken on a certain scruffy splendor. Rose-of-Sharon sat up in bed, pillows plumped behind her back, nursing her baby behind a draped blanket.

The girl's face shone with a light all her own, and Juliana felt a swift pang of pure envy.

Ben took Lincoln's coat from Juliana's shoulders and told her to help herself to coffee and biscuits, explaining that Tom had done the baking.

"I'll be back as soon as we've fed those cattle," he added, putting on his own coat and hat and leaving the cabin.

Ravenous, Juliana poured coffee into a mug, took a steaming biscuit from the covered pan on top of the stove. She sat beside the bed, in last night's chair, while she ate.

When she'd finished nursing the baby, Rose-of-Sharon righted her nightgown and lowered the quilt to show Juliana her son. He was wrapped in a pretty crocheted blanket.

He seemed impossibly small, frighteningly delicate. His skin was very nearly translucent.

"Do you want to hold him?" Rose-of-Sharon asked when Juliana had finished the biscuit and brushed fallen crumbs from the skirt of the blue dress.

The only thing greater than Juliana's trepidation was

her desire to take that baby into her arms. Carefully, she did so, her heart beating a little faster.

"My mama sent that blanket," Rose-of-Sharon said. "All the way from Cheyenne. Ben says he'll take me and the baby home to Wyoming for a visit come spring so we can show him off to the family."

The baby gave an infinitesimal hiccup. He weighed no more than a feather. "Have you given him a name?"

Rose-of-Sharon smiled. "I wanted to call him Benjamin, for his daddy, but Ben'll have none of it. Never liked the name much. So we picked one out of the Good Book—Joshua."

"Joshua," Juliana repeated softly. She pictured the walls of Jericho tumbling down. "That's a fine, strong name."

"Joshua Thomas Gainer," Rose-of-Sharon said.

Juliana looked up.

"Yes," Rose-of-Sharon told her. "For Tom Dancingstar. Did Ben tell you I didn't want him looking after me, because it ain't proper for an Indian to tend a white woman?"

Juliana didn't speak. She did shake her head, though. Ben hadn't told her, and she was glad.

"If Joshua had been a girl," Rose-of-Sharon went on, more softly now, holding out her arms for the baby again, "I'd have chosen your name." She wrinkled her brow curiously, and Juliana, surrendering Joshua with some reluctance, thought of Angelique, wondered if she and Blue Johnston had gotten married. "What *is* your name, anyhow?"

She laughed. "Juliana."

"That's right pretty."

"Thank you. So is Rose-of-Sharon."

Rose-of-Sharon blushed a little. "I'm obliged to you," she said. "The hardest thing about having a baby was being so far from Mama—or at least that's what I thought until it started hurting."

Juliana smiled, tucked the blankets in more snugly around both Rose-of-Sharon and the baby. "You'll forget the pain with time," she said.

"I ain't yet," Rose-of-Sharon said devoutly, and with a little shudder for emphasis. She yawned, and her eyelids drooped a little. "I'm plum worn down to a nubbin," she added.

"Get some rest," Juliana urged gently.

"What if I roll over on Joshua while I'm sleeping?" Rose-of-Sharon fretted. "He's such a little thing."

"I'll make sure you don't," Juliana promised. There was no cradle, but she spotted a small chest of drawers in a corner of the cabin. Removing one drawer, she lined it with a folded quilt, set it next to the bed where Rose-of-Sharon could see and reach, and carefully placed the baby inside.

With no more quilts or blankets on hand, Juliana used several of Ben's heavy flannel shirts to cover little Joshua.

Satisfied that her baby was safe, Rose-of-Sharon slept.

Juliana sat quietly through the morning, her mood introspective.

At half past one that afternoon, the men returned, chilled and red-faced from the brisk wind, and Ben took over the care of his wife and son.

Juliana wore Lincoln's coat, and as they stood in front of the cabin door, he carefully did up the buttons, his gloved hands, smelling of hay, lingering on the collar, close against her face.

"Tom will ride to town and ask after the justice of the peace," he said, "if you're agreeable to that."

Juliana gazed up at him. She had not had time to fall in love with this man—he certainly hadn't swept her off her feet, not in the romantic sense, anyway—but she respected him. She *liked* him.

Was that enough?

It seemed that someone else spoke up in her place. "I'm agreeable," she said.

His smile was so sudden, so dazzling, that it nearly knocked her back on her heels. "Good," he said huskily. "That's good."

A cloud crossed an inner sun. "This—this dress—"

"Beth's mother sent crates full of them, every so often," he told her, his eyes gentle, perceptive. "She never got around to wearing it."

Juliana absorbed that, nodded.

Lincoln took her hand. "Let's get that Christmas tree set up," he said with a laugh, "before Gracie pesters me into an early grave."

Minutes later, while Juliana and the children took boxes of delicate ornaments from the shelves of a small storage room off the parlor, Lincoln went to the woodshed to get the tree, Joseph right on his heels.

It was so big that it took both of them to wrestle it through the front door, its branches exuding the piney scent Juliana had always associated with Christmas.

Billy-Moses and Daisy stared at the tree in wonder, huddled so close together that their shoulders touched, and holding hands. Juliana remembered Mr. Philbert, and knew in a flash of certainty that he would come for them one day soon.

Tears filled her eyes.

She would be Mrs. Lincoln Creed by then, most likely, and with a husband to take her part, it wasn't likely she'd be arrested. Still, when Mr. Philbert took Daisy and Billy-Moses away, it would be as if he'd torn out her heart and dragged it, bruised and bouncing, down the road behind his departing buggy.

"Juliana?"

She looked up, surprised to see Lincoln standing directly in front of her.

He cupped her elbows in the palms of his hands, kissed her forehead. "Let them have Christmas," he said.

Either he was extremely perceptive, or he'd seen the worry in her face.

She nodded. Dashed at her eyes with the back of one hand.

It took all afternoon to festoon that Christmas tree, and what a magnificent sight it was, bedecked in ribbon garlands, delicate blown-glass ornaments of all shapes and colors, draped with shimmering strands of tinsel. Even Juliana, who had grown up in a Denver mansion with an even grander tree erected in her grandmother's library every December, was awestruck.

Tom appeared at dusk, while Lincoln was doing the chores in the barn. He carried a large white package under one arm.

Juliana, peeling potatoes and trying to think what else to prepare for supper, couldn't help looking past him to see if he'd brought the justice of the peace along.

She was both relieved and disappointed to see that he was alone.

He smiled, as though he'd read her thoughts again, and set the parcel on the counter. "Chickens," he said. "All cut up and ready to fry."

Mildly embarrassed, Juliana reported that she'd looked in on Rose-of-Sharon and little Joshua earlier, and they were doing well.

Moving to the sink to wash his hands, Tom nodded. Although, since his back was turned to her, and Juliana couldn't be sure, she thought he was smiling to himself.

He brought lard and a big skillet from the pantry, set the pan to warming on the stove, then rolled the chicken parts in a bowl of flour. They worked in companionable silence, Juliana finishing up the potatoes and putting them on to boil.

The savory sizzle of frying chicken soon brought the children in from the front room, where they'd been admiring the Christmas tree.

"We'll need an extra place set at the table," Tom commented mildly, after Theresa had counted out plates and silverware for everyone. His dark eyes twinkled as Juliana turned to him. "For the circuit preacher. He's out in the barn with Lincoln."

Juliana nearly gasped aloud, and before she could think of a response, the back door opened and Lincoln came in, closely followed by a very large white-haired man in austere black clothes and a clerical collar.

The circuit preacher's eyes were a pale, merry blue, in startling contrast to his sober garments, and before Lincoln could make an introduction, he lumbered over to Juliana like a great, good-natured bear, one hand stuck out in greeting.

"This must be the bride!" he boomed.

Juliana's face flamed. She fidgeted, unable to meet Lincoln's gaze, and shook the reverend's hand.

Gracie piped up. "This morning when I went into Papa's room—"

Theresa put one palm over the child's mouth just in time.

The reverend turned to look at Tom, drawing in an appreciative breath. "Is that fried chicken I smell?"

Tom laughed, nodded.

"And me just in time for supper!" the reverend roared.

Just then, Daisy crept up beside the big man and tugged at the sleeve of his coat. "Are you Saint Nicholas?" she asked, almost breathless with her own daring.

The reverend bellowed out a great guffaw at that. Daisy started, but didn't retreat.

"Why, bless your heart, child," the preacher thundered, "nobody's ever mistaken this ole Bible-pounder for a saint!"

"That's Reverend Dettly, silly goose," Gracie informed Daisy solicitously. "Saint Nicholas always wears red."

"You'll spend the night, won't you, Reverend?" Lincoln asked, taking the preacher's coat. "It's dark out there, and mighty cold, even with the thaw."

"I reckon I'll burrow into a hay pile out in your barn, all right," Reverend Dettly said. "A belly full of ole Tom's chicken ought to keep me plenty warm."

"Surely we can offer you a bed," Juliana said shyly.

Reverend Dettly smiled down at her. "I won't be putting anybody out of their beds," he said. "If a stable was good enough for our Lord, it's sure as all get-out good enough for me."

CHAPTER SIX

TOM TOOK PLATES out to the cabin for Ben and Rose-of-Sharon as soon as supper was ready. When he returned, everyone was already seated around the table, Reverend Dettly waiting patiently to offer up the blessing.

Juliana sat at Lincoln's right side, stomach jittering with fearful anticipation and hunger. Soon, she would be his *wife*. Mrs. Lincoln Creed. Would he expect her to share his bed that night, or would he give her time to get used to being married?

Did she *want* time to get used to it?

The reverend cleared his throat once Tom had joined them, held out his great pawlike hands and closed his eyes to deliver the longest and most exuberant blessing Juliana had ever heard. Behind closed eyelids, her head dutifully bowed, she imagined the gravy congealing, the mountainous piles of fried chicken going cold, and still the preacher went on, thanking God for everything he could think of, from seeds germinating in the earth under their blanket of snow, to the cattle on a thousand hills. When someone's stomach rumbled loudly and at length, Dettly laughed and shouted a joyful "Amen!"

"Thank God," Lincoln agreed.

Juliana elbowed him.

During that meal, it seemed there were two Julianas—one seated next to Lincoln at the table, laughing and talking and enjoying the savory food, and one standing back a ways at the edge of the lantern light, wringing her hands and fretting.

"So," the reverend said, turning to Juliana when he'd eaten his third and apparently final helping of everything, "I'm told there's to be a wedding. I've known Lincoln here since he couldn't see over the top of a water trough, but I don't believe I've ever made the bride's acquaintance."

Juliana felt her cheeks warm, and it took some doing to meet that direct blue gaze, kindly but penetrating, too, head-on. She told him her name, though Tom had probably done that long since, and that she'd been the teacher at the Indian School until it closed down.

"You look good and sturdy," the preacher observed, as though she were a calf he might buy at a stock sale.

Juliana wasn't offended, but she *was* amused. "I have good teeth, too," she said with a twinkle.

Reverend Dettly laughed, but his eyes took on an expression of solemnity as he continued to regard her. "You're amenable to this, Miss Mitchell? Getting married is a serious thing, with eternal consequences. Mustn't be too hasty about it."

Was having no other viable choice the same as being amenable? Juliana didn't know. Her heart seemed to be getting bigger and bigger, sure to burst at any time, and it all but cut off the breath she needed to answer.

"I'm willing to marry Mr. Creed," she said. Even if she didn't get arrested, Mr. Philbert would probably see that she never taught in any school again. If she went home to Denver, it would be on Clay's terms, and she would essentially be a prisoner. She imagined herself growing more and more eccentric as the years passed, until she finally ended up wild-eyed and confined to the attic.

The thought made her shudder.

The children were unusually quiet. Juliana couldn't hear the big wall clock ticking, though she knew it was because she'd climbed up onto a stool and wound it herself earlier with a brass key.

"Very well," the reverend said, evidently satisfied, "let's get on with it, then." In remote areas like Stillwater Springs, Montana, where loneliness and hard work were the order of the day, he probably performed the marriage ceremony for all sorts of unromantic reasons.

Juliana cast a look up and down the table. "As soon as we've washed the dishes—"

"Hang the dishes," Lincoln said, taking her by the hand and pulling her to her feet. "Let's get this thing *done*." With that, he all but dragged her into the front room, the children and Tom following single file like goslings, Reverend Dettly bringing up the rear.

Lincoln stood with his back to the Christmas tree, Juliana at his side. Suddenly, it seemed to her that the whole scene was taking place under water, or inside one of those pretty crystal globes that produced snow flurries when they were shaken. Dettly pulled a small, oft-used prayer book from the pocket of his suit coat, cleared his throat ponderously.

Tom and Joseph were appointed as witnesses; Gracie insisted on being one, too.

The ceremony was amazingly brief; Juliana heard it all through a dull pounding in her ears, responded whenever Lincoln squeezed her hand. The reverend had to repeat himself a lot.

There were no rings and no flowers.

The dress Juliana wore belonged to someone else, and was too tight in the bodice.

For all that, she felt cautiously hopeful, if dazed, and perhaps even happy.

Reverend Dettly pronounced them man and wife, and that, Juliana thought, was that. Until Lincoln turned her to face him, cupped his hands on either side of her face and kissed her so soundly that she had to grasp at his shirt to keep herself from floating away.

When that kiss was over, Juliana stared up into her husband's face, confounded by all he'd made her feel. Fiery sparks leaped within her, and there was this odd sense of *expansion,* embarrassingly physical but going well beyond that into realms of mind and spirit she had never previously comprehended, let alone explored.

The earth shifted beneath her feet, heaven trembled above her.

She was different.

Everything was different.

Lincoln frowned slightly, looking puzzled and a little concerned. "Are you all right?" he asked.

She nodded. Shook her head. Sagged a little, as though she might swoon—she who had *never* swooned until last night, after helping with a difficult birth—causing Lincoln to slip an arm around her.

"Juliana?"

"I'm—we're—married," she said stupidly.

Lincoln's concern softened into a smile. "Yes," he said.

Gracie tugged at the skirt of Juliana's dress. "May I call you Mama now, please?" she asked.

Juliana's heart turned over; she glanced at Lincoln, but saw no urging, one way or the other, in his face. They were strangers to each other, she and Lincoln, and the decision to marry had been made out of expediency on Lincoln's part and desperation on her own. Suppose, in a month or a year, they found they could not tolerate each other? Gracie, thinking of Juliana as a mother, would be crushed.

Looking down into those hopeful eyes, though, Juliana knew she couldn't refuse. "Yes, darling," she said softly. "If you want to call me Mama, you may. But you had another mother—wasn't she 'Mama'?"

"Does a person only get one mama?" Gracie asked, looking worried.

Juliana was at a complete loss. She and Gracie both turned to Lincoln for an answer. He looked flummoxed.

Gracie took charge. "My first mama died," she said. "I loved her—she was pretty and she smelled nice—but she's gone. I won't see her again until I get to heaven, and that might be a long, long time from now. So I need another mama to get me through till then."

Juliana's eyes stung, but she smiled. She couldn't help it; Gracie had her thoroughly bewitched. "All right, then," she said, praying she would never have to let this trusting child down. "It's a bargain. I'll be the best mama I can."

Gracie wasn't finished. Placing her hands on her hips, she said, "Theresa told me that she and Joseph are going home to North Dakota as soon as they can raise the train fare. Couldn't Billy-Moses and Daisy stay here with us and be Creeds, too?"

Juliana closed her eyes.

"Go and help with the washing up," Lincoln told his daughter mildly.

"But you didn't *answer* me, Papa."

"Go."

She left, the reverend in tow, and Juliana and Lincoln were alone, as a married couple, for the first time. The tree sparkled behind Lincoln; a strand of tinsel caught in his hair. Without thinking, Juliana reached up to remove that thin silvery strip, draped it on the closest branch. Her touch was tender.

She'd done a fairly good job of setting aside her fears for the youngest of her charges, but now Gracie's question echoed in her heart like the peal of distant church bells. *Couldn't Billy-Moses and Daisy stay here with us and be Creeds, too?*

"What happens now?" she asked, unable to hold the words back any longer.

Lincoln put his arms around her waist loosely and drew her closer. Ducked his head to kiss the tip of her nose. "Now," he said throatily, "we take things slowly. I want you in my bed, Juliana Creed, I won't deny it. But I won't ask you for anything you're not ready to give— you have my word on that."

Juliana Creed. That was who she was now. It seemed remarkable, as though she'd lived all her life as one person and then suddenly turned into another. As she looked up at Lincoln, she wondered if what she felt—the crazy tangle of longing and sweet sorrow and myriad other things too new to be named—might be love.

Surely that was impossible. She had only known Lincoln for a few days—how could she have learned to love him in such a short period of time?

"I'm—I'm not sure when I'll be ready, Lincoln," she confessed. "I've never— I mean, John and I didn't— wouldn't have—"

He ran a hand lightly down the length of her braid,

gave it a gentle tug. "We'll take our time, Juliana," he reiterated. A sparkle lit his brown eyes. "Not too *much* time, mind you."

A lovely shiver went through her, but then she remembered tales she'd heard other women relate, concerning intimate things that happened between a man and a woman, and frowned.

"What?" Lincoln asked. How he favored that one-word question. He was not one for long speeches, that was for sure.

Juliana flushed with tender misery. "Will it hurt?"

Gently, he ran the backs of his fingers along her cheek. "Maybe a little, the first time or two. But I'll be careful, Juliana. That's a promise."

She believed him. She might not know Lincoln Creed very well, but there *were* things she was sure of where he was concerned. Many men would have packed Gracie off to live with relatives after her mother died—Juliana's own father, for instance—or shipped her away to some distant boarding school, but he'd kept her at home. He clearly loved his daughter, but she wasn't spoiled. He'd brought a strange woman and four Indian children into his home, just because they'd needed someplace to go. He'd stood by, ready to do whatever he could to help, while a young wife gave birth to her first child amid screams and blood, and every morning, without fail, no matter how bitterly cold the weather, he rose before dawn and made sure the range cattle didn't go hungry.

Rising on tiptoe, she kissed his cheek, felt the stubble of a beard against her lips. "I'd better put Daisy and Billy-Moses to bed," she said. "Would you mind if I gave them a bath first?"

Lincoln smiled, touched her lower lip with the tip of

one finger. "This is your house, too, Mrs. Creed. You don't have to ask permission to use the bathtub or anything else I own."

A niggle of worry snaked along the bottom of Juliana's stomach. "Speaking of Mrs. Creed," she said, after working up her courage, "what will your mother say when she finds out you've taken a wife?"

"I don't really care," Lincoln replied easily. "My guess is she'll be a little testy for a while, thinking I ought to have consulted her first, and then she'll get to know you better and come to like you. Anyhow, she won't be back from Phoenix for months—she hates the cold weather, and every year she threatens to stay there for good, since there's no 'culture' in Stillwater Springs, and she dreads being stuck out here on the ranch for weeks at a time. I think the only reason she comes back at all is because she's afraid Gracie will grow up to cuss, chew tobacco and wear pants if she's left with Tom and me for too long at a stretch."

Juliana smiled at the image of Gracie acting like a man. One thing was for certain; Gracie Creed would never be ordinary. "*I* think you and Tom have done a fine job making a home for that little girl."

He grinned, gave her braid one more tug. "I'll go light a fire in the boiler and make sure there's water for a bath," he said. With that, he turned and walked away.

Juliana watched him until he'd vanished into the corridor on the other side of the front room, then took herself to the kitchen.

Tom and the reverend were doing up the dishes while Joseph read aloud from *Oliver Twist*. Theresa was wiping the table with a damp cloth while Gracie sat on the floor near the stove, entertaining Daisy and Billy-Moses with the alphabet blocks.

"That's your name," she said, lining up the blocks to spell *Daisy.*

Daisy stared at the letters in uncomprehending wonder. She was only three, after all. Gracie, with her bright hair and agile mind, must have seemed like a living oracle to her.

"Make *Bill,*" Billy-Moses urged.

"It's time for your bath," Juliana interceded.

Daisy, who loved baths, was on her feet in a moment. Billy-Moses's small face took on an obstinate expression.

"I don't *want* a bath," he said, folding his arms.

Reverend Dettly turned from the sink, his big hands dripping with suds, smiling. It struck Juliana that his life was probably a very solitary one when he wasn't preaching, but traveling from place to place and sleeping in people's barns. No doubt he enjoyed evenings like this one, being around children and eating a home-cooked meal.

"This is not a question of what you want, Billy-Moses," Juliana said firmly. "You *are* going to have a bath, and then you are going to bed. Period."

"Are you going to sleep in Papa's room again tonight?" Gracie asked innocently. This time, Theresa hadn't been close enough to cover her mouth.

Juliana's face flamed, and she couldn't have looked at Reverend Dettly to save her very life. "Yes," she said, because there was nothing else *to* say.

Lincoln had to pump and carry water to fill the boiler over the bathtub, and then it had to heat. When it was finally ready, Juliana bathed Daisy first with Theresa's help, put her to bed and went in search of Billy-Moses.

By that time, Reverend Dettly had retired to the barn, and Tom and Joseph to their shared room off the kitchen. Only Lincoln was there, seated at the table, reading a newspaper.

"Have you seen…?" she began.

"He's hiding in the pantry behind the flour bin," Lincoln said, taking in his harried bride. The front of the marvelous blue dress was soaked from Daisy's happy splashing in the tub, and her hair was popping out of the braid like a frayed rope sprouting bristles.

"Oh, for heaven's sake," Juliana answered, starting in that direction. Normally, she was not easily exasperated, but the day had been a long and eventful one, and it wasn't over.

Lincoln leaned in his chair, caught hold of her hand and stopped her. Rising, he said, "I'll do it. Brew yourself up a cup of tea. Ma likes the stuff, and there's a tin of it around here somewhere."

Juliana sank into a chair.

"Bill," Lincoln said, approaching the pantry door. "Quit fooling around, now. It's time to scrub you down a layer."

Billy-Moses appeared in the pantry doorway, still looking petulant. "*Joseph* didn't have to take a bath," he protested.

"Reckon he'll get around to it tomorrow sometime," Lincoln said easily. Then he bent, hooked Billy-Moses around the waist with one bent arm and carried him through the kitchen.

Billy-Moses squealed with a little boy's joy, kicking and squirming, and it was a sound Juliana had never heard him make before.

As soon as she was alone, Juliana folded her arms on the tabletop and rested her head on them.

Mr. Philbert would come, and soon. She could almost feel him bearing down on Stillwater Springs, on her, full of righteous wrath. How would she explain to Billy-Moses, only four, and Daisy, just three, that he would be taking them far away, handing them over to strangers? Would he even give her a *chance* to explain?

She stood slowly, crossed to the sink and pumped water into the teakettle, found the tin Lincoln had mentioned earlier and a yellow crockery pot. By the time the brew was ready, he'd returned to the kitchen, grinning, his shirtfront soaked with water.

"Bill's been bedded down," he said. "I've wrestled yearling calves with less fight in them."

Juliana smiled. Here, then, was the reason Billy-Moses hadn't asked Gracie to spell out his whole name with her alphabet blocks earlier that evening; he'd wanted "Bill." Because that was what Lincoln called him.

"Thank you," she said, warming her hands around her cup of tea.

Lincoln poured lukewarm coffee for himself, drew back his chair and sat down. With a slight nod of his head, he answered, "You're welcome, Mrs. Creed."

Once again, the name soothed her, and conversely that very fact made her uneasy. "Do you think the reverend will be warm enough in the barn?"

"He's bunking in between two bearskins, Juliana, and the animals put out a lot of body heat. The barn's warmer than the house a lot of the time."

Body heat. What an intriguing—and disturbing—term. She looked away, her tea forgotten.

And that was when Lincoln's hand, calloused by years

of ranch work, came to rest on hers. "Maybe you ought to turn in for the night," he suggested.

She swallowed, nodded. Could not pull her hand out from under his, even—*especially*—when he began to stroke the backs of her knuckles with the rough pad of his thumb, setting her on fire inside.

Was this passion, this ache he aroused in her with the simplest touch of his hand?

Juliana was not prepared to find out.

"I'll be along in a while," Lincoln told her.

She stood.

He stood, too.

"Juliana?"

She met his gaze.

"Don't be afraid," he said.

How *not* to be afraid? She'd never experienced anything more daring than John's hand-patting and chaste pecks on the cheek during their brief and bland engagement.

She nodded and turned to leave.

Lincoln had lost interest in the newspaper. The *Stillwater Springs Courier* came out once a week, if Wes got around to writing the articles and setting the type. As often as not, he didn't—but he was a good writer when he had something to say, and Lincoln usually enjoyed his brother's sly but often lethal wit. Hell, even some of the obituaries were funny, and the opinion pieces kept things stirred up around town.

With a sigh, Lincoln pushed the paper away and rose from his chair. He carried his cup and Juliana's to the sink and left them there, stood with his hands braced against the counter, staring out the window, looking past his own reflection and into the darkness.

Flakes of snow drifted down, and he wondered if they'd stick or melt away by morning.

He felt restless. He knew he wasn't tired enough to lie down beside Juliana and keep his hands to himself. He'd wanted a wife—someone to share his bed, bear him more children, provide the motherly affection Gracie craved—but not one who touched his heart. No, he had not planned on that part.

Resigned, he went to the door, took his hat and coat from their pegs and put them on. Quietly left the house.

He moved past the privy, past the Gainers' cabin, past the bunkhouse. The night air was cold, sweeping inside him somehow, scouring like a bitter wind.

He needed no lantern; even with the moon disappearing behind the clouds, enough light came through to illuminate the snow. Besides, he'd lived on this ranch all his life; he could have found any part of it with his eyes closed.

He reached the orchard—years ago, when they were boys, he and Micah and Wes and Dawson had helped to plant those apple and pear trees—then made his way, sure-footed, over ground he knew as well as the back of his own right hand.

Beyond the orchard was the little cluster of gravestones and markers where his father, his brother, the two lost babies—and Beth—were buried.

He didn't pause beside Josiah Creed's grave, walked right past Dawson's, too, even though he'd loved his brother.

Beth's resting place was marked with a stone angel, now cloaked in snow.

Lincoln brushed off the shoulders and the wings with one hand. He crouched, ran his right forearm across his face. How many times had he come here, said goodbye to Beth? Sooner or later, there always seemed to be something more that wanted saying.

And she wasn't even here.

Gracie believed her mother was in heaven.

Lincoln flat didn't know where dead people went, or if they went anywhere at all. Most likely, though, the journey ended in a pine box under six feet of dirt, but of course he wouldn't have said that to Gracie.

Graves weren't really for the folks who'd passed on, he supposed. They gave the ones left behind a place to go and remember, that was all.

"I got married today," he said, feeling foolish, but needing to say the words all the same. They came out sounding gruff. "Her name is Juliana, and Gracie—Gracie wants to call her Mama."

A raspy chuckle escaped Lincoln then. If that grave had been some kind of passageway between this world and the next, Beth would have clawed her way right up out of it and given him what-for.

"I loved you," he went on, sober again. "I probably always will. But I've been too lonesome, Beth, and so has Gracie. I need somebody to wake up beside, somebody waiting when I come in off the range after a long day. I want Gracie to have a woman to look to so she doesn't grow up to smoke cigars like Ma says she will. I know you can't hear me, and wouldn't like what I've got to say if you could, but I still had to say it."

As he stood again, Lincoln wondered what he'd expected—an answer? Beth's ghost, absolving him of his promise to leave his heart buried with her?

The snap of a branch in the nearby orchard alerted him that someone was approaching—as it had probably been meant to do. He almost expected a specter, though he knew who had tracked him even before he saw Tom moving across the snowy ground toward him. If that old Indian hadn't wanted him to hear, he wouldn't have.

Lincoln waited, without speaking, as his friend drew nearer.

"She's not here, Lincoln," Tom said. "Beth is not here."

"Don't you think I know that?" Lincoln demanded, rubbing the back of his neck with one hand. "Where *is* she, Tom? With the Great Spirit? Or down in that hole in the ground?"

"Why are you doing this to yourself?" Tom asked reasonably. "Coming out here in the dark and the cold when you've got a pretty bride waiting back at the house? Is it because you didn't count on *feeling* anything for Juliana?"

"I think Juliana is beautiful," Lincoln said tersely. "I think she's smart and brave, and I want her. But that's *all* I feel, Tom. I loved my wife."

"Your wife is dead."

"So I hear."

Tight-jawed, eyes flashing, Tom reached out with a palm and shoved hard at Lincoln's chest, so he had to scramble to keep his footing. "Let Beth go," he almost growled. "Juliana doesn't deserve to go through what your mother did."

"What the hell is *that* supposed to mean?"

"It *means,* you damn fool, that your pa married your mother for pretty much the same reasons you married Juliana. He and Micah were alone after his first wife died, and he wanted to give the boy a mother. He never loved Cora, always mooning over his poor lost Mary, and your ma's life was a misery because of it."

Lincoln's mouth dropped open. He took a second or two to get his jaw hinged right so it would shut again. It was the first he'd heard of any of this, and that chafed at something raw inside him. It also explained why Cora couldn't keep the names of Micah's four sons straight, why she never visited them in Colorado or even wrote them letters. Maybe it even explained why Micah had lit out for another state the way he had and never looked back, as far as Lincoln could tell.

"Why tell me this now?" he asked bitterly, but his mind was still reeling, still scrabbling for some kind of purchase. Micah was his father's son, but not his mother's? In that moment, he understood what folks meant when they said they'd had the rug pulled out from under them.

"Because you need to know it."

"I would have appreciated somebody's mentioning this before Micah left home for good," Lincoln said, fighting down the old hurt. "I looked up to him. I didn't even get to say goodbye. One day, he was just—gone."

"Micah didn't leave because things weren't good between him and Cora. He left because he'd always had leaving in him."

"And because his mother's folks lived in Colorado," Lincoln guessed.

"Yes," Tom said.

Lincoln thrust out a sigh, felt a letting-go inside him. "Well, I don't have to wonder what I did wrong anymore, I guess. Does Wes know all this?"

A nod. "He knows."

"Am I the only one who didn't?"

"Let it go, Lincoln. Wes is a little older. He overheard more, that's all."

"I suppose now you're going to tell me my ma was so lonesome, you had to comfort her, and I'm *your* son, not Josiah Creed's." For a brief moment, Lincoln held his breath, hoping it was true.

Tom clenched a fist, looked as though he might throw a punch. "If you were my son," he said, through his teeth, "I'd have claimed you a long time ago. No woman ever loved a man more than your ma loved Josiah Creed. She bore him three healthy boys and raised the one he brought with him when they married. When Dawson was killed, Josiah told her it was her fault, because it was one of her kin that pulled the trigger. To the day he died, he never had a kind word for her."

Lincoln closed his eyes for a long moment, let out the breath he hadn't realized he'd been holding. "But *you* loved my mother all these years, didn't you, Tom? That's why you stayed."

"I stayed because that's what I chose to do," Tom said coldly.

Lincoln started back toward the house, and Tom fell into step beside him.

They walked in silence with nothing more to say.

THERESA, BILLY-MOSES AND DAISY were sound asleep in Mrs. Creed's bed. Careful not to wake them, Juliana tucked the blankets in close and added wood to the fire in the stove.

She looked in on Gracie next, found her sleeping, too. Felt her heart seize with love for this child, the fruit of another woman's womb. It was a dangerous thing, caring so much, but it was too late. Just as it was with Daisy and Billy-Moses, Theresa and Joseph.

Juliana adjusted Gracie's covers and tiptoed out into the corridor.

In Lincoln's room, she lit a lamp. Slowly undressed, took her own nightgown from her satchel and put it on. After drawing a deep breath, she pulled back the covers and climbed into bed.

There, she waited.

Lincoln had promised to wait until she felt ready to give herself to him. That should have lessened her fears, but it didn't, because it wasn't the prospect of his love-making that frightened her most. It was her own desire to give herself up to him with total abandon.

He came in quietly, with the smell of the outdoors on his clothes—snow, pine, fresh, cold air. Feigning sleep, she watched through her eyelashes as he lowered one suspender, then the other.

"I know you're awake," he told her. "Most folks don't hold their breath when they're sleeping."

Juliana huffed out a sigh and opened her eyes.

After looking down at her for a long moment, he chuckled and reached to extinguish the lamp. "Move over, Mrs. Creed," he said. "I'm going to need more than an inch of that mattress."

Juliana scooted closer to the wall, her heart pounding. Lincoln was not going to force himself on her, she knew that if little else. He wouldn't touch her in any intimate way without her permission.

She ought to relax.

But she couldn't. What did married people say to each other at night when they got into bed?

He continued to undress. Dear God, did the man sleep naked? He didn't seem the sort to don a nightshirt.

She tried to take her thoughts in hand, but they wouldn't be governed. Instead, they scattered in every direction like startled chickens, squawking and flapping their wings.

Sure enough, she felt the bareness of his flesh, the hard warmth with its aura of chill.

He gave a long sigh. "Good night, Juliana," he said.

They both lay sleepless in the dark for a long time, neither one speaking, careful not to brush against each other.

Juliana should have been relieved.

Instead, she bit her lower lip hard, and hoped he wouldn't hear her crying.

CHAPTER SEVEN

LINCOLN WAS ON the range the next morning, having bid the Reverend Dettly farewell, his muscles aching from a long night of self-restraint, wanting Juliana and not taking her, when Wes rode up, looking as rumpled and dissolute as ever. The cattle had been fed and Lincoln was there alone, he and his horse, just looking at the herd and wondering if those critters were worth all the grief they caused him.

"Came to get my mule," Wes said. "Tom told me you were out here."

There were bulging bundles tied where his saddlebags should have been. Gifts for Gracie and the other children, no doubt—Wes and Kate were always generous at Christmas and on birthdays, having no kids of their own.

Lincoln didn't say anything. Wes had known all along about Josiah's first wife, Micah's mother, and he'd never bothered to raise the subject. Now, after talking to Tom, he probably meant to make some kind of speech.

"A wire came for Miss Mitchell," Wes said, surprising him. "I thought I'd better bring it out here."

"She's not 'Miss Mitchell' anymore," Lincoln said, his tone flat and matter-of-fact. "I married her yesterday."

Wes gave a bark of pleased laughter at the news. "So *that's* why I met the reverend on the road out from town this morning," he said. "Congratulations, you lucky son of a gun."

"Thanks." He gave the word a grudging note.

Wes pulled a yellow envelope from the inside pocket of his coat, squinting against the glare of sunshine on snow. Watched as Lincoln tucked away the telegram without looking at the face of it.

"It's from the Bureau of Indian Affairs, Lincoln," Wes said quietly.

Trouble, of course—telegrams rarely brought good news. Lincoln swallowed and braced himself for whatever was coming. He'd been enduring things for so long, toughing them out, that he'd learned to dig in whenever a problem appeared. "You'd damn well better not have read it," he said.

"I didn't have to," Wes answered easily. "The telegraph operator told me what it says. By now, half the town knows that that Indian Agent Philbert means to show up in Stillwater Springs some time before New Year's and stir up a ruckus. The new Mrs. Creed is out of a job for sure, but I don't suppose that matters now, anyhow, what with the wedding and all."

Even though he'd expected something like that, the knowledge buffeted Lincoln like a hard wind. Made him shift in the saddle. "What else?" he asked, still avoiding his brother's gaze.

"He's bound on taking the kids back to Missoula," Wes said.

Lincoln closed his eyes. Didn't speak.

He'd get Joseph and Theresa on their way back to North Dakota before Philbert showed up, no matter what he had to do. Take them to the train depot at Missoula if it came to that, and put them onboard himself. Juliana had prepared herself for that particular parting—it was best for them to be with their own folks—but things were different with the two little ones. Orphans, the both of them. Somewhere along the line, Juliana had taken to mothering Daisy and little Bill, and letting go would be a hard thing, for her and for them.

"Tom told you the family secret, I hear," Wes said, when Lincoln had been silent too long to suit him.

Lincoln turned his head then. Looked straight at his brother. "Why didn't *you* tell me, Wes?"

"Ma asked me not to," Wes replied with the solemnity of truth.

Still, Lincoln had to challenge him. "Since when are you so all-fired concerned with doing what Ma wants?"

Wes's smile was thin, and a little on the self-disparaging side. "I chopped down a Christmas tree and hauled it out here on a mule's back because she told me to, didn't I?"

"You did that for Gracie."

Wes sighed, stood in the stirrups for a moment, stretching his legs. "Mostly," he admitted gruffly. Then, after a long time, he added, "Things weren't always so sour between Ma and me, Lincoln. You remember how it was after Dawson died—she was half-mad with the sorrow. Doc Chaney had to dose her up with laudanum. I was pretty torn up myself—we all were—but I felt sorry for her. I wanted to do what I could to help, and God knew there wasn't much."

Lincoln took that in without speaking. He remembered how his ma used to howl with grief some nights, during those first weeks after the shooting, and how his pa had slammed out of the house when she did.

Saddle leather creaked as Wes fidgeted, leaning forward a little, looking earnest. "There was another reason I didn't tell you," he said, sounding reluctant and a little irritated.

"What was that?" Lincoln bit out, in no frame of mind to make things easy for his brother. Whatever Wes's reasons for keeping that secret, he, Lincoln, had had as much right to know as anybody.

"You tend to hold on to things you ought to let go of," Wes said, reining his horse around, toward the main house, looking back at Lincoln over one shoulder. "People, too."

"Beth." Lincoln sighed the name.

"Beth," Wes agreed. Another silence fell between them, lengthy and punctuated only by snorts and hoof-shuffling from their horses and the chatter of the passing creek. "Of the four of us, Lincoln, you're the most like Pa. Tougher than hell, and too smart for your own good or anybody else's. You've held on to this ground, just like he did, and made it pay, in good times and bad. But you take after the old man in a few other ways, too. If I hauled off and swung a shovel at your head—and I've wanted to more than once—it would be the shovel that fractured, not your skull."

"That was quite a sermon, Wes."

"Don't get out of your pew yet, because I'm not finished. Right now, because you're still young, that stubborn streak serves you pretty well—you probably think of it as 'determination.' Trouble is, over time, it might just harden into something a lot less admirable."

As much as Lincoln would have liked to disregard the warning, he couldn't. It made too much sense. He'd mourned Dawson in a normal way, but since Beth had died, he'd boarded over parts of himself, knowing it would hurt too much if he let himself care.

"What do you suggest I do?" he asked moderately, just to get it over with. Wes was going to tell him anyhow; he'd worked himself up into a pretty good lather since talking with Tom.

"You remember how different Pa was when we were little? How he'd haul one or another of us around on his shoulders, let us follow him practically every place he went? How he laughed all the time, even though he worked like a mule? Back then, he wouldn't have believed it if somebody had told him he'd wind up turning his back on all of us, but he did. You know why, Lincoln? Because he decided to go right on loving a dead woman, when he had a living, breathing one right in front of him. It took a while, but that decision—that one bone-headed decision—poisoned his mind, and eventually, it poisoned his soul, too." Wes paused for a few moments, remembering, maybe gathering more words. "Never mind Juliana. She's prettier than Ma was, and she's got a lot more spirit. She'll be all right, even if you're fool enough to keep your heart closed to her. But what about Gracie? She's already got a mind of her own, and she's only seven—what do you think she'll be like at sixteen? Or eighteen? She'll make a lot of choices along the way, and I guarantee you aren't going to like some of them. You're bound to butt heads—I suppose that's normal—but if you aren't careful, you might find yourself treating your daughter the same way Pa did us. Do you want that?"

Lincoln's throat had seized shut. He shook his head.

Wes had finally run down, having reeled out what he had to say. He nudged at his horse's sides with the heels of his boots and rode back toward the house to drop off the things stuffed into those bags tied behind his saddle and collect his mule.

Conscious of the telegram in his pocket, Lincoln waited awhile before following.

JULIANA WAS CROSSING THE YARD, returning from a brief visit to Rose-of-Sharon and baby Joshua, when she saw her brother-in-law leading his mule out of the barn. Tom, meanwhile, carried two burlap bags, stuffed full of something, toward the woodshed.

Because she liked Weston Creed, she changed course, smiling, and went to greet him.

His smile flashed, but his eyes were solemn, almost sad. "My brother," he said, "is a lucky man."

Juliana blushed. She wasn't used to compliments; schoolmarms didn't get a whole lot of them. "We've got two big turkeys for Christmas dinner," she told him, feeling self-conscious. "I hope you'll join us."

He slipped a loop of rope around the mule's neck and paused to look toward the house. "Is Kate welcome, too?" he asked. Without waiting for an answer, he moved to stand beside his horse and tied the other end of the rope loosely around the horn of the saddle.

"Of course," Juliana said.

"Do you know anything about her?" Weston asked, and while the inquiry sounded almost idle, Juliana knew it wasn't.

"I suppose she's your wife."

He chuckled, but it was a bitter sound, void of amusement. "Something like that," he said. "Kate owns the Diamond Buckle Saloon. She and I have been living in sin for some time now."

"Oh," Juliana said. She was intrigued at the prospect

of meeting such a colorful personage, but perhaps she should have spoken to Lincoln before she'd issued the invitation.

"Yes," Weston said wryly. "Oh."

Juliana's cheeks stung with embarrassment. When she'd asked Lincoln for permission to bathe Daisy and Billy-Moses the night before, he'd said the ranch house was her home, too, and she didn't need his permission. She hoped that liberty extended to other things. "We'll sit down to dinner around two o'clock," she said. Since she wouldn't be roasting the turkeys, the hour was a mere guess. "But whatever time you and Kate arrive, we'll be glad to see you."

He rounded the horse to stand facing Juliana. His mouth, sensuous like Lincoln's, twitched at one corner. "You do realize, Mrs. Creed, that the roof will surely fall in, either the instant Kate sets foot over the threshold or when my mother finds out?"

Even without meeting the woman, Juliana was a little afraid of Cora Creed. Just the same, she wasn't one to let fear stop her from doing anything she thought was right. Raising her chin a notch, she replied, "I guess we'll have to take that chance."

Lincoln's brother chuckled again, but this time, it sounded real. "Brave words," he said. "But I think you might just mean them."

"I never say anything I don't mean, Mr. Creed."

"Call me Wes," he said, grinning now.

"Only if you agree to call me Juliana," she retorted.

He leaned in, kissed her forehead. "Welcome to my brother's life, Juliana," he told her. "God knows, he needs you."

Something made her look up then. She saw Lincoln

approaching on horseback, a distant speck, moving slowly. Her heart quickened at the sight. "What makes you say that?" she asked Wes.

Wes sighed, and after glancing back over one shoulder, favored her with a sad smile. "He's lost a lot in his life. Beth, of course, and two babies. Pa and our brother Dawson. He's a good man, Lincoln is, but he's—well, he's mighty careful with his heart, as a general rule."

Juliana laid a hand to her chest; she had been too careful with her own heart, until Daisy and Billy-Moses and other special students had somehow gotten past the barriers.

Wes turned, stuck a foot in one stirrup and mounted the horse. After glancing in Lincoln's direction once more, he said, "I'll be going now. We've had a few words, my brother and I, and there will be more if I stay." He tapped at his horse's sides with the heels of his boots, tightened the rope to urge the mule into motion. "Unless there's another blizzard," he added, "Kate and I will be here Christmas Day."

Juliana smiled, though she was a little troubled by talk of he and Lincoln "having words." "Come early," she said.

Wes nodded and started off, the mule balking at first, then trotting obediently along behind his horse.

Although it was sunny out, the weather was cold. Juliana huddled inside one of her mother-in-law's cloaks, hastily borrowed, and waited for her husband.

When he rode up to the barn, she approached, slowly at first, and then with faster steps.

The confession burst out of her. "I've asked Wes and Kate to come for Christmas dinner," she said, all on one breath.

He swung down from the saddle, stood looking at her with amusement on his mouth and sadness in his eyes, just as Wes had done. "Did he accept the invite?" he asked.

She took a breath, let it out and nodded quickly.

He laughed then, and hooked one stirrup over the saddle horn, so he could unbuckle the cinch. "Well, Mrs. Creed," he said, "you've succeeded where I failed, then. I've never been able to persuade Kate to set foot on this ranch, let alone sit down to Christmas dinner, and if she stays in town, so does Wes."

Juliana took a single step toward him, stopped herself, reading the set of his face. "Something is wrong," she said. "What is it?"

He went still for a long moment, then reached into his coat pocket and brought out a small yellow envelope.

Seeing it, Juliana felt her blood run cold. She was suddenly paralyzed.

Lincoln held out the envelope to her, and her hands trembled as she accepted it. Fumbled as she tried to unseal the flap.

"Wes brought it out from town," Lincoln said.

Juliana began to shiver, finally shoving the telegram at Lincoln. "Please," she whispered. "Read it."

Lincoln tugged off his gloves, opened the envelope and studied the page inside. "It's from the Bureau of Indian Affairs," he said. From his tone, it was clear that he'd known that all along. "'Miss Mitchell. You are hereby—'" Lincoln paused, cleared his throat. "'You are hereby dismissed. I will be in Stillwater Springs by the first of January at the latest. At that time, you will surrender any remaining students now in your custody for placement in appropriate institutions.' It's signed 'R. Philbert.'"

Juliana stood absolutely still, though on the inside, she felt as though she were set to bolt in a dozen different directions.

Lincoln took hold of her shoulders, the telegram still in one hand, and steadied her. "Take a breath, Juliana," he ordered, his voice low.

She breathed. Once. Twice. A third time.

"Listen to me," Lincoln went on calmly. "We're going to handle this, you and I. Together."

Juliana's mind raced, but there was a painful clarity to her thoughts just the same. Mr. Philbert had effectively warned her by sending her a telegram announcing his intention to visit Stillwater Springs, which might mean he planned to come earlier, hoping to forestall any attempt she might make to flee with the children.

"Wh-what are we going to do?" she faltered.

"First, we've got to get Joseph and Theresa to Missoula, put them on a train east. As for Daisy and Bill—well—I've been thinking about what Gracie said yesterday. Now that we're married, we could adopt them, and then they'd be Creeds. They could stay with us."

Juliana was grateful for his hold on her shoulders, because her knees wanted to buckle. "You'd do that?" she whispered, marveling. Surely there wasn't another man on the face of the earth quite like this one.

His eyes were shadowed by the brim of his hat, but she saw a quiet willingness in them even before he answered. "Yes."

"Why?"

"For them. For Gracie. Most of all, for you." Gently, he turned her toward the house. Spoke close to her right ear, his breath warm against her skin. "Go on inside before you catch your death in this cold. I'll be in as soon as I get this horse put up."

Juliana took a cautious step, found that her legs were still working.

Inside, the children, having finished the day's lessons, were pestering Tom to let them go out to play. Juliana gave her permission, with the stipulation that they must all bundle up as warmly as possible and not make noise near the Gainers' cabin because Rose-of-Sharon and the baby needed peace and quiet.

There was a flurry of coat-finding—Gracie was so excited, she could hardly stand still to let Juliana lay a woolen scarf over the top of her head and tie it beneath her chin. Tom found knitted caps for the other children, and they all raced for the front door.

Once they were gone, Tom asked straight out, "You're pale as a new snow, Juliana. What's the matter? What's happened?"

Haltingly, she told him about Mr. Philbert's telegram.

His face hardened as he listened. "What did Lincoln have to say about that?"

"He wants to get Joseph and Theresa to the train in Missoula as soon as possible." She didn't mention the adoption; she still wasn't sure she'd actually heard Lincoln correctly, where that was concerned.

Tom nodded. "Missoula's half a day's ride from here, if the weather holds," he said. "If it doesn't, Philbert probably won't make it to town until the roads are clear."

Lincoln came in just then, looked from Juliana to Tom without speaking, took off his hat and coat and hung them up the way he always did. His expression remained grim.

"I'll take Joseph and Theresa to Missoula," Tom said. "Ride back to North Dakota with them to make sure they get there all right and folks are ready to take them in on the other end."

Sadness moved in Lincoln's face, but he nodded. Looking distracted, he said, "I'll be at my desk." Pausing in the doorway to the front room, he turned around. "You'll come back, won't you, Tom?" he asked.

Tom didn't smile. "I'll come back," he said very quietly.

Later, when the children had worn themselves out playing games in the front yard and returned to the house, bright-eyed and glowing from the cold, Juliana brewed up a batch of hot chocolate in a heavy cast-iron kettle and gave them each a cup. While they enjoyed the treat, she went in search of Lincoln.

He was where he'd said he'd be, seated at his desk in a corner of the front room, surrounded by thick books, all of them open. As she approached, he dipped a pen in a bottle of ink and wrote something on a sheet of paper.

Needing to be near him, she set a mug of hot chocolate beside him. "Thanks," he said.

Juliana's fingers flexed; she wanted to work the tight muscles in Lincoln's neck and shoulders, but refrained. Yes, he was her husband, but touching him, even in such an innocuous way, seemed too familiar. Even a little brazen.

Still, she could not bring herself to walk away, any more than she could have left a warm stove after walking through a blizzard.

"If you're going to linger, Juliana," he said mildly, without looking up from the paper and the books, "please sit down."

She moved to a nearby armchair, sat down on its edge, knotted her fingers together. And waited.

Lincoln finally sighed, shoved back his chair and turned to look at her. "Everything will be all right, Juliana," he said.

He didn't know Mr. Philbert. "Today," she ventured nervously, "out by the barn, I thought you said—"

He waited.

"I thought you said you would be willing to adopt Daisy and Billy-Moses."

Lincoln smiled. "I did say that, Juliana."

She gripped the arms of her chair. "How?"

"I'm a lawyer," he answered. He gestured toward the books on his desk. "I'm drawing up the papers right now."

"You didn't mention that. Being a lawyer, I mean."

"There are a lot of things I haven't gotten around to mentioning," Lincoln said reasonably. "I haven't had time."

She stood up, sat down again. "You could—you could get into trouble for sending Joseph and Theresa to North Dakota," she fretted.

"I'm no stranger to trouble," Lincoln told her. "In fact, I like a challenge."

"I need something to do," she confessed.

Lincoln opened a drawer in his desk, brought out a second bottle of ink and a pen. Gave her several sheets of paper. "Write to your brother," he said. "Tell him you're married now, and if he doesn't come here first, I'll be paying him a visit one day soon."

The thought of Clay and Lincoln standing face-to-face unnerved her a little, but she accepted the pen and ink and paper, and went back to the kitchen. Tom and

Joseph were gone, and Theresa, Gracie, Daisy and Billy-Moses sat in a circle on the floor, playing with a tattered deck of cards.

She took a chair at the table, opened the ink bottle and awaited inspiration. After a quarter of an hour, all she'd written was "Dear Clay." Finally, out of frustration, she stopped trying to choose her words carefully, dipped the pen, and began.

As you have long wished me safely married, I am happy to inform you that yesterday, December 22, I entered into matrimony with Mr. Lincoln Creed, of Stillwater Springs, Montana—

Juliana went on to describe Lincoln, Gracie, the house and what she'd seen of the ranch. She extended sincere felicitations for a happy Christmas and prosperous New Year. Why, it would be 1911 soon. Where had the time gone?

The letter filled three pages by the time she'd finished.

She closed with "Sincerely, Juliana Mitchell Creed," and when the ink was dry, she carefully folded the letter, her earlier trepidation having given way to relief. She could not predict how Clay would respond to the missive, if he responded at all, but that took nothing away from her sense of having turned some kind of corner, found some new kind of freedom.

The rest of the day ground by slowly.

The younger children took naps without protest.

Theresa read quietly in the rocking chair, next to the stove.

When she grew restless, Juliana avoided the front room, where Lincoln was still working, and donned the borrowed cloak and went to the Gainers' cabin again, knocking lightly on the door. When Ben answered, whispering that Rose-of-Sharon and the baby were asleep, she smiled to cover her disappointment and promised to come back later.

She visited the barn and spoke to the cow and all the horses.

She went into the woodshed, planning to peek into the two burlap bags Tom had left there, but the idea pricked at her conscience, so she dismissed it.

She was chilled, but too wrought up to return to the house.

Spotting the orchard nearby, Juliana headed in that direction. The trees were gnarled and bare-limbed, and she paused, laid a hand to a sturdy trunk. Late the following summer, there would be fruit. In the meantime, perhaps Tom would teach her to make preserves.

At first, glimpsing the stone angel out of the corner of her eye, Juliana thought she was seeing things. As she drew nearer, though, she realized she'd come upon a small cemetery.

The angel marked the final resting place of Bethany Allan Creed.

Juliana's throat tightened. Beth. Lincoln's first wife, Gracie's mother. Careful of her skirts—she was wearing the blue dress again—she dropped to her haunches. Brushed away a patch of snow, and the twigs and small stones beneath.

She couldn't have said why she felt compelled to do such a thing. "I'm going to take very good care of your little Gracie," she heard herself say. "She's so smart, and so pretty and so kind. I fell in love with her right away."

A breeze, neither warm nor cold, played in Juliana's hair. "I'll make you a promise, Beth, here and now. Gracie won't forget you, won't forget that you're her real mother."

Behind her, a twig snapped.

Startled, Juliana stood and, forgetting to lift her hem, spun around.

Lincoln stood at the edge of the orchard, wearing his round-brimmed hat and his long black coat. From that distance, she couldn't read his expression.

Feeling as though she'd been caught doing something wrong, Juliana didn't move or speak.

Lincoln came toward her slowly. Even when she could see his face clearly, she found no emotion there. No anger, but no smile, either.

"There are wolves out here sometimes, Juliana," he said. "In the summer, the bears like to raid the orchard. It isn't safe to wander too far from the house alone."

Juliana fought to speak, because her throat was still closed. "You must have loved your wife very much," she said, brushing the angel's wing with a light pass of her hand.

"Beth's father sent the marker," he said. "Nothing but the best for his daughter. Not that he bothered to come all the way out here to the wilds of Montana to pay his respects or meet his granddaughter."

Juliana didn't know what to say. And she probably couldn't have spoken, anyway. Despite Lincoln's lack of expression, the air felt charged with emotion.

"I did love Beth," he continued, when she held her tongue. "The strange thing is, if I met her today, for the first time, I mean, I'm not sure I'd do more than tip my hat."

Juliana reached out without thinking and touched his arm. Was relieved when he didn't pull away. "What do you mean?" she asked softly.

"I was a different man back then," he answered.

Although she was still puzzled, Juliana didn't ask for clarification. Instinct told her to listen instead.

"I wanted different things than I want now."

Juliana waited, her hand still resting on the sleeve of his coat.

He was quiet for a long time. When he broke the silence, his voice sounded hoarse. He told her about his father, his mother, his three brothers. He told her about going off to college in Boston, how homesick he'd been for the ranch and his family, about studying law and meeting Beth when he went to work in her father's firm.

He told her about Gracie's birth, and the two babies who hadn't lived—a boy and a girl. They'd never given them names, and now he wished they had, because then they'd have had identities, however brief.

Juliana didn't look away, though she would have liked to hide the tear that slipped down her right cheek.

Finally, he reached out, took her hand. Led her toward home.

Tom had made supper—bear-meat hash—and Juliana was surprised to find that she had an appetite. Most likely, it was all that fresh air.

She washed the dishes by herself that night, while Theresa got the three younger children ready for bed. Tom and Lincoln sat at the table with Joseph, making plans for the journey to North Dakota.

Juliana listened, knowing that the ache of missing Joseph and Theresa would be with her for a long, long time. They belonged with their family, though—shouldn't have been taken from them in the first place.

She finished the dishes, hung the dish towel up to dry. Left the kitchen.

Gracie had climbed into bed with Daisy and Billy-Moses. Theresa sat cross-legged on the foot of the mattress, reading aloud from, of all things, the Sears, Roebuck catalog.

Juliana stood in the open doorway for a while, unnoticed, while the children listened raptly to descriptions of china platters, teacups and silverware. The words, she realized, didn't matter. It was the sound of another human voice that held their attention.

She slipped away. In Lincoln's room, she filled the china basin with fresh water from the matching pitcher and scrubbed her teeth with a brush and baking soda. She washed her face, unplaited her hair, brushed it thoroughly, and plaited it again.

Her nightgown felt chilly, so she draped it over the screen in front of the fireplace where a cheery blaze crackled. Lincoln must have lit the fire just before supper.

She unbuttoned the blue dress, stepped out of it. Took off her shoes and rolled her stockings down and off. Untied the laces of her petticoat and let the garment fall.

She was standing there, in just her camisole and bloomers, when the door opened and Lincoln came in.

He went still at the sight of her.

She imagined that the firelight behind her had turned her undergarments transparent, and that sent a rush of embarrassment through her, but she made no move to cover herself.

Lincoln started to back out of the room.

"Wait," Juliana said with dignity. "Don't go. Please."

He stepped over the threshold again, closed the door behind him. The conflict in his handsome face might have been comical, if she hadn't been so concerned with the pounding of her heart. He opened his mouth to speak, but when no sound came out, he closed it again.

"You asked me to tell you when I felt ready," she reminded him. Fingers trembling, she began untying the tiny ribbons that held her camisole together in front.

"And?" He rasped the word.

"I'm ready."

CHAPTER EIGHT

LEANING BACK AGAINST the bedroom door, Lincoln shook his head once and gave a raspy sigh. "I'm not so sure about that," he said. "Your being ready, I mean."

Was he rejecting her? Quickly, cheeks throbbing with heat, Juliana stopped untying the camisole ribbons and stood frozen in injured confusion. Without intending to, she allowed her deepest fear to escape. "Don't you— don't you want me, Lincoln?"

He blew out a breath. "Oh, I *want* you, all right," he said.

"Then, why…?"

"My brother said some things to me today that I need to think about," Lincoln explained calmly. "And, anyway, you've been through a lot lately. I won't have you doing this because you think you ought to, or because you want to get it over with."

"Get it over with?" She was astounded, but she probably sounded angry.

His powerful shoulders moved in a shruglike motion. "Making love can be painful for the woman the first time," he reminded her. "And it'll be more so, in a lot of other ways, if you're offering yourself to me for the wrong reasons."

He was such a—*lawyer,* building a case against what they both needed and wanted. *"What* wrong reasons?"

she demanded, careful to keep her voice down, so none of the children would overhear. Earlier, he'd found her visiting his first wife's grave. Did he think she was trying to exert some kind of *claim* on him, somehow supplant Beth's memory? Use her body to push the other woman out of his heart and mind?

Lincoln raised one eyebrow. "Well," he began, "you could be grateful, because I'm willing to adopt Daisy and Bill and raise them as our own."

Indignant, Juliana snatched her nightgown off the fireplace screen and pulled it on over her head, meaning to remove her undergarments later, when he was gone. As luck would have it, though, she got her arms tangled in the sleeves somehow and ended up flailing about like a chicken inside a burlap sack.

Lincoln laughed; she heard him come toward her, his footsteps easy on the plank floor.

She felt him righting the nightgown.

When he tugged it down so her head popped through the neck hole, his eyes were dancing.

"Don't you *dare* make fun of me!" Juliana sputtered.

He chuckled again, but there was something tender in the way he held her shoulders. "I wouldn't do that," he said.

As if she weren't humiliated enough already, hot tears sprang to her eyes.

"Listen," Lincoln said, after placing a light kiss on the top of her head. "Once we've made love, there will be no going back. It's got to be right."

She stared at him, aghast. *Once we've made love, there will be no going back.* Was he having second thoughts, thinking of annulling the marriage on the grounds that they had yet to consummate it?

"May I remind you, Mr. Creed, that getting married was *your* idea?"

"I'm well aware of that," he said affably.

"But now you want to make sure there's a way to *go back?*"

Surprise widened his eyes. "Hell, *that* isn't what I meant," he said.

Relief swept over Juliana, leaving her almost faint. She hoped to high heaven her reaction didn't show, because she'd made enough of a fool of herself as it was, behaving with such wanton abandon. "I practically *threw myself* at you," she fretted, "and you might as well have flung a bucket of cold water all over me!"

He sighed, yet again. "Oh," he said.

"Oh," Juliana repeated, in the same tone Wes had used when he'd repeated the word back to her that afternoon, in reference to Kate's reasons for avoiding the ranch.

Lincoln shoved a hand through his hair. "Maybe we ought to just start over—"

"Maybe," Juliana shot back, "you should go off by yourself and *think* about whatever it was that your brother said to you, out there on the range."

Something flickered in his eyes. "I believe I've come to terms with that," he said, and his voice sounded different. It was lower than before, and gruff in a way that made Juliana tingle in peculiar places. Her mouth went dry.

She waited for him to explain further, but, of course, he didn't, being a man and used to keeping his own counsel. He raised his hands to the sides of her face, the way he'd done after the marriage ceremony, and then he kissed her.

The wedding kiss had rocked her, but this one was even more intense. He parted her lips and used his tongue, and the pleasure of that was so startling that Juliana would have cried out if her mouth hadn't been covered.

She slipped her arms around his neck and rose onto her tiptoes, caught up in her response like a leaf swept up into a whirlwind.

His tongue.

The way his body fit against hers.

The way her own expanded, ready to take him in.

All of it left her dazed, and when he finally stopped kissing her, he had to grab her shoulders again, because she swayed.

Blinking, she stared up at him.

"*That,* Mrs. Creed, should settle any question of whether I want you or not."

It had certainly settled the question of whether or not *she* wanted *him.* She most definitely did, and the consequences be damned.

"Then you'll make love to me?" she asked, brazen, flushed with desire.

"Inevitably," he answered, but he was releasing her shoulders, turning to leave the room. Only her pride, or what remained of it, kept her from scrambling after him, begging him not to leave.

"When?" she croaked.

He paused without turning to face her, and tilted his head back, considering. "When it's right," he finally replied.

And then he was gone.

Juliana felt like some wild creature, caught and caged. She stood there trembling with rage and frustration for

a few moments, then took up her brush, undid her braid
and brushed her hair with long, furious strokes that left
it crackling around her face like fire.

Once she'd regained her composure enough to risk
leaving the room, she went to look in on the children.
Billy-Moses, Daisy and Gracie lay curled against one
another like puppies, sleeping soundly. Theresa was in
Gracie's bed with her eyes closed.

Just as Juliana would have closed the door, though,
the child spoke.

"Miss Mitchell—I mean, Mrs. Creed? Will you sit
with me—just for a little while?"

Juliana approached the bed, sat down on its edge.
Smoothed Theresa's dark hair with a motherly hand.
"Sure," she said softly. "Is something bothering you?"

A stray moonbeam played over the girl's face, was
gone again. "Joseph remembers the folks at home," she
said. "I do, too, sort of, but mostly I remember going
away and living in a lot of different schools."

Juliana simply waited.

"What if we get home, Joseph and me, and they can't
keep us for some reason? Or don't want us after all?"

Juliana's heart ached. "You saw the letter they sent,"
she said gently. "They want you."

"But maybe somebody like Mr. Philbert will come
and take us away again."

"I don't think that will happen," Juliana said. Although unlikely, it *was* possible. "Tom is going with you,
remember. He'll make sure you and Joseph get settled,
and keep you safe all along the way."

"Folks might be mean to us. After all, Mr. Dancingstar is an Indian, too."

That, too, was possible. Juliana wished she could

make the trip with the three of them, and stand guard over them, but of course she couldn't. Gracie and Daisy and Billy-Moses needed her—if Wes Creed could be believed, so did Lincoln. She had to face Mr. Philbert and settle things, once and for all, so she and Lincoln could go on with their lives.

"Don't worry, Theresa," she said. "That won't change anything. And Mr. Dancingstar *will* take care of you."

"I almost wish I could stay here with you, but I'd miss Joseph something fierce, and he might forget to practice his reading if I don't keep an eye on him."

Juliana blinked back tears. "Will you write to me when you get home? Tell me all about the trip, and what things are like in North Dakota?"

Theresa nodded and reached up with both arms for a hug.

She and Juliana clung together for a little while.

"Will you write me back?" Theresa asked finally, settling back onto her pillow. "Long, long letters?"

"Long, long letters," Juliana promised, choking back more tears. She leaned over, kissed the girl's smooth forehead. "Now, go to sleep, Theresa. Tomorrow is Christmas Eve."

"You don't think I believe all those stories about Saint Nicholas, do you?" Theresa asked in a whisper. "I'm twelve, you know. Besides, Joseph says it's all malarkey and I oughtn't to expect anything much."

With yet another pang, Juliana tucked the covers under Theresa's chin. "You mustn't stop hoping for things," she said. "Not ever. That's what keeps us all going."

"But Saint Nicholas *is* just a story?"

Juliana thought of the presents hidden in the top of

Mrs. Creed's wardrobe. They were simple things, but seen through the eyes of these children, who'd never owned much of anything, they would gleam like Aladdin's treasure. "Yes," she admitted. "There was a real Saint Nicholas, once upon a time, and a lot of legends have grown up around his life, but they're just that, legends. Still, there *are* people in the world who have generous hearts."

Lincoln was one of them. Wes Creed was another. And, of course, Tom Dancingstar.

Theresa sighed, closed her eyes and settled into her dreams.

Juliana waited until she was sure the child was asleep, kissed her cheek and returned to the corridor.

She'd left the bedroom door open; now it was closed.

She stopped, put a hand to her throat before reaching to turn the knob.

The room was dark except for the flickering glow cast by the fireplace. Lincoln was already in bed, but sitting up with pillows behind his back. His chest was bare, she could tell, but his face was in shadow, making his expression impossible to read.

"I wondered if you'd come back to this room after our—discussion," he said.

"There is nowhere else to sleep," Juliana answered, and the formal tone she employed was at least partly an act. She wasn't angry with Lincoln, just confused. "Unless, of course, you'd prefer I retired to the barn like Reverend Dettly did."

Lincoln gave a snort. "The reverend is a man," he reminded her. "And despite being on a first-name basis with the Good Lord, he carries a gun in his saddlebags, right alongside his Bible."

Juliana folded her arms, keeping a stubborn distance from Lincoln Creed's bed, even though it was the very place she most wanted to be at that moment. "If you're going to be argumentative, perhaps *you* should sleep in the barn," she said, jutting out her chin. It was all bravado, and everything she said seemed to be coming out wrong—thinking one thing, saying quite another. What was the matter with her? "I was prepared to forgive you for your rudeness, Mr. Creed, but now I'm not so sure."

He chuckled, a low, rumbling sound, entirely masculine and not entirely polite. "That's very generous of you, *Mrs.* Creed," he answered. "Especially since I was trying to look out for your best interests, and if anybody ought to be apologizing around here, it's you."

"You were looking out for your own interests, not mine!" she whispered accusingly.

He patted the mattress. "Get into bed, Juliana. I'm tired and I won't be able to sleep with you standing there like you've got a ramrod stuck down the back of your nightgown."

Since her side of the bed was against the wall, she would have to crawl over him to get there, perhaps even straddling his limbs in the awkward effort. She wasn't *about* to do any such thing.

"Juliana," he repeated.

"The least you could do is get up and allow me to obey your *orders* with some semblance of dignity!"

He laughed then, though quietly. "You really want me to throw back the covers and stand up?" he teased. "Under the circumstances, that might be more than you bargained for."

Juliana reasoned that if she couldn't see Lincoln's face, he couldn't see *hers,* either, and that was a mercy, since she knew she was blushing again. It was the curse of redheaded women. "Oh, for heaven's sake!" she blurted, going to the side of the bed and scrambling over him, trying to keep her nightgown from riding up in the process.

Lincoln chortled at her predicament, and that made her want to pause long enough to pummel him with her fists. Once she'd crossed him, like some mountain range, she plopped down hard on her back and hugged her arms tightly across her chest, staring up at the ceiling.

He rolled onto his side, his face only inches from hers. "I'd like to propose a truce," he said. "I didn't mean to insult you, Juliana."

She didn't turn her head, but she did slant her eyes in his direction. "Do you apologize?"

Lincoln rose onto one elbow, cupping the side of his head in his palm. "Hell, no, I don't apologize. I didn't do anything wrong."

She turned away from him, onto her side.

He turned her back.

"All *right*," he growled. "I'm sorry."

"You are not!"

That was when he kissed her again. She struggled at first, out of pure obstinacy, but he just kissed her harder and more deeply, and she melted, driven by instincts that came from some uncontrollable part of her being. Plunged her fingers into his hair and kissed him right back.

She felt his manhood pressed against her thigh as he shifted on the mattress, and the sheer size of it caused her eyes to pop open in alarm, but then that strange, weighted heat suffused her again. She sank into helpless wanting.

"God help me," he murmured, almost tearing his mouth from hers.

Juliana ran her hands up and down his back, loving the feel of hard, warm muscle under her palms.

Lincoln let his forehead rest against hers. "Woman," he said, "if you don't stop doing that, I won't be responsible for my actions."

She raised her head, nibbled at his bare shoulder and then the side of his neck.

With a groan, Lincoln shifted again, poised above her now, resting on his forearms to keep from crushing her. "Juliana," he ground out, but if he'd been planning to say more, the words died in his throat.

He kissed her tenderly this time, tugging at her lower lip, wringing a soft moan from her. Then, with one hand, he caught hold of her nightgown and hauled it upward, past her thighs, past her waist, past her breasts—and then over her head.

Casting the gown aside, Lincoln sat back on his haunches, the covers falling away behind him.

He moved to straddle her now, his knees on either side of her hips. Firelight danced over her skin, and he seemed spellbound as he looked at her.

When he took her breasts gently into his hands and chafed the nipples with the sides of his thumbs, Juliana was lost, already transported far beyond the borders of common sense.

She couldn't bear too much waiting, not this first time, when she was in such terrible, wonderful suspense, and he seemed to know that.

He deftly dispensed with her undergarments, parted her legs, and she felt that most intimate part of him, pressed against her.

"You're sure, Juliana?" he whispered.

She nodded.

He eased inside her, in a long, slow stroke, and there *was* pain, but the pleasure was so much greater, a fiery friction, inflaming her more with every motion of their bodies, blazing like a little sun at her core. She clutched at Lincoln, gasping, rising to meet him, and he soothed her with gruff murmurings even as he drove her mad.

She was straining for something, wild with the need of it, and then it was upon her, and at the same time, it was as though she'd somehow escaped herself, given herself up entirely to sensation.

Her body dissolved first, and then her mind, and then their very souls seemed to collide. Lincoln covered her mouth with his own, muffling both their cries.

When it was over—it seemed to go on for an eternity, that melting and melding of so much more than their bodies—Lincoln collapsed beside her, gathered her in his arms. Propped his chin on the top of her head.

After a long time, he asked hoarsely, "Did it hurt?"

"Yes," she told him honestly. Surely he'd been aware of her responses, of the pleasure he'd given her. She felt transformed, even powerful.

"I'm sorry."

Juliana turned onto her side, facing him. Touched his cheek. "Don't be sorry, Lincoln," she said. "It was the most *wonderful* thing."

He chuckled, kissed her lightly. "Now will you go to sleep?"

She laughed. Kissed him back. "Now I will go to sleep," she conceded.

With his arms still around her, Lincoln soon drifted off, his breathing deep and slow, his flesh warm. Perfectly content, Juliana lay there in the fire-lit darkness, marveling at all she had not known before this night.

AFTER THE CATTLE had been fed the next morning—the weather remained mild, though Lincoln felt a rancher's wariness and made good use of it while he could—he rode to town.

At the mercantile, he mailed Juliana's letter to her brother and bought presents—a wedding band for his wife, along with several ready-made dresses and a bright green woolen cloak with a hood. He chose coats for the four children, too, guessing at their sizes, and because he'd so often seen Theresa reading, he added a thick book to the pile. There were other things, as well—a stick horse with a yarn mane for little Bill, a music box for Daisy, good pipe tobacco for Tom and a few things for the Gainers and their new baby.

While Fred Willand was wrapping it all in tissue paper, Lincoln crossed to the newspaper office, found it locked up and made for the Diamond Buckle Saloon.

Since it was early in the day, and Christmas Eve to boot, there were no customers. Kate, with her too-blond hair and low-cut dress, sat at one of the card tables, drinking coffee.

"Lincoln!" she said, beaming, starting to rise.

He motioned for her to stay in her chair, joined her at the table after placing a brotherly kiss on her rouged cheek. Like Wes, Kate was something worse for wear, a little tattered around the edges, but there was a remarkably pretty woman under all that paint and pretense.

"Is my brother around?"

Kate made a face. "He was up late, skinning honest working people out of their wages at five-card stud," she said. "Then he decided to write a piece for the paper on how the Bureau of Indian Affairs does more harm than good. Last time I saw him, he was under the blankets, snoring for all he was worth."

Lincoln chuckled at that. Wes had always been more alive at night—daylight was something he tended to wait out, like a case of the grippe—while Lincoln, a born rancher, wrung all the use he could from the hours between sunrise and sunset. "My new bride tells me you and Wes will be at the home place for Christmas Day," he said.

Kate looked worried now, as though he'd forced her into a corner and started poking at her with a cue stick from the rack next to the pool table. "Wes shouldn't have said we'd come," she said, her voice small and sad. She looked down at her gold satin dress, and the cleavage bulging above and behind her bodice. "I don't have anything proper to wear."

Lincoln reached out, took her hand. She wore a lot of cheap rings, and a row of bracelets that made a clinking sound whenever she moved her arm. "Juliana is going to be mighty disappointed if you don't come," he told her. "Gracie, too. It doesn't matter what you wear, Kate."

"What do you know? You're a man."

He sighed. "All right, then. There are trunks full of dresses out at the ranch, up in the attic. Take your pick."

"Beth's dresses," Kate scoffed, but there was hope in her hazel-colored eyes. "Lincoln, she was a little bitty thing and you know it. I'd never fit into anything she wore."

That, Lincoln thought, was probably true. "How about something of Ma's, then?" he suggested.

Wes appeared on the stairway just then, shirt untucked, feet bare, hair rumpled from sleep. He plunged his hands through it a lot when he was composing one of his hide-blistering opinion pieces for the *Courier*.

He scowled at Lincoln, even as Kate gave a throaty little chuckle. "Wouldn't *that* stick under the old lady's saddle like a spiky burr?" Lincoln remarked.

"What the devil are *you* doing here?" Wes grumbled at Lincoln, reaching the table, hauling back a chair next to Kate and falling into it as heavily as a sack of feed thrown from the back of a wagon. He winced when he landed, and closed his eyes for a moment, probably suffering his just deserts after a night passed drinking, gambling and puffing on cigars.

"I came to tell you that you were right about what you said yesterday," Lincoln said, enjoying the visible impact this announcement had on Wes.

He opened his eyes, narrowed them suspiciously. Kate got up to head for the kitchen and fetch coffee for both of them. Lincoln could have done without, but Wes was plainly in dire need.

"Hold it," Wes ground out, grinning a little and working his right temple with the fingertips of one hand. "You just said I was *right*. Will you swear to it in front of witnesses?"

"Kate was a witness," Lincoln pointed out.

"I'm putting it on the front page. Two-inch headline. This is the biggest thing since McKinley's assassination, if not Honest Abe's."

Lincoln smiled, picked up a stray poker chip left behind after some previous game and turned it between his fingers. When he spoke, though, he looked serious, and he sounded that way, too. "I'm in love with Juliana,

Wes," he confided. "And I'll be damned if I know how to tell her."

Wes leaned a little, laid a hand on Lincoln's shoulder, squeezed. "Same way you told Beth," he said quietly. "You just look her in the eye, open your mouth and say 'I love you.'"

Lincoln shifted uncomfortably in his chair, wishing Kate would come back with that coffee, even though he didn't want it, so the conversation might turn in some easier direction.

"You *did* tell Beth you loved her, didn't you?" Wes challenged, looking worried.

"I thought she knew it," Lincoln confessed. "By the things I did, I mean."

"Keeping a roof over her head? Buying her geegaws and putting food on the table? Sweet Jesus, Lincoln, you're even more of a lunkhead than I thought you were."

Kate returned, a mug of steaming coffee in each hand and a big smile on her face—he'd struck home with that suggestion that she wear one of his ma's dresses to Christmas dinner, evidently—but her arrival didn't change the course of the conversation the way Lincoln had hoped it would.

She set a cup in front of each of them, and Wes scooted back his chair, caught hold of her hand and tugged hard so she landed, giggling like a girl, on his lap.

"I love you, Katie-did," he said.

"So you claim," Kate joked, blushing right down to the neckline of her faded dress. "But you've yet to put a gold band on my finger, Weston Creed."

He feigned surprise. "You'd actually hitch yourself to a waster like me?"

"You know I would," Kate said softly, looking and sounding wistful now.

"Then the next time the reverend comes through, we'll throw a wedding."

Lincoln, though pleased, wished he was elsewhere. The trouble with Wes was, he had no idea what was appropriate and what wasn't, but he seemed to be sincere enough, all things considered.

"Is that a promise?" Kate asked cautiously.

"It's a promise," Wes replied, setting her on her feet again, swatting her once on the bottom for emphasis. That done, he pivoted on his chair seat to look straight at Lincoln. "See, little brother? That's how you tell a woman you love her."

Lincoln merely shook his head. He reckoned Fred had the presents wrapped by then, and he was eager to get back out to the ranch. After all, Christmas was coming, and this one was special.

He stood. "You might want to ride out with me," he told his brother. "Kate's going to borrow one of Ma's dresses, and she'll need time to take it in a little first."

Wes gave a guffaw of laughter that made Kate jump and got to his feet. "That," he said, "will be worth seeing. But I'll meet you at the ranch later on—I've got to put on boots and get my horse saddled, and I don't want to hold you up."

"See you there," Lincoln agreed with a nod. He was halfway home, with his sack of presents tied behind his saddle, when Wes rode up alongside him.

They didn't speak of serious things—there had been enough of that and it was almost Christmas—except when they reached the barn. Lincoln unsaddled his horse, Wes didn't.

"Are you really going to marry Kate?" Lincoln asked, half-afraid of the answer. She'd be mighty let down if Wes's proposal turned out to be a joke, and by Lincoln's reckoning, Kate had had more than her share of disappointments as it was.

"Didn't I say that I would?"

"You say a lot of things, Wes."

"This time, I mean it."

Lincoln nodded. "I hope so," he replied, and that was the end of the exchange.

Inside the house, Wes was greeted with an armload of Gracie, launching herself from the floor like a stone from a catapult, while the other kids hung back, looking stalwart and shy.

Wes noticed the way Juliana was glowing right away, and cast a sly look in Lincoln's direction before kissing her soundly on the forehead.

After that, the two brothers headed straight for their mother's bedroom and plundered the big mahogany wardrobe for a dress that would suit Kate without too much tucking and pinning. Flummoxed by the choices, they finally consulted Juliana, who chose a dusty-rose velvet day dress with a short jacket, pearl buttons and a nipped-in waist.

"Been a while since Ma could squeeze into *this*," Wes observed, holding the getup against his front as if he meant to try it on himself.

"It will look fine on Kate," Lincoln said drily. "Personally, I think you'd look better in blue."

Juliana took the dress from Wes, carried it to the kitchen and proceeded to fold it neatly and wrap it up in leftover brown paper, tying the parcel closed with thick twine.

Gracie, having worked out that her beloved uncle and Kate were coming out to the ranch to share in tomorrow's celebration, issued an invitation of her very own. "Come *early*," she pleaded, "because Papa probably won't let us see what Saint Nicholas brought until you get here."

Wes laughed, tugged at a lock of her hair. "Just what time is 'early'?" he asked. Of all the people in the world, Gracie was probably the only one he would have rolled out of the hay for. Lincoln had known him to sleep until four o'clock in the afternoon.

Gracie considered. "Six o'clock," she said.

Wes gave a comical groan.

"Uncle Wes," Gracie said firmly, "it's *Christmas*."

"You could come out tonight," Lincoln suggested carefully. "Sleep in your old room."

Behind his grin, Wes went solemn, no doubt remembering how it had been when their father was still alive, and testy as an old bear with ear mites.

"Bed's wide enough for you and Kate," Lincoln added. "Since you and Micah used to share it."

"Maybe," Wes said thoughtfully.

"Say yes," Gracie ordered, hands resting on her hips.

"Maybe," Wes repeated. He glanced sidelong at Lincoln, an unspoken reminder of the warning he'd given out on the range the day before, probably. Gracie definitely *did* have a mind of her own, and as she grew up, she'd be a handful.

Nothing much was said after that. Wes took the gown, wrapped in its brown paper, and left.

Lincoln went to work on the adoption petition he'd been drafting, and Juliana visited the Gainers. The kids, having been given the day off from their lessons because it was Christmas Eve, chased one another all over the front yard until Juliana rounded them up on the way back from the cabin and brewed up another batch of hot cocoa.

For the rest of the day, Lincoln had half his mind on the petition and half on Juliana. The way she moved. The way she hummed under her breath and looked like she was all lit up from the inside.

Mentally, he rehearsed the words he wanted to say. *I love you.*

By sunset, the children were all so excited—except for Joseph, who showed a manful disdain for the proceedings—they could barely sit still to eat supper.

New snow drifted past the windows, and for once, Lincoln didn't dread it.

The dishes were done, the fires were stoked for a cold night.

The kids were all in bed, asleep. Or so they wanted him to believe.

Just as Lincoln was about to extinguish the lanterns and join Juliana in their bed—he'd been looking forward to that all day—he heard a rig roll up outside.

He grinned, put on his coat and hat. There would be a wagon to unhitch, a team to put up in the barn.

Juliana appeared, still wearing her day dress, just as he was opening the door to go outside.

"Wes and Kate are here," he said.

Juliana beamed, as happy at the prospect of company as any country woman would be. "I'll start a pot of coffee."

CHAPTER NINE

CHRISTMAS MORNING WAS joyful chaos, the younger kids tearing into their packages and squealing with delight at the contents. Juliana watched them with a smile, as did Lincoln and Tom, Wes and Kate. Ben and Rose-of-Sharon had joined them for breakfast with the baby, and so had the other ranch hands.

Theresa opened her gifts slowly, while Joseph examined the first one—a set of watercolors Lincoln had given him—leaving the others unwrapped beside him on the floor.

Juliana, quietly happy, paused often to admire the gold wedding band Lincoln had given her late the night before in their bedroom. They'd made love afterward—Lincoln had taken his time pleasuring her, and the wonder of it still reverberated through her, when she let herself remember, like the aftershocks of an earthquake.

There had been no pain, only a little soreness afterward. Juliana had been as voracious as Lincoln, reveling in eager surrender, but that hadn't been the best part, nor had the ring.

When they'd gone to their room, after several hours spent visiting with Wes and his shy but delightful Kate around the kitchen table, Lincoln had sat her down on the edge of the bed, knelt before her and taken her hands into his.

He'd looked directly into her eyes, cleared his throat out of a nervousness she would always remember with tenderness, and said, "Juliana, I love you."

And she'd replied in kind. If she hadn't already loved him, that declaration, and the way he made it, would have sealed the matter for sure.

They were midway through dinner, Tom having roasted the two turkeys to perfection, when the inevitable happened.

A buggy appeared in the side yard beyond the kitchen windows, and Mr. Philbert drew back hard on the reins.

Juliana barely stifled a gasp.

Laughing at a raucous story Wes had just told, no one else had seen or heard the buggy's approach.

Lincoln, catching sight of the look on Juliana's face, turned in his chair and saw the small man alighting, righteous indignation apparent in his every move. "Is that him?" he asked.

Juliana nodded, afraid she'd burst into tears if she spoke.

Mr. Philbert had reached the back step. He pounded on the door, his fist still raised when Lincoln swung it open.

Everyone fell silent, and Daisy and Billy-Moses both rushed to Juliana and scrambled onto her lap, clinging to her.

The Indian agent wore an avidly righteous expression as he stepped past Lincoln, all his attention fastened on Juliana. Triumph sparked in his tiny eyes, behind the smudged lenses of his spectacles; he'd planned to arrive early all along, just as she'd feared, hoping to take her unawares, circumvent any steps she might take to avoid him. She *had* hoped to have Joseph and Theresa safely away from Stillwater Springs before he got there, but that was not to be.

Tom and Wes both slid back their chairs to stand.

Kate, sitting next to Theresa, slipped a protective arm around the girl's shoulders.

Philbert ignored them all, his gaze riveted on Juliana, trying to make her wilt. Jabbing an ink-stained index finger in her direction, he finally spoke. "I have half a mind to charge you with kidnapping!"

"Watch what you say to my wife," Lincoln said evenly.

Wes stepped in, exuding charm and hospitality. "Sit down," he told Mr. Philbert. "Have some of our Christmas dinner."

A silence fell. Clearly, Mr. Philbert had not expected the invitation.

Wes found a clean plate and silverware. Gave up his own chair so the unwanted guest would have a place to sit.

Looking baffled and taking in the spread of food with undisguised hunger, Mr. Philbert sat down.

Lincoln, after exchanging glances with Wes, returned to his own chair. Reached for Juliana's hand and squeezed it reassuringly.

Tom took Mr. Philbert's plate and filled it to overflowing with turkey, mashed potatoes, green beans and rolls still warm from the oven in the cookstove.

Mr. Philbert hesitated, and then, to Juliana's amazement, began to eat.

"My wife and I intend to adopt Daisy and Bill," Lincoln said after a few moments. "I've drawn up the papers, and I'll see that they're filed right after Christmas."

Both Daisy and Billy-Moses looked at Lincoln curiously, not understanding, but probably instinctively hopeful. Both of them adored Lincoln; he had a way of including them in the expansive warmth of his attention and affection without excluding Gracie.

Juliana held the little ones tightly in both arms.

His mouth full of mashed potatoes, Mr. Philbert couldn't answer.

Joseph spoke up. "I'm taking my sister home," he said. "And if you try to stop us, we'll just run off the first chance we get."

Mr. Philbert chewed, swallowed. He was red in the jowls, and his muttonchop whiskers bobbed. He waved a dismissive hand at Joseph. "Good riddance," he said. "I've got all the problems I need as it is."

Juliana's heart rose on a swell of relief, even though his attitude stung. Was that all *any* of the children whose lives and educations he oversaw were to him? Problems? Daisy and Billy-Moses huddled closer, and Gracie came to stand at her side, staring at Mr. Philbert.

"You have a big nose," the child remarked charitably.

"Gracie," Juliana said. "That will be enough."

"Well, he does. And it's purple on the end."

"Gracie," Lincoln admonished.

Gracie subsided, leaning against Juliana now. She hadn't been deliberately rude; there was no meanness in her. She'd merely been making an observation.

Juliana shifted so she could wrap one arm around the little girl without sending Daisy toppling to the floor.

"Children," Mr. Philbert said with a long-suffering sigh. "They are such troublesome little creatures."

Juliana longed to refute that statement—there were a thousand things she wanted to say, but she held her tongue. It would not do to give the man a reason to dis-like her even more than he already did.

"Nevertheless," he went on, taking clear and unflat-tering satisfaction in his power over all of them, "duty is duty. Adoption or none, I intend to take the little ones back to Missoula with me for the interim. I have to ac-count for them, you know."

Tom's face turned hard, and he started to rise.

Wes, standing just behind him and to the side, having given up his chair to Mr. Philbert, laid a warning hand on Tom's shoulder.

"Now, why would you want to go to all the trouble to drag them all the way to Missoula?" Lincoln asked, with a sort of easy bewilderment. "They're fine right here, part of a family."

Mr. Philbert reddened again, stabbed his fork into a slice of turkey. "According to the storekeeper in town, you and Mr. Creed are married now. Is that true, Juli-ana?"

He'd spoken to Mr. Willand, Juliana concluded discon-solately. That was how he'd known about the marriage—the reverend had probably scattered the news far and wide—and where to find her and the children.

"It's true," Juliana said.

"Awfully convenient," Mr. Philbert remarked, with an unpleasant smile. "Wouldn't you agree?"

Gracie took issue. "Don't you talk to my mama in that tone of voice," she warned.

That time, neither Lincoln nor Juliana scolded her.

Mr. Philbert raised his eyebrows, took the time to fork in, chew and swallow more turkey before respond-ing. The law was on his side, as far as Juliana knew. He had the upper hand, and he wasn't going to let anyone forget that.

Daisy, uncomprehending and frightened nonetheless, turned her face into Juliana's bodice and began to cry silently, her small shoulders trembling. Juliana kissed the top of her head, stroked her raven-black hair.

"I don't think I've ever seen an Indian cry before," Mr. Philbert mused, sparing no notice for the child's obvious grief and fear.

Tom started to his feet again; Wes stopped him by putting that same hand to his shoulder and pressing him back down.

"Daisy," Lincoln said to Mr. Philbert, his voice measured, the voice of a lawyer in court, "is a *child*. She's three years old. You're scaring her, and that's something that I won't tolerate for any reason."

"I have legal authority—"

"So do I," Lincoln broke in evenly. "This is my house. This is my ranch. And if you want to take these children anywhere, you're going to need a court order and half the United States Army to help you. *Do* you have a court order, Mr. Philbert?"

Mr. Philbert sputtered a little. "Well, no, but—"

"You'd better get one, then. Before you manage that, I'll have been to Helena to file the petition and Daisy and Bill will be Creeds, as much my children in the eyes of the law as Gracie here."

Mr. Philbert considered that, gulped, then worked up a faltering smile and asked, "I don't suppose there's any pie?"

An hour later, having topped off his meal with two slices of mincemeat pie, the agent handed Juliana a bank draft covering her last month's salary, warned her that if she should ever apply for any teaching position, any-where, she should not give his name as a reference.

And then, blessedly, he was gone.

TAKING NO CHANCES, lest Mr. Philbert had a change of heart, Tom and Lincoln were up even earlier than usual the next morning. They hitched up the team and wagon while Juliana helped Joseph and Theresa pack for their journey. Once the two young people were on board a train east, with Tom to escort them, Lincoln would travel to Helena, stand before a judge and enter the petition to adopt Daisy and Billy-Moses.

Juliana was afraid to hope the Bureau of Indian Affairs would not step in. At the same time, something within her sang a silent, swelling song of jubilation.

Although she tried to keep up a good front, Juliana despaired as she watched Joseph and Theresa buttoning up the new coats Lincoln had given them for Christmas. They would miss her and the other children, she knew, but the joy of going home, of truly belonging somewhere, shone in their faces.

Juliana hugged both of them, one and then the other, but avoided looking through the window after they'd gone out, unable to watch as they got into the wagon. There would be letters, at least from Theresa, but considering the distance, it was unlikely that she would ever see them again. Eventually, their correspondence would slow, however good everyone's intentions were, and finally stop.

Gracie, standing at Juliana's side, took her hand. "Don't be sad, Mama," she said. "Please, don't be sad."

But Juliana couldn't help crying as she took Gracie into her arms.

Lincoln returned to the house to say goodbye. "I'll be back in a few days," he said. "Ben and the others will look after the cattle and the chores. If Philbert comes back here, send somebody to town to fetch Wes."

Juliana nodded, barely able to absorb any of it. The parting from Lincoln was, in some ways, the hardest thing of all.

He gave her a lingering kiss.

Then he, too, was gone.

Billy-Moses, who had sat quietly near the stove during all the farewells, stacking blocks, knocking them down and then stacking them again, suddenly hurtled toward the door, flinging himself at it, struggling with the latch and uttering long cries of angry sorrow. Juliana hurried to the child, knelt beside him, pulling him into her arms, stroking his hair, murmuring to him.

He wailed for Theresa, for Joseph, for Lincoln, sobbing out each name in turn, between shrieks of despair. Weeping herself, while Gracie and Daisy looked on with forlorn expressions, each clasping the other's hand, Juliana lifted Billy-Moses up and carried him to the rocking chair.

He was a long time quieting down, but Juliana rocked him, holding him tightly long after he'd stopped struggling. Eventually, he fell into a fitful sleep.

Gracie came to lean against the arm of the chair, her face earnest. "Doesn't Billy want to be my brother? Doesn't he want to be a Creed?"

Juliana, more composed by then, smiled and tilted her head so it rested against Gracie's. "Of course he does, sweetheart," she said very quietly. "He misses Joseph and Theresa, that's all. And your papa and Tom, too."

Gracie nodded solemnly, but quickly braced up. "Papa

said he'd come back, and Papa always does what he says he's going to do."

"Yes," Juliana agreed, heartened. "He does."

The next day, Wes returned to the ranch, bringing a telegram from Lincoln, sent that morning from Missoula. Tom, Theresa and Joseph had boarded the train; they would be in North Dakota within the week.

To keep busy, Juliana divided her time between giving Gracie reading, spelling and arithmetic lessons at the kitchen table, visiting Rose-of-Sharon and the baby, and poring over a collection of old cookery books she'd found in a pantry cabinet.

Lincoln sent another telegram the following day when he reached Helena, promising that he'd be home soon.

Determined to use the waiting time constructively, Juliana bravely assembled the ingredients to bake a batch of corn bread, followed the directions to the letter, and almost set the kitchen on fire by putting too much wood in the stove.

On the third day, the previously mild weather turned nasty. Snow flew with such ferocity that, often, Juliana couldn't see the barn from the kitchen window, even in broad daylight. She knew that Lincoln planned to return to Missoula from Helena by rail, once he'd completed his business in the state capital, reclaim his wagon and team from a local livery stable and drive back to the ranch. With what appeared to be a blizzard brewing, Juliana was worried.

He could get lost in the storm, even freeze to death somewhere along the way.

In an effort to distract herself from this worry, Juliana carefully removed all the decorations from the Christmas tree, packing them away in their boxes. When Ben

Gainer brought a bucket of milk to the back door that evening, shivering with cold even in his warm coat, Juliana made him come inside and drink hot coffee.

Somewhat restored after that, Ben dragged the big tree across the floor and out the front door. Later, it would be chopped up and burned.

The storm continued through the night, and snow was still coming down at a furious rate in the morning, drifting up against the sides of the house, high enough that if she'd been able to open a window, Juliana could have scooped the stuff up in her hands.

Ben brought more milk, and told Juliana he hoped the snow would let up soon, because he and the other two ranch hands were having a hard time getting the hay sled out to the range cattle, even with the big draft horses to pull it.

One question thudded in the back of Juliana's mind day and night like a drumbeat that never went silent.

Where was Lincoln?

She tried to be sensible. He'd probably had to stay in Missoula to wait out the storm, and sent another telegram informing her of that. Since the road between Stillwater Springs and the ranch was under at least three feet of snow, Wes wouldn't be able to bring her the message, like he had the others.

There was nothing to do but wait.

Juliana tried the corn bread recipe again, and even though it came out hard as a horseshoe, at least this time smoke didn't pour out of the oven. Soaked in warm milk, the stuff was actually edible.

The next day, Ben strung ropes from the house to the cabin and the cabin to the barn; it was the only way he could get from one place to the other without being lost in the blizzard. The draft horses knew the way to and from the cluster of trees where the herd had taken shelter; otherwise, the cattle would have gone hungry.

On the fifth night, Juliana lingered in the kitchen, long after the children had gone to sleep, watching the clock and waiting.

At first, she thought she'd imagined the sound at the back door, but then the latch jiggled. She fairly leaped out of her chair, hurried across the room and hauled open the door.

The icy wind was so strong that it made her bones ache, but she didn't care. Lincoln was standing on the back step, coated in ice and snow, seemingly unable to move.

Juliana cried out, used all her strength to pull him inside and managed to shut the door against the wind by leaning on it with the full weight of her body.

"Lincoln?"

He didn't speak, didn't move. How had he gotten home with the roads the way they were? Surely the team and wagon couldn't have passed through snow that deep—it would have reached to the tops of the wheels.

She had to pry his hat free of his head—it had frozen to his hair. Next, she peeled off the coat, tossed it aside.

She thought of tugging him nearer the stove, but she recalled reading about frostbite somewhere; it was important that he warm up slowly.

His clothes were stiff as laundry left to freeze on a clothesline. She ran for the bedrooms, snatching up all the blankets she could find that weren't already in use and hurried back to the kitchen.

Lincoln was still standing where she'd left him; his lips were blue, and his teeth had begun to chatter.

"Whiskey," he said in a raw whisper.

Juliana rushed into the pantry, found the bottle he kept on a high shelf. Pouring some into a cup, she raised it to his mouth, holding it patiently while he sipped.

A great shudder went through him, but he wasn't so stiff now, and some of the color returned to his face.

"Help me out of these clothes," he ground out. "My fingers aren't working."

She pulled off his gloves first, and was relieved to see no sign of frostbite. His toes could be affected, though, and even if they weren't, the specter of pneumonia loomed in that kitchen like a third presence.

She unbuttoned his shirt, helped him out of it, then pulled his woolen undershirt off over his head, too. She immediately wrapped him in one of the blankets. He managed to sit down in the chair she brought from the table, and she crouched to pull off his boots, strip away his socks.

His toes, like his fingers, were still intact, though he admitted he couldn't feel them.

He seemed so exhausted just from what they'd done so far that Juliana gave him another dose of whiskey before removing his trousers and tucking more blankets in around him.

"How did you get here?" she asked as he sat there shivering, a good distance from the stove. "My Lord, Lincoln, you must have been out in the weather for hours."

Remarkably, a grin tilted up one corner of his mouth. "I rode Wes's mule out from town," he answered slowly, groping for each word. "Good thing that critter can smell hay and a warm stall from a mile off."

"You rode Wes's mule?" If Juliana hadn't been so

glad he was home, she would have been furious. "Lincoln Creed, are you insane? If you got as far as Stillwater Springs—and God knows how you managed that—you should have stayed there!"

"You're here," he said. "Gracie and Bill and Daisy are here. This is where I belong."

"You could have frozen to death! What good would that have done us?"

He didn't respond to that question. Instead, he said, "You'd better get some snow to pack around my feet and hands, or else I might lose a few fingers and toes."

The action was contrary to every instinct Juliana possessed, but she knew he was right. After bundling up, she took the milk bucket outside and filled it with snow.

Returning to the kitchen, she marveled that Lincoln had been able to travel in that weather, probably for hours, when she'd been chilled to her marrow by a few moments in the backyard.

The process of tending to Lincoln was slow and, for him, painful. It was after two in the morning when he told her there had been enough of the snow packs. She led him to their room, put him to bed like a child, piling blanket after blanket on top of him.

Still he shivered.

She built the hearth fire up until it roared.

Lying in the darkness, under all those blankets, he chuckled. "Juliana, no more wood," he said. "You'll set the house on fire."

There was nothing more she could do except put on her nightgown and join him. He trembled so hard that the whole bed frame shook, and his skin felt as cold as stone.

She huddled close to him, sharing the warmth of her own body, enduring the chill of his. When he finally slept, she could not, exhausted as she was, because she was so afraid of waking up to find him dead.

For most of the night, she kept her vigil. Then, too tired to keep her eyes open for another moment, she drifted off.

When she woke up, his hand was underneath her nightgown.

"There's one way you could warm me up," he said wickedly.

He was safe.

He was warm again, and well.

And Juliana gladly gave herself up to him.

EPILOGUE

June 1911

JULIANA CREED STOOD in Willand's Mercantile, visibly pregnant and beaming as she read Theresa's most recent letter through for the second time before folding it carefully and tucking it into her handbag. She and Joseph had attended a small school on the reservation since their return to North Dakota, but now they would have the whole summer off. Joseph had a temporary job milking cows on a nearby farm, while Theresa would be helping her grandmother tend the garden.

Juliana looked around the store for her children.

Billy-Moses—now called just Bill or Billy most of the time, a precedent Lincoln had set—was examining a toy train carved out of wood, while Daisy and Gracie browsed through hair ribbons, ready-made dresses with ruffles, and storybooks.

With all of them accounted for, her mind turned to the men. Tom was at the blacksmith's, having a horse shod, and Lincoln had gone to the *Courier,* looking for Wes.

Marriage had changed Weston Creed. He was, as Lincoln put it, "damn near to becoming a respectable citizen." Remarkably, given the long estrangement between her and Wes, the elder Mrs. Creed had returned to Stillwater Springs for the wedding back in April. While she hadn't been happy about having a saloonkeeper for a daughter-in-law, she'd behaved with remarkable civility.

Cora had stayed long enough to size Juliana up, decided she'd do as a wife for Lincoln and a stepmother for Gracie, and then she'd announced that she was taking up permanent residence with her cousins in Phoenix. She was too old, she maintained, to keep going back and forth.

Although they'd been a little stiff with each other at first, Juliana had soon come to like her mother-in-law. While Cora had been cool to Kate, she *had* made the long journey home to attend the wedding. During her stay at the ranch, she'd treated Daisy and Billy as well as she had Gracie.

Before her departure, though, Cora and Juliana had agreed, in a spirit of goodwill, that one Creed woman per household was plenty.

When the little bell over the mercantile chimed, Juliana turned in the direction of the door, expecting to see Lincoln, or perhaps Tom.

Her heart missed a beat when she recognized Clay.

Their eyes met, but neither of them spoke.

Clay stood just over the threshold, handsome in his well-tailored suit. His hair was darker than Juliana's, more chestnut than red, but his eyes were the same shade of blue.

Watching her, he removed his very fashionable hat. "Juliana," he said gravely, with a slight nod.

"Clay," Juliana whispered. And then she ran to him, threw her arms around him.

Tentatively, he put his arms around her, too. After a stiff moment, he hugged her back. "You're looking well," he said, his voice gruff with emotion.

Juliana blushed, confounded by joy, pushing back far enough to look up into her brother's face. "When you didn't answer my letter, I thought—"

He smiled, glancing down at her protruding middle. "You did say you were married?" he teased.

She showed him her wedding ring. "How long have you been in town? The train came through three days ago."

"I've been staying at the Comstock Hotel, trying to work up the courage to hire a buggy over at the livery stable and drive out to the ranch to see you."

"Oh, Clay—surely you knew you'd be welcome."

"I *didn't* know," he replied. "According to my wife, I've been behaving like an ogre ever since you refused to marry John Holden, and I'm afraid Nora's right about that."

Juliana's eyes misted over. "I've missed you," she said.

He kissed her forehead. "I'd like to meet this husband of yours," he told her. "Your letter made him sound like a paragon."

The door opened again, and Lincoln was there.

Still tearful—tears came more easily with her pregnancy—Juliana moved to Lincoln's side. He put an arm around her, regarding Clay curiously and then with a grin of recognition.

"You must be Clay Mitchell," he said. "With eyes that color, you have to be related to Juliana."

Clay nodded in acknowledgment. "And you're Lincoln Creed," he replied.

"Papa!" Billy yelled, racing across the store to be hoisted into Lincoln's arms. Lincoln ruffled the boy's hair and laughed.

Clay's eyes widened momentarily, but then he smiled again.

"Daisy," Juliana called, "Gracie—come and meet your uncle Clay."

He charmed those two little girls by executing a gentlemanly bow. "Ladies," he said solemnly, making them giggle.

Still carrying Billy, Lincoln excused himself and went to the counter to speak to Fred Willand about their grocery order.

"You will come out to the ranch and stay with us for a few days, won't you, Clay?" Juliana asked quietly.

"I'd be glad to," Clay assured her.

On the way home, having collected his bag from the hotel, Clay rode on the wagon seat next to Juliana with Lincoln at the reins, while Gracie, Billy and Daisy bounced along in back like always, seated among crates of groceries.

"He doesn't seem so bad to me," Lincoln said much later, when he and Juliana had retired to their room for the night. They'd talked right through supper, the three of them, and for a couple of hours afterward.

"This is the Clay I knew before," Juliana said, choking up a little. The change in her brother seemed miraculous.

Sitting on the edge of the bed, Lincoln pulled off one boot and then the other. Juliana remembered the night he'd ridden a mule through three feet of snow, nearly losing his fingers and toes, if not his life.

"I've never had a sister," Lincoln said, "but I can imagine that if I did, I might have some pretty hardheaded opinions about what she should and shouldn't do."

Juliana stood in front of the mirror, brushing her hair. "We were so young when our mother died," she mused.

She'd long since told Lincoln all about her family history, John Holden and his daughters, secretly studying to be a teacher when her grandmother believed she was in finishing school. "Clay's a little older, and I guess I expected him to be strong, maybe our grandmother did, too. But he was really a child, as scared and lost and hurt as I was. I hate to think what must have gone through his mind when our father left us at Grandmama's that day. Clay knew, even if I didn't, that Father wasn't coming back—and that meant he had to be a man from then on."

Lincoln came to stand behind her, bent his head to kiss her right ear. His hands caressed her round belly. "That corn bread you served at supper tonight was pretty good," he said.

She laughed. "It should have been," she replied. "I've been practicing for six months."

He took the brush from her hand, set it aside on the bureau, turned her around to face him. "Tom says you'll make a fine cook one of these days."

Juliana smiled. Tom had been giving her cookery lessons, and she was making progress. "He also says I try too hard." She slipped her arms around his middle and leaned against him. "What else can I do? I want to keep my husband happy."

Lincoln tasted her mouth, once, twice, a third time. "Your husband," he said, "is *very* happy."

She looked up at him. "I love you, Lincoln Creed. Just when I think I couldn't possibly love you more than I already do, something happens to prove me wrong."

"I love you, too," he replied, tracing the length of her cheek, and then her neck, with the lightest pass of his lips. He eased her toward the bed, still nibbling at her.

He put out the lamp.

"Lincoln, you're not listening to me," Juliana said, laughing a little, as delightfully nervous, in some ways, as she'd been on their wedding night.

He lowered her to the bed. "You're right," he said, kissing her again. "I'm not."

Already cherishing their unborn child, Lincoln was unspeakably tender as he caressed her belly and then slowly raised her nightgown, first to her knees, then her thighs, then her shoulders. With a groan of welcome, she raised her arms so he could slip the garment off over her head.

He kissed her distended stomach, his lips warm and faintly moist.

Juliana groaned again, rolled her eyes back in contentment and closed them, giving herself up to Lincoln, body, mind and spirit.

He loved the fullness of her breasts, kissed and nibbled at her taut nipples until she said his name in a ragged whisper.

Then he moved down along her breastbone, over her middle, pausing at her abdomen before using his fingers to part the nest of curls at the juncture of her thighs. She whimpered as he stroked her with a slow, gentle motion of his hand, and although her eyes remained shut, she felt the dark burn of his gaze on her face. She knew he was silently asking her permission, and she nodded.

He made a sound that was wholly male, low in his throat.

In Lincoln's arms, Juliana had learned a sort of pleasure that she'd never imagined, and that night was no exception. Even before they'd conceived this child they both wanted so much, he'd always been careful, raising her to an explosive ecstasy and at the same time making her feel utterly safe.

For a time, he simply made slow circles with his fingers, and Juliana began to writhe in need and surrender, in triumph and exultation.

Her breath became shallow and rapid as he teased her. Then the first release came, shattering and sweet, leaving her shuddering. Knowing there would be more—much more—before the night was over, only increased her wanting.

Lincoln used his mouth on her next, and though it was scandalous, Juliana gloried in the intimacy of it, in the helplessness and the sheer power of the sensations he wrought in her, with every nibble, every flick of his tongue.

Again, she broke apart in a million fiery pieces, a primitive cry of satisfaction escaping her throat, but going no further than the thick log walls of their bedroom.

Only when Lincoln was certain he'd untied every knot in Juliana's still-quivering body did he mount her, and ease into her depths with that heartrending tenderness she'd come to expect of him.

They rocked together, and she reached yet another pinnacle, softer and yet more intense than the others that had gone before. When Lincoln finally let himself go, Juliana finally opened her eyes, stroking his strong shoulders, his chest, his sides, her hands moving in ways that both soothed and inflamed.

Then he tensed upon her, and she felt life itself spill within her, the life that had brought their child into being, and Gracie, as well.

"I love you," Juliana whispered.

He sighed, kissed her cheek, her neck. Fell beside her. "And I love *you*, Juliana Creed."

IF JULIANA HAD YET to master cooking and housekeeping, she *had* learned to drive a buggy. On the morning of Clay's departure for Denver, she was the one who drove him to the depot in town.

"I've got eyes," Clay said, grinning, as they pulled up to await the train, "but I still need to hear you say it. Are you happy, Juliana?"

She kissed his cheek. "Ecstatic," she said, meaning it.

He reached into the inside pocket of his coat—his fine clothes made him stand out like the proverbial sore thumb in rustic Stillwater Springs—and brought out a thick envelope. Offered it to her.

In the distance, the train whistle shrilled.

Puzzled, Juliana looked at the envelope, then at Clay's face. "What…?"

"Your inheritance," Clay said. "These documents transfer full control to you. You're a rich woman, Juliana. Now that I've taken Lincoln Creed's measure, I know you'll be all right."

Stunned—it had been a long time since she'd given a thought to money—she accepted the papers. Then she beamed. "Now we can build a hay barn right on the range," she chimed in happy realization. "And the cattle will have somewhere to take shelter when the snows come."

Clay laughed. "Some women would want diamonds, or fine dresses."

The train chugged into view, and Juliana saddened a little at the sight, not willing to be parted from this brother she had loved for so long. "You'll come back when you can, won't you? And bring Nora and the children?"

He touched her cheek. "We'll be here," he said. "And you're welcome at our place anytime, Juliana. You and Lincoln and this brood of yours."

With that, he climbed down from the buggy, took his traveling case from under the seat. He looked up at her, winked, and then turned away, walking purposefully toward the depot.

Juliana waited until the train had pulled out before heading for home.

Lincoln was there, having minded the children while she was gone, and Ben and Rose-of-Sharon sat at the table, baby Joshua in his mother's arms. For all the difficulties of his birth, the infant was thriving.

Once the Gainers had left, Juliana took the envelope from her handbag and laid it on the table.

"What's this?" Lincoln asked.

"Open it," Juliana said lightly, "and read for yourself."

Lincoln hesitated, then did as he was told. His eyes widened as he read. "That's one hell of a lot of money," he said finally. "You are a wealthy woman, Juliana."

"*We* are wealthy," she clarified.

He grinned, and only then did she realize how tensely he'd held his shoulders while he read. Had he thought, for the briefest moment, that she'd leave him now that she was a woman of independent means?

She went to him, slipped her arms around his lean, hard waist. "I told Clay we'd be building a big hay barn out on the range, first thing."

Lincoln chuckled. "Speaking of the range, I'd better get out there. We've still got a few calves taking their time to get born."

Juliana began rolling up her sleeves. "I'll have supper ready when you get back," she said.

He gave a comical wince, and she slapped at him playfully.

Once he'd gone, Juliana took a deep breath. It was time to make another attempt at corn bread.

From the *Stillwater Springs Courier*:

September 18, 1911
This editor is proud to announce the
birth of a nephew,
Michael Thomas Creed.
Welcome.

* * * * *

Books by Patricia Davids

HQN Books

The Amish of Cedar Grove
The Wish

Love Inspired

North Country Amish

An Amish Wife for Christmas
Shelter from the Storm

The Amish Bachelors

An Amish Harvest
An Amish Noel
His Amish Teacher
Their Pretend Amish Courtship
Amish Christmas Twins
An Unexpected Amish Romance
His New Amish Family

Don't miss *The Hope,*
the next book in the Amish of Cedar Grove series
from HQN Books.

Visit the Author Profile page
at Harlequin.com for more titles.

THE DOCTOR'S BLESSING

Patricia Davids

To Terrah in Kansas City
and to Rachel in Poland, Ohio.
Bless you both for all your help.
This book is dedicated to nurse-midwives
everywhere. Women helping women
bring healthy babies into loving families.

My little children, let us not love in word,
neither in tongue; but in deed and in truth.
—*1 John* 3:18

CHAPTER ONE

"AMBER, YOU WON'T believe who's here!"

The agitated whisper stopped Amber Bradley in her tracks halfway through the front door of the Hope Springs Medical Clinic. She glanced around the small waiting room. The only occupant was her wide-eyed receptionist standing at her desk with one finger pressed to her lips.

Amber whispered back, "I give up, Wilma. Who's here?"

The tiny, sixtysomething woman glanced toward the hallway leading to the offices and exam rooms, then hurried around the corner of her desk wringing her hands. "Dr. Phillip White."

Oh, no. Amber closed the door with deliberate slowness. So the ax was going to fall on their small-town clinic in spite of everyone's prayers. What would they do now? What would happen to their patients? Her heart sank at the prospect.

Please, dear Lord, don't let this happen.

Composing herself, she turned to face Wilma. "What did he say? Is Harold worse?"

"He said Harold is the reason he needs to meet with us, but he wanted to wait until you were here before going into details."

Dr. Harold White was the only doctor in the predominantly Amish community of Hope Springs, Ohio. Four weeks earlier, he'd taken his first vacation in more than twenty years to visit his grandson, Phillip, in Honolulu. While there, a serious accident landed the seventy-five-year-old man in intensive care.

Wilma leaned close. "What do you think he's doing here?"

"I have no idea."

"You think he's here to close the office, don't you?"

Amber couldn't come up with another reason that made more sense. Harold's only relative had come to close the clinic and inform them that Harold wouldn't be returning.

At least he was kind enough to come in person instead of delivering the news over the phone.

Amber had been expecting something like this since she'd learned the extent of Harold's injuries. Chances were slim a man his age could make a full recovery after suffering a broken leg, a fractured skull and surgery to remove a blood clot on his brain. Still, Harold hadn't given up hope that he'd be back, so neither would she.

Summoning a smile for her coworker, Amber laid a hand on Wilma's shoulder. "When I spoke to Harold last night, he assured me the clinic would stay open."

"For now." The deep male voice came from behind them.

Wilma squeaked as she spun around. Amber had a better grip on her emotions. Wilma hurried away to the safety of her oak desk in the corner, leaving Amber to face the newcomer alone. She surveyed Harold's grandson with interest.

Dr. Phillip White was more imposing than she had expected. He stood six foot at least, if not a shade taller.

His light brown hair, streaked with sun-bleached highlights, curled slightly where it touched the collar of his blue, button-down shirt. His bronze tan emphasized his bone structure and the startling blue of his eyes.

He was movie-star gorgeous. The thought popped into Amber's brain and stuck. She licked her suddenly dry lips. When had she met a man who triggered such intense awareness at first glance? Okay, never.

Rejecting her left-field thoughts as totally irrelevant, Amber tried for a professional smile. Moving forward, she held out her hand. "Welcome to Hope Springs, Dr. White."

His grip, firm and oddly stirring, made her pulse spike and her breathing quicken. He held her hand a fraction longer than necessary. When he let go, she shoved her hands in the front pockets of her white lab coat, curling her fingers into tight balls.

Striving to appear unruffled, she said, "Your grandfather speaks of you frequently. I never saw him so excited as the day he learned of your existence."

His expression remained carefully blank. "I'm sure my happiness was equal to his."

Little warning bells started going off in Amber's brain. He wasn't here to make friends. Her smile grew stiff. "Of course, it can't be every day a grown man discovers he has a grandfather he never knew about."

Up close, Phillip's resemblance to Harold was undeniable. They shared the same intense blue eyes, strong chin and full lips. But not, it seemed, Harold's friendly demeanor. Still, she cast aside any lingering doubts that the whole thing was a hoax. They were obviously related.

She said, "Isn't it strange that both of you became family practice doctors. It must be in the genes. I'd love to hear the whole story. Harold was vague about the details."

A cooler expression entered Phillip's eyes. "It's a personal matter that I'm not comfortable discussing."

Oops! It seemed she'd stumbled on a touchy subject. "I'm sorry Harold's holiday with you ended so badly."

"As am I." His lips pressed into a tighter line.

Amber indicated their receptionist. "I take it you've met Mrs. Nolan? Wilma has worked for your grandfather since he came to Hope Springs over thirty years ago."

He nodded in Wilma's direction. "Yes, we've met."

"And I'm Amber Bradley." She waited with bated breath for his reaction. She knew Harold had told his grandson about their collaborative practice.

Phillip's expression didn't change. "Ah, the midwife."

There it was, that touch of disdain in his voice that belittled her profession, dismissed her education and years of training as if they were nothing. She'd heard it before from physicians and even nurses. It seemed young Dr. White didn't value her occupation the way his grandfather did.

She stood as tall as her five-foot-three frame allowed. "Yes, I'm a certified nurse-midwife. It's my vocation as well as my job."

"Vocation? That's a strong word."

"It is what it is."

Was that a flicker of respect in his eyes? Maybe she had jumped the gun in thinking he disapproved.

Bracing herself, she asked the unspoken question that hovered in the air. "What brings you to Hope Springs, Dr. White?"

He glanced around the small office. "Harold is fretting himself sick over this place."

Amber tried to see the clinic through Phillip's eyes. The one-story brick building was devoid of frills. The walls were painted pale blue. The chairs grouped around the small waiting room had worn upholstery. Wilma's desk, small and crowded by the ancient tan filing cabinets lined up behind it, didn't make much of a statement.

Their clinic might not look like much, but it was essential to the well-being of their friends and neighbors. Amber wouldn't let it close without a fight.

"Harold shouldn't worry," she said. "We're managing."

"Grandfather's doctors can't keep his blood pressure under control. He's not eating. He's not sleeping well. He needs to concentrate on his recovery and he's not doing that." Deep concern vibrated through Phillip's voice.

A pang stabbed Amber's heart. "I know Harold's concerned about us, but I didn't realize it was affecting his health."

"Unfortunately, it is. The only way to relieve his anxiety was to find someone to cover his practice. In spite of my best efforts to hire temporary help, I've had no success. Clearly, working in a remote Amish community is not an assignment most physicians are eager to take on. In the end, I had to obtain a temporary license to practice in the state of Ohio. I'm here until the tenth of September or until a more permanent solution can be found."

"You're taking over the practice?" Amber blinked hard. While she was delighted they were going to have a physician again, for the life of her she couldn't understand why Harold hadn't mentioned this tidbit of information. It ranked above bad hospital food and clueless medical students, the subjects of their conversation last night.

Her shock must have shown on her face. Phillip's eyes narrowed. "Harold did tell you I was coming, didn't he?"

Amber glanced at Wilma, hoping she'd taken the message. Wilma shook her head. Amber looked back at Phillip. "Ah, no."

"I shouldn't be surprised. His mind wanders at times. This is additional proof that he is incapable of returning to work."

Amber wasn't sure what to think. Harold sounded perfectly rational each time she'd spoken to him on the phone. Could he fool her that easily?

Compelled to defend the man who was her mentor and friend, she said, "Perhaps his pain medication muddled his thinking and he forgot to mention it. He will bounce back. He loves this place and the people here. He says working is what keeps him sane."

Phillip didn't look convinced. "We'll see how it goes. For now, I'm in charge of this practice."

He jerked his head toward the parking lot visible through the front Plateglass window. A gray horse hitched to a black buggy stood patiently waiting beside the split-rail fence that ringed the property. "Do we put out hay for the horses or do their owners bring their own?"

His satire-laden comment raised Amber's hackles. The Amish community was tight-knit and wary of outsiders. Harold had earned their trust over thirty years of practicing medicine by respecting their ways, not by poking fun at them.

She crossed her arms over her chest. "I thought you

were joining some big practice in Honolulu. I'm sure Harold told me that before he left."

"Under the circumstances my partners have agreed to let me take a two-month leave of absence."

Wilma finally found the courage to pipe up. "But what if Dr. Harold isn't back in two months?"

"Then I imagine he won't be back at all. In that case, the clinic will be closed until another physician can be found. I'm aware there is a real shortage of rural doctors in this state, so you ladies may want to think about job hunting."

Wilma gasped. Amber wasn't ready to accept Phillip's prediction. The community needed this clinic. She needed Harold's support for her nurse-midwife practice. The people of Hope Springs needed them both.

She chose to remain calm. There was no use getting in a panic. She would put her faith in the Lord and pray harder than ever for Harold's recovery.

Phillip didn't seem to notice the turmoil his words caused. He said, "I found the coffeepot but I can't find any coffee."

His abrupt change of subject threw her for a second. Recovering, she reached in her bag and withdrew a package of Colombian blend. "We were out. I stopped at the store on my way here."

"Good. I take mine black. Just bring it to my office."

Was he trying to annoy her? Everyone was equal in this office. That was Harold's rule. The person who wanted coffee made it and then offered it to the others. He never expected anyone to wait on him. And it wasn't Phillip's office anyway. It still belonged to Harold.

"When can we begin seeing patients?" The object of her ire glanced at his watch.

Wilma advanced around the corner of her desk with a chart in hand. "There is a patient here to see Amber now."

His frown deepened to a fierce scowl. He pinned Amber with his gaze. "You're seeing patients?"

Amber knew the legal limits of her profession. She didn't care for his tone.

Her chin came up. "I *am* a primary care provider. I do see patients. If you mean am I seeing obstetrical patients, the answer is no. I haven't been since Harold left. Edna Nissley is sixty-nine. She's here for a blood pressure check and to have lab work drawn."

"I see." His glower lightened.

"People knew Harold was going to be gone, so our schedule has been light. Those patients outside my scope of practice have been sent to a physician in a neighboring town."

"Plus, we painted all the rooms except Harold's office and had the carpets cleaned," Wilma added brightly.

Amber continued to study Phillip. He was a hard man to read. "Someone had to be here to refer patients and fax charts to other doctors. We haven't exactly been on vacation. We've both traveled a lot of miles letting people know what has happened."

He raised one eyebrow. "Wouldn't a few phone calls have been easier?"

Smiling with artificial sweetness, Amber said, "It would if our patients had phones. The majority of our clients are Amish, remember?"

"Edna is waiting in room one," Wilma interjected.

Amber started to walk past Phillip but stopped. She pressed the bag of coffee into his midsection. "I take cream and one sugar. Just leave it on my desk."

Phillip took the bag. "I'll let you get to work, Miss

Bradley, but there will be changes around here that you and I need to discuss. Come to my office when you're done."

Amber didn't like the sound of that. Not one bit.

CHAPTER TWO

PHILLIP WATCHED AMBER'S stunning blue-green eyes narrow. She was right to worry. He wasn't looking forward to the coming conversation. He'd rather see the charming smile she'd greeted him with earlier than the wary expression on her face at the moment.

She was pretty in a small-town-girl kind of way. Her pink cheeks and slightly sunburned nose gave her a wholesome look. She wasn't tall, but she had a shapely figure he admired. He knew from his grandfather that she wasn't married. Seeing her, he had to wonder why.

Phillip had listened to his grandfather singing the praises of Nurse-Midwife Bradley for the past year but this woman was nothing like he'd imagined. He had pictured a plump, gray-haired matron, not a pretty, petite woman who didn't look a day over twenty-five.

Her honey-blond hair was wound into a thick bun at the nape of her neck. How long was it? What would it look like when she wore it down?

Intrigued as he was by the thought, it was her blue-green eyes that drew and held his attention. They were the color of the sea he loved. A calm sea, the kind that made a man want to spend a lifetime gazing over it and soaking in the beauty.

Such romantic musings had to be a by-product of his jet lag. He forced his attention back to the matter at hand.

He was going to be working with Miss Bradley. He had no intention of setting up a workplace flirtation. Besides, he'd be lucky if she was still speaking to him by the end of the day.

He didn't believe in home deliveries. In his opinion, they were too risky. She wasn't going to be happy when she learned his stance on the subject.

He hefted the coffee bag. Perhaps it was best to give her this small victory before the confrontation. "Cream with one sugar. Got it."

He left her to see her patient and retreated to the small refreshment room beside his grandfather's office. Making coffee took only a few minutes. As he waited for the pot to fill, he studied the array of mugs hanging from hooks beneath the cabinet. Which one belonged to Amber?

He ruled out the white one that said World's Greatest Grandma in neon pink letters. Beside it hung two plain black mugs, one with a chipped lip. Somehow he knew those belonged to his grandfather. That left either the white cup with yellow daises around the rim or the sky blue mug with *1 John* 3:18 printed in dark blue letters.

1 John 3:18. He pulled down the mug. He didn't know his Bible well enough to hazard a guess at the meaning of the passage, but he filed it away to look up later.

Studying medicine, working as a resident and then setting up a practice had consumed his life. All of which left him time to eat or maybe sleep, but rarely both. Even his surfing time had dropped to almost nothing. Bible study had fallen by the wayside, but it looked as if he'd have some free time now. How busy could he be in a small town like this? The next two months stretched before him like an eternity.

He'd do his best while he was here. He knew how much this place meant to his grandfather. Taking over until things were settled was the least he could do. After all, it was his fault Harold wasn't here.

Putting aside that painful memory, Phillip carried the blue mug to the coffee dispenser. If this wasn't Amber's cup, at least it was clean. He filled it, then added the creamer and sugar. Taking down the grandmother mug, he filled it, too. After stuffing a couple of sugar and creamer packages in his pocket, he carried the cups to the front desk.

Wilma was on the phone, so he set her cup on the corner and held up the condiments in a silent query. She shook her head and mouthed the words, "Just black." She reached for the mug, took a quick sip, then continued her conversation. That left him with Amber's cup in hand.

He'd already discovered the clinic layout when he'd arrived early that morning. He knew Amber's office was the one beside his grandfather's, while two exam rooms occupied the opposite side of the short hallway.

Entering her office, he took note of the plain white walls devoid of pictures or mementos. The starkness didn't seem to fit her vibrant personality. Her furniture was another story.

Her desk was a simple-yet-graceful cherrywood piece with curved legs and a delicately carved matching chair. Her computer sat on a small stand beside the desk, as if she couldn't bear to put something so modern on such a classic piece. Everything about the room was neat and tidy. He liked that.

After setting her cup on a coaster at the edge of her desk, he returned to his grandfather's office. Nothing in it remotely hinted at neat or tidy.

Stacks of medical journals, books and file folders sat on every flat surface. Some had meandered to the floor around his grandfather's chair. The tall bookcases on the back wall were crammed full of textbooks. A number of them had pieces of paper sticking out the tops as if to mark important places.

Harold's computer sat squarely in the middle of his large oak desk. On either side of the monitor were two pictures. Phillip reached past the photo of himself standing by his surfboard to pick up a framed portrait of a young man in a marine dress uniform.

He'd seen this picture before. One like it hung in his grandfather's house where he'd spent the night last night. A third copy sat in a box at the back of his mother's closet. The young marine was the father he never knew.

Phillip searched the face that looked so much like his own. All his life he'd aspired to be a person his father would have been proud of. He got good grades, played baseball, learned to surf, things his mother told him his father had done or wanted to do. His dad was even the reason he'd become a physician.

As a child he'd hungered for any crumb of information his mother would share about his dad. Those crumbs were all too rare. Whenever he would ask questions about his father, her reply was always the same: it was too painful to talk about that time of her life.

He could understand that. Much of his early life was painful to talk about, too.

Engrossed in the past, he didn't hear the door open. He thought he was alone until Amber spoke. "You look like him."

He set the picture back in its place. "So I've been told."

Amber moved to stand at his side. "I can see it in the

arch of your brow and your square chin, but especially your eyes."

"Did you know he was killed in action?"

"I asked Harold once what happened to his son. He said he didn't want to talk about it. I never asked again."

"My father was killed in some third world country trying to rescue American citizens who'd been kidnapped."

"You must be very proud of him."

It was hard to be proud of an image on paper. Yet it had been the picture that led Phillip to his grandfather. Finding Harold had been like a gift from God.

What Phillip still didn't understand was why his mother had kept his grandfather's existence a secret for more than thirty years. She'd been furious when he announced he had contacted Harold. She wouldn't say why.

Many of his questions about his father had been answered in the long phone conversations he and Harold had shared, but like his mother, Harold refused to talk about his relationship with his daughter-in-law. It seemed the reason for the family breakup might never come to light.

Amber cleared her throat. "You wanted to talk to me?"

Her voice broke his connection with the past and catapulted him into the present. Face-to-face with a task he knew would be distasteful.

How was she going to take it? He hated scenes. His mother had made enough of them in his life.

He lifted a stack of medical journals from a chair and added them to a precarious pile on the desk. "Please, have a seat."

When she did, Phillip hesitated a few seconds, but quickly decided there was no point beating around the bush. Pulling out his grandfather's chair, he sat behind the desk and faced her. "I've been doing some research on Ohio midwifery."

A look of surprise brightened her eyes. "That's great. It's very important that I resume my practice as soon as possible. I have four patients due this month. Without Harold available, I've had to send them to a clinic that's twenty miles from here. That's a hardship for families who travel by horse and buggy. I can't tell you how relieved I am to be getting back to my real work."

He hated knowing he was about to crush her excitement. "You have a collaborative practice agreement only with my grandfather, is that correct?"

"Yes, but I can easily modify the agreement, listing you as my primary backup. I'll print off a copy ASAP. You can sign it and I can start seeing patients again."

"I'm afraid I can't do that."

A puzzled look replaced the happiness on her face. Then she relaxed and nodded. "Yes, you can. In this state, I'm not required to partner with an OB/GYN. I can legally work with a Family Practice physician."

"I'm aware of that. I'm telling you I won't sign such an agreement. I strongly believe the safest place for a woman to labor, give birth and recover is in a hospital or a well-equipped birthing center near a hospital."

Amber shot to her feet. "Are you serious? Do you know what this means?"

Sitting forward, he steepled his fingers together. "It means you can't legally deliver babies or treat patients as a midwife unless you agree to do so in a hospital."

It took less than a second for the storm brewing behind her stunning eyes to erupt. She leaned forward and braced her arms on the desktop. Each word could have cut stone. "Your grandfather and I have worked diligently to get the Amish women in this community to use a certified nurse-midwife instead of an illegal lay midwife. There are still numerous Amish midwives practicing under the radar in this area. Some of them are highly skilled, but some are not. I have the equipment and training to handle emergencies that arise. I'm well qualified. I've delivered over five hundred babies."

"All without complications?"

Her outrage dimmed. Caution replaced it. "There have been a few problems. I carry a cell phone and can get emergency services quickly if they're needed."

"I'm sorry, this isn't open for discussion. As long as I'm here, there will be no home deliveries. However, I'd like you to remain as my office nurse. We'll talk later about you handling hospital deliveries."

Pushing off his desk, she crossed her arms. "Does Harold know you're shutting down my practice?"

He thought he was being patient with her, but now he glared back. "I don't intend to worry my grandfather with the day-to-day running of the office nor should you. His recovery depends on decreasing his stress level."

"Oh, rest assured, I won't go tattle to him. But you're making a big mistake. You can't change the way the Amish live by dictating to them. If I'm not doing home deliveries, someone else less qualified will."

Spinning on her heels, she marched out of the office, slamming the door behind her.

Clenching his jaw, Phillip sat back. He had hoped Miss Bradley would be reasonable about this. It seemed he was mistaken. Too bad. He wasn't about to back down on this issue. No matter what the lovely nurse-midwife wanted.

CHAPTER THREE

"IF THAT MAN thinks I'm gonna lay down and take this, he has another think coming!"

Three days after her first unhappy meeting with Phillip, Amber was still fuming. They had been working together getting the clinic back up and running full-time, but things remained tense. He refused to alter his stance on home births.

Amber sat at a back booth in the Shoofly Pie Café with her friend, Katie Lantz, across from her. Katie was dressed in the traditional Plain style with a solid green dress, white apron and a white organdy prayer *kapp* covering her dark hair. Amber knew outsiders would never suspect Katie had once lived in the English world. The room was empty except for the two women.

"What can you do about it?" Katie's lilting voice carried a rich Pennsylvania Dutch accent. She took a sip of hot tea from a heavy white mug.

"I'm thinking." Amber drummed her fingers on the red Formica tabletop.

"You'll lose your license if you deliver babies, *ja*?"

"*Ja*. Unless I find another doctor who'll support me."

Katie brightened. "Why not ask Dr. Drake over in Haydenville?"

"Because Doctor Drake, great doctor that she is, is a DO, a Doctor of Osteopathic Medicine. The state requires my backup to be a Family Practice physician or OB/GYN. Most clinics and MDs won't partner with a midwife who does home births. They don't want to pay the huge malpractice insurance fees that go along with it. Dr. Harold is one of the few physicians who'll take the risk."

"Because the Amish do not sue."

"Right."

"This is not so easy a problem to solve." Katie tapped her lower lip with one finger.

Propping an elbow on the table, Amber settled her chin on her hand. "I wish I could talk to Harold about it."

"Why can't you? It is his office. He should have some say in how it is being run."

"The last thing he needs is to hear his beloved long-lost grandson and I are at loggerheads. In that respect, Phillip is right. Harold doesn't need more stress. When he's better and comes home, things will get back to normal. In the meantime, I'll keep looking for a doctor who'll partner with me. Until then, I'll have to bear with Dr. Phillip while I work on changing his mind."

"I have met your doctor. He had lunch here yesterday. He's a handsome man."

Amber rolled her eyes. "Is he handsome? I hadn't noticed."

"For an Englisher, he's not bad. Those dark eyes are hot."

"They're blue, and a good Amish woman should not say a man is 'hot.'"

Katie giggled. "I am Amish, I am not dead. If you know what color his eyes are, you've been looking, too."

"Okay, I noticed he is a nice-looking man, but handsome is as handsome does. What he's doing isn't handsome."

"You're right. Elam's sister, Mary, will be so upset if she must go to the hospital to have this baby. She didn't have a good experience there with her first child."

Elam Sutter was a special someone in Katie's life. He and his mother, Nettie, took her in when she had returned from the English world destitute and pregnant. That act of kindness had blossomed into love for the pair. His sister, Mary Yutzi, had only recently become a patient of Amber's.

"Elam's mother convinced Mary you would do a better job. For less money, too."

A smile tugged at the corner of Amber's mouth. "I'm glad Nettie Sutter thinks I do good work. Thank her for the recommendation."

It had taken years but Amber was finally finding acceptance among the majority of the Amish in the area. People like Nettie Sutter were the key. Older and respected, their word counted for a lot with the younger women in the community.

Amber took a sip of her tea, letting the warmth of the gourmet blend soothe away some of her irritation. "Two of my expectant mothers have appointments today. I'll let them know what's going on when they come to the office. As for the rest of my clients, I can visit their homes on Sunday to explain things and prepare them."

"It is our church Sunday. Everyone will be at Levi Troyer's farm. It will save you some miles if you come there after the service."

"Thank you. If you're sure it's all right, I'll drop in. Of course, I might not need to. In this tight-knit community, the word may have spread already."

"*Ja*, you could be right."

"How is Elam, by the way?" Amber smiled in spite of her unhappiness as a blush bloomed in Katie's cheeks.

A soft smile curved her lips. "He is well."

"And the wedding? When will it be?"

Katie's eyes grew round. "What?"

Amber started laughing. "The whole countryside is talking about how much celery Elam planted this year. It won't come as a surprise to anyone when you have the banns read."

Creamed celery was a traditional food served at every Amish wedding. Leafy stalks of it were also used to decorate the tables. When a family's garden contained a big crop of celery, everyone knew there would be a wedding in the fall.

Blushing sweetly, Katie dropped her gaze. "We don't speak of such things before the time comes."

Amish marriage banns were read only a few weeks before the wedding. Until then, the engagement was kept a secret, sort of. Speculating about who would be getting hitched during the months of November and December was a popular pastime.

Amber said, "I'm sorry to tease."

Katie glanced around, then leaned close. "Not all of the celery is for Elam and me."

"Really?" Amber was intrigued. Elam lived with his widowed mother. All his sisters and older brothers were already married.

Sitting back, Katie smiled. "I will say no more."

"Now you've got me curious. Is someone courting Nettie?"

"Perhaps, but she isn't the only one with a new beau."

Leaning forward, Katie tipped her head toward her boss. Emma Wadler was busy cleaning behind the counter.

"Emma and who?" Amber whispered.

Katie refused to comment. Knowing when to give up, Amber said, "I'm sure you and Elam will be very happy together."

"And Rachel."

"That's right, we can't forget little Rachel. She was my five-hundredth delivery. Did I ever tell you that?"

"No. Looking back all those months ago, I thought it was the worst night of my life. I was unwed, homeless and without family. I didn't see how things could get much worse. I couldn't see it would become the best night of my life. I met Elam, I met you, my friend, and I had a beautiful baby girl. *Gott* has a plan for us even when we can't see it."

"If you're trying to tell me God will take care of my troubles, I already know that. But I can't sit idly by. I've got to take action. Get my own ox out of the well, if you will."

Katie stirred a drizzle of honey into her tea. "I might be able to help."

"How?"

"Perhaps I should talk with some of Elam's family before I say anything. This may be a matter to bring before the church district."

Frowning in concern, Amber said, "I don't want you to do anything that will cause trouble for you, Katie. I know you recently took your vows and were baptized into the Amish Church."

"Don't worry about me. Worry about the women who are depending on you."

They were the reason Amber was upset, not for herself. She glanced at her watch. "I should get back to the office. Dr. Phillip is trying to organize some of Harold's files. Truthfully, they need it. Harold has a terrible time putting things in their place."

"A day with the *furchtbar* Dr. Phillip and old files. Sounds like poor fun to me."

"He's not terrible. I'm wrong to make him sound that way. The community needs a doctor while Harold is gone and Phillip has put his own career on hold to come here."

"*Ja*, we do need a doctor."

"Even if he's a wonderful doctor, I just can't like him. He's so different from Harold," Amber muttered, knowing it made her sound like a petulant third grader.

Rising, Katie chuckled. "We must forgive those who trespass against us, Amber."

"I know," she admitted. "I'm working on it."

"And I also must get back to work."

"I haven't asked before, but do you like your job here at the Inn?" The café was part of the Wadler Inn, run by Emma and her elderly mother.

"Emma is a good woman to work for. Her mother enjoys watching Rachel while I work. It does fine for me now."

"Until you marry and become a stay-at-home wife and mother."

Grinning, Katie nodded. "*Ja*, until then."

Amber paid her bill and headed for the door. Being a wife and mother was something she'd always wanted, but it hadn't come her way.

Not that it was too late. She was only twenty-nine. So what if most of her Amish clients that age already had three or four children? Meeting an eligible man who wasn't Amish was as likely as finding hen's teeth in Hope Springs.

As she opened the door, Amber saw Phillip coming out of the hardware store across the street. He caught sight of her at the same moment. She either had to be civil or pretend she was in a hurry and rush away. Tough choice.

PHILLIP HALTED AT the sight of Amber framed in the doorway of the Shoofly Pie Café, an unappetizing name if he'd ever heard one. Once again he was struck by how lovely she was. Today she wore a simple yellow dress with short sleeves. Her hair hung over her shoulder in a single braid that reached her waist. Now he knew how long it was. Obviously, she hadn't cut it in many years. It was a nice touch of old-fashioned feminine charm.

They stood staring at each other for several long seconds until a man with a thick black beard and a straw hat stopped in front of Phillip. Realizing he was blocking the door, Phillip stepped out of the way. By the time he looked back, Amber was on her way down the sidewalk heading toward the clinic. He sprinted after her, cutting between two buggies rolling down the avenue.

He and Amber had both been doing their jobs at the clinic, but it didn't take a genius to see she was still upset. Her icy stares and monosyllablic replies weren't going unnoticed by their patients. Somehow he had to find a way to break through her anger. Phillip couldn't handle the practice by himself. There was more to medicine than treating symptoms.

Good medicine had physical, emotional and spiritual components. Amber had what he didn't yet have in Hope

Springs. A familiarity with the people he would be treating and knowledge of the inner workings of the town.

He needed to reach some kind of common ground with her if she could get past his stance on home deliveries. As much as he hated to admit it, he needed her help to keep his grandfather's clinic running smoothly.

Besides, the last thing he wanted was to tell Harold that he'd driven away the irreplaceable Miss Bradley. During their brief phone conversation last night, Harold once again sang her many praises. If Phillip didn't know better, he might have thought the old man was playing matchmaker.

After crossing the street at a jog, Phillip reached Amber's side and shortened his stride to match hers. "Morning, Miss Bradley."

"Good morning, Doctor."

"Are you on your way to the office?"

"Yes."

He glanced at his watch. "You're a little early, aren't you?"

"Yes."

In spite of the warm summer sun there was no sign of thawing on her part. He said, "We didn't see many patients yesterday. Can I expect our patient load to be so light every day?"

"No."

This didn't bode well for the rest of the day. "The weather has been agreeable. Are summers in Ohio always this nice?"

"No."

Getting nowhere, he decided to try a different tack.

Phillip saw an Amish family walking toward them. The man with his bushy beard nodded slightly. His wife kept her eyes averted, but their children gawked at them as they passed by. One of them, a teenage boy, was a dwarf. A group of several young men in straw hats and Amish clothing walked behind the group. None of the younger men wore beards.

When they were out of earshot, Phillip asked, "Why is it that only some Amish men have beards?"

He waited patiently for her answer. They passed two more shops before she obliged him. "An Amish man grows a beard when he marries."

"Okay, why don't they have mustaches?"

"Mustaches were associated with the military in Europe before the Amish immigrated to this country so they are forbidden."

"From what I understand, a lot of things are forbidden... TV, ordinary clothes, a car."

She shot him a sour look and kept walking.

That was dumb. Criticizing the Amish wasn't the way to mend fences. "Sorry, that was a stupid remark. Guess I'm nervous."

She kept walking, ignoring his bait. Either she had great patience, grim determination or a total lack of curiosity about him.

He gave in first. "I'm nervous because I know you're upset with me."

"Ya think?" She didn't slow down.

Spreading his hands wide, he waved them side to side. "I'm getting that vibe. People say I'm sensitive that way."

Had he coaxed a hint of a smile? She looked down before he could be sure.

"Amber, we've gotten off to a bad start. I know you must blame me for Harold's injuries. I blame myself."

She stopped abruptly. A puzzled frown settled between her alluring eyes. "Why would I blame you for Harold's accident?"

CHAPTER FOUR

STUNNED BY AMBER'S question, Phillip could only stare. She didn't know? How was that possible? More to the point, once she found out would it kill any chance of a better working relationship? He had opened a can of worms and didn't know how to shut it. She was waiting for his answer.

"Harold hasn't told you how the accident happened?" Phillip cringed at the memory.

"He said he foolishly stepped into the path of an oncoming car."

Phillip stiffened his spine, bracing for the worst possible reaction from Amber. "I was driving that car."

When the silence lengthened, he expected an angry or horror-filled outburst. He didn't expect the compassion that slowly filled her eyes.

Encouraged, he forged ahead. "It was the last night of his visit. We'd had an argument. I dropped him off at his hotel. I was angry and waiting impatiently for a chance to pull out into the heavy traffic. When a break came, I gunned it."

He'd never forgive himself for what happened next. "I should have been paying more attention. I should have seen him, but he rushed out from between two parked cars right in front of me. I couldn't stop."

She laid her hand on his arm. "That must have been terrible for you."

"I thought I killed him." Phillip relived that terrifying moment, that horrific sound, every time he closed his eyes.

Quietly, Amber said, "Thank you for telling me. I can understand how hard it was for you. I want you to know I don't blame you. An accident is an accident. Things happen for a reason only God knows."

Phillip's pent-up guilt seeped out of his bones, leaving him light-headed with relief. "Now, can we work together without those frosty silences between us?"

He knew he'd made a mistake when her look of compassion changed to annoyance. "I don't blame you for what happened in Hawaii. I do blame you for making me feel marginalized and ridiculed for my career choice. For brushing aside my years of training and my skills as if they were nothing. I'm proud to be a nurse-midwife."

Taken aback, he snapped, "Wait a minute. I did not ridicule you. I stated my opinion about home childbirth. An opinion that is shared by the American Medical Association, as I'm sure you know."

"And so far, not upheld by the courts, as I'm sure *you* know. Childbirth is not a medical condition. It is a normal, natural part of life." She started walking again.

Catching up with her, he said, "But it can become a medical emergency in a matter of minutes. I'm sorry we can't agree on this. However, if we're going to be working together we need to agree on some other important issues."

She shot him an exasperated look. "Such as?"

"That my grandfather's practice is important to him.

Both you and I are important to him. He wouldn't want us at odds with each other."

He detected a softening in her rigid posture. Finally, she admitted, "That's true."

"Right. We can also agree that the clinic needs to run smoothly, that I don't know where to buy groceries in Hope Springs and I haven't found a barbershop. Can you help a guy out?"

She did smile at that. "The grocery store is at the corner of Plum and Maple. Take a left at the next block and go three blocks east. The barbershop backs up to our building. Go through the alley to Vine Street. It'll be on your left. And yes, the clinic needs to run smoothly. Our patients deserve our best."

"Thank you."

"You're welcome."

It was grudgingly given, but he'd won a small victory. "I also don't know what labs Mrs. Nissley had done. I couldn't find her chart."

"I was checking her hemoglobin A1c. She's a diabetic. Ask Wilma for any charts you can't find. She has her own system of filing because so many of our patients have the same names."

"Why is that?"

"Most Amish are descendants of a small group who came to this country in the seventeen hundreds. It is forbidden to marry outside of their faith so very few new names have come into the mix."

By now they had reached the clinic. He held open the door and she went in ahead of him. To his surprise he saw they already had a waiting room full of people. Word was getting around that there was a new doctor in town.

It seemed that more one-on-one time with Amber would have to wait. He should have walked more slowly.

She leaned over and said quietly, "Something you should know. The Amish don't run to the doctor for every little thing. They are usually quite sick when they come to us. When they find a 'good doctor,' they send all their family and friends to him."

"And if I'm not a good doctor, in their opinion?"

"We'll lose Amish clients very quickly and we'll be out of business in no time. So, no pressure."

"Right. No pressure."

The day passed quickly. True to Amber's prediction, many of the patients Phillip treated had been putting off seeing a doctor since his grandfather's departure. Two bad cuts had become serious infections. A young mill worker with a gash on his arm and a high fever had to be sent to the hospital in Millersburg for IV antibiotics.

After that, he saw a young Amish woman who'd come to see Amber for her prenatal visits. After he explained the current situation, his patient got up and left his exam room without a word. In the waiting room, she spoke to a second expectant mother. The two left together. Amber followed them outside and talked with them briefly.

Was she smoothing things over or throwing gasoline on the fire?

His next patient was a three-year-old Amish girl with a severe cough. The shy toddler was also a dwarf, and she wanted nothing to do with him. She kept pushing his stethoscope away each time he tried to listen to her chest.

Mrs. Lapp, her worried mother, apologized. Amber moved forward to help restrain the child. "Doctor, Helen doesn't speak English yet. She won't learn it until she goes to school. The Amish speak Pennsylvania Deitsh at home, a German dialect."

Glancing up at her, he said, "I thought it was Dutch."

"It's commonly called Pennsylvania Dutch but that's an Americanization of the term *Deitsh*," Amber replied.

He said, "Don't hold her down, it will only frighten her. What we need is a little help from Doctor Dog."

Reaching into a drawer on the exam table, he withdrew a hand puppet, a fuzzy brown dog with floppy ears, a white lab coat and a miniature stethoscope around his neck. Looking down at the toy, Phillip said, "Dr. Dog, I'd like you to meet Helen Lapp."

"Hello, Helen," the puppet chirped in a falsetto voice as he waved one stubby arm.

Phillip heard Amber giggle behind him. Helen sat up with a hesitant smile on her face.

The puppet scratched his head with his paw. "What's wrong with you, Helen? Are you sick?"

Helen's mother translated for her. The girl nodded, never taking her eyes off the toy.

Swinging the puppet around to face himself, Phillip asked in his puppet voice, "Aren't you going to make her better, Dr. White?"

"I'm trying but Helen is afraid of me."

"She is?" Turning to face the little girl, Dr. Dog asked, "Are you afraid of Dr. White?"

Her mother asked her the question in Pennsylvania Dutch. Helen glared at Phillip and nodded.

Dr. Dog rubbed his nose. "But you aren't scared of me, are you?"

When her mother stopped speaking, Helen shook her head. Reaching out tentatively, she patted the dog's head then giggled. Her laughter quickly became a harsh cough.

Dr. Dog asked, "Can I listen to your chest?"

Helen leaned back against her mother but didn't object. Using Dr. Dog to grasp his stethoscope, Phillip listened to the child. When he was done with the exam, Dr. Dog thanked Helen, shook hands with her and her mother, then returned to his drawer. Helen continued to watch the drawer as if he might pop out again.

As Phillip wrote out a prescription for Helen, Amber leaned close. "Very clever."

More pleased than he should have been by that simple compliment, he continued with his work. Helen had him deeply concerned.

Turning to her mother, he handed her the prescription and said, "I hear a loud murmur in Helen's heart, a noise that shouldn't be there. I'd like for her to see a specialist."

The woman stared at the note in her hand. "Will this medicine make her better?"

"I believe so, but she needs to see a heart doctor. I'll have Amber make an appointment. I believe Helen's heart condition is making her cough worse."

The mother nodded. Relieved, he looked to Amber. She said, "I'll take care of it."

He saw several more townspeople after that with assorted coughs and colds. Then two young Amish brothers came in with poison ivy from head to toe. Their mother explained her usual home remedy had failed to help.

He asked for her recipe and jotted it down. He then ordered a steroid shot for each of the boys. Afterward, he gave their mother a prescription for an ointment to be used twice a day, but encouraged her to continue her own treatment, as well.

When they left, Amber remained in the room.

"Yes?" He kept writing on the chart without looking up.

"Why didn't you have her discontinue her home remedy? It clearly isn't working."

"There was nothing in it that would interfere with the medication I prescribed. It should even give the boys some added relief. Mostly, it will make her feel better to be doing something for them." He snapped the chart shut. "What's next?"

His final patient of the day turned out to be an Amish woman with a badly swollen wrist.

Amber stood by the counter as Phillip pulled his chair up beside the young Mrs. Nissley. Her first name was Martha. She held her arm cradled across her stomach.

Phillip said, "May I see your wrist, please?"

Taking it gently, he palpated it, feeling for any obvious breaks. "Tell me what happened."

"The dog scared my *Milch* cow, and she kicked. She missed the dog but hit me."

He winced. "Sounds painful."

"*Ja.* That it is."

He admired her stoicism. "You're the first cow-kick victim I've treated in my career. In spite of that, the only way to be certain it isn't broken is to get an X-ray. Are you related to Edna Nissley?"

"Which Edna Nissley?"

He struggled to find a description since they dressed alike and seemed so similar. "She's an older lady. Short, kind of stout. Oh, she drives a gray horse."

"That is my husband's uncle's wife. The other Edna Nissley is the wife of my husband's cousin William. Little Edna Nissley is the daughter of my husband's youngest brother, Daniel."

"Okay." A confusing family history if he'd ever heard one. He glanced at Amber. "I'll need AP and Lateral X-rays of the left wrist. Mrs. Nissley, is there any chance you may be pregnant?"

"*Nee.* At least, I don't think so."

He looked at Amber. "Make sure she wears a lead apron just in case."

"Of course."

Ten minutes later he had the films in hand. Putting them up on the light box, he indicated the wrist bones for his patient to see.

"I don't detect a break. What you have is a bad sprain and some nasty bruising. I'll wrap it with an elastic bandage to compress the swelling. Rest it and ice it. I want you to keep the arm elevated. Is there a problem with doing any of those things?"

"Can I milk the cow?"

He tried not to smile. "If you can do it with one hand or with your toes."

She grinned. "I have children and a helpful husband."

"Good. Here's a prescription for some pain medication if you need it. See me again if it isn't better by the end of the week."

When Mrs. Nissley left he saw the waiting room was finally empty. A glance at his watch told him it was nearly four in the afternoon. More tired than he cared to admit, Phillip retreated to his grandfather's office and sank gratefully into Harold's padded, brown leather chair. If his seventy-five-year-old grandfather kept this kind of pace, he was hardier than Phillip gave him credit for.

After only five minutes of downtime, a knock sounded at his door. Sighing, he called out, "Yes?"

Amber poked her head in. "I have a ham sandwich. Would you like to share?"

His stomach rumbled at the mention of food, reminding him he'd had nothing but one cup of coffee since he'd left the house that morning. "I'd love a sandwich. Thank you."

She entered and whisked a plate from behind her back. "I thought you might say that."

He took her offering and made a place for the paper dinnerware on his desk. "Why don't you and Wilma join me?"

"Wilma has gone home."

"Then will you join me?" He held his breath as he waited for her reply.

AMBER HESITATED. IT was one thing to work with Phillip. It was a whole other thing to share a meal with him.

He said, "Don't tell me you've never joined Harold for a late lunch."

"Of course I have."

"Then what's the problem? Afraid I'll bite or afraid you won't be able to resist stabbing me with a knife?"

"All I have is a plastic fork, so you're safe on that score."

"Good." He lifted the upper slice of bread and peered inside. "You didn't lace this with an overdose of digoxin, did you?"

"And slow your heart until it stopped?" She snapped her fingers. "Wish I'd thought of it. Then Dr. Dog could take over. Thanks for the idea."

Grinning, Amber left the room and returned to the break room to get her half of the sandwich. It seemed Dr. Phillip had a sense of humor. It was one more point in his favor. The most impressive thing about him, good looks aside, was how he dealt with patients.

During the long, exhausting day he had listened to them. He discussed his plans of care in simple terms. And he was great with children. She liked that about him.

He could be a good replacement for Harold. If only she could change his mind about her midwife services.

Looking heavenward, she said, "Please, Lord, heal Harold and send him back to us quickly. In the meantime, give me the right words to help Phillip see the need the Amish have for my work."

With her plate in hand, she returned to his office. She saw he'd been busy clearing off another spot on the opposite side of the desk. She pulled over a chair and sat down. Closing her eyes, she took a deep breath then silently said a blessing over her meal.

"Sitting down feels good, doesn't it?" Phillip asked.

She nodded. "You can say that again."

"Is the clinic normally this busy?"

"We serve a large rural area besides the town. Today was busier than usual but not by much."

He took a big bite of his sandwich. "This is good," he mumbled with his mouth full.

"I picked it up at the café this morning."

"Okay, I have to know. Why is it called the Shoofly Pie Café?"

"You've never heard of shoofly pie?"

"No."

"Wait here." Rising, Amber returned to the break room and pulled a small box from the bottom shelf. Returning to Phillip's office, she set it in front of him with a pair of plastic forks.

He popped the last bite of sandwich into his mouth

and cautiously raised the lid of the box. Swallowing, he said, "It looks like a wedge of coffee cake."

"It's similar. No dessert in the world says 'Amish' like shoofly pie. It's made with molasses, which some people say gave it the name because they had to shoo the flies away from it. It's a traditional Pennsylvania Dutch recipe but it's served in many places across the South."

"Interesting."

"Try some." She pushed it closer.

He shook his head.

"Are you a culinary chicken, Dr. Phillip?"

"It must be loaded with calories. I don't indulge in risky behaviors."

"That from a man who surfs the North Shore of Oahu?"

His eyes brightened. "You follow surfing?"

"A little." And only since Harold told her it was his grandson's favorite sport.

Phillip sat back and closed his eyes. "The North Shore is perfection. You should see the waves that come in there. Towering blue-green walls of water curling over and crashing with such a roar. The sandy shore is a pale strip between the blue sea and lush tropical palms. It's like no place else on earth."

"I'd like to see the ocean someday," she said wistfully.

His eyes shot open in disbelief. "You've never been to the seashore?"

"I once saw Lake Erie."

"Sorry, that doesn't count. What makes you stick so close to these cornfields?" He picked up the fork and tried a sample of pie.

"I was born and raised in Ohio."

"That's no excuse." He pointed to the box with his fork. "This is good stuff."

"Told you. I was raised on a farm in an Amish community about fifty miles from here. My mother grew up Amish but didn't join the church because she fell in love with my father, who wasn't Amish. They owned a dairy farm. That means work three hundred sixty-five days a year. I don't think I traveled more than thirty miles from our farm until I was in college."

"What made you go into midwifery?"

"I always wanted to be a nurse. I liked the idea of helping sick people. Becoming a CNM wasn't my first choice. I was led to become a nurse-midwife by my older sister, Esther. You would have liked her."

Thoughts of Esther, always laughing, always smiling, brought a catch to Amber's voice. He noticed.

"Did something happen to her?" he asked gently.

"Unlike mother, Esther longed to join the Amish church. She did when she was eighteen. After that, she married the farmer who lived across the road from us."

"Sounds like you had a close-knit family."

"Yes, we did. Esther had her first child at home with an Amish midwife. Everything was fine. Things went terribly wrong with her second baby. The midwife hesitated getting Esther to a hospital for fear of repercussions. By the time they did get help, it was too late. Esther and her baby died."

"I don't understand. How would that make you want to become a midwife?"

"Because a CNM has the skills, training and equipment to deal with emergencies. There are a lot of good lay midwives out there, but as a CNM I don't have to be afraid to take a patient to the hospital for fear of being arrested for practicing medicine without a license. I can save the lives of women like my sister who want to give birth at home because they truly believe it is the way God intended."

"Had your sister been in the hospital to start with, things might have turned out differently."

He didn't get it. She shouldn't have expected him to. "Maybe, or maybe God allowed Esther to show me my true vocation among her people."

Amber helped herself to the small bite of pie he'd left. "My turn to ask a question."

"Why won't I allow you to do home deliveries? I don't believe it's safe."

She leaned forward earnestly. "But it is. Home births with a qualified attendant are safe for healthy, low-risk women. Countries where there are large numbers of home births have fewer complications and fewer deaths than here in the United States. How do you explain that if home births aren't safe?"

"The American College of Obstetricians and Gynecologists do not support programs that advocate home birth. They don't support individuals who provide home births."

"Is that for safety reasons or financial ones? I'm taking money out of their pockets if my patients deliver at home."

"You think the majority of doctors in the ACOG put money before the safety of patients? I doubt it. We could argue this point until we're both blue in the face. I'm not changing my mind."

Frustrated, Amber threw up her hands and shook her head. "This isn't a whim or a craze. This has been their way of life for hundreds of years. At least listen to some of the Amish women who want home births. Hear their side of the story. This is important to them."

All trace of humor vanished from his face. "What part of *no* don't you understand, Miss Bradley?"

They glared at each other, the tension thick enough to cut with a knife.

Suddenly, Amber heard the front door of the clinic open. A boy's voice yelled, *"Doktor, doktor, komm shnell!"*

She leapt to her feet. "He says come quick."

CHAPTER FIVE

PHILLIP JUMPED TO his feet and followed Amber out to the office lobby. An Amish boy of about eight began talking rapidly. Phillip couldn't understand a word. He looked at Amber. "What's he saying?"

She shushed him with one hand until the boy was done. Then she said, "Their wagon tipped over in a ditch. His mother is trapped."

"Did he call 911?"

She gave him a look of pure exasperation. "How many times do I have to tell you? They don't have phones."

Running back to his office, Phillip grabbed his grandfather's black bag from a shelf beside the door. Returning to the lobby, he saw Amber had a large canvas bag slung over her shoulder.

He said, "I'll get the car. Try to find out from him how badly she's hurt and where they're located so we can get EMS on the way."

Taking the boy by the hand, Amber followed Phillip out the door and climbed into his black SUV. She said, "It's Martha Nissley, the woman we treated today. They overturned near their farm. It's a quarter of a mile from the edge of town. Should I drive?"

"You navigate and try to keep the boy calm. Is he hurt?"

She spoke briefly to the boy in Pennsylvania Dutch.

He shook his head. To Phillip, she said, "I don't think so. He's just out of breath from running and from fright. Turn left up ahead and then take the right fork in the road."

Phillip did as instructed. He wanted to hurry but he knew he had to drive safely. He'd heard horror stories from his grandfather about buggy and automobile collisions on the narrow, hilly roads.

"There, that's the lane." Amber pointed it out to him as she was dialing 911 on her cell phone.

Topping a rise, Phillip saw a group of four men freeing the horses from the wagon. Both animals were limping badly. The wagon lay on its side in a shallow ditch. Phillip pulled to a stop a few yards away.

Turning to Amber, he said, "Make the boy understand he needs to stay in the car."

"Of course." After giving the child his instructions, Phillip and Amber got out.

Martha was lying facedown in the ditch, trapped beneath the wagon. A man knelt beside her. Phillip assumed he was her husband.

Only the broken spokes of the front wheel were keeping the wagon from crushing her completely. The rear wheel bowed out dangerously. If either wheel came off, she wouldn't stand a chance.

He knelt beside her. "Martha, can you hear me?"

"Ja," she answered through gritted teeth.

"Where are you hurt?"

"My back burns like fire. I can't move my legs."

His heart sank. "All right, lie still. We'll get you out."

"Where is my boy, Louis? Is he okay?"

"He's sitting in my car. I told him to stay there."

"Goot." She began muttering what he thought was a

prayer. Amber scrambled down in the ditch beside them. Quickly, she checked Martha's vital signs. Then, to Phillip's horror, she lay down and wiggled as far under the overturned wagon as she could.

After a minute, Amber worked herself backward and Phillip helped her gain her feet. He said, "Don't do that again."

"Martha's bleeding profusely from a gash on her left thigh. I couldn't reach it to put pressure on it, but it's bad."

He wanted to wait for the fire department and EMS. They'd likely have the Jaws of Life to lift the vehicle. But if she were hemorrhaging as badly as Amber thought, time was of the essence. "Okay, we'll have to get the wagon off of her."

Phillip turned to the men gathered around. The one kneeling beside Martha rose and joined them. "I'm David Nissley, Martha's husband. We were afraid to move the wagon and do Martha more injury."

"You were right. However, we need to move it now."

Mr. Nissley pointed up the lane. "My boy, Noah, is coming with the draft team."

What Phillip wouldn't give for a forklift or at least a tractor…something he knew had enough power and wouldn't bolt in fright and pull the heavy wagon on top of his patient. He considered trying to use his SUV but there was no room to maneuver on the narrow road.

He said, "We need some way to brace the wagon in case that wheel comes off."

"We can use boards from there." Amber pointed to the white painted fence running alongside the road. An instant later, Mr. Nissley and the men were dismantling the boards by using their heavy boots to kick them loose from the posts.

Phillip watched the activity impatiently. "Once we have it braced so it can't fall back, we'll try pulling it off her."

A boy of about fifteen came racing down the road with a pair of enormous gray horses trotting at his heels. Sunlight gleamed off their shiny flanks as their powerful muscles rippled beneath their hides. They made a breathtaking sight.

The boy quickly backed them into position. They stood perfectly still as they waited for their harnesses to be hooked to the wagon. Feeling dwarfed by the massive animals, Phillip decided a tractor wouldn't be necessary.

He turned back to Mrs. Nissley just as Amber was once again working herself under the broken vehicle, this time with her bag. He caught her foot. "What do you think you're doing?"

Her voice was muffled. "Once the weight comes off her leg, someone has to put pressure on that gash. It's oozing bright red blood."

"You think it's a severed artery?"

"I do."

He didn't like the danger she was putting herself in. He let go of her ankle because he knew she was right. The weight of the wagon on Martha might be stemming the flow of blood. Once it came off, she could bleed out rapidly.

Mr. Nissley alternated between speaking comforting words to his wife, directing the men making braces and instructing his son on the best way to attach the horses to the rig.

In less than five minutes, they were ready. Mr. Nissley spoke briefly to his wife, then took the reins from his son.

The boy said, "I can do it, Papa?"

"Nee, das ist für mich zu tun."

Phillip looked at Mrs. Nissley for an explanation. "He said, 'This is for me to do.' If it falls back, he doesn't want my son blaming himself."

Another man called the boy over to help with the braces. Mr. Nissley coaxed the big horses forward. The wagon creaked ominously but lifted a few inches. The men standing by instantly moved in with the fence boards to prop it up. Squatting beside Amber's feet, Phillip prepared to drag her out of harm's way if need be.

The wagon inched upward with painful slowness, but finally Martha was free. Amber was already staunching the flow of blood with a heavy pad as the team dragged the broken wagon across the road. Phillip rushed to help secure the pad with a heavy elastic bandage. Amber was right. It was arterial blood. Martha would have bled to death if they'd delayed any longer.

The Amish woman was conscious but pale. Phillip said to Amber, "What supplies have you got in your bag?"

"IV supplies, pain medication, sterile drapes, suture, anything you'd need for a regular delivery. I'm going to start an eighteen gauge IV with Ringer's Lactate."

"Once that's done give her a bolus of morphine if you've got it. Martha, are you allergic to any medications?"

"Nee."

All color was gone from her cheeks and her breathing was shallow. Phillip's concern spiked. She was going into shock.

"Amber, hurry with that IV."

"Should we try to turn her over?" Amber asked as she rapidly assembled her equipment, donned gloves and started prepping Martha's arm for the needle.

"I'd rather wait for EMS and their backboard." Phillip grabbed his stethoscope from his bag and listened to Martha's lungs through her back. They were clear of fluid. One thing in her favor.

Amber slipped the IV line in and started the fluids. Gesturing to one of the men nearby, she gave him the bag to hold.

After handing over the reins of his horses to his son, Mr. Nissley returned to his wife's side. Once there, he sat beside her and simply held her hand without saying a word.

Relief ripped through Phillip when he heard the sound of a siren in the distance.

Within minutes, the ambulance arrived on the scene, followed by a sheriff's department cruiser. Standing beside Amber, Phillip felt her grasp his hand as they loaded Mrs. Nissley aboard.

Louis jumped out of Phillip's SUV and raced to his mother's side. She patted his head and told him not to worry. One of his sisters took his hand and coaxed him away. Mr. Nissley climbed in beside Martha. Soon they were on their way to the hospital in Millersburg, red lights flashing.

Together, Phillip and Amber watched the vehicle disappear in the distance. As the adrenaline drained away, Phillip grew shaky. Looking down, he noticed Amber still gripped his hand.

FOLLOWING PHILLIP'S GAZE, Amber realized her fingers were entwined with his. Suddenly, she became aware of the warmth traveling up her arm from where they touched. It spread through her body in waves and made her skin tingle like a charge of static electricity.

Their eyes met. An intense awareness rippled around them. Her breath froze in her chest. Her eyes roved over his face, soaking in every detail and committing it to memory.

Sweat trickled down his cheek. His hair was mussed, his clothes dirty. None of that diminished the attraction drawing her to him.

Behind her, someone spoke and a discussion about where to take the wagon broke out. She let go of Phillip's hand and wrapped her arms across her chest. It had to be the adrenaline ebb. Holding his hand surely wasn't making her weak in the knees, right?

He said, "I should follow them to the hospital. She's my patient, after all."

Amber struggled to get herself together. "We'll need to make arrangements for the family to travel there, too."

Phillip reached into his pocket and pulled out his cell phone. "Who shall I call?"

"Samson Carter has a van service." She gave him the number and after someone answered, he handed the phone to the oldest Nissley boy. When the boy was finished with the call, he handed the phone back and then gave instructions to his younger brothers and sisters. Already, the neighbors who had come to help were busy repairing the fence. The sheriff was interviewing them.

"Will these kids be all right?" Phillip asked quietly as they made their way toward his SUV.

Walking beside him, Amber nodded. "Yes. Word will spread quickly, and they will be smothered with help. Men will come to do the chores and women will come to take charge of the house. An Amish family never has to worry about what will happen to them in an emergency. It's a given that everyone in the Church will rally around them."

"That's good to know. Martha shouldn't have been driving that big wagon with her arm in a splint."

"She wasn't driving. Her son was."

"That little one who ran to our clinic?"

"Yes, but it wasn't his fault. Some teenage boys driving by in a pickup threw firecrackers under the wagon and spooked the horses."

He stopped. "Does the officer know that?"

Amber glanced over her shoulder. "I doubt it. They won't talk to the authorities about it. They will forgive whoever has done this. It is their way."

"Someone should tell the officer. Can you get a description of the vehicle from them?"

"No. They won't talk to me about it. I'm an outsider, like you."

"But you've lived here for years."

"That makes no difference. I'm not Amish."

The sheriff came over to them. Tall and blond, with eyes only a shade lighter than Amber's, he smiled at her fondly. "Hey, cuz. Can you give me any information about what happened here?"

"Hi, Nick. I can tell you what I overheard but not much else." She relayed her story while he took notes.

After a few minutes, he put his notepad away. "Thanks. Not much chance of solving this but I'll give it my best shot. How about you, Doc? Can you add anything?"

"Sorry, no."

Amber said, "Dr. White, this is Nicolas Bradley, my

cousin. Nick, this is Harold's grandson. Phillip's taking over the clinic until Harold gets back."

The two men shook hands. Nick said, "Sorry we didn't meet under better circumstances. Ordinarily, this is a pretty quiet place. If you'll excuse me, I've got to get back to work. Amber, see you later."

As he went to finish interviewing the witnesses, Amber turned to Phillip. "We should get to the hospital."

Reaching out, he gently brushed some dirt from her cheek. "I should get to the hospital. You should get home."

Her heart turned over and melted into a foolish puddle. *Don't do this. Don't go falling for a man who'll be gone in a few weeks.*

It was good advice. Could she follow it?

Drawing a quick breath, she forced her practical nature to the forefront. This rush of emotion was nothing more than a reaction to their working together during a crisis. It would soon fade.

With a logical explanation for her irrational feelings, Amber was able to smile and say, "Dr. White, you can't find your way to the grocery store. How are you going to find your way to Millersburg?"

He looked as if he wanted to argue. Instead, he nodded toward his car. "Get in."

CHAPTER SIX

PHILLIP TRIED TO concentrate on the road ahead, but he couldn't ignore the presence of the woman seated beside him. Her foolish bravery, her skill and quick thinking under pressure impressed him to no end. He saw now why his grandfather valued her so highly.

He said, "You did a good job back there."

"Thanks. It's not the first horse-drawn vehicle accident I've been to. Although there's usually a car involved."

"If they're so unsafe, why do the Amish continue to use their buggies?"

"It's part of being separate from the world. It's who they are. Turn left at the next corner. You handled yourself well. Your grandfather would be proud of you."

"I hope so."

"He means a lot to you, doesn't he?"

Phillip glanced at her. "Yes. More than you can know. How did you end up working for him?"

"Long story."

"Longer than the drive to Millersburg?"

Her smile slipped out. "Probably not."

"So tell me."

"When I finished my nurse-midwife program, I started looking for a place to set up my practice. I knew I wanted to do home deliveries among the Amish. I know you don't approve. Rest assured, you aren't the only doctor who feels that way."

"But my grandfather sees things differently."

"Yes. I began talking to Amish families at local farmers' markets and other gatherings. It was at the produce market in Millersburg that I heard about your grandfather. He's held in very high regard in the Amish community."

"He's devoted more than thirty years to these people. They should think highly of him. I'm sorry. Go on." He might not approve of their lifestyle, but he had to remember she did.

"I came to Hope Springs and explained to Harold how I wanted to practice. He was delighted. We both knew it wouldn't be easy building a practice for me, so he hired me to work as his office nurse, too. Those first couple of years he mentored me every step of the way."

"I envy you knowing him so well and working so closely with him." Surprised that he'd admitted that out loud, he checked for her reaction.

"Your grandfather has taught me so much. The Amish say if you want good advice, seek an old man. It is true— but don't tell Harold I called him old."

Phillip laughed. "It will be our secret. I wish I could get him to act his age."

"How is he supposed to act?"

"The man is seventy-five years old. He should be retired and enjoying his golden years."

She waved a hand, dismissing his assumption. "If Harold is able, he'll be back. We need him."

Phillip needed him, too. He'd longed for a father figure all his life. His mother's string of "Uncles" who lived with them over the years hadn't filled that need. If anything, they made it worse. Meeting Harold in person had finally started to fill the hole in Phillip's life.

All he'd wanted was to spend more time with his grandfather. Their weeklong visit had been drawing to a close far too quickly. Phillip's suggestion that Harold think about relocating to Hawaii had been met with an unexpectedly harsh response.

His grandfather had made it *abundantly* clear that his place was in Hope Springs. Harold's anger seemed entirely out of proportion to the suggestion. Phillip still didn't know why. Was he wrong to want his grandfather near him for what few years the man might have left? Were these backward Amish more important than Harold's own flesh and blood?

Phillip glanced at Amber. "Harold has given enough of his life to this backwater burg. He deserves a few years of peace and relaxation."

Her smile faded, replaced by a puzzled frown. "I think that's up to Harold to decide."

Phillip reined in his sudden anger because he knew she was right. For the rest of the ride, neither of them spoke. When they pulled into a parking space outside the hospital's ER, Phillip turned off the engine. Sitting with his hands still gripping the steering wheel, he said, "I'm sorry I snapped at you. I have issues with my family but that's no reason to take it out on you."

She stared at him for a long moment. The spark of annoyance in her eyes gradually died away.

"You're forgiven. Care to talk about what happened between you and Harold in Hawaii? I'm getting the impression that something is seriously bothering you."

"So you're a mind reader as well as a midwife?"

She waved her hands back and forth. "Some people say I'm sensitive that way."

He chuckled at his own line being thrown back at him. "I appreciate the offer, but I've got to deal with things in my own fashion."

Reaching out, she laid her hand over his where it rested on the steering wheel and asked gently, "Are you sure that's best?"

The touch of her hand made his heart stumble, miss a beat and then race like it did when he was surfing into the pipeline at Oahu. And like being inside the curl of a giant wave, Phillip knew he'd just entered dangerous waters.

His next move could shoot him into the clear or send him headlong into a painful battering.

AMBER MEANT HER touch to be comforting, an offer of friendship. It turned into something more in an instant. The warmth of his skin sent her heart racing. She couldn't tear her gaze away from his. What was he thinking? Did he feel it, too, this strange and wonderful chemistry that sparked between them? On some purely feminine level, she knew he did.

The attraction both thrilled and frightened her. She'd never reacted to any man this way, and she'd been in a few relationships over the years.

The ambulance pulled out of the ER bay as they sat staring at each other. Phillip slowly withdrew his hand. Looking out the window, he said, "We should go in and find out how Martha is faring."

Embarrassment flooded Amber to her very core. Did he think she was making a pass at him? She'd only known him a few days. He was her boss. Nothing had been further from her mind, but that might not be the way it looked to him. She quickly opened her car door and got out.

Inside the ER doors, the charge nurse came to greet them. "Hello, Amber. I heard about your excitement."

"Yes. Give me pregnant women and crying babies any day. Gloria, this is Dr. Phillip White, Harold's grandson. Dr. White, this is Gloria Bender. She's the head of the ER department."

The two shook hands. Gloria said, "Dr. White, I received the notice just this morning that you've been granted privileges here."

"Excellent. Where is Mrs. Nissley and who's seeing her?"

"Dr. Kline was on duty when Mrs. Nissley came in. X-rays confirmed a spinal fracture. She's been taken to MRI to assess the complexity of her injury. The two of you did a good job stabilizing her in the field. It made our work much easier."

Wearily, Phillip rubbed a hand over his face. "Thanks. Do we know yet if her spinal cord is compressed or if it is severed?"

"I haven't heard. Dr. Kline started her on steroids to reduce any swelling. I know he wants to speak to you as soon as he's done. His plan is to take her straight from MRI to surgery where he'll clean out and close the gash on her leg. If she needs spinal surgery, she'll be airlifted to Akron." Glancing at her watch, she noted, "They should be finished in about thirty minutes."

"Thank you." He sighed heavily. Amber could sense his frustration.

Gloria returned to her office, leaving them alone once more. Phillip's face mirrored the same worry running through Amber. If Martha's spinal cord was severed, she'd never walk again.

He said, "Thirty minutes. Guess that leaves us enough time to get a cup of coffee."

"It's not gourmet, but the coffee in the cafeteria here is drinkable. Let me tell Gloria where we'll be and then I'd like to wash up first."

He smiled and looked her over. "Good idea. You've got grass in your hair."

"What?" she squeaked as her hands flew up and brushed at her scalp.

"Come here." He pulled her over and plucked the offending blades from where they'd lodged in her braid.

She kept her gaze riveted to the floor.

I'm not going to blush and babble like a teenage girl with a crush on the top jock. I'm a professional and I can act like one.

Phillip took a step back. "There, I think that's all of it."

"Thank you." Without looking at him, she made her escape to the ladies' room, where she splashed water on her heated face.

Staring into the mirror for a long time, she said, "I can't hide in here forever. I'm going to be working with the man. I've got to get a handle on my emotions." Standing up straight, she added, "Right? Can do!"

Bucked up by her personal pep talk, Amber exited the room.

PHILLIP ALSO TOOK the time to wash up and sternly remind himself that he and Amber shared a professional relationship. He couldn't allow it to become anything else.

Unfortunately, it was easy to forget that when he looked into her compelling eyes. Determined to stick to his professional standards of behavior, he left the washroom.

Amber was waiting for him but avoided looking him in the eyes. Together, they walked out of the ER and took the elevator to the lower level of the hospital.

Stepping out, they walked without speaking down a short hallway to a wide set of double doors. Amber pushed one open to reveal a small, cozy room where a dozen round tables were covered with red-checkered tablecloths. Several Amish men sat at one of the tables near the back of the room. They glanced up, then resumed their quiet conversation.

Phillip said, "This doesn't resemble any hospital cafeteria I've eaten in and I've eaten in plenty."

"It is homey, isn't it?"

The smell of fresh-baked bread and fried chicken filled the air. A young Amish woman wearing a dark maroon dress under a white apron with a white organdy cap on her head stood behind the low counter.

Amber approached her. "Hello, Barbara."

"Hello, Amber. How's Martha Nissley doing?"

"She's still in surgery. Can we get a couple cups of coffee?"

"Sure. Have a seat anywhere and I'll bring some out."

Phillip realized he was hungry. The half sandwich he'd shared with Amber hadn't been enough to fill the void in his midsection. He pointed to a chef's salad under glass in the serving area. "Let me have one of those and give Miss Bradley anything she'd like."

"I'll take one of your wonderful cinnamon rolls, Barbara."

"Icing or no icing?"

"Are you kidding? The icing's the best part."

Phillip eyed her petite figure in surprise. "It's refreshing to meet a woman who isn't afraid of a few calories. Shoofly pie and now a cinnamon roll?"

Amber giggled. "Oh, Barbara doesn't put any calories in her rolls, do you?"

Smiling shyly, the Amish waitress shook her head. "Not a one."

While she went to get their order, Phillip led the way to a table near the back corner. As he sat down, the elder of the two Amish men approached him. Phillip recognized him as Martha's husband.

"I thank you both for your kindness to my wife today. *Gott* was *gut* to send you in her hour of need."

Phillip nodded. "You're welcome. I'm glad we were still in the office when your son arrived. He must have run like the wind."

"He wanted to help his mama. He felt bad about the accident but it wasn't his fault. Also, I want to tell you we are praying for your grandfather. He has done much for the Plain People hereabouts. We praise *Gott* for bringing him to us."

A lump rose in Phillip's throat, making it hard to speak. He had been harsh in his judgment of these people and he had been wrong. "Thank you."

Barbara arrived with their food. Mr. Nissley nodded to them and returned to his own table. After Barbara set the plates down, Amber asked her, "How is your Grandmother Zook doing? Is she taking her heart medication like she should?"

"Mammi is *gut*. She has more energy every day."

After the waitress left, Phillip watched Amber dig into her steaming roll. "Do you know everyone around here?"

"Not everyone, but many of the Amish. I delivered Barbara's two youngest sisters."

"It must be odd." He cut a hard-boiled egg in half and forked it into his mouth.

"What?"

"Knowing everybody. Having them know you."

"Why do you think that's odd?"

He shrugged. "It just is. Can I try of bite of your roll? It looks good."

"Sure." She pushed her plate toward him. When he'd cut himself a generous piece, she said, "I take it you've never lived in a small town?"

"I've lived in three or four. Just not for long."

"You moved around a lot?"

"Yes, you could say that." He couldn't count on both hands the number of schools he'd attended before his mother settled in Hawaii and he started college.

After taking a sip of coffee, Amber glanced at the large round clock on the wall behind him. "Gloria said thirty minutes. That was ten minutes ago. We should hear something soon."

He closed his eyes as he savored his sample of roll. "There are some very good cooks around here. Is it difficult working among the Amish?"

"It can be challenging. Many don't readily accept an English midwife."

Puzzled, he glanced at her. "English?"

"It's what they call anyone who isn't Amish."

"I used to think my grandfather's Amish stories were exaggerations."

She grinned at that. "Harold is a talented storyteller. I don't doubt he has embellished some things."

"The Amish really don't allow their children to go past the eighth grade in school?"

"That's true."

"It's hard to believe anyone in this day and age is opposed to higher education."

"They aren't opposed to it. They just don't want it for their children. They believe in on-the-job training for skills that will keep their family and community together. They aren't all farmers, you know. Many are successful small-business owners. Their work ethic and craftsmanship skills are second to none. Employers love to hire the Amish. They work for less and work hard."

"You sound like you approve of this."

She cocked her head to the side. "Don't you believe in freedom of religion?"

"Of course I do."

"Do you believe a person has the right to choose his own lifestyle?"

"Yes." He didn't like feeling he was in the wrong somehow.

"The Amish lifestyle *is* their religion. They do not separate the two."

Her intenseness reminded him of his mother's Pomeranian standing guard over his food dish. Phillip wasn't looking to get bitten. He'd had enough trouble for one day. "I defer to someone who knows them better than I ever will."

After they finished eating, they returned to the ER waiting area and were soon joined by Dr. Kline. Shaking hands with the big, burly man in blue scrubs, Phillip immediately had the feeling that Martha was being well taken care of.

"Good news. The spine isn't severed. A bone fragment is compressing it. That's why she can't move her legs. I've already placed a call for an airlift to Akron."

Dr. Kline continued with a description of Martha's injuries. Phillip conferred with him over some of her interim care and then left the hospital knowing she was getting the best possible treatment.

As he walked to his SUV with Amber at his side, he said, "My grandfather told me the Amish don't believe in health insurance. How are Martha and her family going to pay for her care?"

"It's true that they don't believe in insurance of any kind. If a man gets insurance, that means he doesn't have faith in God's protection. Whatever happens is God's will. On the flip side of that, they don't sue for bad outcomes. Such a thing is also *Gottes Wille*.

"As far as the Nissleys are concerned, the Church community will take up a collection for them. A notice will be sent to the Amish newspaper and donations will come from all over. Their bills will be paid."

Phillip had to admire people who cared so well for their own. While he thought they were some of the most backward people on the planet for refusing modernization, he had to admit that their sense of community was impressive.

The drive back to Hope Springs was made in silence. They were both too tired to make small talk. The only time Amber spoke was when she gave him directions to her home. It was nearly dark when he pulled up in front of her house.

She hesitated before getting out. Taking a deep breath, she said, "I'm glad you came to Hope Springs. We needed you."

"It's not the type of medicine I want to practice, but I'll admit it isn't boring."

Turning to face him, she asked, "What type of medicine do you want to practice?"

He sensed her unwillingness to leave, and it made him feel good. "I want to practice cutting-edge medicine. I want the newest and best equipment and procedures available for my patients."

"We don't have that here."

"No, but you've got mighty big horses." That coaxed a tiny smile from her. She looked beautiful in the fading light.

She acted as if she wanted to say something else. Instead, she abruptly got out. She gave a little wave and said, "Good night, Dr. White. See you on Monday."

He watched her walk inside the white, narrow, two-story Victorian and felt a sharp sense of regret. He'd missed his chance to escape her dangerous undertow. He was well and truly in for a nasty dunking. Amber Bradley was as beautiful as the sea and every bit as dangerous to his peace of mind. Shifting his SUV into reverse, he backed out of her drive, determined not to think about her the rest of the night.

He hadn't gone half a block before the memory of her last little smile slipped into his mind and stayed there.

CHAPTER SEVEN

BESIDE AMBER'S FRONT DOOR, Fluffy sat waiting to get in. She picked up the overweight white cat. "How did you get out?"

A yellow tabby darted past her feet and raced down the steps. Amber recognized Ginger, her neighbor's cat. Apparently, she had broken up a feline tryst.

Inside her house, Amber put the cat down and flipped on the kitchen light. Crossing the room, she dumped her purse on the table. Fluffy began rubbing against Amber's legs. She picked up the big cat again and cuddled him close, taking comfort from his happy, rumbling purr.

"Did you see the guy in the car? This is nuts, Fluffy. I don't understand why I'm so attracted to that man. He's standing in the way of my life's work. One minute I want to strangle him, the next minute I'm wondering what kissing him would be like. What is wrong with me?"

Putting the cat down, Amber puttered around her cheery yellow kitchen. She had only one object in mind, to get so tired that she couldn't think about Dr. Phillip White anymore. On the one hand, she was furious with him for stopping her midwife practice. On the other hand, she was honest enough to admit she was deeply drawn to him.

Why, she had no idea. Sure, he was a good physician, but she'd met plenty of those. He wasn't the best-looking man she'd ever met. Close maybe, but looks weren't everything. Phillip had more going for him. Even if he didn't understand the Amish, he seemed willing to learn. Could he learn to love this place as she did?

She banged her hands on the countertop. "Stop obsessing about him!"

Her shout startled Fluffy and sent the long-haired white cat dashing out of the room.

"Great. Now you'll be stuck behind the sofa, and I'll spend the night listening to you yowl. One more mark against the oh-so-handsome Dr. Surfer Boy," she shouted after the cat.

Fluffy's ample girth made it impossible for him to turn around and get out of his favorite hiding place. He would simply yowl until someone moved the heavy sofa away from the wall or pulled aside the even heavier bookcase that blocked one end of his tunnel.

Ignoring her cat, Amber began vigorously scrubbing her kitchen sink. Unfortunately, the exercise only took a couple of minutes. Next, she washed the kitchen floor. Another ten minutes gone. By now, Fluffy had started mewing loudly. "All right, I'm coming."

After freeing her pet, Amber glanced at the clock. It was time to call Harold. Settling herself in her favorite chair, she dialed the long-distance number.

Each day she called and got an update from Harold to share with his friends. The entire county was praying for his recovery. He was improving slowly but not as quickly as he wanted.

As she listened to the phone ring, she wondered what she could tell Harold that wouldn't upset him. Should she mention that things in Hope Springs weren't the same without him?

It was true, yet if the accident hadn't occurred, Amber never would have met Phillip.

There was no way she was going to tell Harold she might be falling for his grandson. Even a hint of that would have him planting a whole garden of celery. She had stopped counting the number of times he'd told her she needed to find a husband and raise some kids of her own.

Like it was as simple as picking out a ripe melon at a roadside produce stand.

Amber wasn't opposed to finding a man who could win her heart and soul, but she didn't want one who lived in Hawaii. She wanted someone who loved this community the way she did.

When Harold answered at last, she knew what she would do. She'd fill Harold in on the things happening in Hope Springs. That was the truth. She could only hope that he wouldn't dig deeper.

"KEEP IT ABOUT the work," Phillip muttered as he entered his grandfather's house and closed the heavy oak door behind him. Sure, Amber was cute, intelligent, quick thinking and dedicated. What was so unusual about that?

"Okay, she's the kind of woman any man would want to know better, but she's completely off-limits."

Talking to himself about it sure wasn't a good sign. With the pressures of school and setting up his practice, the only relationships he'd had in the past few years were uncomplicated. Short-term relationships where both parties wanted nothing deeper than an occasional movie date, a dinner partner or someone to go surfing with. Amber was anything but uncomplicated.

He'd ruled out taking a wife a long, long time ago. Too

many times as a kid he'd seen his mother weeping uncontrollably when her latest lover left her brokenhearted. He'd seen it often enough to know he'd never risk doing that to any woman. If his father had lived, would it have been different? He would never know.

At least his mother was happy now, or as happy as she could be. Her current husband, Michael Watson, was a good and decent man. After spending years with one toad after another, she'd finally found her prince. However, the emotional toll of her former life stayed with her. She suffered from a deep-seated fear of abandonment.

His mother met Michael when Phillip was a junior in high school. Michael provided the things she desperately longed for—safety, security, a nice home and a man who loved her. Although Phillip wasn't sure she truly loved Michael in return, she worked hard to be a good wife.

Phillip owed his stepfather a great deal. Without Michael's help, med school would have remained a pipe dream. Phillip never would have come to know God without his stepfather's gentle encouragement. That had been Michael's greatest gift, but one Phillip had let slide recently. He would remedy that while he was in Hope Springs.

He glanced at the clock above his grandfather's mantel. With the five-hour time difference, his stepfather should be getting home from work in another twenty minutes. That left Phillip enough time to check on his grandfather first.

After dialing the number to his grandfather's room in the rehab hospital in Honolulu, Phillip settled himself on the sofa and waited for Harold to pick up. When he finally did, he was anything but cordial.

"It's about time you called. How are things? I want to know what's going on."

"Things are fine. Like they were yesterday when I spoke to you. I came to Hope Springs so you would stop worrying. If you're not doing that, I might as well go home and get a little surfing in."

"And then what would become of my people?"

It was a good question. One Phillip hesitated to suggest an answer for, but he did anyway. "You could advertise for a partner or for someone to take over the practice."

"Ha! Don't you dare try to sell my practice out from under me. I'll fight you every step of the way."

"I'm not trying to sell your clinic out from under you. It's just that I've seen how much work is involved here. You're not a spring chicken anymore."

"There's a little crowing left in this old rooster. I'll be back there before you know it."

"I hope so. I really do. How's the physical therapy going?"

"They just like to torture people here. I might have fractured my skull but my mind still works."

"I can tell. What did you do today? Besides grump at the therapists." Harold chuckled. Phillip was happy to hear that sound again.

"I've been putting square pegs in round holes. I picked up numerous small objects and transferred them to different types of containers. Joy, joy. I went up three steps with my crutches but that was all I could manage. I can't seem to make my legs work right."

"Harold, that's a lot more than you could do a week ago. What did your doctor have to say?"

"He says I can't come home yet. What does he know?"

"He's one of the best in Honolulu. He knows a lot. You're making progress."

"Maybe so. It's just hard to be here and not there. Everyone writes, though. I've gotten lots of mail. So tell me, who did you see today?"

After describing the patients he'd seen in the clinic and their conditions, he recounted Martha Nissley's accident.

"Yes, Amber told me about that. It's a shame. Martha kept house for me years ago, before she was married. I don't know why some teenagers think it's fun to torment the Amish. They are such gentle people. They'd never hurt anyone. I will pray for her recovery."

"The family wouldn't make a police report."

"It's their way."

"That's what Amber told me."

There was a long pause on the line, then Harold asked, "How are the two of you getting along?"

"Fine." Phillip wasn't about to get into details when he wasn't sure what his feelings were.

"Yes, that's what Amber said, with exactly that same tone in her voice."

Phillip felt like a college freshman pumping his best friend for information about the cute girl in English class. "What did she have to say about me?"

"Nothing much."

"Oh." He hoped he didn't sound as disappointed as he felt.

"She did mention you were a nice-looking guy."

"She did?" That was promising.

"I think what she actually said was that you look a lot like me."

"Gray-haired and wrinkled? Oh, joy!" he replied with teasing sarcasm.

Harold laughed out loud. "Tell me what you think of her."

"Are you going to repeat this conversation to her?"

"Maybe."

"Then I'm not telling you a thing. Except she's a very good nurse. She's brave, incredibly foolish, stubborn to a fault and—"

"And what, Phillip?"

He searched for the right word but came up short. "I don't know. Sweet."

"She's pretty as the day is long, too. Don't you think?"

Now Phillip was sorry he'd gotten himself into this conversation. "I hadn't noticed."

The sound that came through the phone had to be a snort. "Didn't know you were thickheaded, boy."

"Okay, she's cute, but being a skilled nurse is a lot more important to me."

"She's the best midwife I've ever worked with."

Phillip decided it was best to avoid that topic. "Is there anything you need, Harold?"

"No, your stepdad has been here every day to check on me and bring me some decent food. Some of this Hawaiian stuff is good. Have you had poi?"

Phillip chuckled. "Many times."

He hesitated a moment, then asked, "Has my mother been to see you?"

"No, and she won't."

"Don't you think it's about time one of you told me what happened between you?"

A long silence followed Phillip's question. Finally, Harold said, "That's between her and me."

"It certainly affected me. We could have known each other for thirty additional years. I could have learned so much more about my father from you!" He was almost shouting as his resentment surged to the forefront.

Calmly, Harold said, "Phillip, you have to let go of your father. Nothing you learn can bring you closer to him or bring him back. All you can do is live your life for God and others and pray you will see him in heaven."

Sighing heavily, Phillip struggled to gain control of his raw emotions. It was hard to admit, but he said, "I know you're right."

"But you can't accept it."

"Not until I know why my mother kept me away from you all these years. Nothing you tell me can be worse than the things I imagine."

"I wouldn't be too sure of that. Tell Amber I'm thinking of her and hoping Sophie Knepp has an easy delivery. The poor woman has already lost two of her seven children before they turned two."

"You're changing the subject, sir."

"Yes, I am. Good night, Phillip." The line went dead.

CHAPTER EIGHT

By Sunday morning Amber had complete control of her emotions. Her feelings for Phillip were a silly infatuation and nothing more. Once she had spent a few more days working with him, this odd attraction would die a natural death. They had bonded because of their danger-filled rescue of Martha Nissley. It was a common occurrence between people in tension filled situations. Such intense emotions rarely lasted. Satisfied that she understood what was going on, she headed with light steps toward the Hope Springs Fellowship Church.

It was a beautiful summer morning. Late July could be frightfully hot in Ohio but the temperature had been mild lately. The sky was clear except for rare fleecy clouds floating past.

They reminded her of Fluffy. The cat who was most likely curled up at home asleep on Amber's blue sofa. A few white hairs on the furniture were a small price to pay for such a loving companion. Looking toward the white spire of the church silhouetted against the sky, Amber allowed the peace she always felt on this day to soak into her soul.

That peace lasted until she reached the church steps. At the top of them, Phillip stood talking to Pastor Finzer as he greeted his flock. Her hope to slip inside unnoticed was dashed when the minister caught sight of her.

"Amber, look who's joining us this morning."

She nodded in their direction and slowly climbed the steps. "Pastor, good morning. Dr. White, nice to see you."

Beaming a bright smile at the two of them, the friendly young pastor said, "We're delighted to have Dr. White as a visitor to our church while he's in town. I'm sure Amber will introduce you around, Phillip, and help you feel at home. Won't you, dear?"

"Of course." The smile on her face was fake. She hoped neither of the men realized it.

As they passed through the doors, Phillip leaned down and softly said, "Sorry about that. I know you didn't want to get stuck with me on your day off."

Was that how he was feeling? That he was stuck with her? She couldn't hide the sting of disappointment she felt. "Don't worry, Dr. White. I'll find somebody to pass you off to quickly."

"That wasn't what I meant."

Amber spied the perfect candidate sitting to the left of the aisle. Stopping beside an ample woman in a pink suit with a matching pink hat, Amber said, "Mrs. Curtis, how lovely to see you're feeling well enough to attend church today."

"Thank you, Amber dear. I struggled this morning. I don't know how I managed, but the Lord gave me strength."

"Mrs. Curtis, I'd like you to meet the new doctor in town. Dr. White, this is Gina Curtis. She's one of your grandfather's most frequent visitors."

"Dr. White, do have a seat." Gina scooted over to make room for him, her eyes bright with interest.

After he sat she said, "You know, I've been having this terrible pain in my neck. What do you think it could be? Oh, and my left heel hurts dreadfully when I stand up in the mornings. What can cause that? Your grandfather has never been able to figure out what ails me."

Amber felt a little ashamed, but if Phillip was going to be practicing in Hope Springs, he had to take the good with the bad. He might as well get his first meeting with Gina over with. She'd stop listing her ailments as soon as Pastor Finzer began the service.

Amber suspected the spinster harbored a secret crush on the good-looking blond preacher who was at least thirty years her junior.

Amber started to turn away, but Phillip grasped her wrist. "Please, sit with us."

It wasn't so much a request as a command. Unless she wanted to make a scene by twisting away from his firm grip, she had no choice. With another false smile in place, she said, "I'd be delighted."

He stood to let her in the pew. "I doubt it," he muttered as she slipped past and sat down

Gina leaned forward to look past Amber. "Isn't this cozy?"

"Very," Phillip replied, a twinkle of amusement in his eyes.

Amber took her punishment like a big girl. For the next ten minutes she listened to Gina's litany of complaints and answered the odd medical question aimed her way. Phillip got the brunt of them. Between Mrs. Curtis's painful heel, clicking knee, sciatica and the nervous twitching of her right eye that only happened during the late show, she put Phillip through his paces.

Amber glanced his way once and saw his eyes about to glaze over. Taking pity on him, Amber turned to Gina.

"How is your nephew in Cleveland getting along? Didn't he have surgery not long ago?"

"Oh, honey, you don't *even* want to know the things that went wrong for Gerald. First, they checked him into the wrong wing of the hospital."

Before Amber had to hear the entire story, Pastor Finzer entered and the congregation rose to its feet. Opening her hymnal to the first song, Amber softly joined in the singing. She couldn't carry a tune very well, but the Lord only asked for joyful noise. Phillip had no such trouble. His deep baritone rang out clear and strong.

She had been surprised to see him standing on the church steps earlier. He hadn't struck her as a religious person. The moment the thought crossed her mind she amended it. *She* wasn't being very Christian this morning.

Determined to do better, she gave her full attention to the sermon when it started. Pastor Finzer spoke eloquently on suffering for being a Christian and the prejudice that existed in their own small town.

Once or twice, well, okay, four or five times, she glanced at Phillip out of the corner of her eye. He was listening intently, not fidgeting or yawning as a few others in the congregation were doing. It warmed her heart to know he was truly listening to God's word.

Since first meeting him, she had cast Phillip in the role of a villain because his decision played havoc with her career. He wasn't a bad guy, and she owed him an apology.

When the closing hymn began, he glanced down at her and smiled. She smiled back before she could stop herself. Clearly, it was time to admit that she liked this man in spite of their professional differences.

When the service ended and they began filing out,

Amber saw her chance to separate Phillip from Mrs. Curtis when the woman stopped to compliment Pastor Finzer on his sermon. Grabbing Phillip's hand, Amber tugged him toward the corner of the building. Once they were out of sight, he pulled her to a stop.

"Miss Bradley, you should be ashamed of yourself."

"I am. I'm so sorry. She's one of our town characters."

"Remind me to look up late show twitching tomorrow so I can at least sound like I know something."

"Okay, but I warn you, it will be her left shoulder that hurts or her right thigh the next time you see her. Gina's ailments travel from one place to the next."

He nodded. "She must be lonely."

Tipping her head to the side, Amber said, "You're right. She is. Her family is gone or moved away."

"She needs a hobby or, better yet, a cause."

"A cause?"

"Yes, doing something for others helps diminish our own troubles."

"Very wise. Did Harold teach you that?"

"No, my stepfather. He got my mother involved in raising money for a women's shelter shortly after they were married."

"Sounds like a worthy cause."

"It is."

"What's your cause?" She was curious about every aspect of his life.

"Me? Getting my practice up and running and hitting the beach when I can."

Disappointed, she said, "Not very altruistic."

"Maybe I'm trying to maintain the stereotype of surfers as self-centered thrill seekers."

She raised her eyebrows. "I'm familiar with stereotyping."

Grinning, he said, "I thought you might be. If you must know, I'm on the board of a private relief agency called Surf Care. It's an agency that combats diseases inside the prime surfing areas of Indonesia."

"I've never heard of it."

"I'm not surprised. A friend of mine, a doctor named Jake Taylor, started Surf Care. Jake wanted to show our thanks to the people of Indonesia for allowing us to surf in their islands. Jake was horrified at the poverty and suffering he saw when he first traveled there. He quickly saw that ninety percent of the suffering could be prevented with simple medications."

"That's very noble of him, and of you."

"Thanks. We've been working together on the project since day one. To date, we've raised more than one million dollars for treatment teams and supplies."

He had surprised her once more. In a good way.

Tipping his head, he regarded her intently. "So what is your cause, besides mothers and babies?"

"I'm active in my Ohio midwifery chapter, and I foster animals for the local Humane Society."

"No kidding? Are you like a dog whisperer person?"

"No, I'm the woman with the food bowl."

He laughed. The masculine sound of pure joy sent a thrill straight to her heart. Still chuckling, he asked, "How many animals do you have?"

A number of other families were gathering in the area so they began walking toward a small footbridge that arched over the stream behind the church.

Amber said, "I've had as many as four. Right now I have one. A big white cat named Fluffy."

"How original." Humor danced through his voice. His smile brightened his often-stern face and made him even more attractive.

Shaking her head, Amber said, "I didn't name him. The shelter did."

"How does fostering an animal work?"

"The shelter has a limited amount of space. When they have more pets than they have room for, they send them to foster families. Sometimes they stay a week, sometimes a month, but they always go back and then to good homes."

They had reached the bridge and Amber stopped to lean on the wooden railing. The water in the small stream slipped like quicksilver over and around the stones in its race down the hillside from its birthplace in the bubbling spring that had given the town its name.

Phillip stopped beside her and leaned his forearms on the rail, too. "This is a pretty little spot."

"It's one of my favorites."

Amber kept her gaze on the water. How did he do this? How could he twist her around so easily? Each time they were together she started out annoyed with him, and for good reason. Then before long she was sharing a sandwich or cinnamon roll or her favorite spot with him and wishing their time together wouldn't end. It was perplexing in the extreme.

He turned around and leaned against the railing. "I've found some very lovely things to admire in Hope Springs."

She stared at her hands. "Now you're making fun of us. Hawaii is much more beautiful."

"Each place has its own unique beauty, just as each person does."

Surprised, she gazed up at him. "That's so true."

Their eyes locked, his darkened with emotion. "Yes. There are some very, very lovely things in Hope Springs."

He slowly lowered his head toward her. Amber knew he was going to kiss her. Her heart began to race.

CHAPTER NINE

IT COULD HAVE been the sun on her upturned face, or the wind that toyed with a few wisps of her hair at her temples that made Phillip want to kiss her. It could have been the secluded bridge with the sound of the brook babbling underneath and the smell of mossy rocks and pine needles in the air.

It could have been anything, but it wasn't just anything. It was those beautiful mermaid eyes looking up at him. Eyes a man could get lost in.

He bent toward her slowly, giving her time to realize what was happening. That was his mistake.

She leaned toward him a fraction. He sensed her willingness and tilted his head to meet her. Abruptly, she pulled back and took several steps away. A rosy blush flooded her cheeks with color.

She looked down, her hands fluttering nervously as she gestured toward the church. "I have to get going. I... I need to visit my clients today and tell them I won't be delivering their babies."

Spinning around, she hurried away from him and back up the grassy lawn toward the building.

Heaving a heartfelt sigh, he leaned against the rail again. "Phillip, old boy, you messed that up big-time."

AMBER RAN TO her car without stopping. She didn't care about the odd looks being thrown her way by the congregation members still visiting near the church steps. She had to get away.

Why had he tried to kiss her? Did he think that was what she wanted?

Okay, maybe it was. The thought of what it would be like to kiss him had entered her mind, but she was sure she'd been careful not to let on. Hadn't she? Had he seen through her pretense? Oh, please, no.

Reaching the sanctuary of her blue station wagon, Amber quickly started the engine and drove home. When she pulled into her own driveway, some of her panic started to fade. She turned off the engine and sat in the quiet car. Leaning forward, she rested her forehead against the steering wheel.

How was she going to face him again? How was she going to work with him after this? She sat back slowly and pressed her fingertips to her lips.

What *would* it be like to kiss him?

Would it have been as wonderful as she imagined? Closing her eyes, she relived those moments. The way the sunlight brought out the highlights in his hair. The way his blue eyes matched the color of the sky beyond. She'd never forget the quiet way he said, "There are some very, very lovely things in Hope Springs."

She knew by the way he was gazing at her that he wasn't talking about scenery. He'd been talking about her.

"He thinks I'm lovely." No one had ever said that before. Reaching up, she turned the rearview mirror to see her reflection. What she saw couldn't be described as beauty.

She had nice hair when she kept the curl contained. It

was a light blond color that was as common as dirt among the Amish communities. Her nose was short and turned up at the tip. A classical beauty wouldn't be caught dead with a nose like that. Her eyes were a muddle of blue and green without being either. If she had her way, she'd have dark, mysterious eyes like her friend Katie Lantz.

"Oh, skip it. I'm not lovely. He was playing with me."

Readjusting the mirror, she shook her head at her own foolishness. He was a good-looking man who found himself stuck in a tiny town with nothing to do. It was no wonder he decided to set up a flirtation to ease the boredom.

Well, she would not be his plaything. She was better than that. She would let him know the next time she saw him that he'd stepped over the line. She got out of the car and slammed the door shut.

With purposeful steps she marched toward her front door. When she reached the porch, she opened the door and saw Fluffy waiting by his food bowl. The cat let out a mournful meow. "Fluffy, you won't believe what that man tried to do today."

The cat meowed again and circled his bowl. It was clear he didn't care what was troubling his human companion. Tossing her purse on the kitchen table, Amber opened a cabinet and pulled out a can of cat food. As the opener ran, she tried to think of something scathing to say.

About what? About an almost, maybe kiss? She was more mature than that.

No. She wouldn't mention a thing to Dr. Phillip. She'd carry on as if nothing *had* happened because nothing had happened. He hadn't kissed her.

"That's right. He didn't kiss me."

As she knelt beside Fluffy's bowl, the cat rubbed against her legs.

Spooning the salmon-flavored food into the dish, Amber said, "Maybe he'd simply been leaning forward to scratch his knee, and I completely misread his intentions."

How embarrassing would it be to rake him over the coals for something he hadn't done or intended to do?

Banging the spoon against the edge of the bowl to get the last morsel out, she said, "Nothing happened and that's that."

Rising to her feet, she drew a deep breath. "Good. Now I need to let my clients know that I won't be seeing them until Harold is back or until I can change Phillip's— I mean *Dr. White's* opinion about home births. I'll go to work as usual at the office. I won't say a thing unless he says something because nothing happened."

Looking down, she said, "Do you hear me, Fluffy? Nothing happened."

The cat didn't stop eating to reply.

By Monday morning, Phillip had an adequate apology prepared and rehearsed. It had taken most of a sleepless night to compose, but he felt he'd achieved the right tone of repentance mixed with a touch of humor. Although he wasn't eager to deliver it, he found he *was* eager to see Amber again.

At eight o'clock, he left his grandfather's house and walked with quick steps the two blocks the office. As he rounded the last corner, he stopped in surprise. The parking lot in front of the office was filled with horses and buggies. A crowd of Amish people stood grouped near the front door.

Had there been some kind of epidemic outbreak to bring so many people in at once? As he walked toward the door, one elderly man with a long gray beard stepped forward and approached Phillip.

"I am Bishop Zook. May I have a word with you, Dr. White?"

"What's going on, Bishop? Are these people sick?"

"No. We've come today to ask you to reconsider your decision to stop Nurse Bradley from delivering our babies."

Phillip looked over the sea of Amish faces, both men and women, waiting for his reply. Many of the women had children at their sides or babies in their arms. None of them were smiling.

Amber had put them up to this. And to think he'd lost sleep planning to apologize for wanting to kiss her.

Shaking his head, he said, "I'm sorry, Bishop Zook. On this issue I cannot change my mind. The safest place for a woman to have a child is in the hospital."

The bishop eyed him silently for a long moment. "A high court of Pennsylvania upheld our right to have our children at home and to use midwives."

"This is Ohio, not Pennsylvania, sir."

"We are a peaceful people, Doctor. It is not our way to make trouble. Your thinking on this matter jeopardizes our way of life. We must be separate from the world, a peculiar people set apart by our faith. Home births are natural and in keeping with God's design."

"I understand and admire your religious principles, but I have principles of my own. They won't allow me to change my mind on this issue. Amber won't be delivering babies. I will. Your women will have to go to the hospital or birthing clinic in Millersburg."

"I am sorry you feel this way, Doctor. We will no longer be needing your services." Turning around, he spoke to the crowd in Pennsylvania Dutch, leaving Phillip clueless as to what he was saying. Whatever he said, it started a buzz of low conversation in return.

"What's going on here?"

Phillip spun around to see Amber standing a few feet away. "Oh, like you don't know."

"Sorry?" She stepped closer, a frown making a deep crease between her brows.

"Now you're going to try to tell me you didn't arrange this mob?"

"What are you talking about?"

He pointed to Bishop Zook. "Ask him."

"I will. I'm sure he'll at least be civil in his answers."

Walking past Phillip, she stopped beside the bishop. They spoke in low tones and in the language Phillip couldn't understand, but it was easy to see Amber was becoming upset.

Phillip crossed his arms over his chest and waited. If she hadn't arranged this, he might have thought she was pleading with the church elder. After a few more minutes, the bishop turned and walked away. One by one, the buggies drove out of the parking lot until only one man was left standing by the door. It was David Nissley, Martha's husband.

The look of indecision on his face moved Phillip to approach him. "Mr. Nissley, how is Martha?"

"Some better. She can move her legs now. Again, I wish to offer my thanks for your help that day. I say this now because I will not speak to you again." He turned away, climbed into his buggy and left.

Phillip turned to Amber. "What does he mean?"

"It has been decided that you are an outsider who seeks to disrupt their ways. They will no longer have communication with you or do business with you."

"I'm being shunned?"

Amber shook her head. "Only someone who departs from the teaching of the Amish faith is shunned. You're being avoided. I can't believe this. The Amish make up over fifty percent of our patient base."

"You can't believe this? Aren't you the one who arranged it?"

She rounded on him with a deep scowl. "Why would I arrange this?"

"Payback because I won't sign your collaborative practice agreement."

"Are you serious? You think I'd do this?"

"Did you or did you not visit your clients and tell them I stopped you from making home deliveries?"

"I did. But I didn't plan this."

They were still glaring at each other when Wilma drove in and parked her old sedan beside the front door. She got out and gave them a funny look. "What's going on?"

"I'm being shunned," Phillip said, daring Amber to correct him.

Wilma shook her head. "You can't be shunned. You aren't a member of the Amish faith."

He blew out a huff of pure frustration. "Okay, I'm being avoided."

Wilma looked at Amber. "For real?"

Nodding, Amber said, "For real."

"That's not good." Wilma pressed her hands to her face. "That's *really* not good. The Amish are half our patients. We aren't going to be able to make our expenses if they stop coming to the clinic. We're barely making it as it is. Why, we could be broke in a matter of weeks."

Phillip walked over and laid a hand on her shoulder. "Don't panic, Wilma. I'm sure this is a bluff on their part. People can't do without medical care."

Amber walked past them, shaking her head. "You underestimate the Amish, Dr. Phillip. Word will spread and the Amish will stop coming here. They've resisted changes that threaten their way of life for hundreds of years. They aren't going to make an exception for you."

Normally shy Wilma surprised Phillip when she shook off his hand and shouted at him, "You're trying to shut this place down, aren't you? Is that what you want? Well, you might get it. Then see how proud Harold is of you."

CHAPTER TEN

WHEN AMBER ARRIVED at the clinic the following morning, the walkway was lined with Amish women, most of them her clients. Almost all of them had their children with them. Katie Lantz stepped forward. She held her four-month-old daughter in her arms.

Katie said, "We have come to show our support for you. Dr. White must allow you to continue your work among us. It is God's will."

Amber's hopes that Phillip hadn't arrived yet were dashed. She glanced toward the clinic and saw him staring out the window in her direction. His usual frown was back in place.

Turning to Katie, Amber reached out to touch Rachel's little bare feet where they stuck out of her blanket. "*Danki*, Katie."

Mary Yutzi, Katie's future sister-in-law, patted her round stomach. "We know you have a good place in your heart for our babies."

Another woman said, "You have done so much for us, Amber. We wish to give back."

Although she didn't know if their tactics were helping or hurting, Amber was deeply moved by their support. Tears stung her eyes. Glancing around at the women, she said, "My thanks to each of you. I can't tell you what this means to me."

After delivering their promises of prayers and well wishes, the women left and Amber walked inside. Phillip, black coffee mug in hand, was still standing by the window.

He said, "You have a lot of friends."

"Yes, I do."

"Another group was waiting outside my house this morning. They gave me copies of the Pennsylvania court decision allowing their midwife to continue practicing in that state."

"It was a huge victory for their way of life. Many hundreds of Amish showed up on the courthouse steps in support of the midwife on trial."

"For practicing medicine without a license, I believe."

"Yes, but the court ruled—"

He threw up his hands. "I know how the court ruled. You still claim you had nothing to do with these assemblies?"

Fisting her hands on her hips, Amber shouted, "I did not arrange this! What part of that don't you understand?"

Shocked, he took a step back. "Isn't this out of character for the quiet and simple Plain People?"

Crossing her arms, she reined in her anger and tried to sound reasonable. "Not really. When something threatens their teachings or way of life, they are willing to take peaceful action. When the states tried to make them send their children to high school, many were jailed for refusing to comply. They took their case all the way to the U.S. Supreme Court and won."

Phillip took a sip of his coffee. Then without another word, he walked back to his office and shut the door.

Amber had no idea if he believed her claim or not.

By Friday afternoon, Amber knew the boycott of the clinic had become the talk of the town. Several non-Amish patients canceled their appointments to show their support of their neighbors.

None of the merchants in town wanted to upset the Amish by taking Phillip's side. Most employed Amish men and women and many of their businesses depended on either the Amish themselves or the tourists who came to see them.

Even the mayor made a visit to Phillip asking him to reconsider. He stressed how the Amish were good for tourism and how tourism was good for the entire community. As far as Amber could see, Phillip remained unmoved.

Reluctantly, Amber admired the way he stuck to his principles in the face of so much pressure.

By late afternoon on Friday, the one patient that showed up was Gina Curtis. After taking her vital signs, Amber listened to her describe her usual recurring, traveling pains and made a few quick notes on her chart. Phillip was waiting outside the door when she left the room. She didn't speak to him as she handed over the chart.

Still annoyed over the fact that he believed she had set up the confrontation with the Amish, she tried her best to ignore him. Seating herself on the corner of Wilma's desk, she noticed that Wilma's long face matched her mood.

"How tight are the expenses, Wilma?"

"We've had very little income since Harold left. Our checking account is almost empty."

"But the business has a reserve fund, doesn't it?"

"Only enough to run the place for another month. You know how Harold is about his charities."

"He'd give away the shoes off his feet."

"And his smelly socks, too." Wilma leaned forward. Worry set deep creases between her eyebrows. "What are we going to do?"

It was the same question that had been keeping Amber up at night. She gave Wilma the only answer she had. "We're going to pray and we're going to hold on until Harold gets back."

"What if he doesn't come back?"

"He has to. He just has to."

Amber heard the exam room door open and stood up.

Phillip came down the hall with a look of deep concentration on his face. "I want to set up an appointment for Mrs. Curtis with a rheumatologist. Is there one Harold normally uses?"

"Dr. Abe Snider in Akron," Amber said.

"Fine. See how soon they can get Mrs. Curtis in."

He started to turn away but Amber wanted more of an explanation. "Why are you sending Gina to a rheumatologist?"

He stopped and looked over his shoulder. "Because I suspect she has fibromyalgia. I think she's been dismissed as a crackpot for years instead of getting the workup she deserves."

Amber stared at him, aghast. "Are you insinuating your grandfather inadequately treated one of his patients? How dare you. Harold loves the people of this town. He'd do anything for them."

Phillip stared at the chart in his hands for a long moment, then looked at her. "I'm not insinuating anything. I'm flat-out telling you. This woman has the symptoms of a real disease and she's been left untreated. Because she complains a lot doesn't mean she isn't sick."

Amber was speechless. Phillip handed her the chart. "I've ordered lab work, and I'm starting her on some medication for her pain."

Turning to Wilma, he said, "I want to see Gina back in three weeks to assess if the medication helps her. Please put her on the schedule."

With that, he walked away and left Amber staring openmouthed behind him.

"Harold is a fine doctor," Wilma stated emphatically. "He's been the salvation of this town for more than thirty years."

Still staring down the hall, Amber replied quietly, "Our only salvation is the Lord."

"You know what I mean."

"I do, Wilma. I'm going to be in my office for a while. Call me if you need anything."

Walking down the hall, Amber paused outside the exam room door. She heard muffled voices but she couldn't make out what they were saying. Turning aside, she entered her office and sat at her computer.

For the next thirty minutes, she did an extensive search for information on fibromyalgia. After reading through the literature and surfing the websites, she conceded Phillip might be right.

Some of the stories from patients were heartwrenching. Many had been ignored by their physicians and made to feel like they were crazy or simply attention seekers. After proper treatment many had drastically improved lives.

Turning off her computer, Amber sat with her chin in her hand and her elbow on the desktop. Surely Harold had done a proper workup on Gina Curtis before deciding she was a hypochondriac. Amber thought back over the years the woman had been coming to the clinic and couldn't recall one.

Had Harold been negligent? As hard as that was to accept, the idea stuck in Amber's mind and couldn't be dislodged. She idolized Harold. To know that he might have let Gina suffer all this time was enough to make her feel sick to her stomach. She rose from her desk and walked down the hall to Phillip's office.

His door was open. He was seated at the desk studying a spreadsheet on Harold's computer and making notes. He glanced up as she entered.

Looking around, she said, "I see you've made some inroads in taming the disorder."

Waving to the stack of folders on the corner of the desk, he shook his head. "I've still got a long way to go."

Picking up a journal that had fallen to the floor, Amber rolled it into a tight cone. "You know Harold will complain for months that he can't find anything."

"Then we will be even. I can't find anything in here now."

She walked over and sat in the chair across from him. "Have you had an update on Martha Nissley?"

"They were able to repair the fractured spine and she has recovered some use of her legs."

Amber chewed the corner of her lip, then asked, "Do you think Harold blew off Gina's symptoms?"

Phillip rubbed his forehead. "I don't know. I can't find evidence that he sent her for a workup, and Gina says she's only seen Harold. Ignoring complaints from people with this disease is more common that you think because of the vague and changing symptoms they have."

"So I've learned as I've been reading. I feel horrible about this."

Leaning back in his chair, Phillip gazed at her intently. "I'm not saying you and Harold are entirely to blame. These textbooks must be more than twenty years old. Many of the journals look like they've never been opened. I can't tell if he's done any online research."

Unrolling the journal in her hand, she stared at the cover. "He hates using the computer. He told me he'd rather have real paper in his hands. There were never enough hours in the day to catch up on his reading."

"I'm sure there weren't. From what I've seen of this practice, I can't imagine how a seventy-five-year-old man could manage it by himself."

Rolling his eyes, he gave her a half smile. "This week being the exception, of course. Has Harold ever tried to get a partner?"

"We had a young resident drop in last year and ask about joining us but Harold turned him down."

"Do you know why?"

Shrugging, she said, "I assumed Harold didn't think there was enough work for the both of them."

"That might be true now."

Amber gritted her teeth and decided it was best to get it out in the open. "When I said I had nothing to do with the meeting Monday, that may not have been the entire truth."

His eyebrows rose. "Oh?"

"I didn't organize it, but I may know who did. I have a friend, an Amish woman whose baby I delivered a few months ago. She told me she thought she could help by bringing it to the attention of the Church elders."

"And you didn't try to dissuade her?"

"I don't remember the exact conversation. I don't believe I encouraged her. She may have seen it differently."

He waved aside her confession. "What's done is done. My intention was to keep my grandfather's practice going in the event that he could return." He tapped the computer screen. "It looks like I may run it into the ground instead."

Leaning closer to see what he was pointing out, she asked, "What is that?"

"Harold's financial records."

"He did his financials on the computer? That's surprising."

"Wilma does them for him. I nearly had to threaten her with bodily harm to get the password."

"I can imagine. Is it as bad as she says?"

"It is. Harold has taken out a large bank loan using this place as collateral."

Amber was stunned. "Why?"

"It appears he bought a fifty-one percent interest in the Wadler Inn."

"He owns part of the inn? He never mentioned that. I know he takes most of his meals at the café. He likes their cooking. When did he do this?"

"Five years ago."

"Five years ago was when Mrs. Wadler's husband died."

"Maybe he was trying to help out an old friend's widow. Anyway, the loan payment is what's hurting us the most."

Tapping the desk lightly with her journal, Amber gathered her courage and said, "I know this must sound like blackmail, but if you'd allow me to resume my deliveries it would solve a lot of problems."

He sent her a sidelong glance. "You're right. It does sound like blackmail."

Her shoulders drooped. "You don't know how important this is to them."

There had to be some way to make him understand.

CHAPTER ELEVEN

As Phillip stared at Amber, she suddenly jumped to her feet. "We need to take a trip."

"We do?" What was she up to now?

"Yes, we do. You need to meet someone who can tell you what being Amish really means." There was new excitement in her voice.

"I think I already know," he replied drily.

"No, you don't. You've been on the outside looking in. We're going to take a drive to an Amish farm about thirty-five miles from here."

"Won't they shun me, too?"

"They're not from the same church district as the Amish in this area. When I explain why we've come, they'll be happy to educate you."

"What if we get a patient in?"

"Wilma can call us and we'll be back in forty minutes or less."

This was a waste of time. "I don't see what good it will do. I'm not going to change my mind."

Crossing her arms, she gave him a challenging stare. "Okay, then why not come with me? What have you got to lose? The Plain People mean a great deal to your grandfather. Why not learn why?"

Phillip stared at her thoughtfully. What *did* his grandfather see in these people? Why had he chosen to remain here instead of living near Phillip and making up for thirty-four years of lost time with his only living relative?

Maybe Amber was right. Maybe it would be worthwhile to understand them better.

If his stepfather were here, Michael would be telling him to keep his heart open to God's whispering. Perhaps this was one of those times.

"Okay. I'm game," he admitted slowly.

Within ten minutes they were traveling northeast on a winding rural highway in Amber's beat-up station wagon. As they left the town limits, they had to slow down for an open-topped buggy. The high-stepping horse pulling it looked like a thoroughbred trotter.

When the opportunity arose, Amber pulled out and passed the buggy. Phillip said, "That animal looks more like a racehorse than a farm horse."

"He may have been on the track at one time. The Amish frequently buy trotters and pacers who can't make the grade on the racetracks. They've already been trained to pull racing carts. It's a short step to teaching them to pull the family buggy. The one we just passed most likely belongs to a young man of courting age. A high stepper and an open buggy are cool."

"The Amish version of a sports car?"

"Sort of." She smiled at him and he relaxed.

Glancing covertly at Amber as she drove, Phillip realized their on-again, off-again battle was starting to take its toll on him. He was friendless in a strange land. Amber was the one person he'd met that he wanted to count as a friend—and perhaps even something more.

They continued down the highway, slowing occasionally to follow behind a buggy or horse-drawn cart until it was safe to pass. Outside his window he saw farm after farm dotting the rolling landscape of fields and pastures. For the most part, the houses were white and the barns were red. It was easy to tell which farms belonged to the Amish. The lack of power and phone lines was a dead giveaway.

After traveling in silence for a quarter of an hour, he turned in the seat to face her. "What should I know about the Amish?"

"Wow, there is so much it's hard to know where to begin. They immigrated to this country, mostly from Germany and Switzerland in the seventeen hundreds to avoid religious persecution."

"I thought they were Dutch."

"Because their language is called Pennsylvania Dutch?"

"That might lead a person to believe they came from Holland."

"The common explanation was that they were known as the Pennsylvania *Deutsch*, or 'German,' and that the word *Deutsch* morphed into Dutch over time. What they speak is a form of German."

"You speak it, too."

"It was spoken in my home when I was growing up."

"Was it hard growing up in an Amish community not being Amish?"

"Not really. Like most kids I accepted my home life as normal. I knew I dressed differently than my cousins and that I went to a different school. That didn't matter when we were playing together."

"Makes sense."

"Back to your history lesson. In nineteen hundred there were about five thousand Amish in America and Canada. Currently, there are over two hundred thousand.

Ohio and Pennsylvania have the largest settlements. We have about three hundred seventy-five church districts among the dozen or so different types of Amish."

Intrigued in spite of himself, Phillip asked, "What do you mean different types? Aren't they all one religion?"

"Yes and no. They range from ultraconservative like the Swartzentrubers who live without gas, electricity or indoor plumbing and don't even allow cushioned chairs in their homes, to the Beachy Amish. They use electricity and drive cars. However, the cars must be black. They paint the chrome bumpers black so they don't appear 'fancy' or worldly."

"You're kidding, right?"

"Nope. If you're Amish and you must use a computer for your business and your church group doesn't allow it, you can join a more progressive group."

"Do they switch?"

"Not very often. Okay, here we are." She slowed the car, turned onto a gravel lane and drove up to a large, rambling white farmhouse.

An elderly Amish woman sat on a rocker on the front porch surrounded by three young girls of varying ages. They all had large pans in their laps.

The woman's face brightened into a big smile when Amber got out of the car. Putting her pan aside, she held out her hands. Amber raced up the steps and sank to her knees beside the woman. "Hello, *Mammi*."

"My English granddaughter finds time to visit me at last. I thought I was going to have to get a driver to take me into Hope Springs to look for you."

Phillip walked around the hood of Amber's car and stood beside the steps.

Amber laid her hand on her grandmother's arm. "I'm sorry. I will come more often, I promise."

"You must not forget us while you are out in the English world. Who have you brought with you? Your young man perhaps?" She eyed Phillip hopefully. He knew his face had to be turning red.

Amber giggled like a schoolgirl. The sound was adorable. "No, *Mammi*, don't go planting extra celery for me. This is Dr. Phillip White. We work together. Phillip, this is my grandmother, Betsy Fisher."

Betsy studied him with interest. "I thought your doctor was old, like me."

"This is his grandson."

Phillip stepped forward. "How do you do, madam? It's a pleasure to meet you."

"You will stay to supper, *ja*?"

"Unless we get called back for an emergency, I'd love to. I'm finding Amish cooking is full of hidden delights."

"*Gut!* Amber, your *Tante* and *Onkel* should be home soon. They've gone to market."

Amber glanced from Phillip to her grandmother. "I've brought Phillip here today so you can talk to him about Amish ways."

Betsy's eyes brightened. "What is it about our ways that you would like to know?"

"Many things."

She spoke in German to the young girls who were watching the adults intently. The girls set their pans on the floor and went into the house.

Betsy looked at Amber for a few seconds, then said, "Go and help your nieces prepare supper, Amber. They have many questions for you about living in the English world."

"Yes, *Mammi*." Rising, Amber kissed her grandmother's cheek, then followed the younger girls into the house.

Turning her sharp gaze back to Phillip, Betsy scrutinized him long enough to make him squirm. Finally, she patted the chair beside her. When he sat down, she handed him a pan. "Have you snapped beans before?"

"No, but I'm a fast learner."

She chuckled warmly. "A man willing to learn a woman's task is a man I like. Ask your questions, Phillip."

CHAPTER TWELVE

AMBER VISITED WITH her young cousins in the spacious kitchen but kept an eye on Phillip and her grandmother through the big window overlooking the porch. Could her grandmother make him understand that the Amish weren't some strange cult but simply Christians that didn't separate their everyday lives from their faith?

She glanced at her watch. They had been out there for almost thirty minutes.

Taking a sip of tea that had been made for her, Amber blew out a long breath. If her grandmother couldn't make Phillip see how important having a home birth was for an Amish woman, Amber didn't know who could. She glanced out the window again and saw the rocker was empty. Her grandmother and Phillip were nowhere in sight.

"Is he your *boo-friend*?" Lilly, the youngest cousin asked.

Turning her attention back to the three girls ranging in age from seven to twelve who were seated around the table with her, Amber shook her head. "No. He is most definitely not my boyfriend."

The girls were like stair-step carbon copies of each other with blond hair, inquisitive blue eyes and ready smiles for the English cousin they rarely saw.

"Mammi Fisher fears you will become *en alt maedel.*

Will you?" Ruth, at twelve, was in charge of her younger sisters while their parents and brothers were gone.

Amber summoned a smile. Trust kids to ask the most embarrassing questions. "If I find the right man, I'll get married someday."

"Are there no good English men? My friend Kara's *dat* needs a new wife. Kara's *mamm* died last year. Kara has only four brothers and sisters." Ruth looked hopeful.

"Please tell Kara I'm sorry for her loss but I'm not interested in getting married right now. Besides, I'm not Amish. Kara's *dat* would not marry me."

"Mammi says you could be Amish if *Gott* wished it." Rhoda, the nine-year-old, left the table to check on the roast simmering in the oven. The mouthwatering smells of perfectly seasoned beef with roasting carrots and onions filled the kitchen and set Amber's stomach rumbling.

She said, "I believe I'm following the path He has chosen for me."

The door opened and Betsy came in, followed by Phillip. He had three large pans full of snapped beans stacked in his arms. Amber jumped up to help him by taking one. "This is the trouble with visiting my family. They find work for everyone."

"I don't mind. I can add bean snapper to my résumé now." He was smiling and seemed less tense than he'd been at the start of this journey.

After helping him set his burdens on the counter, Amber showed him where to wash up, then waited for him in the living room.

When he returned, she gestured to an empty chair. "Was my grandmother able to answer your questions?"

"She's a very wise woman. Do you know she is worried about you? She wishes you lived closer to home so she could see you more often." There was a touch of longing in his voice that Amber didn't understand.

"I know she worries about me. She doesn't understand I have my work and I love what I do. The Amish view being a wife, a mother and a helpmate to her husband as the only roles for women. Has she helped you see how important my work is?"

"She gave me a lot to think about."

The sound of a buggy coming into the yard sent the girls scurrying outside to help. Amber and Phillip were soon engulfed in introductions as she presented her mother's youngest sister, Maryanne, and her stoic husband, Tobias. While he and his two teenage boys stayed to visit with Phillip, it was easy to see they weren't entirely comfortable with an outsider in their home. When the conversation lagged, Amber leaned over and whispered to Phillip, "Do you like baseball?"

He gave a slight nod.

"So does Tobias," she said with a nod in his direction.

Giving her a thankful wink, Phillip straightened on the sofa and asked, "How do you think the Cleveland Indians will do this year?"

Tobias's face turned bright red. His oldest son sat forward in his chair. "Their pitching staff is deep and they can field a ball. I think they'll do well this year."

"Nee." Tobias shook his head. "They've got good hitters but no consistency."

The conversation quickly turned to local Amish teams and then to the sport Phillip enjoyed. He tried to explain surfing, but it was clear the idea of zipping along in front of a wave on a long board seemed silly to these stoic men. Fortunately, Maryanne came in to announce that supper was ready.

When everyone was seated in the kitchen, Tobias clasped his hands together at the head of the table. The entire family did the same and closed their eyes for his silent blessing over the meal.

He cleared his throat when he was finished. It signaled everyone to begin serving themselves and passing the food to their guests.

For Amber, watching Phillip enjoy her family's home cooking made the trip worthwhile. The roast, fork-tender, was done to perfection, as were the warm dinner rolls served with homemade strawberry jam and fresh butter.

Phillip sat beside Lilly. She watched his every move with wide eyes, especially when he began laying a few of his string beans aside at the edge of his plate. After careful examination of each bean, he chose to eat some and save some. Finally, it was too much for her.

"What are you doing? Are de beans *faul*?" Lilly eyed her own critically.

"Bad," Amber translated.

Pointing to his stack with his fork, Phillip said, "These are my friends. I met them today when I was snapping with your grandmother."

A few chuckles came from the adults at the table, including Amber.

Lilly looked at him in disbelief. "You can't be friends with a bean."

"I can't?"

"*Nee*, and you can't tell 'em apart, neither."

"Are you sure?" He picked up one. "This looks an awful lot like one I snapped today."

"I'm sure."

Phillip tossed the bean in his mouth. "Well, he tastes good, even if he was my buddy."

Lilly put her hands on her hips. "Are you funning me?"

Smiling, he nodded. "*Ja*, just a little."

Lilly looked at her papa. *"Der Englischer ist ab im kopf."*

That made everyone laugh. Amber, seated across from Phillip, explained. "She said you are off in the head. Crazy."

Phillip laughed, too.

When the meal was nearing its end, Betsy brought an applesauce cake to the table. Phillip held up his hand. "It smells wonderful, but I'm too full. Thank you, no."

Cutting a slice, she placed it on his plate. "You must try this. It is my special recipe."

Sighing, he lifted his fork and took one small bite. His eyes grew as round as silver dollars. Swallowing, he said, "This is the best stuff I've ever had."

Seeing her grandmother's delight, Amber was glad she had talked Phillip into coming here.

Later on the way back to Hope Springs, they traveled in companionable silence, both too stuffed to need conversation. The setting sun painted the sky with bands of gold and turned the bottom of the clouds a beautiful pink. When they passed a small cornfield, a flock of black birds rose in unison and wheeled across the sky, circling back and coming to rest again in the place they'd left.

Amber watched them settle in her rearview mirror and knew she was like those birds. No matter where she traveled in life, she would always come back to this place. It saddened her to think that Phillip would be flying away and might never return.

As they were nearing the outskirts of Hope Springs, he said, "I had a wonderful time today."

"I'm glad."

"Meeting your family has changed my perception of the Amish in many ways."

"For the better or for the worse?"

"For the better. But I haven't figured out one thing."

"What?"

"Without TV or radio, how do they keep up on the baseball scores?"

Amber started giggling. "The Amish do love baseball. You'll find games being played in all the districts during the summer. While interest in such worldly things is forbidden, you can find many of the young boys gathered around a radio in someone's store when a professional game is on, with the occasional elder shopping near by. The local newspapers have a sports section for those not willing to risk the censure."

"Ah."

"Dr. White—"

"Please, call me Phillip."

"Very well, Phillip."

"I know what you're going to ask. I'm afraid the answer is still no."

Deflated, Amber didn't know how to respond. She was out of arguments. Driving into the clinic parking lot, she stopped the car and turned toward him. "I'm still glad you enjoyed your visit with my family."

"They have a special charm, don't they? Not only your family but all the Amish. They coexist peacefully in a world that is anything but peaceful. They turn their backs on the basic modern inventions most Americans can't live without, yet they thrive and are happy in their small world."

"Everything they do, everything in their daily lives, is a direct reflection of how they interpret the Bible."

"It's very thought-provoking. Your grandmother's explanation for why they don't use electricity made a lot of sense."

"I imagine she said if electricity comes to a house then all sorts of things come with it, things that pull a family apart. Instead of spending the evening together, they turn on the TV and tune out what is happening around them. Another person may go away to listen to the radio or use a computer. Still another chats on the phone instead of with the family."

"Right, and before long it isn't a family anymore. It has become a group of strangers living in the same house. I've seen the truth of that in my own life, but I still couldn't live the way the Amish do."

"Nor could I, but my respect for their culture is bone-deep."

After a long pause, he said, "I see you inherited your wisdom and strength from your grandmother."

Looking down, Amber shook her head. "I'm not sure I have wisdom, but I do have stubbornness."

"I've noticed, but you are passionate, too, in your defense of these people. I think that's a rare thing."

His soft tone made her look up. When she did, he reached out and gently touched her cheek. "Thanks for a great evening."

Blushing, she shrugged. "And I didn't even have to cook."

Don't get sappy. Don't read more into his touch. Don't think about kissing him. He's your boss.

Looking away, she noticed a light still on in the clinic. "Wilma must be working late."

He withdrew his hand. "Does she do that often?"

"Once a month or so she stays late to catch up on filing and to get old charts ready to be shipped to the storage facility."

"Maybe we should give her a hand after goofing off most of the day."

"Maybe we should." Anything to escape the close intimacy of sitting in the car with him. The scent of his sandalwood cologne stirred her, making her anxious to get away.

Quickly, she pushed open the car door and got out. As she headed for the clinic, he fell into step beside her. When they entered, they found Wilma sealing several cardboard boxes with packing tape. Her disapproval when she caught sight of them was all too easy to read.

Amber felt like a teenager who'd been caught coming home after curfew.

Phillip didn't look troubled in the least. Glancing at the files stacked on her desk and the number of boxes, he said, "I didn't know you had this much work to do. You shouldn't have to work late."

"I've been managing this office for thirty-four years. Your grandfather never complained about my working late."

"I'm not complaining. I hate to see you doing this by yourself. You should have called us to come back."

"Then you should keep your cell phone turned on."

"What?" Reaching for the phone in his pocket, he lifted it up to the light. "It's dead. Wilma, I'm so sorry. Did we have patients? You should have gotten me by calling Amber."

"No patients, just phone calls."

As if on cue, the telephone on the desk rang. She answered it, spoke briefly, then held it out toward Phillip. "It's your grandfather. Again. And he's not happy."

CHAPTER THIRTEEN

PHILLIP PICKED UP the phone. "Harold, is something wrong?"

"I'll say there is! What on earth do you think you're doing, running my practice into the ground?"

Phillip held the phone away from his ear until the shouting decreased in volume. It was then he caught Wilma's self-satisfied smirk. When she realized he was staring at her, she began working industriously.

Speaking into the phone once more, Phillip said, "Harold, I'd rather have this conversation in my office. I'm going to put you on hold."

Some muttering started. Phillip ignored it and pushed the button. Amber moved to stand beside him, a look of worry clouding her eyes. "Is he all right?"

"Once he's finished reading me the riot act, I think he will be."

"Do you think he's heard about the Amish avoiding us?"

"That would be my guess. Go home, both of you. I'll lock up."

"But I have work to finish," Wilma said.

He scowled in her direction. "It can wait."

"Very well." Rolling her eyes, she gathered her purse and headed for the front door.

His annoyance faded as he transferred his gaze to Amber. "You go home, too. I can handle this."

"Are you sure?"

He wasn't. He wanted her to stay. He wanted her help in calming Harold. He just wanted her near him.

For a moment, he wavered, but in the end realized this trouble was of his own making. His principles were under fire. He was the one who needed to face the music.

"Go on home, Amber. I'll be fine."

AMBER LEFT THE building reluctantly. Looking over her shoulder, she said, "I hope Harold isn't too upset."

"Oh, he is." Wilma confirmed Amber's fears.

"You talked to him?"

"Yes. Someone had let him know how things were being handled here. I spoke the truth when he asked me about it."

"You told him we were being boycotted? Why would you do that? You know he needs to rest and recuperate."

Wilma dismissed Amber's concern with a wave of her hand. "Harold already knew. I just wish Surfer Dude Doc had never found Harold. Things were fine the way they were. Don't worry, Amber. I have a feeling you'll be seeing patients again in no time."

Wilma got into her car and drove off, leaving Amber staring after her. Torn between leaving and staying to hear what Phillip had to say, Amber decided it was best to go home. Phillip and Harold deserved their privacy. She drove back to her house with a million questions swirling through her brain.

When she reached home, the cat greeted her at the door. As usual, Fluffy was more interested in his bowl being filled than granting affection. Keeping his mistress company went by the wayside when there was kibble available. When his belly was full, he'd be all about purring and wanting attention.

Tossing her handbag on the dining room table, Amber checked her message machine. It showed a big fat zero. It seemed she wasn't as popular as Dr. White.

In the kitchen, she put the kettle on and grabbed a box of tea from the cupboard. She was pouring the hot water into her cup when her doorbell rang.

When she opened the door, she saw Phillip standing on her steps. In her heart, she had been hoping he would come.

Looking tired and frustrated, he said, "I didn't know where else to go."

She took a step back. "Come in. I just made some chamomile tea. Would you like some?"

"Sounds great, thank you." He followed her into the kitchen and took a seat on one of the bistro chairs at her small round glass table near the bay window.

Fluffy came over to investigate the new visitor. Purring loudly, he wound in and around Phillip's ankles. Phillip picked him up and scratched behind his ears, a maneuver Fluffy loved.

"If he bothers you I can put him up." Amber fixed Phillip his tea and carried it to him.

"No, I like cats. Is this the well-named Fluffy?"

"It is. Of all the animals I've fostered, I like him the best."

Handing Phillip his cup, she sat down opposite him. "What did Harold have to say?"

Phillip put Fluffy on the floor. "The gist was that if I can't run his clinic any better than this, I need to go back where I belong."

"That was harsh and not like Harold."

Propping his elbows on the table, Phillip said, "I spoke to his primary doctor after Harold hung up on me. His doctor says he's been improving rapidly when he isn't worried about his patients here. His doctor and I are both afraid this may trigger a setback."

"Oh, no. I was worried about that, too."

"So you weren't the person who called and updated him on our troubles."

Scowling, she retorted, "No."

"I didn't think so."

Somewhat mollified, Amber said, "It wasn't Wilma, either."

"Rats. She was at the top of my list."

"It doesn't matter who called him."

"Maybe not, but I'd like to find out who it was."

"If you leave, we'll go under anyway."

"It seems we can't stay afloat with or without me. I came here to help my grandfather. I owed him that much. I'm even beginning to understand why he feels so protective of these people, why he loves the simplicity and peaceful lives they lead. But instead of helping him out, I've made things worse."

She wanted to take Phillip's hand, to reach out and hold him and offer him comfort, but she didn't dare. She had no idea where such a move would lead. Her attraction to this man was simply too strong. The last thing she wanted was for him to find out how she felt.

After taking a sip of her tea, she asked, "What are your plans? Will you leave?"

"That may depend on you."

Taken aback, she frowned. "What do you mean?"

He hesitated and suddenly she knew. Happiness

surged through her veins. "You're going to sign a collaborative practice agreement with me."

"Yes, but before you start doing the happy dance, I've got a few restrictions."

Her scowl came back. "Such as?"

"I'll allow home births as long as I'm in attendance. If I'm going to be ultimately responsible for these women and their babies, I want to be there."

This was the last thing she expected. "Let me get this straight; I can do home deliveries, but you have to be there?"

"Yes."

"What about my prenatal and postnatal visits, the birthing classes I hold here and my seeing women at the clinic?"

"All those things can continue. After every delivery, I want to see both mother and baby at the clinic within two days."

"Harold liked to see them at two weeks unless there were problems. Remember, these women have to come by horse and buggy, not in a comfortable car."

"All right, I'll compromise and say one week."

Rising, she carried her cup to the sink and poured out her tea. "What makes you think you're more capable of delivering a baby than I am?"

"I'm an MD."

Spinning around, she glared at him. "How many babies have you delivered?"

"Fifty-four."

"Fifty-four compared to my five hundred and two. You're asking me to give up my autonomy, to project the image that I can't do my job. Why would I want you tagging along?"

"So that you *can* do your job. Being a midwife is what you love, isn't it? I'm offering you the opportunity to get back to it."

Crossing her arms, she leaned back against the sink. "*Will* you let me do my job? Or will you interfere if you see something you don't like?"

"You can do your thing as long as no lives are endangered. If we can't agree on this, it won't matter anyway."

He was right. Amber considered her options. If she didn't work with Phillip, she would remain out of business until Harold returned. *If* he returned.

She had to admit she'd known for some time that Harold needed a partner. He was getting on in years. Finding another doctor who allowed home deliveries would take time. Time she would not have if the clinic went under.

Staring at the tips of her shoes, she said, "Dr. White, I accept your proposal under one condition."

"What's that?"

She looked up. "That you begin searching for someone to take over the practice in the event Harold can't return."

"I've been doing that."

"I don't mean temporary help."

"You mean someone with the same Amish-friendly philosophy that Harold has?"

"Yes."

"I can't guarantee we can find someone or that he or she will permit home deliveries."

"I'll face that when I come to it. This town needs a full-time doctor."

They were both silent for several long seconds. Amber suspected they were thinking the same thing. She asked, "Shall we arm wrestle to see who gets to mention this to Harold?"

A touch of humor glinted in Phillip's eyes. "I'm good with that."

"I was kidding."

"I'm not."

She leveled her most serious gaze at him. "Your mission, Dr. White, should you accept it, is to convince your grandfather that he needs a partner."

"Will this message self-destruct in five seconds?"

"No. I will be here to remind you constantly that God never gives us more than we can bear." A smile tugged at the corner of her lips.

"I still think the suggestion would be better coming from you."

"No."

He crossed his arms. "From both of us then."

"Maybe, but you first," she insisted.

Rolling his eyes, he said, "I've already mentioned something like that once."

"And how did that go over?" she asked with interest.

He shook his head. "Not well."

Her smile vanished. "You'll simply have to keep after him. If he doesn't agree, our clinic could be without a doctor in a few more years. I pray that doesn't happen for a long time, but I have to be practical."

"I'm not sure you know what you're asking me to do."

CHAPTER FOURTEEN

PHILLIP KNEW AMBER was right. Harold needed to start looking for a partner or someone to replace him. Since their last conversation on the subject ended with Phillip accidentally running Harold down with his car, he wasn't eager to broach that subject again. His relationship with his grandfather was tenuous at best. It might not survive many more blowups. And he wanted it to survive.

Amber said, "If you are going to be seeing my patients, you need to get up to speed on their cases. I'll get their files for you."

He hated giving in on this. He'd hate himself more if Harold had a serious setback following his angry outburst tonight. It had never been Phillip's intention to ruin Harold's health, his business or his standing in the Amish community. Yet in the past month he had accomplished just that.

Coming out of her office, Amber handed Phillip a heavy box. "If you look at my outcomes, you'll see how safe giving birth at home is for low-risk pregnancies."

He shook his head. The woman did not give up. "You've won. What more do you want? Is that everything?" He gestured toward the box.

"Yes, even those patients I sent to the hospital because of complications. What I want is for you to accept what

I do. Wait a minute. Before you leave, let me get a few other things for you."

She sat down at her desk and booted up her computer. A few minutes of searching gave her a dozen articles in favor of home deliveries with qualified nurse-midwives in attendance. Handing them to him, she said, "If you won't believe me, maybe you'll believe the data from other experts in the field. Say you'll at least read these."

He looked at the loaded box he held. "Sure, in my spare time."

"It won't be that bad. I've put the charts of the women who are due first on the top."

"Good. So, how do we get the word out?"

"It won't take long. I'll make a few calls."

He cocked his head to the side. "I thought you said they don't use phones."

"No, but the businesses they use do. We can start by putting a notice in the paper and notes up at the grocery and feed stores."

"I can see the headlines tomorrow. Dr. Phillip White Crumples Under Pressure."

Her gaze turned sympathetic. "I realize you're doing this only because Harold insisted, but I do want to thank you."

It was hard to resist her when she was being nice. "I'll admit I've been curious about how you handle the whole thing at someone's home."

"I'm sure your questions will be answered within a few days. I have women due the end of this week and two due the following week."

He patted the top of the box she'd given him. "Then I'd better get my homework done."

"If you have any questions I'll be happy to answer

them. I plan to make this very easy on you." They walked together to her front door.

"Why, after the grief I've given you so far?"

"Because I believe in what I do, and I want you to feel the same way. Birth at home is a beautiful, spiritual experience."

He thought simply looking into her eyes was a beautiful, spiritual experience. He stopped trying to kid himself. He was falling hard for this woman.

The last thing he'd expected to find in Ohio was someone like Amber Bradley. He deeply admired her grace, her humor, her dedication to the Amish people, her skill as a nurse and her profound faith.

Leaving Hope Springs was going to be much harder than he'd anticipated.

It DIDN'T TAKE long for word to get around that Amber was back in business. The first person Amber told was her friend Katie. After several moments of rejoicing in the lobby of the Wadler Inn, Katie declared that she'd be happy to pass on the news.

On Monday afternoon, Bishop Zook arrived at the clinic and had a brief chat with Phillip. Amber was not included. Phillip looked surprised by the fact that she wasn't being asked to sit in. She wasn't. Men dominated Amish society. Only men held Church offices and could work outside the home. Unmarried women could hold jobs to help support the family, but once a woman married she stayed at home.

The bishop, satisfied that Phillip was willing to allow home births, left to share the news with the rest of the Church district. That evening, Amber resumed prenatal visits with her expectant mothers.

Phillip accompanied her. She knew it was important for the families to meet him prior to the big day, but spending so much time alone with him as they traveled the back roads of the county began wearing on her nerves. Each hour she spent with him made it increasingly difficult to maintain a professional attitude. The one thing helping her was the knowledge that he didn't agree with what she was doing.

Sunday morning rolled around on the first day of August with the good soaking rain so many farmers had been praying for. In church, Amber made a point of sitting with Nick and several of her cousins during the service. Looking over her shoulder, she saw Phillip come in.

Nick leaned over to whisper, "I see your special friend is here."

Slanting a glance at her handsome cousin, she caught his mischievous grin and made a face. "He's not my anything, Nick."

"That's not what I've been hearing."

Okay, who had been talking? "Not all gossip in Hope Springs is true, you know."

Nick glanced toward the back of the church then crossed his arms. "The man might think you're avoiding him."

Amber focused her attention on the sanctuary where a large stained glass window depicting a shroud-draped cross was set high in the wall. Instantly, she felt guilty.

It's not that I'm avoiding Phillip, Lord. It's just that... Okay, I'm avoiding him.

Being in Phillip's constant company was making her wish for things that could never be. He was charming and funny. He loved kids. In spite of their many differences, it would be so easy to fall for the guy.

She hadn't fallen for him, but she could feel herself stumbling.

Remember, he isn't staying in Hope Springs. He has a life waiting for him in Hawaii.

She had a wonderful life here. A life she had always wanted. So why didn't it feel as wonderful as it once had?

During the service, she prayed for the strength to keep a level head and her heart intact. After church was over and they all went outside, she remained with her cousins, exchanging small talk and getting updated on family matters. The sun had come out and the air smelled fresh-washed and sweet. She saw Phillip standing off to the side of the church steps. He looked lonely by himself, and very handsome in his charcoal gray suit and pale green dress shirt.

Amber wavered and nearly went to talk to him. The arrival of the mayor saved her. As the tall, lanky public servant pumped Phillip's hand and loudly expressed his gratitude, Amber made a quick escape.

Her respite lasted until Monday. At least they were busy through the morning, which left them little time together. In the afternoon, Phillip sat down with her to finish reviewing the charts of her clients.

Amber was leery that he would be critical of her methods. She knew she did good work, but this collaboration could prove to be difficult if they didn't see eye to eye on the basics.

Closing the last chart, he looked up at her. "You're very thorough. The only patient I question as low-risk is Sophie Knepp."

"Why? Everything about this pregnancy has been great."

"She has lost two children."

"From what Harold and the family told me, those little girls died at the age of two from medical problems. It was before my time here. Her last two pregnancies have gone without a hitch."

"Still, I'm not comfortable with doing a home delivery with her."

"Will you be comfortable with any of them?" Amber snapped. She didn't mean to be snippy but the words were out before she could stop them.

He sat forward in his chair and crossed his arms on the desktop. "You think I'll find something wrong with all your patients?"

"No. I'm sorry I said that."

"We've got some trust issues here, don't we? Maybe we should begin addressing those."

Leaning back in her chair, she studied him intently. "I want to believe you've got my back here but it's a little hard. I know you've been forced into this and it goes against what you believe. Besides that, you aren't invested in these patients because you'll be leaving in a few weeks."

"Fair enough. The only thing I can do is to let my actions speak for me."

Just then her cell phone rang. Opening it, she spoke briefly with the caller and then hung up.

Looking at Phillip, she said, "Here and now you should know this isn't about us anymore. From now on, our focus must be making sure our clients have a wonderful birthing experience."

"And safe."

Nodding, she echoed him. "And safe. Agreed?"

"Absolutely."

Amber rose to her feet. "Well then, you're about to see

your first home birth. That call was from a neighbor of
Mary Yutzi. She's in labor and we need to go."

He picked up the phone. "Wilma, do I have any more
patients scheduled this afternoon?"

Amber grinned. He was going to find balancing office
work and delivering babies to be a real time challenge.

He said, "Cancel Mrs. Curtis and reschedule her for
tomorrow morning."

Hanging up the phone, he rose. "Let's go welcome a
new child of God into this world."

As soon as they arrived at the Yutzi farm, Phillip watched
Amber quickly set up her equipment. Mary was still
walking the floor with her hands pressed to the small of
her back. Her husband was holding her elbow and speaking softly to her as he walked by her side.

After examining her, Amber smiled. "You've got a
ways to go yet."

Getting up from the bed, Mary looked at Amber. "But
you will stay, *ja*?"

"I'll stay. Dr. Phillip and I can make ourselves at
home. Why don't you take a walk outside? It's a beautiful day."

With her attentive husband at her side, Mary went
out the front door.

Amber said, "Walking will move her labor along more
quickly."

She removed her gloves and washed while Phillip
checked over her supplies.

"Clamps, suction bulb, Ambu bag, oxygen, IV fluids,
Pitocin, a baby scale. You've got a whole delivery suite
here." He sounded impressed.

"There's more in the car if I need it. Are you feeling less apprehensive about this?"

"Maybe. Cleanliness isn't an issue here. This home is as neat as a pin."

"That's true for most Amish homes."

It wasn't long before Mary and her husband returned. Phillip stood in the bedroom doorway and watched as Amber helped her lie down. When Mary was comfortable, Amber listened to the baby's heartbeat with her fetoscope. "Everything sounds fine. How are your contractions?"

"Uncomfortable and about every two minutes." She glanced repeatedly at Phillip with a slight frown on her face.

"Good. It won't be long now," Amber reassured her.

Walking over to Phillip, she asked, "Would you like to help?"

"You seem to have everything under control."

"You look like you're ready to jump in at any second."

"I am."

"I'll tell you what you can do to help. I find reading from the Bible will often calm my mothers."

"And nervous doctors, too?"

Smiling, she nodded. "Yes, you, too. I hand out an instruction packet on diet and exercise and what new moms need to expect on my first prenatal visit with a client. The packet also contains some of my favorite Scripture passages."

"Do you do that because they are Amish?"

"No, I do it because I have been called by God to be a nurse-midwife. Praising His name and reading His word while a new life is coming into the world just seems right."

"Would one of your favorite Scriptures be *1 John* 3:18?"

"Yes, how did you know that?"

"Your coffee cup told me. 'My little children, let us not love in word or in tongue, but in deed and in truth.'"

Her eyes softened. "Exactly."

"Would you like me to read to you, Mary?"

"Ja."

Amber said, "I think it would make us less nervous than having you hovering in the background."

He looked about the room. "Do you have a Bible I can use?"

"How good is your German?" Amber asked with a know-it-all grin.

He adored her smile. "I now know *Doktor, doktor, komm schnell* and *Der Englischer ist ab im kopf.*"

Mary and her husband chuckled at that.

Amber slipped past him in the doorway. "I have my Bible in my bag. I'll get it."

When she came back, she handed it to him. Happily, it was an English version. She said, "Read anything you like."

Settling himself on a wooden chair by the bedroom window, Phillip started reading as Amber coached Mary in her labor, checked her progress and kept a good eye on the baby's condition without seeming intrusive.

Later, when it grew dark outside, Mary's husband lit the gas lamp on the bedroom wall. Phillip moved to make use of the soft, warm glow.

Throughout the evening, Mary asked for numerous readings and he was happy to oblige. In amazement, he watched as Mary labored with her husband at her side in the quiet stillness of their own bedroom and by the light of a single lantern. It was a surreal experience for Phillip who had attended many deliveries under bright hospital lights with numerous medical personnel in the room.

At 12:09 a.m. Anna Yutzi arrived, weighing seven pounds, three ounces. She was twenty inches long and as bald as a rock.

"A beautiful and healthy girl," Phillip said after examining the baby. He gave the weighed and measured infant back to her smiling parents. He had usurped Amber's job, but the chance to hold such a precious child wasn't to be missed.

"*Ja*, she is our gift from God. My mother will be excited to have her first granddaughter," Mary replied, never taking her eyes from her baby's face. Her gentle smile warmed Phillip's heart.

It took another hour or so to clean up and make sure both mother and baby were comfortable. Mary's husband assured them Mary's mother would come to stay as soon as she heard the joyful news.

Phillip knew it was the man's way of saying that he and Mary wanted to be alone.

Amber said, "I'll check in on you tomorrow."

"And I'd like to see you in the office in about a week," Phillip added.

As he followed Amber outside to her car a little after two o'clock in the morning, he noticed at once the full white moon shining down on them. A soft breeze stirred the night air and carried to him the scent of roses from Mary's garden and the smell of corn ripening in the fields. He drew in a deep, cleansing breath and blew it out slowly.

"Tired?" Amber asked.

"A little. You?"

"A lot."

"Want me to drive?"

She turned and leaned against the car door, then slipped her hands into her scrub top pockets. "First tell me what you thought of this home birth. How did it compare to your hospital deliveries?"

At a loss for words, he simply shook his head.

"Come on. You must have some opinion. What did it feel like?"

Moving to stand beside her, he rested his hip against the car, too. "It was amazing. To see their all-embracing faith, their absolute trust in God's will, was humbling. There is beauty and serenity in every birth but this was special. Mary was so quiet, I've never seen a laboring woman stay so calm."

"You will find that's the norm among Amish women."

"Really?" He studied her upturned face. Her eyes glittered in the moonlight. Her hair glowed from the touch of moonbeams. Her skin looked flawless and pure. He beheld her ethereal beauty that was so much more than skin-deep.

This time, he wasn't going to mess up. Cupping her chin in his hand, he bent down and kissed her before she could turn away.

CHAPTER FIFTEEN

THE WORLD STOOD still around Amber. The full moon faded away and the stars winked out. The wind died to a soft sigh. Only it wasn't the wind she heard. That wistful sound formed in her own mind. The wonder of the moment swept her away from everything she'd ever known and into enchantment.

Phillip's lips were firm yet gentle as they moved across hers. The rasp of his whiskers on the tender skin around her mouth sent a thrill racing over her, making her want to draw closer. She leaned into the kiss and her arms crept up to encircle his neck.

Nothing in the world existed except the two of them and this wonderful feeling of rightness. Her hands moved up his neck to tangle in his hair. He was a very good kisser.

It took a while but Amber's common sense finally reasserted itself. As hard as she tried to stay in the glorious moment, reality seeped in. It was a wonderful kiss. It was a doomed romance. She couldn't let this go any further.

Moving her hands to Phillip's shoulders, she pushed gently. He loosened his embrace but didn't release her entirely. The kiss lasted one more heart-stopping second before he pulled away.

Drawing a ragged breath, he cupped the back of her head and tucked her face against his neck. "Wow."

It felt marvelous to rest in his embrace. He was so warm and strong and vital. It was the kind of moment she'd dreamed of but never thought would become a reality. She didn't want to lose this marvelous feeling but the sensation was fading. She had to get the two of them back on solid footing.

"Phillip, if you say something stupid like 'I'm sorry,' I'll kick your shin."

He chuckled. The sound reverberated deep in his chest beneath her ear and made her smile. "Amber, of all the things running through my mind right now, *I'm sorry* is not even on the horizon."

"Good."

Where did this leave them? It changed nothing and it changed everything.

"Does this mean we've resolved the trust issues between us?" he asked.

"I'm working on it." If only it were that easy. One kiss and everything became rosy. *Not.*

He leaned back so he could see her face. Amber looked up, hoping her heart wasn't shining in her eyes. Before she could think of anything else to say, he released her and stepped away.

"I think it's time I drove you home."

Without his arms around her, the night air felt cold. She crossed her arms as a shiver ran down her spine. "If you aren't going to kiss me again, we should go."

He paused in the act of opening the car door. "Oh, Amber. Talk about temptation. You've been one since the first day I came to Hope Springs."

His comment pleased her feminine side to no end, but it didn't narrow the chasm that existed between them.

"Okay, home it is," he conceded.

Once in the car, Amber hoped things would return to normal. Her hopes were in vain. He said, "What are we going to do about this?"

What could they do about it? The answer was painfully clear to her. "Nothing."

His gaze jerked toward her. "What's that supposed to mean?"

"Don't get me wrong. It was a wonderful kiss."

"That was the impression I had at the time. Now I'm wondering if I misread something."

"You didn't. It just can't happen again."

By the sudden deep silence, Amber knew he understood. Finally, he said, "It won't."

"We have to work together. You're my boss. Besides that, you're leaving in a few weeks. If we jump headlong into a relationship, we'll end up hurting each other."

"I thought I was practical. You've got me beat hands down. But answer me this, what if we allowed this relationship to take its natural course and see where it leads?"

He had no idea how much she longed to have that happen. One kiss from him was not enough. It would never be enough. That didn't change anything. "Okay, you tell me how this might play out differently."

"We could enjoy each other's company when we aren't working. You know, spend time together. We could get to know each other. Who knows, we might find this is the real deal for both of us."

"And then what? You'd settle down in Hope Springs for the rest of your life? You'd be happy being a family doctor to the Amish and skip the part where you practice cutting-edge medicine with the latest technology?"

She hated driving home the point, but it was a pipe

dream to think what they had between them could ever be more than a breathless kiss in the moonlight.

"You're right," he admitted.

"Of course, I'm right."

He gave in so easily. That hurt a little. He could have offered a few more arguments.

Okay, maybe it was better that he hadn't. This way she could make believe it was nothing more than a simple flirtation.

By now they had reached the edge of town. It didn't take much longer to reach her house. When he pulled up to the curb in front of her home, she turned in her seat to see his face better. Trying to convince herself it hadn't been an important moment didn't cut it. She had to admit the truth. "I'll never forget tonight, Phillip."

Reaching out, he tenderly stroked her cheek with the back of his knuckles. "Neither will I, Amber. Neither will I."

PHILLIP DIDN'T WANT her to go. The delight he'd felt when he held her in his arms was stronger than anything he'd experienced before. She fit so perfectly.

Perhaps those feelings had been caused by the heightened emotions they both shared following Mary's delivery. Perhaps it was because Amber was a remarkable, beautiful woman.

Whatever the reasons, he knew once she stepped out of the car they had to go back to their roles of doctor and nurse. Working side by side, never touching the way he touched her now.

She said, "I should go."

He withdrew his hand. Other than locking the doors

and driving away with her, he couldn't think of any way to stop her from leaving.

Silently admitting defeat, he tried for a normal, friendly tone. "Then I'll see you tomorrow at the clinic."

"You mean today at the clinic."

She was right. Dawn was still a few hours away, but he wasn't in any rush to get home. Sleep would be very hard to come by. He would relive that tender kiss many times before he slumbered. Probably for many nights to come.

"Don't forget, Gina Curtis will be in first thing," she reminded him.

Shaking his head, he said, "I've never seen a person so happy to find out there was actually something wrong with her."

"Poor Gina. I feel terrible for dismissing her complaints so callously."

"What happened in the past can't be changed. What we do from now on is what's important. Get some sleep, Nurse Bradley. I'll need you at your best today."

"Are you sure you don't want me to drop you off at your place?" she asked.

"No, a walk will do me good. It's only a few blocks. Besides, it not like Hope Springs has much of a criminal element."

He got out and came around to her side of the car. Opening the door, he handed her the keys as she got out. "I'll expect you at eight sharp."

"Yes, Doctor," she replied smartly and walked up the steps to her house.

She never looked back. He knew because he waited at the curb until she entered her front door, until the downstairs lights finally went out and until her upstairs bed-room window went dark. Only then did he walk away.

At the corner, he stopped and looked back. How was he going to stay away?

CHAPTER SIXTEEN

AFTER A SLEEPLESS, very short night, Amber arrived at the clinic determined to revert to her normal working relationship with Phillip. The last thing she needed was for things to be strained between them.

By the middle of the morning she knew it wasn't working.

There were all those little things that sparked memories of the kiss. Like when he handed her a cup of coffee when she arrived and their hands touched for a brief moment. The current of attraction that ran between them zinged like lightning. It grew more powerful with each passing moment.

Not long afterward, she came face-to-face with him in the break room door. She froze, unable to move as she stared into his expressive eyes. He was thinking about the kiss, too.

He found the presence of mind to step back and allow her to leave. If he hadn't, she'd still be standing there longing to find out if a second kiss would be as wonderful as the first.

Several times throughout the morning she looked up to find him staring at her. Once, he had the sweetest smile tugging at the corner of his mouth. The next time, he wore a faraway sad look, as if he'd lost something important. Was she important to him? She was afraid to ask. Afraid that he would say yes. Afraid he would say no.

A little before noon, Amber's phone rang. Phillip, having finished with their last patient of the morning, stopped outside her door to wait as she answered it.

It was the husband of Sophie Knepp. Excitement sent Amber's pulse skipping. She loved delivering babies and was grateful God had chosen her for this special work.

After assuring Elijah Knepp that she would be there within the hour, she closed her phone, looked at Phillip and grinned. "Ready to help me bring another child into the world?"

He glanced at the schedule board. "We've got three more patients to see this afternoon."

Sitting back in her chair, she shrugged. "Clue number one as to why Harold lets me do my own deliveries. Not enough hours in the day. I can do this on my own," she offered.

"That's not the agreement we signed."

She smiled sweetly. "Can't blame a girl for trying."

He struggled not to smile but lost the battle. "I'll get Wilma to reschedule. Give me five minutes. Will this one last all night, too?"

"That's not likely. It's baby number five for Sophie Knepp. She's not due for three more weeks, but her other babies have come this early. They did fine."

"Knepp? I remember reading her chart. She's not a candidate for home delivery. She's high-risk." All levity vanished from his face.

Amber bristled. "In my professional assessment, she is not a high-risk mother."

"Then professionally we disagree."

"Yes, I believe we do." To think she'd been feeling sorry for him less than an hour ago.

"Call the Knepps back. Tell them to make arrangements for Mrs. Knepp to go to the hospital in Millersburg. I'll meet them there."

"Yes, Doctor," she snapped. Annoyed, Amber flipped open her phone and poked in the numbers.

After eight rings, she hung up. "There's no answer. It's likely that Elijah called from one of the rural phone booths shared by several of Amish families in his area."

"I thought they didn't use phones."

"Not in their homes. Some who need phones for their businesses share a freestanding booth located centrally to their farms."

"So how do we contact him and tell him about the change of plans?"

"Wilma will know if they have a neighbor with a phone who can deliver that message. If not, one of us will have to go out there." Amber picked up her desk phone and asked Wilma to see what she could find out.

Hanging up, Amber glared at Phillip. "She's looking into it."

"Good. Keep me informed."

Something in his tone pushed her over the edge. "Yes, Dr. White, of course, Dr. White. I shall keep you informed of the situation without delay, Dr. White. How could you think otherwise?"

Turning back to her computer, she said, "Now, if you will excuse me, I have work to do."

She pulled out her keyboard and began typing up her notes from her last delivery. He didn't move. He simply stood in the doorway staring at her. Try as she might, she couldn't ignore him.

With an exasperated huff, she looked up. "Yes, Dr. White, is there something else? Some other mistake I've made that needs to be pointed out?"

"Amber, please."

"Please what? Please don't be annoyed that you can't trust my judgment? You know what? You're right. That little episode of *bad judgment* on my part last night proves your point."

Taking a step toward her, he said, "We need to talk about that."

Nope. That was the last thing she wanted. What if she blurted out how much she enjoyed it?

"I have nothing to say to you. Now, this is still my office. I have work to do. Close the door on your way out." Pushing the print button on the machine at the side of her desk, she focused on the noisy clatter as her notes were transferred to paper.

He didn't reply. When she looked up from her task, her door was closed. Phillip was standing inside with his arms folded across his chest. The look on his face said he wasn't going anywhere.

PHILLIP HAD NO idea how to handle Amber when she was in a mood like this one, but he couldn't leave until they had reached some kind of understanding. She had become too important to him, and he had hurt her.

Trusting God to bring him the right words, he crossed the room and pulled a chair over beside her. He sat down and took her hand. "I'm sorry."

"For what?" She tried to pull away. He held on.

The catch in her voice made him want to kick himself for upsetting her. "I'm sorry for a lot of things. For kissing you last night, not in the least."

"If you're expecting a repeat, you're not getting one."

He chuckled. "How can you be so cute even when you're mad at me?" She opened her mouth but shut it quickly. He turned her hand over and began stroking her palm with his thumb. "*Now* you're speechless?"

"I can't very well say I'm not cute because I am. That doesn't make me less irritated with you."

Her tone, if not her words, showed she was somewhat mollified. It was hard to believe she hadn't pulled her hand away and slapped him. That gave him hope.

"Let's get things out in the open. Maybe then we won't have to tiptoe around each other for the next few weeks."

"That's not necessary."

"I think it is. From my point of view, we were both elated by the beauty of Anna's birth. The moonlight and the scent of roses were utterly romantic. You are a beautiful woman. One thing led to another and we kissed. It wasn't wrong. It was an expression of joy. I'd repeat the event in a heartbeat."

The tension left her shoulders and the wary expression disappeared from her eyes. A shy smile tugged at the corner of her oh-so-kissable lips. "That wasn't exactly an apology."

"No, and I won't offer one. I don't regret that I kissed you. I do regret it's making it difficult for us to work together. Believe it or not, I do understand boundaries."

"You're giving our interlude too much credit. We had trouble working together before then."

Letting go of her hand, he sat back with a grin. "Okay, you're right about that, but we are making progress."

"I know I'm right. I'm right about a lot of things. Including Sophie Knepp."

Leaning forward, he rested his forearms on his knees

and clasped his hand together. "Let's say you are right and her delivery goes off without a hitch. Is it really going to make a difference to this Amish community to have one mother deliver at a hospital just to be on the safe side? Come on, are these people so fragile or so autocratic that they can't accept this?"

He watched the internal struggle going on behind her expressive eyes. Finally, she shook her head.

He sat back. "I've reviewed your charts. I have agreed with all your assessments except this one. Doesn't that prove I think you know your stuff?"

"Maybe."

"Not maybe. Yes or no?"

"Okay, yes, you believe I know my stuff."

"And you will agree that I know my stuff?"

"Maybe."

Shaking his head in exasperation, he said, "Yes or no, Amber?"

"Yes, you're a skilled doctor who has the best interests of his patients in mind."

"Thank you."

"You're welcome."

Reaching out, he took her hand again. "Does this mean we can kiss and make up?"

She yanked her hand away. "In your dreams, buster."

How right she was. She'd been invading his dreams for some time now. He didn't see it stopping anytime soon.

There was a knock at the door. Wilma looked in. "I got hold of the Knepps' neighbor who went right over to give them your message. He just called me back on his cell phone. He was still at their house. Sophie says it was false labor. Elijah jumped the gun by calling. She says she's sorry to have alarmed you."

"Thank you, Wilma."

Rising, Phillip looked at them both. "We've got forty minutes before our next patient. How about lunch at the Shoofly? It's on me."

"I've already had my sandwich," Wilma replied. She left the room, but she made a point of leaving the door open.

Phillip turned to Amber. "What about you? Have you forgiven me enough to join me for lunch?"

"Only if we go Dutch."

It was always small victories with her. Independent, stubborn and passionate about her work, he wouldn't have her any other way. "Dutch it is."

Leaving Wilma to hold down the fort, Phillip walked beside Amber as they traversed the few blocks to the café.

He fought the urge to hold her hand the entire way. He kept his hands inside his lab coat pockets instead.

The day was sunny and warm, but the breeze made it bearable. At the café, the interior was cool and filled with appetizing aromas that made his mouth water. He hadn't realized how hungry he was.

Katie came forward to greet them. "*Willkommen.* I'm afraid we don't have a table for you, but the wait should not be long. Our special today is pork chops with fresh peas and home-baked dinner rolls."

"Sounds wonderful, Katie. What's for dessert?"

Katie grinned, "We have raisin pie. I know you want a slice of that."

"Oh, yes I do."

Phillip nudged Amber with his elbow. "Let's have lunch first before you go diving into dessert."

"All right, but we don't have time to wait for a table. It took us ten minutes to walk here."

"We have some fried chicken ready. I can make you a quick picnic," Katie offered.

"Is that all right?" Phillip asked Amber. He loved the outdoors and the sun on his face. He suspected Amber was the outdoorsy type but he didn't know for certain.

To his delight, she said, "Sounds great. We can eat at the park. It's a block from the clinic."

He liked the sound of that. Amber was being practical. He saw it as the perfect opportunity to spend some quality time with her. Their brief but so-very-sweet kiss left him longing for more. He smiled at the prospect of a repeat.

A hint of wariness crept into her eyes. He wiped the grin from his face. It wasn't like he was planning to kiss her again. He wasn't. Absolutely not. No way.

He turned his attention to the rest of the room. From their spot by the door, he saw the place was indeed packed with a dozen or so English tourists, and numerous Amish families at the other tables.

Phillip leaned toward Amber. "I didn't think the Amish ate out."

"Sure they do. They come for special occasions like birthdays or simply to enjoy a break from home cooking on market day."

At the nearest table, Phillip noticed that two of the children where dwarfs. "I've seen a disproportionately large number of little people since I've arrived."

"The Amish, because of intermarriages, suffer from many inherited diseases such as the dwarfism that those children have."

"For people who don't believe in health insurance, some inherited diseases must place a huge burden on the families."

"They don't see it as a burden. They accept it as God's will. They consider the children who are affected to be gifts from God."

"As they are."

"I'm glad you think so. I've noticed you are very good with the children who come to the clinic."

He folded his arms across his chest. "I almost went into pediatrics."

"Why didn't you?"

"I've wanted to be a family practice doctor since I was ten years old." Memories of his unhappy childhood slipped out to taint the day.

"So young? Did something happen that pushed you in that direction?"

Staring into her sympathetic eyes, Phillip struggled with a difficult decision. Normally, he deflected questions about his early life. Plenty of people had looked down on him in the past. Deeply ashamed of the way he'd grown up and of his mother's behaviors, he preferred to keep those times bottled away.

Amber was someone who made him want to share even the ugly parts of his life. There was something about her that made him believe he could trust her—made him believe that she would understand.

Was he right? Could he take that chance?

CHAPTER SEVENTEEN

KATIE RETURNED WITH their box lunches, giving Phillip a chance to ponder his options. Some inner part of him wanted to share everything about himself with Amber. He had guarded his past so closely for so long, he wasn't sure he could talk about it now. It existed like a bad dream in the back of his mind.

With their lunches and ice-cold bottles of soda in hand, they left the Shoofly and started back toward the clinic. Flashing a sidelong glance at her, he half hoped she would forget about her question.

She hadn't. After taking a sip of her cola, she went right back to the subject. "What happened that made you want to become a doctor?"

He walked in silence for several yards, unable to bring himself to talk about it.

She cast a worried glance his way. "I'm sorry. I didn't mean to pry."

He opened his mouth to say it was a personal matter he didn't care to discuss. That wasn't what came out. "When I was ten, my mother and her current boyfriend had a birthday party for me. I can't remember his name. She had so many men in her life that they all run together in my head."

Looking down, he expected to see repugnance. He saw only sympathy in her beautiful eyes. "I'm sorry,

Phillip. I can't imagine what that must have been like for you."

Suddenly, it was as if the floodgates of his emotions broke open. His unhappy past came pouring out. "It was so hard. A new town every few months, a new 'Uncle' just as often. I was always the new kid at school who didn't fit in, who wore dirty clothes. It didn't pay trying to make friends because I knew I'd be leaving."

"Yet you turned out to be a responsible, caring adult. You became a physician, which is no easy task."

"That was due in large part to my stepfather. When I was fifteen, God brought a great guy into our lives. A man who saw how sad Mom was and helped her find a better life. Michael is a devout Christian. He showed me God's blessings in my own life. He made me realize I didn't have to shoulder my burdens alone. I still have a ways to go in being a good Christian, but I'm trying to get there. It was Michael's generosity that allowed me to go to medical school, although I did receive some academic scholarships."

By this time they had reached the park. They found a picnic table in the shade of a pear tree and sat down. The park was deserted except for a few squirrels chattering as they raced from treetop to treetop. The faint breeze smelled of newly mown grass. Phillip opened his box just as Amber held out her hand and bowed her head. He grasped her hand and did the same.

She said, "We thank You, Lord, for the food that nourishes our body. Grant us Your comfort and Your grace as we work to do Your will. Amen."

"Amen," Phillip echoed. Slowly, he released her hand.

"What happened on your birthday?" She took a bite of her drumstick. Her gaze didn't leave his face.

Drawing a deep breath, he said, "Mom's boyfriend asked me what I wanted to be when I grew up. She told him I was going to be a doctor like my father planned to be. It was the first I'd heard that my dad wanted to be a doctor. I cornered her later that night before she and what's-his-name went out to party. I asked her what kind of doctor my dad wanted to be. She hemmed and hawed, but finally told me he wanted to be a family doctor."

"Your father must have wanted to be like his own dad. I'm sure Harold would be happy to know that."

Phillip took a drink, then said, "You once asked me how Harold and I found each other."

"I remember. You said it was personal. I respect that."

"I want to tell you now. Sometimes, when I'm in my grandfather's house, I try to put myself in his place. I try to imagine what it would be like to live alone in that small house for thirty-four years. I stare at the walls and wonder what made him give up a lucrative practice in Boston to come to Hope Springs. I wonder what makes him stay. Did he ever tell you what brought him here?"

"No, and I never asked. By the time I began working here he was already a fixture, like the clock in the town square. I didn't even know he came from Boston. Perhaps it was the death of his only son that made him leave."

He shrugged. "Mother rarely talked about my father although I pestered her for information about him from the time I could talk. I was certain if he had lived my life would have been different. I thought my mother would have been happy. That we would live in a house instead of rented trailers and abysmal run-down apartments."

"It's easy to understand that you wanted to know him."

"That's the easy part. The rest is weird."

"How so?"

"My mother never showed me a picture of my dad. Yet she kept it all those years. Through all the moves and all the crummy boyfriends. When I found it, I didn't know who he was. I turned it over. On the back of the picture he'd written, 'To my wife Natalie with all my love, Brendan.' I was shocked."

"What did she say when you asked her about it? She had to know how much you wanted to learn things about him."

"She gave no explanation other than to say it was a personal item and for me to put it away."

"That is weird. Perhaps it was too painful for her to look at."

"That was always her excuse. Once I knew my dad had been in the military, I started searching his military records for some clues about what kind of man he was. That was how I found out about Harold. He was listed along with my mother as kin. My mother told me that my dad was an orphan, that he had no family."

"Why would she do that?"

"I don't have a clue. She's very good at avoiding uncomfortable situations. From the moment I learned of my grandfather's existence, I spent every free minute and every free dime I had trying to track him down. I looked online, combed through old newspaper articles and public records. It was slow going. I finally hired a private detective in Boston to do the legwork for me."

"And that's how you found Harold?"

"The P.I. was a good investment. Within a week, he sent me Harold's current address and the phone number of this clinic. I can't begin to describe the emotions going through me at that moment."

"To finally find your father's father must have been wonderful."

"My fingers were cold as icicles when I dialed the number. My heart was beating so hard I thought I might stroke out."

Every word of that first conversation remained imprinted in Phillip's mind. After explaining who he was and how he'd found Harold, Phillip waited for his grandfather's reaction.

Amber said, "I imagine Harold was delighted to hear from you."

"His reaction wasn't exactly what I'd hoped for. Harold was hard to convince. Who could blame him? To have me pop up out of nowhere after thirty-four years must have been a shock. I told him about the military records and the P.I. I left my phone number with him, then I hung up and waited."

"He may have sounded hesitant when you were on the phone but I saw him when he came out of his office after speaking to you. There was such joy on his face. He didn't share his news until a few days later but I knew something big was up."

"That's because he hired a P.I. to check me out first."

Her eyes widened. "Really?"

"He's a smart man. A week after our first contact Harold called me. We began a tentative long-distance relationship. After nearly a year of emails and phone conversations, Harold announced he was ready to meet me. We both know how that turned out. I ran him down with my car."

Reaching out, Amber laid a hand on his arm. "You never intended to hurt him, Phillip. It was an accident. You have to stop blaming yourself."

Her gesture of comfort was exactly what he needed. A sense of peace settled in his bones. "You're right. I can't blame myself forever."

AMBER WITHDREW HER hand. The warmth between them cooled as she concentrated on her pie. Words didn't seem adequate but she needed to say something. "Thank you for sharing your story with me. I feel honored."

"Thank you for listening."

They finished their meal in silence. As they gathered their trash and disposed of it, he glanced at his watch. "Time to get back to work."

And time to shift back into her professional mode. If only Phillip didn't make it so hard for her to maintain that persona.

Having him share his unhappy childhood memories with her touched her deeply. Little by little he was creeping into her heart in a way she knew would lead to heartbreak. He'd be leaving in a few weeks. She simply had to get a grip on these emotions.

If only he weren't such a wonderful person. Sure, they disagreed about a few things, important things. She could get downright angry with him but it never lasted long. He had a way of smoothing over the rough spots and making her like him all over again.

Besides being charming, he was wonderful with patients, especially the children. He attended the same church she did. He had strong Christian beliefs. He was growing to accept and care about the Amish and their ways.

Okay, he's an almost perfect man. My mother would fall over backward with joy if I brought him home.

So why had the Lord brought such a wonderful man

into her life if he wasn't going to stay? It was a question she couldn't answer. The ways of the Lord were not for her understanding.

Back at the office, they went through the rest of the day together without any more blowups or exchanged confidences. A little before five o'clock, they were in the lobby getting ready to close for the night.

Phillip said, "I still have to make my rounds at the hospital in Millersburg. I should get going."

"And I need to see Mary and her baby."

"Let me know how they're doing." He held up one hand. "Not because I don't trust your professional expertise. Because I'd like to know how they're getting along."

Amber couldn't help smiling. "I'll call you later tonight."

He stopped on his way to the door and glanced back. "I'll look forward to that."

Just then, the phone rang. Phillip waited as Wilma picked up. After exchanging a few pleasantries with the caller, she covered the mouthpiece with one hand. "It's Harold. He'd like to speak to both of you."

Amber exchanged a worried glance with Phillip. He said, "We'll take it in my office. Thank you, Wilma. You can go home."

"I always miss the good stuff," she grumbled as she gathered her purse.

"I'll fill you in tomorrow morning," Amber promised.

"You'd better." She walked out the door, leaving Amber and Phillip alone.

Amber turned to face him. "Ready to accomplish your mission?"

Stuffing his hands in his pockets, he asked, "What mission?"

"Don't play dumb. Harold needs a partner. You get to tell him."

"I can't believe I gave in to you."

She gave him a playful push toward his office. "Don't worry. I'll be right there beside you."

"You'd better be."

In the office, Phillip pressed the blinking light on the phone and set it to speakerphone mode. Leaning his hip against the corner of the desk, he said, "Hello, Grandfather. How are you?"

"Better than these morons give me credit for. If I were home I'd be doing great."

Speaking up, Amber said, "Harold, I'm sure they know what's best for you."

"Enough about me. How is my practice?"

"It's busy," Phillip said with a questioning look at her.

"And Amber is back to work as a nurse-midwife?"

"Yes," she said quickly. "Mary Yutzi had a little girl last night. Seven pounds, three ounces and twenty inches long."

"Wonderful. What did they name her?" He sounded truly relieved and happy.

"Anna." Phillip answered.

Harold chuckled. "Nettie must be over the moon to finally get a granddaughter. Give Mary my congratulations."

Amber perched on a chair by the desk and leaned toward the speaker. "I will. I'm going out to the farm tonight to check on her and Anna."

Looking at Phillip, Amber nodded toward the phone. He closed his eyes and said, "We've been busy here."

"You mean since the boycott ended."

Phillip flinched. "Even before the boycott, I was amazed at the number of patients you see."

Harold replied, "Of course we're busy. There's a shortage of rural doctors, or haven't you heard that in Hawaii?"

"I've heard. I was simply wondering if you had considered taking on a partner?"

"Ha! Find me one who'll work for peanuts, see patients without insurance and make visits to homes without electricity, and I'll take him on. It has to be a man, though. No offense, Amber."

She grinned. "None taken. I know Amish men won't use female doctors."

Phillip said, "Let me be clear. You are okay with me advertising for a new physician to work with you?"

There was a long silence on the phone. Amber finally asked, "Harold, are you still there?"

"Yes."

"What do you think about Phillip's suggestion?"

"So the pair of you think I can't do the job, anymore, is that it?"

"No!" they said in unison.

Phillip closed his eyes. "You aren't a young man anymore. These people deserve to have your knowledge and skills passed on to someone who can help them far into the future. If you had died, what would have happened to them?"

"Don't think that hasn't crossed my mind, but I'm not ready to hang up my stethoscope."

"Phillip didn't say that you were," Amber replied, trying to be reasonable.

"All right. Go ahead and advertise. You won't find anyone."

Phillip winked at Amber. "Then you should do as your doctors tell you so you can get back here and get to work soon."

"Everyone sends their love and prayers," Amber added.

"Give them my thanks." Harold's tone held a pensive quality that troubled Amber. The line went dead before she could ask him what was wrong.

Phillip rubbed his jaw thoughtfully. "Do you remember the name of the resident who wanted to join this practice?"

"I still have his card somewhere." What was it that Harold hadn't said? Amber couldn't get his tone out of her mind.

Springing to his feet, Phillip said, "Great. Maybe the guy is still interested in working here. I can't believe Harold agreed. That was easy."

Amber continued to stare at the phone. "I'm not so sure."

CHAPTER EIGHTEEN

PHILLIP COULDN'T BELIEVE how quickly the days were flying by. When he'd first agreed to spend two months in Ohio, it had seemed like a prison sentence. He couldn't imagine being away from his beloved ocean for so long. Now he wished he had more time to spend with Amber.

They had done one more delivery together, a first baby for a non-Amish couple. In spite of Phillip's worries, Amber conducted the whole experience so that both the young woman and her nervous husband had a happy and successful birthing experience.

As Amber and Hope Springs worked their way deeper into his heart, it became increasingly clear why Harold refused to give up medicine in this place. There was something so soothing and rich about the way these people lived.

He sat in his grandfather's kitchen, absently tapping a pen on the table. He didn't have to leave. He could be the man to work with his grandfather.

Tempting as the thought was, he knew it wouldn't work. This wasn't the kind of medicine he saw himself doing into his seventies. He imagined himself working in the finest modern medical center, diagnosing diseases and treating his patients with the best tools available.

Coming to Hope Springs had clarified one issue for him. It was the sick children that called to his soul. Sick children like little Helen Lapp with her bad heart. If anyone deserved the finest care, it was children like her.

Wilma was waiting for him when he reached the clinic. Not once since arriving in Hope Springs had he beaten the woman to the office. He wasn't sure that she didn't sleep there. She said, "The Lapp family is here as you requested."

"Good, thank you. Please hold my calls."

He had little Helen's report from the cardiologist. He had asked for a family meeting to discuss it.

In his office, he found Mr. and Mrs. Lapp waiting for him. They looked like any other Amish couple he might pass on the street. She wore a dark blue dress and apron. On her head she wore a dark bonnet with a wide brim.

Her husband had on a dark suit and held his black felt hat in his hands. They could have been any Amish couple in Hope Springs except for the intense worry in their eyes.

Phillip sat behind his desk. "How is Helen?"

"Some better," her mother answered.

"As I'm sure Dr. Yang discussed with you, Helen has a heart defect called an atrial septal defect."

Her father nodded. "*Ja*, she will need surgery soon to fix her heart."

"Yes. In studying her cardiologist's report, I see that her disease is genetic in nature. Do you know what that means?"

They looked at each other and shook their heads.

"She has Ellis-van Creveld syndrome. That means your future children are at risk for the same type of dwarfism and heart defects."

"But I have two fine sons," Mr. Lapp insisted.

"I know. I merely wanted you to be aware of the risks

for any other children. Your sons need to know that their children may have the same problems."

"It was *Gottes Wille* that our daughter was born this way. We accept that." Mrs. Lapp spoke at last. She sat with her hands clasped tightly in front of her, her knuckles white with tension.

Her husband nodded. "If He sends us more children like Helen, we will accept that, too."

Phillip sat back in his chair. "We have no way to cure Helen. Surgery isn't a complete fix. Any colds or coughs can quickly turn serious for her, so please don't hesitate to come see me if she becomes ill again."

"Danki, Doktor." Rising, Mr. Lapp nodded, then walked out the door. His wife hung back.

Looking at Phillip, she asked, "What can be done so that my sons don't have such children?"

"They can be tested for the defective gene. If they don't carry it, their children will not have Helen's disease."

She took a step closer. "And if they do carry it?"

"In that case, the way to prevent them from having a child with her defect would be to screen the women they wish to marry to see if they carry the gene."

"If they both have this gene?"

Sighing deeply, he said, "Their children will have a one in four chance of having Ellis-van Creveld syndrome."

"So God decides?"

"Yes. I'm not an expert on this disease, Mrs. Lapp. If you'd like, I can make an appointment for you to see a genetic specialist."

"No." She left his office and caught up with her husband waiting outside.

Phillip watched them leave and knew they both carried heavy hearts. The specialist believed Helen had only a fifty-fifty chance of reaching adulthood. Phillip prayed God would give them the strength and comfort they needed to deal with such devastating news.

Turning back to his desk, he stared at the books in his grandfather's case. Pulling down one with numerous bits of paper sticking out, he read the title. *Noted Patterns of Human Malformation.*

Leafing though the pages of the text, Phillip saw Harold had made dozens of comments in the margins, mostly dates and occasional names.

"Are you looking for something special?"

He turned at the sound of Amber's voice. She was standing in the doorway. She had on her usual pale blue scrubs and white lab coat. He heard Wilma call out a question to her. Turning around, she stepped into the hall to answer. When she did, he saw that her hair hung to her hips in a shimmering honey-colored curtain. The sight robbed him of breath.

When she turned back to face him, he closed his mouth and asked, "What did you say?"

"I asked if you were looking for something special?"

He focused his gaze on the books. "I was looking for some texts on genetics."

She joined him by the bookcase and reached for a book on the upper shelf. "I'm not sure what Harold has in here. He never alphabetizes anything."

The clean citrus fragrance of her hair slipped around him like a soft Hawaiian breeze. He leaned back to scope her hair out again.

Yep. Every bit as glorious up close.

She should have flowers in it, the way the island

women wore them. It was easy to picture her walking beside him on the beach, her hair flowing in the wind. He itched to feel its softness. To let it glide though his fingers.

Suddenly, she whipped her head around to stare at him. "What?"

He took a step back and crossed his arms. "Nothing."

"You were staring at me."

"No, I wasn't." Even to his own ears he sounded like a kid caught with his hand in the cookie jar.

She arched one brow. Her look said she wasn't buying it.

"Okay, I was admiring your hair, that's all."

Grasping a lock in her hand, she frowned at it. "When I left the house this morning it wasn't dry so I had to leave it down. I'll put it up before I see patients."

"You don't have to do that. It's very lovely."

Her cheeks took on a rosy hue. "Thank you."

He couldn't help himself. Reaching out, he brushed a strand from her shoulder in a soft caress.

AMBER SUCKED IN a quick breath at his touch. Her hair *had* been damp when she left the house, but she could have put it up after she arrived. She never wore it down. It was always confined in a braid or bun. Today had been different. For some inexplicable reason, she wanted Phillip to see it down.

Now she realized she was being vain. Taking a step away from him, she swept it into a rope and began coiling it. "My mother never cut her hair. She called it a hangover from her Amish life. I adopted the habit."

"You don't have to put it up." He sounded sorry to see her do so.

"It's dry now."

"Have you ever cut it?"

Continuing to wind, she said, "It gets trimmed. It pleases mother and my grandmother that I keep it long."

Pulling several large hairpins from her pocket, she slipped them in and patted the roll. "There. Good to go."

"You should wear it down more often. It's beautiful."

He did like it. A thrill of happiness made her smile.

"Amber, have you ever thought of working somewhere else?"

"Like where?"

"Hawaii, for one place." A question hovered in his eyes, a hope that secretly pleased her. She had thought about seeing his island home, but she wasn't ready to admit that.

She turned back to the bookcase. "I sunburn too easily. Genetics, you say? I don't see anything but what you're holding. You can always use the computer to look something up. I know our dial-up can be slow and frustrating."

"I'll drive to Millersburg after work and do some research at their medical library. I need to check on Martha anyway. Are any of your patients in labor?"

"Not a one."

He opened the book and held it out to her. "Do these dates and names mean anything to you?"

She studied the textbook for a few minutes. "I'm not sure." Pointing, she said, "This could be the Zook boy who died two years ago. He had some developmental difficulties from birth."

"What kind of difficulties?"

"I'm not sure."

"He wasn't one of your patients?"

She shook her head. "No, he was born in the hospital in Millersburg. They were visiting family there when she went into premature labor. He never left the hospital."

Turning to a new page, he asked, "What about this one?"

Checking, she shook her head. "Before my time."

"It says Knepp. Could it be one of Sophie Knepp's girls?"

"It could be. We have a lot of Knepps in this state."

He carried the book back to his desk and sat down. It was clear he was deep in thought.

"Your next patient is in room one," she reminded him.

"Fine. Thank you. I'll be there in a minute."

She started to leave but he suddenly spoke again. "Do me a favor, will you? Ask Wilma to get some old charts from storage."

"Sure. Which ones?"

"The one for this Zook boy, and see if she can find a Knepp with this birth date." He scribbled it down and handed her the note.

"It may take a few days. We store our closed charts out of state."

"Tell her to get them as soon as she can."

Throughout the rest of the morning, Phillip remained distracted. He was always attentive to his patients, but in between clients he shut himself in the office.

At noon, Amber stuck her head in to see if he wanted to get some lunch. He didn't, and she went away feeling more disappointed than she should have.

When they closed up that evening, she watched him walk across the parking lot and turn the corner.

"You'll have to get used to that," Wilma said as she came to stand beside Amber.

"Get used to what?"

"Him being gone."

"I know he's leaving soon." It was hard to imagine this place without him. He'd become so much a part of her life. Pushing open the door, she walked to her car and drove home feeling more depressed than she had since she'd first learned of Harold's accident.

At home, Fluffy was waiting eagerly for his food bowl to be filled. Amber obliged the cat then made herself a light supper. She spent the rest of the evening catching up on her midwife journal, reading and trying not to think about Phillip. Or how much she would miss him when he went away.

On an impulse, she went to the computer and began clicking through some of the travel sites that featured Hawaii. She'd always thought the rolling hills, fertile fields and pristine white farmsteads of the Amish made Hope Springs a beautiful place. It paled in comparison to the exotic beauty of the islands embraced by the blue-green sea.

What man in his right mind would give up a home and a practice there to relocate to this wide spot in the road? No, she might wish he would stay but he wouldn't. This wasn't the kind of medicine he wanted to practice. She understood and respected that to the fullest. Phillip would leave in a few more weeks.

Unless Harold asked him to stay.

Was that what Harold had been thinking when he agreed to getting a partner? Was that idea the odd quality she detected in his voice? If it was, he might be in for a heartbreak as big as hers.

Fluffy chose that moment to leap onto Amber's desk in search of some affection. Pulling the cat close, Amber sighed. It was time to stop denying it. She had fallen hard for Dr. Phillip White.

"Do you want to hear how foolish I am, Fluffy? I may not get stuck behind the sofa but I'm a fool anyway. I've fallen in love with Phillip. Stupid, huh?"

The cat meowed softly as if in agreement.

It was foolish. A wonderful kind of foolishness. She'd never felt like this about anyone. She suspected the attraction was mutual. Even if it were, it wouldn't make a difference.

"He didn't come here looking for a relationship, Fluffy. He's doing his grandfather a favor, that's all. He came out of guilt, not because he wanted to work in an Amish community."

Fluffy remained silent this time.

"You're right. I'm going to do myself a favor by forgetting we had this conversation."

Raising the cat to look into his face, Amber said, "I hope you can keep a secret. I'm going to bed now and I'm not going to cry myself to sleep. I'll save that for the night he leaves."

It seemed like she'd barely closed her eyes when her doorbell began ringing incessantly. She glanced at the clock. It was a few minutes after three thirty in the morning.

The doorbell chimed again. Slipping into her robe, she pulled it tight and padded barefoot down the stairs. It was likely that one of her expectant mothers needed her.

Turning on the porch light, she pulled aside the lace panel on the tall window that flanked her entryway.

To her surprise, she saw Elijah Knepp standing outside, his straw hat in his hand. She pulled open the door. "Elijah, what's wrong?"

"It is Sophie. Her time has come."

Amber's heart sank. "Elijah, I can't deliver her. Sophie must go to the hospital in Millersburg."

His brows snapped together in a worried scowl. "We do not wish the hospital."

"I'm sorry, but this is what Dr. White says must happen. Didn't you get his message last week?" She couldn't force anyone to accept medical care. She could only hope to persuade them to agree.

"*Ja*, we got the message. But it is not what we wanted. If you say we must, we will. Her time is close."

"Thank you. Let me grab her chart. The hospital will want it. Why don't you leave your buggy here? I'll drive you back to the farm and take both of you into the city. You can make arrangements for someone to get the buggy home in the morning."

"*Danki*. I will unhitch Dobby."

"You can put him in the side yard."

It wouldn't be the first Amish buggy to be parked in her drive overnight. She'd had a small area privacy fenced at the side of the house for such occasions.

Racing back upstairs to change, Amber wished with all her heart she could give Elijah and Sophie the kind of delivery they wanted. Being able to do home deliveries again was the one good thing that would happen when Phillip left.

Perhaps the only good thing. She would to cling to that bit of comfort.

CHAPTER NINETEEN

THE RINGING OF Phillip's cell phone woke him at a quarter to four. Picking it up, he mumbled, "Dr. White here."

"Phillip, this is Amber."

Her voice brought him wide-awake. "What's up?"

"I'm on my way to Sophie Knepp's home. She's in labor. Her husband came to get me."

He sat up and swung his legs over the side of the bed. "Okay. What's the plan?"

"I'm going to pick her up and drive her to the hospital. Why don't you meet us there?"

"Sounds good. How long?"

"It'll take me at least fifteen minutes to get out to the farm. I'd say we should be in Millersburg in forty minutes."

"All right. I'll meet you there."

Hanging up the phone, he headed for the shower. He couldn't be sure of his grandfather's motivation for allowing Amber to do home births, but if it meant more hours of sleep, it wasn't such a bad idea.

After a quick shower, he dressed and jumped into his car. He did think Sophie was a high-risk patient, but his conscience pricked him. She might not get to experience the calm, spiritual birth that he'd seen with Amber's other home delivery patients. Even so, it was better to be safe than sorry.

Halfway to Millersburg, he dialed Amber's number while he was stopped at a stop sign. It went straight to her voice mail. He left a brief message asking for an update, then snapped his phone shut and drove on. At the parking lot of the hospital, he placed another call to her number with the same results.

Why wasn't she picking up? What was wrong?

Up on the OB floor, he checked in with the night shift charge nurse. The young woman in pink scrubs smiled at him brightly. "How may I help you?"

"I'm Dr. Phillip White. I'm expecting a patient soon. Nurse-midwife Bradley is bringing her in. What room is she going to?"

"This is the first I've heard of an admission, Dr. White."

"Miss Bradley hasn't notified you?" He glanced at his watch. It had been almost an hour since he'd spoken to her last.

"No sir, but we have room six ready. Can I have the patient's name?"

"Sophie Knepp," he replied absently.

"Do you have her chart with you?"

"No. Excuse me a moment." He walked away from the desk and tried Amber's number once more. There was still no answer.

DRIVING ON THE dark roads required all Amber's concentration. In places it was rough and bumpy. It was easy to get lost on some of these twisting lanes. When they finally pulled up to the farmhouse, Mr. Knepp got out first and hurried toward the house. Pausing to grab her bag from the front seat, Amber noticed her phone on the car floor. Picking it up, she dropped it in her jacket pocket and followed Elijah inside.

It took her five seconds to see that Sophie was well into her labor. Her face, sweat streaked and red from exertion, filled with relief when she caught sight of Amber. "The baby is coming."

There was no way Amber was going to put her in a car and risk a delivery on the roadside somewhere between here and Millersburg. Smiling to reassure her, Amber said, "Hi, Sophie. It looks like you've done most of the work already."

Sophie's only answer was heavy breathing as another contraction took hold.

Pulling her phone from her pocket, Amber started to dial Phillip's number, but her phone screen remained blank.

Surprised, she tried again. "This isn't out of my service area. I should still get a signal."

She tapped the phone against her palm. Nothing. She tapped it harder. Still nothing. It couldn't be the battery. She'd put a new one in two days ago. Maybe it had broken when it fell out of her bag.

Sophie spoke up. "I do not want to go to the hospital."

Amber shook her phone again. "I'm sorry, we talked about this. The doctor feels it's best that you do."

Sophie, wide-eyed, shook her head. "There is no time."

Amber slipped her useless phone in her pocket, then took off her jacket and looked for a place to lay it. Elijah took it from her. She muttered her thanks and started laying out her things. Babies didn't care what doctors wanted. They came in their own good time. This one was going to arrive very soon. She needed to get ready.

For another hour, Phillip waited by the hospital maternity desk, drumming his fingers, turning down offers of coffee and pacing. His first instinct was to rush out to the Knepp farm, but he knew he'd never find his way in the dark. He wasn't sure he could remember the way in broad daylight.

He'd spent more time enjoying Amber's company than memorizing the twisting roads when they'd made prenatal visits to her clients. If he hadn't been so smitten with her he'd be more effective now in tracking her down. That irony wasn't lost on him.

When a second full hour had gone by, he couldn't wait any longer. Something was up. She wouldn't blow him off like this. Maybe she'd had an accident. His mind shied away from that thought, but he knew something had gone wrong.

Returning to the desk, he leaned on the counter and spoke to the charge nurse. "How do I contact the sheriff?"

The nurse dialed the emergency number and handed him the phone. When dispatch answered, he quickly explained the situation. After being asked to wait, he impatiently held the line, his fear growing by leaps and bounds. Finally, a man's voice came on.

"This is Nick Bradley. You think something has happened to Amber?"

"She hasn't shown up at the hospital, she's not answering her phone. Did she call 911?"

"We've got no record of that. Stay at the hospital, Doc. I'm on my way. I'll pick you up out front."

AMBER WAS LOADING her supplies in the back of her station wagon when she saw the flashing lights coming up the lane. Oh, dear. Phillip had pulled out all the stops to find her. At least she knew he cared.

When the sheriff's car stopped beside her and an officer got out, she gave him a little wave. "Hi, Nick."

She saw Phillip emerge from the cruiser's passenger side door. Her heart did a funny little flip-flop at the sight of him. He was a tall, lean silhouette against the blood-red sunrise; she couldn't see his face.

The sheriff said, "You okay, cuz?"

"I'm fine, Nick. Sorry you were sent on a wild goose chase."

"When someone tells me my little cousin is missing, I don't take that lightly. What's the story?"

"Yes, Amber. What is the story?" Phillip asked coming up behind Nick.

"It was the weirdest thing. I called you on my cell phone and told you I was on my way here. When I arrived, I tried to notify you, but my phone didn't work. I think it broke when it fell out of my bag."

Nick gestured toward the house. "Everything go okay?"

"Sophie and her new daughter are fine. They were settling down to sleep when I left. Phillip, I was going to call you as soon as I got to a phone. Thanks for sending the cavalry after me. Even if I didn't need it."

He approached and stood close. Softly, he said, "I'm just thankful you're okay."

His voice vibrated with deep emotion. He held out his hand. She took it and he squeezed tightly, as if he'd never let go. Amber wanted to throw her arms around him and reassure him with a kiss. Having her eagle-eyed cousin observing them kept her from doing something so foolish.

Nick opened his cell phone and held it up. "I've got cell service here. I wonder why you can't get it?"

"It wasn't that I didn't have service. The thing was dead. It wouldn't work."

Suddenly, her phone began ringing. Both men looked at her in surprise.

Amber dug it out of her pocket, her surprise equal to the men standing beside her. She opened the phone and said, "Hello?"

"Honey, are you all right?" It was Wilma.

"I'm fine."

"I heard the sheriff's office is looking for you."

"They found me."

"Thank the Lord for that. Where are you?"

Amber saw a scowl begin to darken Phillip's face. "Wilma, I'll give you the details when I get to the office. I've got to go."

Closing the phone, she looked Phillip straight in the eye. "It was not working an hour ago. At least the delivery went off without a hitch. I told you it would."

A remote expression turned his face to stone. "You had to do it your way, didn't you? You had to prove I was wrong."

"What?" Was he implying she deliberately didn't take Sophie to the hospital?

"I never thought you'd risk her life to make a point." Disappointment filled his voice.

Amber stood toe-to-toe with him. "If I planned to attend her at home, why did I call you in the first place?"

"Beats me, but it's clear your phone works. I've seen

people devoted to their jobs, but you take the cake, Amber. What if something had gone wrong?"

Anger sent her pulse pounding. Crossing her arms, she glared at him. "Nothing did go wrong, so I was *right* all along."

"Whoa." Nick stepped in between them. "There'll be no bloodshed on my watch. It makes too much paperwork."

Seething, she said, "Don't worry, Nick. I wouldn't waste my time trying to knock some sense into Dr. White. There's no room in that brain with his overgrown ego taking up so much space."

Phillip's jaw tightened and his eyes narrowed. For a second, she thought she'd gone too far. When he spoke his voice was like ice. "Take the day off, Miss Bradley. We'll manage without you at the office."

"Fine. I'd love to." Marching to her car, Amber got in, slammed the door and started the engine. Her anger began draining away and tears rushed in to fill the void.

How could he think she would play such a trick on him? She pressed the heels of her hands into her stinging eyes to stem her tears. It didn't help.

It had been such a beautiful birth. The calmness, the joy on their faces when they saw their little girl. From their rushed start to the peaceful finish, it had gone without a bit of trouble.

Phillip would have robbed them of one of the most precious moments of their lives because he didn't trust *her* judgment. He didn't believe in her skill. He believed she was capable of underhanded deceit and lying to his face.

Slamming the car in gear, she backed up to turn around in the narrow yard. When she had the car straight, she saw Mr. Knepp coming out of the barn with his oldest son. Each of them carried pails full of frothy milk.

Rolling down her window, she said, "I'll be happy to take your son into town so he can bring your buggy back but I must leave now."

She heard Phillip call her name. She ignored him.

Setting his pails down, Mr. Knepp spoke quietly to his son, handed him something, then spoke to her. "*Danki*. Walter will go with you."

Again she heard Phillip call her name. She refused to look that way. She had no intention of letting him see she was crying.

Walter raced around to the passenger side of the car, eager to ride in the normally forbidden automobile. When he got in, she said, "Buckle up."

After he complied, she stomped on the gas and tore down the dirt lane. She left her window rolled down so the warm air would dry the tears on her cheeks.

Walter, at sixteen, loved everything about cars. He chatted happily on the way to town and changed the radio station a dozen times. Amber didn't mind. It saved her from having to make conversation.

When they reached her home, she got out feeling as if her entire body were made of lead. She couldn't remember the last time she felt so disconnected. Her tears were done but they'd brought on a pounding headache.

Walter went to get the horse and she waited until he returned and harnessed the animal. When he climbed into the buggy, she stepped up to the driver's side. "Please remind your mother that I will be back tomorrow to check on her and your new sister."

"My *dat* asked me to give you this." He held out a note.

She opened the slip of paper. It was a brief apology for

disabling her phone. She looked up at Walter in shock. "Your father tampered with my phone?"

"*Mamm* did not want to go to the hospital. *Dat* took your battery out when you weren't looking and put it back before you were ready to leave. He does it to my phone whenever he finds it."

Lifting his pant leg to show his boot, he pulled a cell phone out of his sock. "I hide it better now, and I keep a spare battery in the barn."

The Amish never ceased to amaze her. She knew that their teenagers often ventured outside the Church rules to use modern gadgets such as phones and radios. Without electricity in their homes, they had to find an English friend or neighbor who would charge the battery-powered devices for them.

While parents often turned a blind eye to such behaviors, Mr. Knepp had apparently learned how to silence his son's unwanted intrusion in his home. The Knepps belonged to the Swartzentruber Amish, the most conservative group. Walter would soon have to give up his worldly ways or face growing Church disapproval of him and his family.

Walter said, "*Dat* is sorry if you were upset."

"Tell your father he is forgiven." There was nothing else she could do.

"*Danki*, I will." He slapped the reins and sent the horse trotting out into the street.

Amber stared at the note. She had proof that she hadn't lied about her phone. When Phillip saw this he'd realize how wrong he'd been.

Suddenly angry, she crumpled the note and tore it into shreds. Phillip shouldn't need a note to prove she was honest. What an idiot she'd been to think she was in love with him. He didn't trust her. How could she love a man like that?

That answer was simple. She couldn't.

CHAPTER TWENTY

"HOW LONG ARE you going to keep giving me the silent treatment?"

Phillip watched as Amber ignored his question, laid the patient chart he'd asked for on his desk and walked out of the room. Apparently, she could be silent a little longer.

Wilma, standing on the other side of his desk, tucked her pencil behind her ear, crossed her arms and scowled at him. "I don't know what you did. I've never seen her this upset."

Shooting her a sour look, he asked, "What makes you think I'm to blame?"

"Because you're a man."

There was no point arguing with her logic. He was beginning to think he had liked Wilma better when she was a timid mouse. Who knew she could become a spitting cat when her friends were in trouble? "Just order those forms and check to see if we have more printer ink somewhere."

"Yes, sir." She rolled her eyes and started to leave, but stopped at the door and turned around.

"What now?" he demanded.

Pointing at him, she said, "Don't be crabby with me, young man. I'm old enough to be your grandmother. I deserve some respect."

She was right. He folded his hands and made himself smile. "I'm sorry, Mrs. Nolan. What is it you wanted to tell me?"

"That young Mennonite doctor who was here last year called after you left last night. He wants to come interview for the position."

Phillip's spirits shot skyward. Maybe he could get Harold the partner he needed. "That's great. Thank you, Wilma. I'll give him a call and we can set something up."

"Maybe he'll be smart enough not to go around upsetting the Amish, Harold and everyone else." She closed the door behind her when she left.

Phillip's elation popped like a balloon hitting a thorn tree. It had been like this for three days. Amber spoke to him only when necessary. Wilma never missed a chance to deliver a jab. If this was how his last three weeks were going to go, he honestly didn't think he could take it.

How was he supposed to run a clinic with a nurse who wouldn't speak to him? Maybe he should have handled the whole thing differently.

He had cooled off considerably by the time Nick Bradley dropped him at the office after leaving the Knepp farm. After all, Amber had been found safe and sound. Mrs. Knepp and her daughter seemed fine. He had checked on them before he left the farm. He'd almost called Amber then to apologize but his pride had held him back. He wasn't wrong. She was.

How often had she insisted Sophie Knepp wasn't a high-risk patient? Unable to change his mind on the subject, she'd gone behind his back and delivered the woman at home anyway. What he didn't understand was why Amber wouldn't admit she'd turned her phone off on purpose. She'd been found out. She had nothing to gain by pretending anymore.

Unless she was telling the truth.

That nagging voice at the back of his brain was getting louder by the hour. He hadn't known Amber very long but she didn't seem like an underhanded person. She was warm and witty and devoted to the people of her community.

Okay, there had been that time at church when she'd seated him with Gina Curtis. That had been a little sneaky but it was nothing compared to this. Was his ability to read a person that messed up?

If she had told the truth, what could he do at this point? He'd already called her a liar. In front of her cousin, no less. Would she even accept his apology?

He glanced at his watch. It was almost four and it was time to end this standoff. They had to work together. He would eat crow. One wouldn't hurt him. There were plenty more out in the cornfields.

He pressed the intercom button. "Wilma, ask Amber to step in here, please."

"Can't."

Letting go of the button, he muttered a few unkind words under his breath, then asked. "Why not?"

"She's with Sophie Knepp and her new baby."

"Sophie wasn't scheduled to come in until Monday. Is something wrong?"

"Oh, yes."

He rose and headed for the door. Before he reached it, it flew open. Amber stood in the doorway with a look of panic on her face. "You need to come quick."

"What's the matter?"

"It's Sophie Knepp. She's hallucinating and muttering that God is taking another child away. She won't let me see that baby."

"Is her husband with her?"

"Yes."

They crossed the hall and Phillip saw Amber wasn't exaggerating. Sophie sat plucking invisible things from the baby's blanket and throwing them away as fast as she could. She kept muttering the same phrase over and over.

Quietly, he asked Amber, "What's she saying?"

"That leaves are falling and covering her baby. She has to keep them away or her baby will be buried."

Phillip looked at her husband. "When did this start?"

"This morning. She picked up the baby and started crying. I couldn't get her to stop." He stood against the wall turning his straw hat around and around in his hands. He looked worried to death.

Phillip sat on a stool and moved in front of her. "Sophie, I'm Dr. White. Do you remember me?"

She didn't answer, didn't make eye contact. He moved closer slowly and touched her hand. "Sophie, I need to see your pretty little girl."

She stopped picking and started crying. Carefully, he withdrew the swaddled child. Laying the baby on the exam table, he opened the blankets. The child looked asleep. To his relief she was clearly breathing. She was also very jaundiced.

He looked at Mr. Knepp. "How long has her skin been so yellow?"

"Since two days after she was born."

Amber broke in. "I told you to contact me if the baby's jaundice got worse."

"When we saw the whites of her eyes were yellow,

too, we knew God was taking her from us as He did our first children."

Puzzled, Phillip asked, "You've had other children with jaundice?"

"Twin girls who both died before they were two years old. Then we had strong sons and more healthy daughters. Why has God put this burden on us again?"

Sophie sat rocking herself and staring into space.

Phillip said, "Elijah, your wife is very sick. This is a rare thing called postpartum psychosis. She needs to be hospitalized, but she will get better."

The man nodded without looking convinced. Phillip turned to Amber. "Call an ambulance, then call the hospital and tell them we need a mental health assessment for Sophie. After that, call the Peds unit and tell them we need triple phototherapy lights for this little one. I also want a total bilirubin level STAT along with standard admission lab."

"Yes, Doctor."

He asked, "Mr. Knepp, do you understand what jaundice is?"

When the man shook his head, Phillip explained. "This is a common thing in newborns. Jaundice refers to the yellow color of the skin and whites of the eyes caused by excess bilirubin in the blood. Bilirubin is a chemical produced by the normal breakdown of red blood cells. We all have a little in our blood. Normally, bilirubin passes through the liver and is excreted as bile by our intestines. This yellow color occurs when bilirubin builds up faster than the baby's liver can break it down and pass it from the body. We treat it by putting the child under a special light. If the level is very high, we may have to do an exchange transfusion. To do that, we take out some of the blood with the high concentration and put in blood with normal levels."

"Will she die from this as our other children did?"

"I'll do everything I can to make sure that doesn't happen."

Within thirty minutes, both Knepp patients were on their way to the hospital. Phillip was getting into his car to follow the ambulance when Amber came running up to him. She grasped his arm in a tight grip. "I have to know, Phillip. Did I miss something? The jaundice was barely visible the day after birth. I told them to bring her in if it got worse."

The look in her eyes tugged at his heart. He didn't want to answer her. He wanted to pull her into his arms, kiss her and tell her everything would be all right, but that might be a lie.

Home deliveries weren't safe. Maybe she hadn't missed anything at the birth, but a woman and her baby need round-the-clock observation for two days after a delivery. Most state laws require a mother and her new-born to stay in the hospital at least that long.

He had tried to make that point. Amber had made it for him.

When Phillip didn't answer, Amber's heart sank. "I saw them the day after delivery and nothing looked out of the ordinary. Lots of newborns have mild jaundice."

She bit her lip as she waited for him to say something, anything.

"Amber, there are too many unknowns for me to start guessing now. We need some solid information. Let's run some lab tests and find out why the baby is so jaundiced at four days old."

"Sophie's blood type is O positive so it can't be an RH incompatibility. Sepsis? The baby didn't act sick or look dehydrated. Maybe it's an ABO problem. And what about Sophie?" Amber knew she was babbling. She couldn't help herself.

He gripped her hand. "Calm down. You'll drive yourself nuts doing this. Postpartum psychosis can occur anywhere from one to three months after delivery. I've not heard of a case starting four days after birth, but I haven't researched it. Were the signs there when you saw her? We may never know. The best thing that could happen is happening now. They're getting the treatment they need."

She withdrew her hand. "You're right."

"Do you want to come with me to the hospital?"

Shaking her head, she stepped back. "I'd only be in the way."

"All right, I have to get going. I'll fill you in when I get back."

After he drove away, Amber went back inside the clinic. Wilma, getting ready to close up, slipped her purse strap over her shoulder. "Is everybody okay?"

"Sophie was sedated enough to go calmly. Elijah looked like a zombie. I don't think he knows what's hit him. The baby was sleeping quietly in the car seat the EMS brought."

"Dr. White will find out what's wrong. Don't worry."

"You think he's a good doctor, don't you?"

"As good as Harold. Maybe better."

Turning around, Amber began pacing across the lobby as she racked her mind for every little detail. "For a baby to get that jaundiced so fast, it must have been worse than I thought when I saw her last. Why didn't I pick up on that?"

"Amber, you're a great midwife. You love your patients. You'd never hurt them."

Pressing her hand to her forehead, Amber closed her eyes. "I remember checking her nose. I always push lightly on the tip of their noses to see what color their skin was underneath. I do that on all newborn checks."

"See? What did I tell you?"

"I was so mad that day. Did my anger at Phillip cloud my judgment? Did I want to be right so badly that I fooled myself into thinking everything was fine? That baby could have permanent brain damage if her jaundice causes kernicterus."

"What does that mean?"

"If the levels of bilirubin in her blood rise high enough to cross the blood-brain barrier, the bilirubin can enter her brain cells and damage them."

Wilma took Amber by the shoulders. "Some things are out of our control. We are human. Only God is perfect. Beating yourself up is not helping. Go home and get some rest."

Dropping her arms to her side, Amber nodded. "I will. First, I need to call Harold."

"That reminds me. The charts Dr. White wanted were delivered a little while ago." Returning to her desk, Wilma picked up a large package and brought it to Amber.

Taking it, Amber said, "I'll see that he gets them."

After Wilma left, Amber retreated to her office and put a call through to the rehab hospital in Hawaii. When Harold came to the phone, she started crying. It seemed like she was always crying. How many tears did she have left?

"Amber? What on earth is wrong? Get a hold of yourself. Has something happened to my grandson?"

The fright in his voice forced her to gain a modicum of control. "Phillip… I mean, Dr. White, is fine. It's nothing like that."

"Thank heaven. Then what is it?"

After blotting her face and blowing her nose, she was able to relate the event of the afternoon with only a few hiccups.

He said, "Another yellow baby for Sophie. I'm so, so, sorry to hear that. The twins she lost were such beautiful little girls."

"What was the cause of death?"

"I'm not sure. It had to be some kind of liver disorder, but all the liver function studies were normal. It was very puzzling. Both Sophie and Elijah said they had family members who had lost children from the same thing. They knew the girls were going to die. I tried everything. Phototherapy and blood transfusions worked for a while, but once we stopped them the jaundice came back. There was nothing left to do but let them take the girls home to die. We accepted it as God's will."

"That must have been awful for Sophie. Seeing this baby getting jaundice may be what triggered her psychosis."

"I imagine you're right."

"I'll let Phillip know what you've told me. I'll pray this isn't the same thing."

"I'll do the same. All those tears over Sophie's illness, that's not like you, Amber. What's going on?"

"We need you back," she moaned, then pressed her fingers to her lips. She had no intention of telling him that his grandson was breaking her heart.

"I'm getting better by leaps and bounds."

"Are you? Honestly?"

"Okay, now you've got me worried."

"Don't be. Things are…okay here. I'm tired. I miss you."

"Are you sure there isn't something else you want to tell me? Are you and Phillip still not getting along? Wilma told me he accused you of doing deliveries without his consent. I'm gonna have to have a talk with that boy."

"No," she said promptly. "Just…just get well soon. Everyone misses you."

"Okay." He didn't sound convinced but he hung up.

Amber settled the handset back in the cradle and lowered her head on her folded arms. She did miss Harold. Things were okay at the clinic. It was only her heart that was broken.

She'd seen the look in Phillip's eyes. The look that said she had messed up big-time. Exactly the way he had expected.

Sitting up, she dried her face on her sleeve. After leaving her office, she locked up the building and got in her car. She didn't drive home.

CHAPTER TWENTY-ONE

WHEN PHILLIP PULLED into his grandfather's driveway it was well after eleven o'clock at night. He'd had a long day and an even longer evening.

Getting out of the car, he headed for the front steps. Someone rose from the wrought iron bench that circled the maple in the front yard and came toward him. He saw it was Amber when she stepped into the light coming from the front porch.

She had her hands clenched tightly in front of her. "How are they?"

"Both of them are doing better."

He heard her sigh of relief. "I'm so glad."

They stood staring at each other like strangers in the near darkness. How had their relationship gotten so out of whack?

"Amber, you should go home."

"I needed to know how they are."

He walked toward the bench and sat down. She joined him but left some distance between them.

Running his hand through his hair, he said, "Sophie has been admitted to the psychiatric unit. Little Grace had a bilirubin level of twenty-six milligrams per deciliter. We did an exchange transfusion and got it down to sixteen."

"That's still a long way above a normal of four."

"She'll stay under triple lights for now. We're doing a workup to see if this is an infection. It doesn't look like it."

"Will she have brain damage from such a high level?"

"You mean will she want to be a doctor when she grows up?" He didn't get the smile he was hoping for.

"Phillip, please. Tell me."

"She's lethargic but she isn't showing the more serious symptoms of kernicterus. They'll check her bili level again at midnight. I came home to get a change of clothes. I'll be spending the night at the hospital."

She nodded slightly. "I talked to Harold about Sophie's other children who died. He thinks it was some kind of liver disorder."

"All Grace's liver studies are normal. You know that in some cases the reason for a high bilirubin is never found and the child recovers. Grace was a little dehydrated. I think she'll be fine in a few days. Stop worrying."

"I can't help feeling guilty."

He hated to add to her burden, but he didn't believe in sugarcoating the truth. "To have a bili level this high this soon after birth, she had to have had some symptoms when you saw her."

Clasping her arms across her middle, Amber stood. "I'm so sorry. I thought it was ordinary newborn jaundice. I should have gone back to see her again."

"Amber, mistakes happen." He rose and reached for her. She stepped away. She wouldn't look at him.

"You'll stop all my home births, won't you?" She sniffed and wiped her face with the heels of her hands.

"I have to. You know that." He hated giving her this news on top of everything else.

She gave a short, quick nod. "I knew you would."

Picking up a mailing envelope, she held it out to him. "These are the old charts you wanted."

He took them, wondering what he could say to make this whole thing better. No words came to him.

She said, "Thanks for giving me an update on Sophie and Grace. I'll see you on Monday."

Before he could stop her, she vanished into the darkness.

PHILLIP KEPT CLOSE tabs on Grace overnight. Her bilirubin levels dropped as expected. With no sign of infection or other underlying problems, he thought he'd be able to send her home in a few days.

By early in the morning, he was able to gradually drop the number of blue lights to one. Her level stayed low and steady. He went home.

He wanted to call Amber then, but he wasn't sure what to say. In spite of being exhausted, he slept poorly. The phone rang shortly after six thirty the next morning. The news was good. Grace's levels were much lower.

He'd had the nursing staff take the lights off for six hours and recheck her. She might have some rebound but he didn't expect much.

Waiting was the hardest, so he called to get an update on Sophie. The report he got for her was good. Sophie continued to improve with medication, but she remained under the care of her psychiatrist. It might be several more days before she could be reunited with her baby.

Getting dressed, Phillip got ready to go into work, eager to see Amber and find out how she was doing. The answer, as it turned out, was not well.

She came in to work but remained aloof and withdrawn. He missed her smile more than he missed the sea. When he tried to talk with her, she found something to do elsewhere.

A little after one o'clock, Wilma came toward him with a sheet of paper in her hand. "The hospital called over these lab reports for you."

"Thank you."

Just then Amber came out of the exam room. She muttered, "Excuse me." Then she slipped between them and went into her office and shut the door without another word.

He stared after her. "Wilma, what are we going to do with her? I hate to see her like this."

Patting his arm, Wilma said, "She'll come around. She feels responsible. She's going to have to learn to live with that. Medicine is not for the faint of heart."

"Amen to that."

"How are you doing?"

"Me? I'm fine."

"Are you?" Wilma nodded toward Amber's door. "I ask because you've got the same hangdog look on your face that she's wearing."

As Wilma walked away, he glanced at the lab report in his hands. Grace's bilirubin level had shot back up. Her jaundice had returned.

This was not right. Puzzled, he went to his phone and called the pediatric unit with orders to restart the lights and retest her in six hours.

Sitting at his desk, he noticed the old chart files he'd been too busy to review. He opened them and began to study them.

The first chart he picked was the child named Knepp. As it turned out, it wasn't one of Sophie's children. The parents were Otto and Norma Knepp. Their child had died at eighteen months from persistent jaundice. As he read the lab reports and notes by his grandfather, he became more and more intrigued. It was as if he were reading Grace's chart. The similarities were too close to ignore.

There was a soft knock at his door. Amber looked in, staring at a point over his head. Each time she couldn't bring herself to look him in the face, another piece got shaved off his heart. He had no idea how to mend it.

She said, "I'm getting ready to leave. Do you need anything before I go?"

A kiss, a hug, a smile. I want you back, Amber. How do I do that? Help me, God. Help me find a way through this wall she's put up between us.

He glanced at the chart in his hands. Medicine was her life. Somehow, the answer was in their work.

"Amber, do you remember a child of Otto and Norma Knepp who died about eight years ago?"

He saw the hesitation in her face, but her curiosity won out. "I do. The funeral was held the day after I arrived here. Why?"

"I started reading this old chart and found that this Knepp child died of severe jaundice at eighteen months of age."

Amber stepped inside the room. He wanted to shout for joy. Instead, he kept his gaze down. She asked, "Was it liver failure?"

Leafing though the chart, he said, "Not according to these lab reports. Do you know if Otto and Elijah are related?"

"I believe they're first cousins. Actually, I think Norma and Sophie are second cousins." She came to peer over his shoulder at the papers he held.

His heart raced at her nearness. It was a struggle to keep his voice level. "Sophie's twins, this child and now Grace, all related. This suggests we are dealing with some kind of inherited disorder."

"Like what?"

"I'm not sure. Maybe something like Dubin-Johnson or Rotor's syndromes, maybe—" He spun around to the computer and began typing.

Pulling a chair up, she sat beside him. "Maybe what?"

His frustration at the slow speed of the dial-up connection was offset by Amber's nearness. He wouldn't care if it took an hour to get online as long as she stayed beside him.

Nudging him with her elbow, she repeated, "Maybe what?"

"Maybe it's Crigler-Najjar Syndrome."

Her eyebrows shot up. "Why does that sound familiar?"

"It's a very rare recessive genetic defect. The actual incidence is less than one case per one million live births."

"One in a million?" she repeated. "And you think we've had four suspected cases in our town? That's kind of a stretch."

"No, it's not. There are only about two hundred cases of Crigler-Najjar Syndrome in the world. There are nearly forty cases in the United States. Care to guess where the majority of those are found?"

He saw the lightbulb come on. She leaned toward him eagerly. "A recessive gene disorder would occur more frequently in a population with limited common ancestors."

"Bingo. Old Order Amish and Mennonite communities." The computer finally connected. She bumped him with her elbow to gain access to his keyboard.

Happily, he allowed it, grinning like a schoolkid. This was the woman he'd come to love, determined, smart and eager to help. She typed quickly and pulled up the website for the Pennsylvania Clinic for Special-Needs Children.

Tapping the screen with her finger, she said, "This is where they're doing wonders with genetic research among the Amish. They are working on treatments and, someday, maybe even cures."

"How do you know this?" He stared at her in amazement.

"I read everything I can about my mother's people. This is the contact information for the clinic." She pointed to a number scrolling at the bottom of the screen.

Leaning close to look, he inhaled the clean, citrus scent of her hair and the fragrance that was uniquely her own. It sent his head swimming. He reached for the mouse at the same time she did. His hand covered hers.

Her gaze flew to his face, those beautiful mermaid eyes widened with wonder. He'd never wanted to kiss anyone so badly in his whole life.

NEVER HAD AMBER wanted a man to kiss her as much as she wanted to be kissed by Phillip. He knew it. She saw it in his gaze.

He was so close. If she moved a fraction of an inch toward him it would be the impetus he needed. The temptation was so great it formed a physical ache in her chest.

"Amber." He breathed her name into the air with such longing.

Turning her face away, she concentrated on keeping her wild emotions in check.

He squeezed her hand. "Tell me you feel the way I

do about you. Tell me I'm not imagining this…thing we have."

"Phillip, there's no future for us."

Taking her chin in his hand, he tipped her face toward him. "Are you sure about that?"

"Maybe," she whispered, wishing for some way to keep this wonderful man in her life.

His tender smile was her undoing. Closing her eyes, she raised her lips to his. His kiss, featherlight at first, slowly deepened as his hands cupped her face. This was how it was meant to be between two people in love.

Pulling away at last, he drew a ragged breath. "You rock my world, Amber. We can work this out, darling. I know we can."

"How? Do you give up your dreams or do I give up mine? How long before one of us starts to feel cheated? To wonder if it was worth it? I won't do that to you. I won't do it to myself."

How she wanted to snatch her words out of the air and take them back. She couldn't because they were the truth.

"I understand." His voice grew rough as he withdrew his hand in a soft caress. "I don't like it, but I understand."

Clenching her jaw, she refused to acknowledge the stinging behind her eyes. She forced her attention back to the computer screen. "This may not be what Grace has."

When he didn't say anything, she chanced a glance in his direction. He stared at her with a lost, sad look in his eyes.

After a moment, he blinked hard, then focused on the computer and took control of the mouse. "I'll have to do some further research on this disorder, but I think we're on to something."

He clicked through to information and symptoms of the disorder. "It says high levels of unconjugated bilirubin in the presence of normal liver function is characteristic of CNS. That's exactly what I've found with Grace. The cause of CNS is a missing liver enzyme. That explains a lot."

Amber forced herself to concentrate on the computer screen and not on her breaking heart. A child needed their help. "Grace's liver functions normally, but without that specific enzyme, the production of bilirubin in the blood can't be controlled by her body."

"Right. Nothing we've tested for so far could detect that."

One more click brought up the picture of a child resting in a crib under intense blue lights. A mirror on one side of the crib reflected the light around the sleeping infant.

Phillip said, "The current treatment is twelve hours of phototherapy a day for their entire lives. With the type 1, which sounds like Grace's illness, patients will die before they are two years old without these special blue lights."

Amber couldn't imagine trying to sleep one night under such intense lamps, let alone a whole lifetime.

He leaned closer to the screen. "These people are doing some fascinating work. In rural Pennsylvania, of all places. How strange is that? They've identified more than thirty-five different diseases that Amish children can be born with. Wow. What I wouldn't give to tour their facility."

"Is there anything else that can be done for Grace?"

"Sorry, I got off on a tangent for a second. It says a liver transplant provides the only known cure."

Sitting back, he shook his head. "A transplant exchanges one set of problems for another. Costly antire-jection drugs, infections, a whole host of other potential complications."

"But it can save her life?"

He looked at her. "Yes. Would the Amish consent to a liver transplant for one of their children?"

"Harold told me they won't accept heart transplants. I do know someone who had a kidney transplant. Yes, I believe most of them would allow it. They're not op-posed to modern medicine."

Rubbing his chin with one hand, he studied the screen. "She would need home phototherapy lights like the ones in the picture in order to survive until she's old enough for a transplant."

Amber sat back with a sigh. "I see one big hurdle with that."

"What?"

"The Amish have no electricity in their homes."

"That is a big problem. Would they make an excep-tion for this?"

"I'm not sure. What is the likelihood of matching Grace for a liver?"

"We're getting ahead of ourselves. First we need to confirm that this is what she has." He picked up the phone and began dialing.

"Who are you calling?"

"The physicians at the Pennsylvania Clinic for Special Needs Children. I want to pick their brains."

Rising to her feet, she stared down at him with pride and sadness. She deeply admired his intensity, his knowl-edge and his desire to help patients. He was a fine doc-tor. She would be sorry to see him leave—for that reason and many others.

As she headed for the door, he softly called her name. When she looked back, he said, "Thank you."

She gave him a half smile and a short nod. He was a good man but he wasn't the man for her.

The eagerness in his voice as he spoke with the genetic specialist and the questions he fired off proved to her he'd never be happy practicing small-town medicine. His vocation lay in another direction.

Her calling was here among the Amish. Only, how could she be happy in Hope Springs without Phillip?

CHAPTER TWENTY-TWO

AT THE SOUND of her phone ringing, Amber laid aside her duster to answer it. Even a telemarketer would be a welcome break from her Saturday morning housecleaning. How did things get so dirty in a week?

Snatching up the portable handset, she pressed it to her ear. "Hello?"

"Amber, I'm glad I caught you." The cheerful voice belonged to Jennifer Hart, the director of the county animal shelter.

A sinking sensation hit the pit of Amber's stomach. Crossing to her kitchen table, she parked herself on one of the chairs. "What's up?"

"We have room at the shelter now for the cat you are fostering."

Oh, no. Amber knew this day was coming, but she still wasn't prepared. "Jennifer, I don't mind keeping Fluffy a little longer. I've been thinking about adopting him myself."

"We've had an inquiry about him from our website. A family in Toledo believes he's the cat they lost when they were on vacation. They're driving down to see him tomorrow. I'm sorry, Amber. Is there any way you can bring him in today?"

Fluffy had a family searching for him. Adopting him was out of the question now. Amber fought back sudden, unexpected tears. What was wrong with her? She should be thrilled for her pet and the unknown family. "Sure. I can bring him in."

Ten minutes later, Amber could barely see the front door for her tears. She didn't want company but the persistent knocking would not stop. Setting her now-damp cat down off her lap, she wiped her swollen eyes with a paper towel and jerked open the door. "Yes?"

It was Phillip. Why did it have to be him?

"Amber, you're crying. What's wrong, honey?"

Sympathy was the last thing she needed. She started boo-hooing again.

Without another word, he stepped inside and took her in his arms. One hand cupped the back of her head and tucked her face against him. The other arm held her tight as she cried out her heartbreak. Softly, he swayed and rocked her as if she were a child. Over and over, he murmured that it would be okay.

No, it wouldn't.

Her sobbing slowed to an occasional hiccup, but she didn't move. She simply rested in the gentleness of his embrace, soaking in his masculine smell and warmth. He would be gone soon. When he was, she would remember this moment of kindness for a long, long time.

He leaned back to look down at her. "What happened?"

"It's just the last straw." She fought back a new flood of tears.

Slipping a finger under her chin, he raised her face to his. "What was the last straw?"

"The Humane Society wants Fluffy back. I have to take him there this afternoon." Her lip started quivering.

"I'm so sorry. Can't you adopt him?"

"He has a family already."

"You're his family."

"No, the family that lost him wants him back. I knew I wouldn't keep him but I didn't know how attached I was going to get, either."

That, in a nutshell, was what was wrong with her whole life. The things she loved were gone or going away. Her practice, unless Harold came back, her cat, this wonderful man—it wasn't fair.

Moving out of his arms was the last thing she wanted to do. She forced herself to do it anyway. "What are you doing here, Phillip?"

"I need your help."

Rubbing her cheeks with her palms, she cleared her throat and tried to look like a calm, reasonable woman instead of a wreck. "Sure. What do you need me to do?"

"I'm meeting with Elijah Knepp and some of his Church elders at five o'clock tonight. I'm sorry for the short notice. We were right about Grace having Crigler-Nijjar syndrome. I got confirmation this morning."

"Oh, no. I hoped we were wrong." Her heart ached for Grace and her parents. Returning Fluffy paled in comparison to such heartrending news.

"Elijah was at the hospital this morning. Sophie has been released. Both of them came to see the baby. When I explained what Grace would need to go home, they said no. Can you believe that?"

Putting her own troubles aside, she gestured toward the living room. "Have a seat. Let me wash my face and we can talk about this."

"I'm sorry to bring this to you but I didn't know who else could help."

After Amber made herself presentable, she joined

Phillip in the living room. Agitated, he paced back and forth in front of her bay window. Taking a seat in one of her chairs, she asked, "Can I get you something to drink? A soda? I have iced tea made."

He stopped pacing and turned around. "No, I'm fine. Tell me why these people won't allow electricity in their home to save their child's life."

How could she explain it to him? "Phillip, the Amish believe they are commanded to be separate from the world. Literally. Having power lines come to their home makes them connected to the world at large."

"Grace will die without those lights."

"We all die. The Amish understand that and accept it in a way that is foreign to many people. They know that Grace will be in a better place, a place without pain or want. They love their child as any parent loves their child, but they believe they will be with her in heaven. She will not be lost to them."

He turned to stare out the window. "You were supposed to help. How can I argue against that when it is what I believe as a Christian?"

She rose and moved to his side. "I'm not suggesting we give up. I'm simply saying we have to work within their system."

Rubbing the back of his neck, he asked, "How do we do that?"

"Do you know why my phone didn't work the night Sophie gave birth?"

"Why?"

"Because Elijah slipped the battery out when I wasn't looking and put it back in before I left."

Looking stunned, he pressed the fingers of one hand

against his temple. "Okay, two questions. Why? And how did he know *how* to do that?"

"The why was because Sophie didn't want to deliver at the hospital. He knew how because his son uses a cell phone. The cell phone operates on a battery and is not connected to landlines so some Amish are accepting them."

"That seems contradictory."

"Welcome to the Amish world. What we need is a way to provide the power for Sophie's light without electric lines to the house." Amber started pacing.

"A generator?" he suggested.

"That may not work. The Knepps belong to an ultra-conservative church district that doesn't allow the use of gas."

"How do the Amish feel about solar power?"

Returning to her chair, Amber sat forward and laced her fingers together around her knees. "Solar might be okay. It's light from God to power the world. Maybe that's the right angle. If their Church elders don't agree to the lights, then Sophie and Elijah will have to abide by that decision or be shunned."

"It doesn't seem right." He shook his head in frustration.

"For the Amish, it is not about the individual. It is about the good of the whole."

"Then the good of the whole is the angle I need."

"I'd say so."

He sat in the armchair opposite her. "Let's think this through."

Folding her jean-clad legs under her, she stared at the floor. "My mind is a blank."

"I'm sorry. I know you're upset about your cat. I shouldn't have come running to you."

She waved aside his concern. "I don't have to leave for a while yet. I'm glad you came."

He rose and started pacing again, his brow furrowed in concentration. She didn't envy him his task. His words today might mean the difference between life and death for little Grace.

Turning to her, he said, "I think I've got an idea. Listen to this."

PHILLIP ARRIVED AT the home of Elijah Knepp at five minutes before five o'clock. On the porch, he saw eight straw hats hanging from pegs along the side of the house. He took a second to wonder how each man found his own hat when he left. They looked identical to him.

The elders were already waiting for him inside. Seated in a semicircle, the men all wore dark suits or pale blue shirts under dark vests. Most wore wire-rimmed glasses. All had gray beards that reached to the middle of their chests.

After the introductions were made, Phillip took a seat. "Thank you for meeting with me today."

The man on the end said, "It is a serious thing you are asking Elijah to do. It is forbidden."

"I understand that. I do not ask lightly. Without these special lights, his daughter will die. As did his first daughters and in the same way."

"It was *Gottes Wille*," said one on the other end.

"He had need for my daughters to be with Him in Heaven," Elijah replied, his voice heavy with sorrow.

His suffering was painful to watch. Phillip had no doubt he loved his child. "Grace has a terrible disease, but one that can be treated by the very first gift God gave the world. *Genesis* 1:3-4, 'And God said, Let there be light: and there was light. And God saw the light, that it was good: and God divided the light from the darkness.'"

A stern-faced man in the middle said, "We know the Bible."

"Forgive me. What I want to show you is that God has given us the knowledge to understand how His gift, His light can save Grace."

Pulling a prism from his pocket, Phillip moved to where the sunlight was streaming in the south window. Holding the glass to the light, he threw a rainbow on the opposite wall.

"Light is made up of all these colors. The blue you see is the color that will make Grace better. Blue fluorescent lamps generate specific wavelengths of light that help break down the chemical in her blood, the bilirubin. As the light shines on her skin it changes the bilirubin into water-soluble components that are excreted."

He put the prism back in his pocket. Did they understand or was he talking over their heads? "If Grace could stay outside all day, without clothes on, all year 'round, and let God's light touch her skin, her jaundice would be controlled. You men know what it is to be outside all day summer and winter."

"It would not be possible for a child to live like this." The elder on the end stroked his beard.

Phillip knew he was reaching them. "That's right. That's why we take the blue light and bring it inside and let the sick children sleep under it at night. By using a solar panel, we can change sunlight into electricity to run the lights."

"But this will not cure her," Elijah said mournfully.

Phillip returned and sat on the edge of his seat. "No, but work is being done in the Amish community in Lancaster County, Pennsylvania, to understand this disease and find a cure. It will be found, but not in time to help Grace. Right now, the only cure for her will be a liver transplant when she is old enough to have one."

Elijah's bishop, who had been sitting quietly among the other elders, spoke up at last. "You have given us much to consider. Thank you for coming."

He was being dismissed. Deflated, Phillip tried one last thing. "Because this defective gene comes from both her father and mother, we know there will be more children with this disease in your community. We have already seen it in Elijah and Sophie's families. When the children of those families grow up and marry, they will pass this gene along to their children and their grandchildren. More Amish children will be sick. It is within your power to save them by using the first gift God gave the world. How can you turn your backs on them?"

He held his breath as he waited for their reply.

WILMA WAS ALREADY at the clinic when Phillip arrived there early on Monday morning. To his surprise, Amber was there, too.

He knew he'd never tire of seeing her face. The thought that he'd be leaving in two weeks was as painful as a knife in his heart. How could he leave her? How could he not?

His new partners in Hawaii were eagerly awaiting his return. Their busy practice needed him there full-time. They had been generous in granting him a two-month leave, but he couldn't ask them for more time.

Harold was progressing so well that he'd be able to

return in a month or so. The clinic might have to close for a few weeks, but it would survive until Harold's return. It might even prosper if Harold took on a partner of his own.

Phillip wondered if Amber would be as sorry to see him go as he was to leave.

"Well?" Wilma demanded. "What did they decide?"

"I don't know. I haven't heard." He came into the room and parked himself on the corner of her desk. Amber moved to settle herself close beside him.

"When will you hear?" she asked.

"I'm not sure. Soon, I hope."

Amber laid her hand on his arm. "What if they say no?"

"I won't think like that."

Smiling, she nodded. "God brought you here for this reason."

He had such a short time left in Hope Springs. He was going to make the most of every minute with this wonderful woman. He had a lifetime worth of memories he needed to make.

"But what if they do say no?" Wilma asked.

"If they say no, I have a tough choice ahead of me. I'll either have to release the child from the hospital to go home and die, or I can petition the court to have her removed from her parents' custody. In that case, she would go to foster care, but at least she'd be getting the treatment she needs. I'm sure the Amish would take us to court over such a move. They might even win."

Amber's hand tightened in a gesture of sympathy. "What will you do?"

He gave her a soft smile. "I honestly don't know."

The clatter of hooves outside announced the arrival of

a buggy. Phillip stood and waited with his heart pounding as Elijah Knepp walked in. The farmer pulled his hat from his head. "I must speak with you, Phillip White."

"Please, come to my office." Phillip led the way and when they were inside the room, he offered Elijah a chair.

"*Nee*, I must get back to my fields. I wish to tell you the Church elders have come to a decision regarding Grace."

"I see." Phillip swallowed hard. "What was their decision?"

"Grace may have the lights."

Phillip's mouth dropped open in relief. Rounding the corner of his desk, he slapped the man on the back. "That's great news."

Elijah grinned. "*Ja*. It is *goot*. My Sophie is happy today."

"I'm sure she must be. I don't want you to worry. I'll take care of getting the equipment ordered."

"My Church will pay for what is needed."

"Fine. As soon as it's installed in your house, Grace can come home." Phillip knew he was grinning like a fool, but he couldn't stop.

At the door, Elijah said, "My thanks for your efforts to help my daughter and my wife. You have been a gift from *Gott* to my family."

Pulling open the office door for him, Phillip said, "I'm glad I could help."

Elijah looked down at his hat and then back to Phillip. "This cure they are looking for, you will help them find it?"

"I'm afraid I must leave that to more qualified doctors." What he wouldn't give to be part of that battle.

As the man walked away down the hall, Phillip stared

after him. He did want to be a part of finding answers and cures, not waiting for others to do the work. He'd never be content to send grieving parents out his door without being able to give them hope.

Suddenly, he realized he'd been heading down the wrong career path.

Perhaps this had been God's purpose in bringing him to Hope Springs. To show him where his true calling lay. Not in family medicine like this, but in genetic research.

Amber once said God used her sister's tragedy to reveal her true calling. In his heart, Phillip knew he was being called, too. Not to follow in his father's footsteps, but to forge a new path for himself.

I'm listening, Lord. I'm finally listening.

Excitement percolated through his body. He'd need a new degree. It would mean more years of study. He knew just where to make it happen. At his alma mater, the University of Hawaii at Manoa.

The door beside his office opened. Amber peeked out. "Well?"

Wilma came rushing down the hall. "Don't keep me in suspense."

Phillip stepped back into his office. The women crowded in. Holding his arms wide, he grinned. "They said yes."

Happy screams almost raised the roof. Phillip found himself the center of a group hug and joyful jumping.

Wilma broke away first. "I've got to call my husband. We've been praying about this all weekend." She dashed out of the room and headed for her desk.

Shyly, Amber smiled at Phillip and placed both her hands on his chest. "You done good."

"With your help." His heart turned over and he pulled

her close. She had become as important to him as breathing. How could he live without her?

He loved her. He loved her with all his heart. Would she leave this place and come with him to Hawaii if he told her that? He braced himself to find out.

The outer door of the office opened. Expecting Wilma, he looked over Amber's head and his mouth dropped open.

Harold, leaning on crutches, stood in the doorway scowling at them. "Don't let me interrupt. On second thought, what's going on here?"

With a squeal of delight, Amber tore away from Phillip to embrace his grandfather. "Harold, I'm so glad you're back. Why didn't you tell us you were coming?"

Wilma squeezed through the door behind them shaking with excitement. She, too, threw her arms around the man. "God has answered my prayers. It hasn't been the same without you."

He hugged both women close. "I'm happy to be back. I don't think I'll ever leave this town again."

"Good," Wilma stated firmly, patting his chest. "Now, maybe things can get back to normal around here."

Phillip stood back, allowing them their long-awaited reunion. Finally, his grandfather looked up and met Phillip's gaze over the women's heads. Harold said, "That's my plan. I'm here to make sure that things get back to normal as soon as possible."

CHAPTER TWENTY-THREE

AMBER WALKED SLOWLY toward Phillip's office the following morning. The door stood open.

Harold's office, she corrected herself. It would take some time to get used to that again. She stopped in the doorway and watched the man she had come to love more than anyone in her life. Busy packing his few belongings, he didn't see her.

The dreaded moment was here at last. She wouldn't cry. She wouldn't. "You're leaving?"

He looked up. His eyes were filled with the same pain and longing that was tearing her heart to shreds. "Yes."

"When?" She took a step inside the room.

"I've got a flight out of Cincinnati at two o'clock. I can make it if I hurry."

"Today?" He heard the despair in her voice because he stopped packing and came to take her in his arms. Huddled against his chest, she said, "I don't want you to go."

If she told him that she loved him, would he stay? Did she have the right to ask him?

He whispered, "You could practice as a CNM in Hawaii. It's a beautiful, special place."

Those were the words she both longed and dreaded to hear. "There are no Amish in Hawaii."

The strength ebbed out of his embrace. "Why are they so important to you?"

"I don't really know—except I believe this is where God wants me to be." She looked up. "Why don't you stay? You know Harold could use the help."

"Not according to him. He's in a rush to get back in the saddle. I'm in the way. I've changed things."

"He's bluffing. He does need help, especially now. He can barely walk."

"Even if I didn't have commitments in Hawaii, I wouldn't stay longer."

"Of course. It was silly of me to ask."

He held her at arm's length. "Let's not make this any harder than it already is. We knew from the start that I was only here for a short while."

Her throat ached with unshed tears. "Somehow, I forgot that."

Gently, he stroked her cheek. "So did I. I never meant to hurt you, Amber."

"I know that."

"You are the most amazing person I've ever met in my life. Knowing you has been an honor. I've learned so much from you about the Amish, about birthing babies and a great deal about myself. If you ever change your mind, you'll be welcome in Hawaii."

"I thought we weren't going to make this harder than it already is?" Her voice caught on the last word and she pressed a hand to her lips as she struggled not to cry. "I'd love to see your island, but Harold is going to need me more than ever. I can't run out on him now."

"No, and I shouldn't ask you to do that." Defeat laced his words. She stepped away from him and wondered why life had to be so difficult.

Just then, her cell phone rang. As much as she wanted to ignore it, she couldn't. One of her patients needed her.

The longer she stayed with Phillip the harder it became to say goodbye.

Holding up the phone, she said, "I have to take this."

She silenced the ringing and put the party on hold. Taking another step away, she said, "Have a wonderful flight. I know you'll be a great doctor in Hawaii. Send me a postcard of the ocean."

She turned and ran before the tears started falling again.

PHILLIP PRESSED HIS fingertips to his eyes to ease the burning pain behind them. Why had God allowed him to find the most perfect woman in the world only to put her out of reach?

A tap at the door made him look up. Harold stood in the doorway. "May I come in?"

"It's your office." Phillip turned away to finish putting his few personal belongings in his carry-on case. The last item to go in was Doctor Dog. Phillip drew his hand over the puppet's silky ears before putting him away.

Harold cleared his throat nervously. "I'm hearing good things about what you did while you were here. I'm a little sorry now that I rushed back."

Phillip glanced at his grandfather with concern. "Are you well enough to be back to work?"

Holding out his leg cast, Harold said, "I'll need some physical therapy when this comes off, but they tell me I'll be as fit as ever. The old noggin gets headaches. Hopefully, those will fade." Stepping close, Harold said, "I know you didn't have an easy time here, but I'm proud of the way you handled yourself. Your father would have been proud of you, too."

"I hope someday I can become as good a doctor as he hoped to be."

Harold drew back, a puzzled frown on his face. "Your father never wanted to be a doctor."

Stunned, Phillip stared at his grandfather. "Wait a minute. What are you saying?"

"My boy wanted to be a musician from the time he could reach the piano keys. I know you idolized him, but he drifted from club to club playing his saxophone and guitar. He was always broke, never had a decent place to live. I prayed for him. I paid for his college but he blew that, too."

"Why didn't anyone tell me this?" It was like Phillip's world had tipped off its axis.

"Was it your mother who told you Brendan wanted to be a doctor?"

"Yes."

"What else did she tell you about him?"

"That he loved baseball."

"I wouldn't say he loved it, but he enjoyed Little League."

"And did he surf?"

"As far as I know, he never tried it."

Phillip sat down, his knees suddenly weak. His entire life he'd done things because he believed they were the things his father wanted to do. It had all been a lie. Why?

He thought back to those times. When his mother wanted him to play ball, he refused at first. Telling him his father had loved the sport had changed his mind. Shortly after that, she began dating his coach.

She'd never brought up the subject of surfing until they moved to California. She had hooked up with more than one beach bum during those years.

He looked up at Harold. "Why did my father join the Marines?"

"Your mother should tell you that."

Phillip stood and picked up his bag. "This time she will."

He started to leave, but Harold grabbed him in a fierce hug and clung to him as if for dear life. "I'm going to miss you, my boy. I love you, more than I thought possible. I loved your father, too. Remember that and don't think badly of me."

"I could never think badly of you."

Sniffing once, Harold straightened. "It was great getting to know you. Thank you for everything you've done to keep this practice going. It's all I have left in the world."

Pulling a card from his pocket, Phillip handed it to him. "This is the number of a young doctor who'd like to go into practice with you. You should give him a call. The Amish deserve to have someone here after you're gone. Hopefully, that won't be for many years so you can train him up the way you want."

Harold took the card. "God bless you, Phillip."

"And you, too, sir." With a nod of goodbye, he walked out to the lobby. Wilma rose from her desk and came around to shake his hand and wish him well.

Out in the parking lot, he tossed his bag on the front seat of his car, then glanced toward the building once more. Amber stood at the window in the first exam room. She raised her hand and pressed it to the glass.

He raised his hand briefly in return, then got into his car and drove away.

HIS FLIGHT WAS long and tedious, giving him plenty of time to rehash every decision he'd made in Hope Springs.

Right or wrong, he still wasn't sure. He put his pain and unhappiness in God's hands. The Lord had a plan for his life that he couldn't see yet. He had to believe that.

After seventeen hours in a cramped airline seat, he was more than happy to get off the plane. To his surprise, his mother was waiting near the gate.

"Mom! I wasn't expecting you." He gave her a quick hug.

"When my baby is gone for two months, do you think I wouldn't want to see you the moment you got off the plane? Tell me about your stay in that frightful place."

Petite, with an artfully styled riot of red curls that wasn't her natural color, Melinda Watson tried never to look her age, yet tonight she looked much older than he remembered. There were carefully disguised dark circles under her eyes.

He wasn't ready to talk about his time in Ohio. "Mom, what I want is a hot shower and to sleep for a week."

"I thought you could use a lift back to your apartment."

"I could have grabbed a cab. Where's Michael?"

"I didn't tell him you were coming today. I thought you and I could visit for a while."

"All right. Let me get my bags." He was tired, but he didn't want to dampen her happiness. Besides, he had questions he needed to ask her.

"Marvelous." She clapped her hands together. "Why don't we have dinner at the Maui Fire? I hear it's the hot new place."

After catching his bags off the carousel, he followed his mother outside into the warm, tropical evening air. He could smell the sea. For the first time in his life it didn't make him want to pick up his board. It reminded him of Amber…and her sea-green eyes glistening with tears.

How was he going to function if he couldn't cross the airport parking lot without missing her so much his heart felt like a jumble of broken glass?

His mother continued to chat aimlessly on the drive. Watching the familiar sights of high-rise hotels and waving palm trees, he couldn't help comparing the glitter and glitz to the simple rolling hills and plain white farmsteads of the Amish countryside.

"You're very quiet," she said, sneaking a peek at him.

"I'm tired."

"A good dinner will perk you up in no time."

He didn't want food. He wanted answers. "Why did you tell me my father wanted to be a doctor?"

"Because he did!"

"Was that before or after he wanted to form his own rock band?"

She didn't answer. Instead, she slowed the car and turned into the parking lot of one of the popular beaches, stopping the car where they faced the ocean. The waves came sweeping in, each topped with a whitecap of foam. His stomach was churning in much the same fashion.

After rolling down the windows, she turned the car off. Gripping the steering wheel, she stared straight ahead. "Phillip, I wasn't a very good mother when you were young. I know that. I do."

She turned to gaze at him. "But I've been a good mother since I met Michael, haven't I? I love you. You know that, don't you?"

"You've always done your best, Mom. I love you, too."

"I know how excited you were to find your grandfather, but he isn't a good man. Believe me, I know."

Phillip drew a deep breath. Was he finally going to get to the bottom of this? "He is a good man, Mother. He's kind and devoted to the Amish and his community."

"Well, he wasn't always that way. Your father and he never got along. Nothing Brendan did was good enough for Harold. Finding out that Brendan and I were planning to get married infuriated him. I wasn't good enough for his only son." Scorn dripped off her every word.

Phillip wasn't sure he liked where this conversation was leading. "Some parents have trouble accepting their child's new spouse at first. It normally changes over time."

"Harold didn't want his son tied down with a family at such a young age. He knew Brendan couldn't handle it, that it would destroy his life. We were only nineteen and I was pregnant. We were as poor as dirt, living in Brendan's van half the time. Oh, Brendan's father had plenty of money. He could have helped us but he wanted his son to earn his own way."

Phillip tried to imagine what his mother had gone through back then. "I'm sorry things were so difficult for you. I never knew."

"And I never wanted you to know but there's no point in hiding it any longer. Your grandfather came to me and offered me a lot of money."

Phillip's heart sank. "He paid you to leave my father?"

"He paid me to get rid of you."

The blood rushed to Phillip's brain and sent his head pounding. "I don't believe it!"

Calmly, she replied, "It's true. When Brendan found out, he flipped. He and your grandfather had a terrible fight. Brendan told his old man he'd find a way to support his wife and a child. Then he stormed out of the house and stopped at the first recruiting station he could find."

"That's why he joined the Marines?"

"Yes. We were married before he shipped out and he was killed three months later. It's your grandfather's fault that your father is dead."

Leaning his head back against the seat rest, Phillip listened to the waves and struggled to digest all the information he'd been given. Had he wanted his grandfather to be a wonderful man so badly that he'd been blind to Harold's faults? Perhaps that had been true, at first.

Phillip realized that he'd spent his life longing for something he could never have. He'd never have his father watch him at a ball game or sit in the audience at his graduation. Maybe he'd gone to medical school because he thought that was what his father would have wanted, but medicine was where Phillip belonged. It was his vocation.

Images of Amber slipped through his mind, quieting the turmoil inside him. Amber knew where she belonged in life. Now he finally did, too.

He couldn't stay in Hawaii. He had to confront his grandfather, to find out if this was the truth or more of his mother's manipulations.

Then he needed to tell Amber that he loved her. He'd been a fool to leave without telling her how he felt. If she returned his love, somehow he would to find a way to keep her in his life.

He looked at his mother. "Thanks for telling me this, Mom. I'd like to go to your house now. There are some important things I want you and Michael to hear together."

CHAPTER TWENTY-FOUR

PHILLIP GOT OUT of his rental car in front of Harold's home late on a Saturday afternoon. It had been almost three weeks since he'd left Hope Springs. Because it was the weekend, Phillip was reasonably sure Harold would be in. He hadn't called in advance. He wasn't sure what he was going to say now that he was here. After knocking, he waited outside the door.

Thumping of crutches and grumbling on the other side alerted him before Harold yanked it open. The elderly man's annoyed expression changed to happiness, then to guarded surprise. "Phillip. What are you doing here?"

What was he doing here? What did he hope to learn? The truth? Or more carefully crafted secrets? "I need to talk to you."

The light died in Harold's eyes. His face went ashen. "Your mother told you, didn't she?"

"I want to hear your side of the story."

The man seemed to grow older in front of Phillip's eyes. "Then you'd better come in. I can't be up long or this miserable leg begins to swell."

Following his grandfather inside, Phillip sat on the sofa and waited until Harold settled himself in his recliner. He sighed loudly as he grimaced and leaned back. "Thought you might like to know that Martha Nissley got to come home."

"That's great. How is she doing?"

"She got all the feeling back in her legs. Looks like she'll make a full recovery."

"That's great to hear." Phillip nodded toward Harold's walking cast. "How are you managing at the clinic?"

"I get around in a wheelchair for the most part. That young whippersnapper, Dr. Zook, is helping a lot."

"I'm glad to hear he took the job."

"He's got his head on straight, but don't tell him I said so."

"I'll leave that to you. I'm sure he'd like a little encouragement." Any would be more than Harold had given Phillip.

Harold dismissed the idea with a wave of his hand. "I don't need to give him pats on the back. Amber and Wilma do it for me."

"How is Amber?" Phillip was almost afraid to hear the answer but he was dying for any information about her.

"She has changed. She's not herself, although she tries to be. Some of the light has gone out of her."

Phillip dropped his gaze to his feet. He was to blame. "She's a wonderful, strong woman. I'm sure she'll be fine."

"You didn't come here to talk about Amber, did you?"

Raising his head, Phillip stared at Harold. "I came to get some straight answers."

"All right. Ask away."

Phillip hesitated. His mother had lied to him and manipulated him so many times in the past. Why should he trust what she'd told him about Harold? Would it alienate his grandfather to be accused of such horrible motives? Was that her plan all along?

Well, he hadn't come all this way for nothing. "Is it

true you tried to bribe my mother to get an abortion and to leave my dad?"

Harold closed his eyes. "Stupidest mistake I ever made. I had no idea how much Brendan loved her. What a terrible fight we had when he found out."

"At least they wanted me." Phillip couldn't keep the bitterness out of his voice.

Harold folded his hands across his abdomen. "Did your mother tell you she took the money?"

Phillip blinked hard. Why wasn't he surprised? No wonder she hadn't wanted him to contact Harold. "She left that part out."

"I never dreamed Brendan would enlist. I always thought we'd be able to mend things between us. Then he was killed. You are so like him. Looking at you is like looking into my past."

"Why didn't you take care of us after he died?"

"When Brendan was killed, your mother blamed me. At his funeral, the only time we saw each other again, she told me she'd gone through with the abortion and she never wanted to see me again. You have to understand. I held her responsible for my son's death instead of accepting my share of the blame. I didn't know and didn't care where she went after that."

Phillip struggled to find the words for what he was feeling. "We lived a hard life. She drank heavily. She got into drugs. I can't count the times we were evicted from one rattrap or another. I can't count the number of men she brought home. If it hadn't been for Michael, I don't know what would have happened to us."

"Believe me when I tell you I'm glad your mother has found some happiness. I came to realize Brendan's death and the loss of his child was my punishment for putting my own desires ahead of his love. In spite of what you think, I was doing what I thought was best for my son. Had I known about you, I would have moved heaven and earth to find you."

Seeing the sincerity in his grandfather's eyes, Phillip felt he had the truth at last. "I believe that."

"After your father died, I couldn't stay in Boston. Everything reminded me of him and my horrible mistake. My wife had died when Brendan was five. There was nothing to keep me there. I sold all I had and came here. I hoped to find forgiveness and peace working among these simple and faithful people."

Phillip wasn't done with his questions. "When I suggested you retire and come live near me, why did you become so upset?"

Harold rubbed his jaw with one hand. "Because I was terrified my sins would come to light. I didn't want to lose you the way I lost your father."

"When you ran in front of my car, why were you trying to stop me?"

"I realized I couldn't come back to Hope Springs and live among the Plain People with that terrible secret in my heart. I had to tell you the truth." The corners of his mouth quirked upward. "I honestly had no intention of getting run down."

"I thank God each day you weren't killed."

"I thank God He has given me the chance to right the terrible wrong I did you and your mother."

Harold struggled to stand. Phillip moved to assist him. When he was on his feet and steady, he gripped Phillip's arm and looked into his eyes. "Can you forgive me?"

Phillip had the truth now. More than he wanted to know. It was all so sad and so unnecessary. He had it within his power to lay a lifetime of unhappiness to rest, for both of them.

Phillip covered his grandfather's hand with his own. "Yes, I can."

The old man's eyes closed and he swayed. Frightened, Phillip quickly helped him into his chair. "Are you all right, Grandfather?"

"I'm fine. I'm fine for the first time in a long while. Thank you."

"Can I get you something?"

"Great-grandchildren."

Phillip's worry slipped away. Relief made him smile. "I was thinking along the lines of a glass of water."

Harold sat up and took a deep breath. "That would be nice, too. You are going to marry Amber, aren't you? She loves you. You're a fool if you don't know that."

AMBER WAS BONE-TIRED by the time she returned home. The delivery had gone well. Both mother and child were happy and healthy. She should have been thrilled, but all through the long hours of labor she kept thinking about the time she and Phillip spent with Mary and her family. Remembering their time together was still painful but she didn't cry as often anymore.

After parking in her driveway, Amber walked toward the house with lagging steps. Everything took more energy since Phillip had gone. Walking, eating, getting out of bed, it was all so hard to do. How much longer would this malaise affect her? It already felt like a lifetime had passed since he went away.

At the steps, she heard a meow from the end of the porch. For a second she thought it was Fluffy, then she remembered that her cat was gone, too. It had to be one of the neighborhood cats.

Fluffy was back with the family who loved him. At least that had ended well. When Amber reached the front door, she heard a second meow.

Turning to see whose cat had come for a visit, she froze in shock. Phillip sat in her wicker chair with a box at his feet. Afraid to blink in case he vanished, she kept staring, trying to make herself believe it was true.

Rising to his feet, he said, "Hello, Amber."

He wasn't a figment of her imagination. Her heart thudded painfully against the inside of her chest. It took every ounce of self-control she possessed to keep from flinging herself into his arms. "Phillip? What are you doing here?"

He smiled but she saw the uncertainty in his eyes. "I had to see you again."

Looking away before he could read the longing on her face, she fumbled to get her keys out of her purse. Finally, she found them and attempted to open her lock. When they tumbled out of her shaky fingers she knew there was no use pretending she was okay.

She closed her eyes and leaned her head against the door. "I can't do this again, Phillip."

In a few steps he was beside her, not touching her, but surrounding her with his masculine warmth. "I'm sorry. I had to see you."

Bending down, he picked up her keys. She stayed strong until he placed them in her palm and tenderly closed his fingers over hers. He whispered, "I've missed you, Amber."

His soft words were her undoing. She melted into his

arms as he gathered her close. "Oh, Phillip, I've missed you so much."

"I love you. I never want to leave you again."

"I can't bear it, Phillip. I can't stay here without you."

Brushing her damp cheeks with his knuckle, he asked in surprise, "You would come to Hawaii?"

"Yes, if you want me. I can't be more unhappy there than I've been here these past three weeks."

"My poor darling. I don't want you to be unhappy anywhere. I don't want you to give up the things you love most."

She buried her face against his chest. "I love you the most. So we are right back where we started from because I know you will never be happy practicing small-town medicine."

He rocked her gently in his embrace. "We're not exactly back where we started from. I know that I love you and I know that you love me."

"True."

Leaning back, he looked down at her. "I have something for you."

"What?" Wiping her face with both hands, she took a step back, already missing the warmth of his body and the comfort of his arms around her.

Picking up the box by the chair, he held it out. "Open it. Doctor's orders."

As she started to take the top off, she heard a tiny meow. It was then she noticed the holes poked in the sides of the box. Phillip said, "I know you miss Fluffy."

The moment the top came off, a white kitten raised its head over the lip. Amber gasped in delight. "Oh, he's beautiful."

Phillip looked quite pleased with himself. "I'm glad

you like him. He's all yours. No one is going to take him back."

"He's just what I've been needing. What a wonderful gift. Thank you."

"I'm not done." Phillip put the top on the box and took it from her. The kitten protested as he set it aside. Drawing a deep breath, he withdrew several packets from his jacket and offered them to her.

Puzzled, Amber took them. Tilting them toward the porch light she saw they were celery seed packets. Her lip quivered as she pressed a hand to her chest. "Oh, Phillip."

He dropped to one knee in front of her. "Amber Bradley, will you marry me?"

Speechless, she stared at him as happiness strummed the cords of her heart. Joy unlike anything she'd ever known sent her blood humming. On the heels of that intense joy came a quick downer dose of common sense.

She bit her lower lip. What should she do? If she said yes, one of them would have to give up their dreams. Yet how could she bear to say no and lose his wonderful love? Finally, she said, "Maybe."

He sat back on his heel. "Maybe? I thought your only choices were yes or no."

"I want to marry you, but I'm afraid."

"Of what?" He rose to his feet and took her in his arms once more.

"I'm afraid I'll be miserable away from the Amish and I'll make you miserable, too." If they could only stay this way forever, encircled in each other's arms, surrounded by love.

He took her face in his hands. "I don't want you to come to Hawaii. I want you to stay here."

In a flash, she realized he was giving up his dream for her. "You can't resign from your practice in Hawaii."

"I already have."

"But you won't like practicing medicine here. You know you won't."

"I'll be happy wherever you are, but you're right. I wouldn't be content practicing general medicine. Anywhere."

"Then I don't understand."

"I have been mistakenly trying to fulfill my father's dreams, not my own. God brought me to this town to meet the most wonderful woman in the world." He flicked the tip of her nose with his finger.

She chuckled. "I'm glad you think so."

"And He brought me here to show me my true calling. I'm going to be a pediatrician in a new diagnostic center for children with special needs that will open in Hope Springs sometime in the next few years."

He wasn't kidding. She knew by the joy in his voice. "A new clinic here?"

His eyes danced with eagerness. "I've just come back from Pennsylvania and their genetic research facility for special needs children. It's a wonderful place. They are doing cutting-edge genetic research among the Amish there. Besides research, they treat children with all types of inherited diseases and they don't limit their service to just the Amish. They are eager to find out more about the Knepp baby and her parents, and they want to develop a second clinic in this area."

"You and Dr. Dog will make wonderful pediatricians. But that means you'll have to go back to school."

"Believe me, I've been looking into it. There's a combined human genetics and pediatric residency at Cincinnati Children's. It's only three hours away. We can see each other on my days off. It's a five-year program, but I'll be board certified in both genetics and pediatrics when I'm done. I've already applied. So, you can see why I'm going to need a wife with a good job."

Pulling back, she asked, "You're okay with me continuing as a nurse-midwife here?"

"Honey, I know you give your patients the very best of care. I know that because I've seen your passion and your skill. I may never be convinced that home deliveries are best, but I will support *you* one hundred percent."

Circling his neck with her arms, she smiled softly. "Oh, I think in fifty or sixty years I can get you to come around."

"What method of persuasion will you be using?" He tightened his hold and gave her a heart-stopping grin. The love in his eyes sent a tingle clear to her toes.

Leaning close, she whispered, "Kisses, lots of kisses."

Phillip pulled back a little. "Does this mean you've changed your maybe to a yes?"

"Yes, yes, yes," she whispered as she drew his face to hers. The heady feel of his arms and his lips sent her heart tripping with delight.

As their lips touched, Amber sent up a silent prayer of thanks. God had truly brought a wonderful man into her life.

After that, she gave Phillip her full and undivided attention.

* * * * *

We hope you enjoyed reading

A Creed Country Christmas
by *New York Times* bestselling author
LINDA LAEL MILLER
and
The Doctor's Blessing
by *USA TODAY* bestselling author
PATRICIA DAVIDS

Both were originally HQN and Harlequin®
series stories!

From passionate, suspenseful and dramatic
love stories to inspirational or historical,
Harlequin offers different lines to
satisfy every romance reader.

New books in each line
are available every month.

Harlequin.com

SPECIAL EXCERPT FROM

*Can a mysterious Amish child bring two wounded
souls together in Cedar Grove, Kansas?*

Read on for a sneak preview of
The Hope *by Patricia Davids*
available December 2019 from HQN Books!

"You won't have to stay on our account, and we can look
after Ernest's place, too. I can hire a man to help me.
Someone I know I can…" Ruth's words trailed away.

Trust? Depend on? Was that what Ruth was going
to say? She didn't want him around. She couldn't have
made it any clearer. Maybe it had been a mistake to think
he could patch things up between them, but he wasn't
willing to give up after only one day. Ruth was nothing if
not stubborn, but he could be stubborn, too.

Owen leaned back and chuckled.

"What's so funny?"

"I'm here until Ernest returns, Ruth. You can't get rid
of me with a few well-placed insults."

She huffed and turned her back to him. "I didn't insult
you."

"Ah, but you wanted to. I'd like to talk about my plans
in the morning."

Ruth nodded. "You know my feelings, but I agree we
both need to sleep on it."

Owen picked up his coat and hat, and left for his uncle's farm. The wind was blowing harder and the snow was piling up in growing drifts. It wasn't a fit night out for man nor beast. As if to prove his point, he found Meeka, Ernest's big guard dog, lying across the corner of the porch out of the wind. Instead of coming out to greet him, she whined repeatedly.

He opened the door of the house. "Come in for a bit." She didn't get up. Something was wrong. Was she hurt? He walked toward her. She sat up and growled low in her throat. She had never done that to him before. "Are you sick, girl?"

She looked back at something in the corner and whined softly. Over the wind he heard what sounded like a sobbing child. "What have you got there, Meeka? Let me see."

He came closer. There was a child in an Amish bonnet and bulky winter coat trying to bury herself beneath Meeka's thick fur. Where had she come from? Why was she here? He looked around. Where were her parents?

Don't miss
The Hope *by Patricia Davids,*
available now wherever
HQN™ books and ebooks are sold.

HQNBooks.com

Love Inspired®

Uplifting romances of faith, forgiveness and hope.

Save $1.00

on the purchase of any
Love Inspired® or
Love Inspired® Suspense book.

Available wherever books are sold,
including most bookstores, supermarkets,
drugstores and discount stores.

Save $1.00

on the purchase of any Love Inspired® or Love Inspired® Suspense book.

Coupon valid until February 28, 2020.
Redeemable at participating outlets in the U.S. and Canada only.
Not redeemable at Barnes & Noble stores. Limit one coupon per customer.

52616509

Canadian Retailers: Harlequin Enterprises Limited will pay the face value of this coupon plus 10.25¢ if submitted by customer for this product only. Any other use constitutes fraud. Coupon is nonassignable. Void if taxed, prohibited or restricted by law. Consumer must pay any government taxes. Void if copied. Inmar Promotional Services ("IPS") customers submit coupons and proof of sales to Harlequin Enterprises Limited, P.O. Box 31000, Scarborough, ON M1R 0E7, Canada. Non-IPS retailer—for reimbursement submit coupons and proof of sales directly to Harlequin Enterprises Limited, Retail Marketing Department, Bay Adelaide Centre, East Tower, 22 Adelaide Street West, 40th Floor, Toronto, Ontario M5H 4E3, Canada.

U.S. Retailers: Harlequin Enterprises Limited will pay the face value of this coupon plus 8¢ if submitted by customer for this product only. Any other use constitutes fraud. Coupon is nonassignable. Void if taxed, prohibited or restricted by law. Consumer must pay any government taxes. Void if copied. For reimbursement submit coupons and proof of sales directly to Harlequin Enterprises, Ltd 482, NCH Marketing Services, P.O. Box 880001, El Paso, TX 88588-0001, U.S.A. Cash value 1/100 cents.

5   65373 00076   2   (8100)0 12433

® and ™ are trademarks owned and used by the trademark owner and/or its licensee.

© 2019 Harlequin Enterprises Limited

BACCOUP92846